CITY OF WONDERS

Eduardo Mendoza

CITY OF WONDERS

Translated from the Spanish by
Nick Caistor

MACLEHOSE PRESS
QUERCUS · LONDON

First published in the Spanish language as *La ciudad de los prodigios*
by Seix Barral, Barcelona, 1986
First published in Great Britain in a translation by Bernard Molloy as *City of Marvels*
by Collins Harvill, London, 1998
This translation first published in Great Britain in 2022 by

MacLehose Press
An imprint of Quercus Editions Ltd
Carmelite House
50 Victoria Embankment
London EC4Y 0DZ

An Hachette UK company

This book was supported by a grant from Acción Cultural Española (AC/E)

A CIP catalogue record for this book is available
from the British Library.

ISBN (MMP) 978 1 5294 1008 2
ISBN (Ebook) 978 1 52941 009 9

10 9 8 7 6 5 4 3 2 1

Designed and typeset in Minion by CC Book Production
Printed and bound in Great Britain by Clays Ltd, Elcograf S.p.A.

Papers used by MacLehose Press are from well-managed forests
and other responsible sources.

For Ana

When the unclean spirit is gone of a man, he walketh through dry places, seeking rest; and finding none, he sayeth: "I will return unto my house whence I came out." And when he cometh he findeth it swept and garnished. Then goeth he, and taketh to him seven other spirits more wicked than himself; and they enter in, and dwell there; and the last state of that man is worse than the first.

Gospel According to Luke, 11:24–6

CONTENTS

CHAPTER ONE

1

The year Onofre Bouvila first set foot in Barcelona, the city was in a frenzy of renewal. The Catalan capital lies in the valley between Malgrat and Garraf, where the coastal mountain range withdraws inland, creating a sort of amphitheatre. The climate is temperate, not given to extremes; the skies are mostly bright and clear; the clouds few and white. Atmospheric pressure is stable, and rainfall infrequent, but on occasion treacherous and torrential.

Although still a matter of debate, it is generally agreed the Phoenicians founded the city not once but twice. What is known for certain is that Barcelona enters History as a colony of Carthage, allied to Sidon and Tyre. It is an attested fact that Hannibal's elephants stopped to drink and frisk about on the banks of the Rivers Besós and Llobregat on their trek to the Alps, where they were decimated by the cold and mountainous terrain.

When they saw these animals, the earliest inhabitants of Barcelona were amazed. "Look at their tusks, their ears, what a trunk or proboscis!" they gasped. This shared sense of wonder and the stories told about it over many years forged a sense of Barcelona's identity as an urban centre – an identity lost until the nineteenth century, when the inhabitants of the city made strenuous efforts to regain it.

The Phoenicians were followed by the Greeks and the Layetani. The former left behind traces of their craftsmanship; to the latter, according to ethnologists, we owe two distinctive characteristics: the tendency Catalans have to tilt their heads to the left when they're pretending to listen, and the tendency the men have to grow luxuriant nasal hair.

Little is known of the Layetani, except that their principal food source was a milk product sometimes referred to as whey or lemonade, which was not very different from our present-day yoghurt. However, it was the Romans who gave Barcelona the stamp of a city and created its definitive structure. And yet everything points to the fact that they felt a haughty disdain for Barcelona. It didn't seem to interest them for strategic – or any other – purposes.

In the year 63 BC a praetor by the name of Mucius Alexandrinus writes to his father-in-law and protector back in Rome complaining at being posted to Barcelona, when he had asked to be sent to the lavish city of Augusta Bibilis, today's Calatayud. After the Romans, it's the Gothic kinglet Ataulf who conquers the city, and it remains in the hands of the Goths until the Saracens take it without a struggle in the year 717 of our era. As is their custom, the Moors do no more than convert the cathedral (not the one we can admire today, but another, older one, built elsewhere, the scene of multiple conversions and martyrdoms) into a mosque, and little else. The French recover it for Christianity in 785, and exactly two centuries later, in 985, Almanzor or Al-Mansur, the Pious, the Merciless, the Three-toothed One, regains it for Islam.

These conquests and reconquests explain the thickness and complexity of the city walls. Straitjacketed between concentric bastions and fortifications, its streets become increasingly winding; this attracts Hebrew Cabbalists from Gerona, who set up branches of their sect in the city. They dig tunnels leading to secret Sanhedrins and purifying baths that were only rediscovered in the twentieth century when the metro was being built. Still visible on the stone lintels of the old quarter are scribbled characters that are passwords for the initiated, formulas for attaining the ineffable, etc. Following this, the city goes through years of splendour and centuries of obscurity.

"You'll be very comfortable here, you'll see. The rooms aren't big, but they're well aired, and as for cleanliness, you couldn't ask for more. The meals are simple, but nourishing," the boarding house owner declared. This establishment, where Onofre Bouvila pitched up shortly after his arrival in Barcelona, was situated on Carreró del Xup. A gentle slope began a few metres further along this side street, the name of which could be translated as "alley of the well". The incline became more pronounced until it reached two steps, then levelled out until it came up against a wall built on the remains of an ancient, possibly Roman, city wall. A thick black liquid oozed constantly from this wall, and over the centuries it had rounded, smoothed, and polished the two steps, making them extremely slippery. The trickle then flowed down a gutter running parallel to the pavement, and finally gurgled into the open drain at the intersection with Calle de la Manga (formerly Calle de la Pera), the only access to Carreró del Xup.

This entirely unremarkable, drab street could boast (although other corners in the same neighbourhood disputed the same dubious honour) of being the scene of a cruel event: the execution of Saint Leocricia on the Roman wall. This saint, probably an earlier one than the Saint Leocricia of Córdoba, figures in some hagiographies as Saint Leocricia, and in others as Lucrecia or Locatis. She was a native of Barcelona or its environs, the daughter of a wool carder, who converted to Christianity as a young girl.

Against her will, her father married her to somebody called Tiburcius or Tiburcinus, a quaestor. Inspired by her faith, Leocricia gave away her husband's possessions to the poor, and freed their slaves. Tiburcius, who had not given permission for any of this,

13

flew into a rage. As a consequence of her actions, and for refusing to renounce her faith, Leocricia was beheaded on top of the wall. Legend has it that her head rolled down the slope and didn't stop, turning corners, crossing streets and causing panic among passersby until it plopped into the sea, where a dolphin or some other large fish carried it off. Her saint's day is 27 January.

At the end of the nineteenth century a boarding house stood on the upper level of this side street. Despite its owner's pretentions, it was a very humble establishment. The lobby was tiny, dominated by a light-coloured wooden counter, with a brass inkwell and a register on it. The register was always left open so that anyone could check the legality of the business by casting an eye over the list of the lodgers' nicknames and pseudonyms. There was also a barber's cubbyhole, a china umbrella stand, and an image of Saint Christopher, the patron saint of travellers before becoming that of motorists.

Behind this counter, at all hours of the day and night, sat Señora Agata. She was obese, half bald, and so worn out she might have been thought dead were it not for the fact that her aches and pains, which obliged her to keep her feet constantly in a washing-up bowl filled with warm water, made her cry out ceaselessly: "Delfina, the wash-basin." Whenever the water grew cold, she came to life once more and called out, and her daughter would pour in steaming hot water from a pan.

Señora Agata did this so repeatedly every day that the water threatened to overflow and flood the lobby. This, however, did not seem to bother the owner of the boarding house, whom everyone knew as Señor Braulio. It was to him that Onofre Bouvila spoke on his arrival. "In fact, if this place were in a better location, it could pass for a hotel with stars," Señor Braulio confided.

Señora Agata's husband and the father of Delfina, he was

uncommonly tall with regular features, and possessed a certain mannered charm. He left the running of the boarding house to his wife and daughter, and spent most of the day reading newspapers and commenting on the news with the long-term lodgers. Novelties fascinated him, and since this was an age of great inventions he was forever exclaiming "Oh!" and "Ah!" Occasionally, as if somebody were insisting he do so, he flung down his newspaper and announced: "I'll go and see what the weather's like."

He would go out into the street and peer up at the sky, then return inside and declare: "Clear" or "cloudy, chilly" and so on. This appeared to be his only occupation. "It's this dreadful neighbourhood that forces us to charge much less than an establishment such as ours merits," he grumbled. At that he raised a cautionary finger: "But we're very careful when it comes to choosing our guests."

Was that a veiled criticism of my appearance, Onofre Bouvila wondered. Although the boarding house owner's friendly attitude appeared to suggest otherwise, Bouvila's fears were well-founded: despite being still a youth, it was plain that he would always be short in stature, with very broad shoulders. He had a sallow complexion, pinched and coarse features and black curly hair. His clothes were patched, crumpled and far from clean: everything spoke of him having travelled for several days wearing them, and that he didn't have any others, except perhaps for a single change in the bundle he had placed on the counter when he arrived, which he now kept glancing at furtively. Whenever he did this, Señor Braulio was relieved; when the young man fixed his eyes on him again, he became alarmed. There's something in his gaze that sets my nerves jangling, he said to himself. Bah, it must be the usual: hunger, confusion and fear, he decided on reflection. He had seen many people arrive in similar circumstances: Barcelona was growing all the time. Yet another one, he thought, a tiny sardine the whale will swallow without even realising it. At this, his nervousness turned to compassion. He's still only a child and he's desperate, he told himself.

"And might one enquire, Señor Bouvila, as to the motive for your esteemed presence in Barcelona?" he asked. This overblown phrase was intended to make a big impression on the youth. And Bouvila was indeed silent for a few seconds: he wasn't sure he had even understood the question.

"I'm looking for employment," he responded timidly. He fixed the owner again with his penetrating gaze, fearing his reply might rebound against him. But Señor Braulio's mind was already elsewhere and he barely paid him any attention.

"Oh, that's good," was all he said, flicking a speck of dust from his frockcoat shoulder. Onofre Bouvila was silently grateful for this lack of interest. He was ashamed of his origins, and above all wanted to avoid having to reveal why he had been driven to leave everything behind and come to Barcelona in despair.

Onofre Bouvila was not born, as some later claimed, on the prosperous, bright, cheerful and somewhat vulgar Catalan coast, but in the wild, dark and harsh Catalonia that extends to the south-east of the Pyrenees, runs down both flanks of the Sierra del Cadí and then levels out round the upper reaches of the River Segre and its main tributaries, before the river joins Noguera Pallaresa and begins the final stage of its journey, flowing into the River Ebro at Mequinenza.

In the low-lying areas these rivers are fast-flowing and flood every spring. Once the water subsides, the flooded fields become unhealthy and yet fertile marshes, infested with snakes but ideal for hunting. These regions of thick fogs and dense forests give rise to many superstitions. Nobody will venture into these murky mists on certain days of the year, when bells can be heard tolling where there were no churches or chapels; the sounds of voices and laughter can be heard among the trees; and sometimes dead cows are seen dancing the *sardana*. Anybody who saw and heard these things was certain to go mad.

The mountains surrounding these valleys are steep and snow-covered almost all year round. In the past, houses were built on wooden stilts, life was tribal, and the rough, surly menfolk still wore animal skins as part of their attire. These men only descended into the valleys with the spring thaw, to find brides at the celebrations of the grape harvest and the slaughtering of a pig. On these occasions they played bone flutes and performed a dance imitating a rutting ram. They continually chewed on hunks of bread and cheese, and drank wine mixed with oil and water.

On the mountaintops lived an even tougher race: they never went down into the valleys, and their only pastime appears to have been a kind of Greco-roman wrestling. The people in the valleys were more civilised; they lived from their vines, olive groves, maize (for the livestock) and fruit trees, cattle and honey. In this region, at the start of the twentieth century, some 25,000 different kinds of bee were counted, of which only five or six thousand survive in our day. These folk hunted fallow deer, wild boar, rabbits and partridge. They also shot foxes, weasels and badgers to ward off their constant incursions. They were adept at fly-fishing for trout in the rivers. They ate well: there was no shortage of meat or fish in their diet, or vegetables and fruit; as a consequence they were a tall, strong and energetic people who didn't tire easily; at the same time they digested their meals slowly and were lethargic. These physical characteristics influenced the history of Catalonia: one of the reasons the government in Madrid gave for refusing its push for independence there was that this would adversely affect the average height of Spaniards. In his report to King Don Carlos III, who had recently arrived from Naples, R. de P. Piñuela calls Catalonia Spain's footstool.

These people could also count on an abundance of timber, cork and a few minerals. They lived in farmhouses scattered around a valley, connected only by the parish church or rectory. This gave rise to the custom of giving the name of the parish or rectory as their birthplace. So, for example, there was Pere Llebre, from Sant Roc; Joaquim Colibròquil from Mare de Déu del Roser, etc. This meant the rectors bore a great responsibility on their shoulders. They were the ones who maintained spiritual, cultural and even linguistic unity in the region. They were also charged with the crucial mission of keeping the peace in the valleys, and between one valley and its neighbour, to avoid outbreaks of violence and endless bloody vendettas. As a result there emerged a kind of clergyman later praised by the poets: prudent, moderate men, capable of enduring extremes of weather and of walking incredible distances carrying the ciborium in one hand and a blunderbuss in the other.

It was probably also thanks to these priests that the region had almost completely avoided the nineteenth-century Carlist wars. Towards the end of the conflict, Carlist bands had used it as refuge, winter quarters, and a supply centre. The locals let them do so. Every so often a dead body appeared half submerged in the furrows or among the bushes, with a bullet in the chest or the back of the head. Everyone pretended not to notice. Sometimes it wasn't a Carlist, but the victim of a personal quarrel resolved under cover of the war.

All that is known for sure is that Onofre Bouvila was baptised on the feast day of Saint Restituto and Saint Leocadia (December 9) in the year eighteen hundred and seventy-four (or seventy-six), that he received the baptismal waters from the hands of Dom Serafí Dalmau, and that his parents were Joan Bouvila and Marina Mont. It is not known, however, why he was given the name Onofre rather than that of the saint whose day this was. On the baptism certificate he is described as being born in the parish of San Clemente, and as the first-born child of the Bouvila family.

"Splendid, splendid, you'll live like a king here," Señor Braulio said. He took a rusty key from his pocket and waved airily in the direction of a gloomy, foul-smelling passage. "The rooms, as you will see . . . Oh, my goodness, you gave me a fright!"

This exclamation was due to the fact that the door he had been about to unlock had suddenly been thrown open from inside. A female silhouette appeared in the doorway, framed against the light from the balcony.

"This is my daughter Delfina," said Señor Braulio, recovering from the shock. "She must have been tidying the room so that it meets your expectations. Isn't that so, Delfina?" When Delfina made no reply, he added, addressing Onofre Bouvila once more: "Since her mother, my wife, is not in the best of health, all the work here would fall on my shoulders were it not for Delfina. She is a real treasure."

Onofre had already seen the young woman in the lobby a few moments earlier, when she was refilling Señora Agata's bowl with hot water. He had barely noticed her then, but now that he was able to study her more closely, she seemed to him utterly repulsive. Delfina was more or less the same age as him; she was skinny and clumsy, with buck teeth, cracked skin and shifty eyes made unusual by their yellow irises.

He soon came to realise that Delfina was the one who in fact carried out all the chores in the boarding house. Dour-looking, filthy, unkempt, ragged and barefoot, she ran at all hours from the kitchen to the bedrooms and back to the kitchen and the dining room, carrying buckets, brooms and floor cloths. In addition, she attended to her mother's constant needs, and served at table for breakfast, lunch and dinner. First thing each morning she went out to do the shopping with two wicker baskets, and returned dragging them along. She never said a word to any of the lodgers; and they in return pretended she wasn't there.

In addition to her sullen nature, she always had a black cat at her heels. Going by the name of Beelzebub, it only tolerated the presence of its mistress: anybody else ran the risk of bites and scratches. The boarding house furniture and walls bore the marks of its ferocious nature.

For now, however, Onofre Bouvila was unaware of any of this. He had just entered his allotted room, and was surveying this cramped, austere cubicle for the very first time. This is my room, he was thinking with a surge of emotion. I'm an independent man now: a true citizen of Barcelona. He was still carried away by the novelty of his situation; like all new arrivals, he was fascinated by the big city. He had always lived in the country, and had only once visited a town of any size.

That visit constituted a sad memory. The town was called Bassora, situated some eighteen kilometres from his home parish of San Clemente or Sant Climent. At the time when Onofre Bouvila visited it, Bassora had been experiencing rapid growth. From being an agricultural and above all livestock centre, it had become an industrial city. According to the statistics, in 1878 there were 36 industries in Bassora: 21 of these produced textiles (cotton and woollen mills, silk spinners, fabric and carpet workshops, and so on); 11 were chemical factories (phosphates, acetates, chlorides, dyes and soaps); three iron and steel works, and one for timber. A railway line linked Bassora and the port of Barcelona, from where Bassora's goods were exported overseas.

Although there was still a regular horse-drawn coach service, in general people preferred to travel to Barcelona by train. Several streets in the town had gas lighting, there were four hotels or inns, four schools, three social clubs and a theatre. A rocky, uneven road linked Bassora and Sant Climent. It crossed the mountains through a pass or gorge, usually blocked by snow in winter. Weather permitting, an old horse and trap made the journey. There was no regularity, timetable or fixed stops on its trips. It brought farming tools to the farmhouses, all manner of supplies, and any correspondence there might be; on the way back to Bassora it carried surplus produce. This was dispatched by the Sant Climent rector to another priest in Bassora who was a friend of his; he in turn saw to it that it was sold, handed over the earnings, generally in kind, and kept accounts no-one asked him for or cared about.

The driver of the trap was called or went by the name of Uncle Tonet. In Sant Climent he spent the night on the floor of an inn that backed on to the church. Before going to bed he would relate what he had seen and heard in Bassora, even though few of his listeners put any store by what he said: he had the reputation of being too fond of wine and of making things up. Nor could anyone see how the wondrous tales he told could alter the course of life in the valley.

Now, however, Bassora itself shrank into insignificance when Onofre Bouvila mentally compared it to the Barcelona he had just arrived in, and of which as yet he knew nothing. This attitude, in many respects rather naive, was not without justification: according to the 1887 census, what is now known as the "metropolitan area" – that is, the city proper and its outskirts – contained 416,000 inhabitants, a total that was increasing year on year by some 12,000 souls. Of this census figure (which some people question), in the city of Barcelona itself there were 272,000 inhabitants. The rest lived in neighourhoods and villages outside the perimeter of the old city walls. As the nineteenth century wore on, it was here that the most important industries were concentrated. Throughout the century, Barcelona had been in the vanguard of progress. In 1818 the first regular coach service in Spain had been established, linking Barcelona and Reus. The year 1826 saw the first trial of gas lighting in the Patio de la Lonja. In 1836 the first "steam engine" was installed, the start of industrial mechanisation. The first railway in Spain had been the one between Barcelona and Mataró, dating from 1848. In addition, the country's first electric power station was built in Barcelona in 1873.

All this meant there was a huge gulf between Barcelona and the rest of Spain, and the impression the city produced on any new arrival was overwhelming. But it had taken an immense effort to produce this development. Now, like the female of some exotic species that has just given birth to a numerous litter, Barcelona lay back exhausted and torn apart. Out of the wounds flowed pestilent liquids; stinking gases made the air unbreathable in streets and homes. The city's inhabitants were weary and pessimistic. Only a few simpletons like Señor Braulio saw everything through rose-tinted spectacles.

"Barcelona is full of opportunities for anyone with imagination and the determination to seize them," he told Onofre Bouvila that first night in the dining room, as the new lodger sipped the colourless, brackish soup Delfina had served him. "You seem honest, bright, and hard-working. I have no doubt you will soon resolve your situation in a highly satisfactory manner. Just think, young man: never in the history of mankind has there been an age such as this: electricity, telephones, the submarine . . . do I need to go on listing its wonders? God only knows where it will all end. By the way, would you mind paying in advance? My wife, whom you've already met, is very particular when it comes to accounts. The poor woman, she's so ill, d'you see?"

Onofre Bouvila handed over all he had to Señora Agata. He paid a week's rent, but was left without a peseta. At first light the next morning, he set off in search of a job.

2

Even though at the end of the nineteenth century it was already a cliché to say that Barcelona lived "with its back turned on the sea", daily reality did not bear out this claim. Barcelona was and always had been a port city. It had lived from the sea and for the sea; it was fed by the sea and gave the sea the fruits of its toil. Its streets led any pedestrian's footsteps down to the sea, and it was the sea that connected it to the rest of the world. Its air and climate came from the sea: the not always pleasant smell, the humidity, and the salt that corroded its walls. The lapping of the sea lulled its inhabitants to sleep for their siestas; ships' sirens marked the passage of time, and the sad, mournful cry of seagulls was a warning that the sweetness of the shade offered by the trees lining the avenues was merely an illusion. The sea peopled its backstreets with outlandish characters who spoke foreign tongues, had a rolling gait and a dark past, and were all too ready to wield a cut-throat razor, pistol or blackjack. The sea covered the tracks of those stealing a body from justice, those who fled leaving behind them heart-rending cries in the night and unpunished crimes. The colour of the houses and squares in the city was the dazzling white of the sea on cloudless days, or the dull grey of stormy ones. All this was bound to attract a man from the hinterland like Onofre Bouvila. The first thing he did that morning was to go down to the port to look for work on the docks.

Although Barcelona's economic development had begun towards the end of the eighteenth century and would continue until the second decade of the twentieth, it had not been without its ups and downs.

Boom periods had been followed by periods of recession. The flow of migrants into the city did not diminish, but demand for workers did; to find work in these circumstances presented almost insuperable difficulties. Despite Señor Braulio's optimism, when Onofre Bouvila headed out into the streets in search of a living, Barcelona had for several years been going through one of these recessions.

A police cordon barred his way to the docks. When he asked what was going on, he was told there had been several cases of cholera among the stevedores, the disease doubtless brought by a ship arriving from distant lands. Peering over the shoulder of one of the policemen, he glimpsed a tragic scene: several dockers had dropped the loads they were carrying and were vomiting onto the flagstones of the quay; others were excreting a yellowish liquid at the feet of the cranes. So as not to lose their day's pay, as soon as the attack was over, they staggered back to work. Those unaffected gave the sick men a wide berth, threatening them with chains and hooks if they tried to approach. The police were violently driving back a handful of women trying to break through the cordon to go to the aid of husbands or friends.

Onofre Bouvila carried on walking in the direction of Barceloneta. In those days, the majority of ships were still under sail. The port installations were also very rudimentary: the wharves did not allow ships to come alongside, but they were forced to moor by the stern. This meant that loading and unloading had to be done using lighters or launches. Swarms of these vessels plied the waters of the port at all hours, fetching and carrying goods. Old sailors with weather-beaten faces thronged the quays and nearby streets, usually wearing trousers rolled up to the knee, striped jerseys, and Phrygian caps. They smoked cane pipes, drank liquor, ate salt meat and hard tack, and sucked avidly on lemons. They had few words to say to others, and avoided all contact, but talked to themselves the whole time. They were quarrelsome, but more often than not were accompanied by a dog, parrot, turtle or some other pet animal on which they lavished care and attention.

In fact, theirs was a tragic destiny: having gone to sea as cabin boys, by the time they returned to their native land they were old men, bound to it only in their memories. Their rootless existence prevented them from having a family or long-lasting friends. Now they were back, they felt like strangers. However, unlike real foreigners, who can more or less adapt to the customs of the country receiving them, these old tars carried the burden of memories distorted by the passage of so many years, so many idle hours wasted in fostering dreams and projects. Faced with a changed reality, these idealised memories made it impossible for them to adapt to the present. To avoid this mismatch, some of them preferred to live out their days in a foreign port, far from their homeland.

Such was the case of an almost one-hundred-year-old seadog called Sturm. No-one knew where he came from, but he had become famous in Barceloneta, where he now lived. He spoke a tongue no-one could understand, not even the professors in the Faculty of Philosophy and Letters, where his neighbours had once taken him. His entire capital consisted of a wad of banknotes that none of the Barcelona banks was willing to exchange, but since it was a very large bundle, people thought he must be rich, and the neighbourhood shops and bars gave him credit. It was said he wasn't a Christian, that he worshipped the sun, and that he kept a pet seal or manatee in his room with him.

Barceloneta was a fishing village that had grown up in the eighteenth century outside the walls of Barcelona. Subsequently absorbed into the city, it had undergone a process of rapid industrialisation, and now contained the main shipyards. Walking along there, Onofre Bouvila came across a group of cheerful, plump women laughing as they sorted the day's catch. Encouraged by this apparent good humour, he went up to them to seek information. Maybe these women can tell me where I might find work, he thought. Women will be more forthcoming with a youngster like me. He soon discovered his mistake: what he had taken for cheerfulness was in fact a nervous tic that made the fishwives laugh uncontrollably for no reason. Deep down inside they were bitter about life, and seethed with anger: without warning they would brandish their knives and throw lobsters and crabs at each other. Seeing this, Onofre took to his heels. He had no better luck when he tried to sign on as a seaman aboard one of the vessels unaffected by the quarantine. When he approached one of these craft, the sailors leaning on the gunwale advised him not to do so. "Don't climb on board lad, if you don't want to die," they warned him, and told him they were all suffering from scurvy. As proof, they showed him their bleeding gums.

At the railway station the porters, crippled with rheumatism, advised him that you had to belong to a certain association to have any chance of obtaining this slave labour. And so on, wherever he tried. At nightfall Onofre returned exhausted to the boarding house. As he was devouring the meagre dinner, Señor Braulio, who was fluttering from table to table, asked how he had got on. Onofre Bouvila confessed he had had no luck. Hearing their conversation, the person who ran the barber's shop in the lobby butted in. "It's as plain as day you're a country boy," he told Onofre Bouvila. "Try the fruit and vegetable market, you might find something there." Ignoring the veiled sarcasm in this remark, Onofre thanked the man, at the same time aiming a kick at Delfina's cat, which had sunk its claws into his calf. The maidservant glared at him; he responded with a look of disdain.

Even though Onofre was loath to admit it, his failures that day had disheartened him. I had no idea things were so bad, he said to himself. Bah, no matter, he continued, I'll try again tomorrow; if I'm patient enough, something will turn up. Anything so long as I don't have to go back home: that to him was the most daunting prospect.

The next day he took the barber's advice and went to Borne, the central fruit and vegetable market. He had no luck there, however, nor on any of his subsequent attempts. So the hours and the days went by, without any tangible result or hope of one. He plodded from one end of the city to the other in sunshine and rain. He knocked on every door in his wanderings, trying to obtain jobs that until then he had not even known existed: cigar-roller, cheesemaker, diver, stonemason, well-digger. In most places there was no work; in others they wanted experience. In a cake shop they asked if he knew how to make wafers; in a shipyard, if he knew how to caulk a boat. Each time, he was obliged to say no. He soon discovered something he had never suspected: of all the jobs in the city, the least onerous was domestic service.

At this period, a total of 15,186 people were employed in this sector in Barcelona. Conditions in other areas of work were terrible: the hours were extremely long; workers had to get up at four or five in the morning to arrive at work on time. Wages were very low. From the age of five, children worked on building sites or in transport; they even helped gravediggers in cemeteries.

In some places, Onofre received a friendly reception; in others they were openly hostile. In a dairy, a cow almost gored him; elsewhere some charcoal burners set their mastiff on him. He saw misery and disease all around him. Whole neighbourhoods were struck down with typhus, smallpox, erysipelas or scarlet fever. He came across cases of chlorosis, cyanosis, dropsy, necrosis, tetanus, pleurisy, afflux, epilepsy and croup. Malnutrition and rickets were rife among children, tuberculosis among adults; syphilis was everywhere. As with every other city, Barcelona periodically suffered from the most terrible plagues. In 1834, cholera carried off 3,521 people; twenty

27

years later, the death toll was 5,640. In 1870 yellow fever brought from the Spanish Caribbean had spread throughout Barceloneta. The whole neighbourhood had been evacuated, and La Riba wharf burned down.

Whenever these plagues happened, the first reaction was panic, followed by dismay. Processions and public demonstrations were organised to beg God for His forgiveness. Everybody took part in them, even those who a few months earlier had burned convents during a riot or had encouraged these barbaric acts. Those who only recently had taken the lead in setting fire to some poor priest's chasuble, had juggled with sacred statues and had even, it was said, cooked *escudella i carn d'olla* stew with the bones of saints, were precisely the most contrite.

These epidemics eventually abated and moved on, but never entirely: pockets always remained where the disease seemed to be at home, to have put down roots. One epidemic followed another before the previous one had completely disappeared: they overlapped. Doctors had to abandon the last cases of one infection to start to deal with the first patients of the next. Their work was never-ending. This meant that charlatans, quacks, herbalists and healers were everywhere. In all Barcelona's squares there were men and women preaching muddled doctrines, announcing the coming of the Antichrist, the Day of Judgement or of some outlandish Messiah who was suspiciously interested in other people's wealth.

Others honestly offered cures or preventative measures that proved useless, if not counter-productive, such as howling under the full moon, tying bells to one's ankles or having the signs of the zodiac or Saint Catherine's wheel tattooed on the chest. Terrified, and defenceless against the onslaught of disease, people would buy talismans and take potions and powders without a murmur, or give them to their children in the belief they were doing them good.

The city council sealed up the homes of those who died, but such was the lack of housing that before long someone who preferred to run the risk of contagion to living out on the streets would occupy the house, contract the disease, and inevitably die. As always happens in these extreme situations, there were cases of great sacrifice. The following story was told, for example: that of a no longer young nun with the hint of a moustache by the name of Tarsila who, as soon as she learned that such and such a person was laid up with some incurable disease, would run to their bedside with her accordion. She did this for decades without ever getting sick herself, however much she was coughed over.

The night Onofre Bouvila's first week at the boarding house was coming to an end, Señor Braulio called him in. "As you know, payment is in advance," he told him. "You need to settle for the coming week." Onofre sighed. "I haven't found work yet, Señor Braulio," he said. "Give me a week's grace and I'll pay you everything I owe once I get my first day's wage."

"Don't think I don't understand your situation, Señor Bouvila," the boarding house owner replied, "but you need to understand ours: not only does it cost us a great deal to provide your meals every day, but we're losing what another guest would pay if your room were free. I know it's hard, but I have no other choice than to ask you to leave tomorrow at first light. Believe me, I'm sorry to do this, because I've grown fond of you."

That evening, Onofre Bouvila could barely touch his food. He was so tired from his day's efforts he fell asleep as soon as he climbed into bed. An hour later he woke with a start, his mind filled with bitter thoughts. To escape them, he got up and went out onto the balcony, taking deep breaths of the damp, salty breeze that wafted the smell of fish and tar up from the port. Down there too he saw an unearthly glow: the light from the gas street lamps reflected on the mist. The rest of the city was in utter darkness.

After a while the cold penetrated his bones and he decided to go back to bed. Lighting the candle stub on his bedside table, from under his pillow he took out a carefully folded yellowing sheet of paper. Unfolding it, he read what was written on it by the flickering candlelight. As he read what he doubtless already knew by heart, his mouth tightened, his brow furrowed, and his eyes took on an ambiguous mixture of resentment and sadness.

In the spring of 1876 or 1877, his father had emigrated to Cuba. Onofre Bouvila was eighteen months old at the time, the only child the couple then had. His father was a talkative, jovial sort, a good hunter but a bit of a daydreamer, according to those who had known him before he set off on his adventure. Onofre's mother, Marina Mont, was a mountain woman who had come down into the valley to wed Joan Bouvila. Tall and wiry, she seldom spoke, but had nervous, brusque reactions. Before her hair turned white, it had been brown; Onofre's eyes were a bluish-grey like hers, although in every other respect he took after his father. Prior to the eighteenth century, Catalans had seldom gone to the Americas, and then only as servants of the Crown. From that date on, however, many Catalans had emigrated to Cuba. The money these emigrants sent back from the Spanish colony had created an unexpected accumulation of capital. This was used to begin the process of industrialisation and to breathe fresh life into Catalonia's economy, in the doldrums since the days of the Catholic monarchs Don Fernando and Doña Isabella.

As well as sending money, some of these emigrants returned: they were the wealthy so-called *indianos or Americanos*, who built extravagant mansions back in their home villages. The more daring among them brought black or mixed-race slaves with whom they obviously had intimate relations. This created such a huge scandal that, pressurised by relatives or neighbours, they often married off these slaves to simple-minded peasant farmers. These marriages produced dark-skinned offspring, outcasts who often ended up entering religious orders. They were dispatched on missions to the far ends of the earth: to the Mariana or Caroline islands, which were still administered by the archbishoprics of Cadiz or Seville.

After a period of time, this migratory flow diminished. There were still people who crossed the ocean in search of a fortune, but these were isolated cases: a second son left penniless due to a hereditary system which meant that all a family's wealth was inherited by the eldest son, known as the *hereu*; a landowner ruined by phylloxera, and so on.

Joan Bouvila didn't fit into any of these categories, and nobody had ever discovered what drove him to emigrate. Some said it was ambition; others that it was because of matrimonial discord. Someone invented the story that soon after their marriage Joan Bouvila had discovered a terrible secret concerning his wife, that at night terrible screams and blows could be heard coming from their house, and that these rows kept the baby awake until they finally died down in the early hours. Apparently, none of this was true. After Joan Bouvila's departure, the Sant Climent rector not only still received his wife in church, but gave her the sacraments just as he did the other faithful, even treating her with special deference.

Shortly after he left, Joan Bouvila wrote his wife a letter. This missive, sent from a stopover in the Azores, was taken to the parish by Uncle Tonet in his trap. The rector had to read it, because Mariana was unable to. In order to silence the wicked tongues once and for all, he read it from the pulpit one Sunday before his sermon. "When I get work and a house and some dough I'll send for you," Bouvila's father declared. "The crossing is fine, today we saw some sharks.

31

They follow the ship in dangerous packs, waiting for a passenger to fall overboard, then devouring him in one go, they chew him with their three rows of teeth. Nothing is left in the sea of the ones they catch and devour." This was the only letter Joan Bouvila had written.

Onofre Bouvila folded the letter again with great care, put it under his pillow, blew out the candle and closed his eyes. This time he slept deeply, oblivious to the hard mattress or the vicious bedbugs and fleas. Shortly before daybreak, however, he was awakened by a weight on his stomach, a growl, and the unpleasant feeling that somebody was watching him. The bedroom was lit by a candle: not the one he had blown out hours earlier, but another one, held by someone he couldn't at first identify, because his attention was elsewhere. On the bedcover stood Beelzebub, Delfina's savage cat. Its back was arched, its tail stiff; its claws were out. Onofre had his arms trapped under the sheets: he didn't dare lift them out to protect his face, afraid his movements might provoke the monster. So he lay completely still, while sweat pearled on his brow and lips. "Don't be afraid, he won't attack you," whispered a voice, "but if you touch me he'll tear your eyes out." Onofre recognised Delfina's voice, and yet he couldn't take his eyes off the cat or utter a single word.

"I know you haven't found work," Delfina went on. There was a note of satisfaction in her voice, either because Onofre's failure had confirmed her opinion of him or because she took pleasure in other people's misery. "They all think I don't know what's going on, but I hear everything. They treat me like a piece of furniture, a useless bit' of junk, and don't even acknowledge me when we pass in the corridor. It's better that way: they're all swine. I'm sure they hope they can get me into bed ... you know what I mean. Let them try: Beelzebub would tear their skin off. That's why they prefer to pretend they don't see me."

Hearing its name, the cat gave a malignant hiss. Delfina laughed triumphantly, and Onofre realised she was not quite right in the head. That's all I needed, he thought. Where's all this going to end? Dear God, don't let it blind me . . .

"You don't seem like the others," Delfina muttered, switching instantly from laughter to being serious, "perhaps because you're still a child. Bah, you'll be ruined soon enough. Tomorrow you'll be out on the street, where you'll always have to sleep with one eye open. You'll wake up frozen and hungry, with nothing to eat; you'll fight over scraps in the garbage. You'll pray it doesn't rain and that summer is on its way. Bit by bit, you'll turn into a scoundrel, like all the rest. Haven't you got anything to say? You can talk if you don't raise your voice. Just don't move your arms."

"Why are you here?" Onofre risked asking breathlessly. "What do you want from me?"

"They think all I'm good for is scrubbing floors and washing dishes," said Delfina, breaking into a scornful smile. "But I'm worth more than that. I can help you if I choose to."

"What do I have to do?" said Onofre, feeling sweat trickle down his back.

Delfina took a step towards the bed: Onofre went rigid, but she didn't come any closer. After a pause, she said: "Listen to me. I have a boyfriend. Nobody knows that, not even my parents. I'll never tell them. And then one fine day, I'll run away with him. They'll look for me everywhere, but by then we'll be far off. We'll never marry, but we'll always live together, and they'll never see me again here. If you reveal my secret, I'll tell Beelzebub to rip your face to pieces, do you hear me?" she said. Onofre swore by God and on his mother's grave that he would keep her secret. Satisfied with his answer, Delfina went on: "Listen: my boyfriend belongs to a group of generous and brave men, determined to put an end to the injustice and misery all around us." She paused to judge what effect her words had on Onofre Bouvila, but when he didn't react, she added: "Have you heard of anarchism?" Onofre shook his head. "Do you know who Bakunin is?" Onofre shook his head again, but rather than flying into a rage as he had feared, she merely shrugged. "It's natural," she concluded: "They're new ideas and few people know about them. But there's no hurry: soon the whole world will become aware of them; things are going to change."

In the 1860s, the anarchist groups that had flourished in Italy during the years of struggle for that country's unification decided to send disciples abroad to spread their message and win converts. The man sent to Spain, where anarchist ideas were already known and held in great esteem, was called Foscarini. A few kilometres outside Nice, the Spanish police, in cahoots with their French counterparts, stopped the train Foscarini was on and boarded it. "Hands in the air," shouted the police, waving their carbines at the passengers: "Which of you is Foscarini?" All of them immediately raised their arms: "I am Foscarini, I am Foscarini," they shouted in unison: for them there was no greater honour than to be taken for this apostle of anarchism. The only one who kept his mouth shut was Foscarini. Endless years spent in clandestinity had taught him to dissemble in cases like this; now he sat staring out of the window whistling cheerfully, as if this police raid had nothing to do with him. This lapse meant the police were able to identify him immediately. They dragged him off the train, stripped him to his underclothes, then tied him up and laid him across the railway tracks, his head on one rail, his feet on the other. "When the nine o'clock express comes through, you'll end your days as a salami, Foscarini," they laughed diabolically. One of the policemen put on the Italian's clothes and re-boarded the train. When he entered the carriage, the passengers thought Foscarini must have fooled his captors, and burst into cheers. The bogus Foscarini smiled and wrote down the names of those applauding most loudly. Once the policeman reached Spain, he began to incite senseless violence to create a tense atmosphere, turn people against the workers, and justify the harsh repressive measures the government was introducing. In fact, he was an *agent provocateur*, Delfina told Onofre.

At almost the same time, there arrived in Barcelona someone diametrically the opposite of the real and bogus Foscarinis. His name was Conrad de Weerd. In his native United States he had been a sports journalist of some renown. A descendant of plantation owners in South Carolina who had lost their fortune in the Civil War, including their estates and their black slaves, De Weerd had tried his hand at journalism in Baltimore, New York, Boston and Philadelphia, but being a Southerner he had found all openings barred to him, apart from the sports pages. He had known personally all the most important figures of his day, such as Jake Kilrain and John L. Sullivan, but in general his career had followed less illustrious lines.

In the mid eighteen hundreds, sport was little more than an excuse to place bets and to indulge mankind's worst instincts. De Weerd covered cock fights, dog fights and rat fights, as well as mixed contests of bulls against dogs, dogs against rats, rats against pigs. He also had to attend exhausting, bloody boxing matches that lasted as many as eighty-five rounds and usually ended up with shots being fired.

In the end De Weerd came to the conclusion that human nature was essentially brutal and cruel, and that only public education could transform an individual into a minimally tolerable being. Spurred on by this conviction, he abandoned the world of sports and dedicated himself to setting up workers' associations with funds provided by some liberal-minded Jewish moneylenders. The aim of these associations was mutual education and the promotion of the arts, especially music. De Weerd sought to incorporate the workers into huge choirs, believing this would stop them being interested in rat fights. He always lived as a poor man: whatever he earned he invested in the upkeep of the choirs he had founded. Bit by bit, however, gangsters infiltrated the choirs, transforming them into mobs. To get rid of De Weerd they packed him off to Europe to spread his message there. Having heard of the existence of the Clavé choirs, he landed in Barcelona on Ascension Day 1876. He soon ran into the crazed followers of the bogus Foscarini, who were proposing the indiscriminate killing of children as they came out of school. This shocked him beyond measure.

Another interesting character, Delfina continued, is Remedios Ortega Lombrices, known as *la Tagarnina*. This intrepid syndicalist happened to be working in the Seville tobacco factory. An orphan at the age of ten, she had been obliged to take charge of her eight brothers and sisters. Two had died of illness, but she managed to raise the others by dint of hard work, and still had the strength to bring up eleven children by seven different fathers. While twisting and rolling cigars, she managed to acquire a thorough knowledge of economic and social theory in an ingenious way: since each girl had to roll a certain number of cigarettes per day, the female workers resolved to cover the quota of one of their companions so that she wouldn't have to work but could read books out loud to them. This was how they learned about Marx, Adam Smith, Bakunin, Zola and many others. She was more militant than De Weerd, less individualistic than the two Italians. Rather than preach the destruction of factories, which in her view would have left the country in absolute misery, she called for them to be occupied and collectivised.

Of course, Delfina explained, each of these leaders had their followers, and yet the distinct factions had always respected each other, however profound their theoretical differences. They had always been willing to co-operate and come to one another's aid, and had never fought amongst themselves. From the outset their bitter enemy had been socialism in all its forms, although sometimes it was hard to distinguish one doctrine from another, she concluded.

As she expounded this naive argument with its glaring contradictions and inconsistencies, her yellow eyes shone with a demented gleam that Onofre found, if not attractive, then at least fascinating, without being able to say why. She was holding the candle aloft like a lantern, oblivious to the drops of wax falling to the floor. By this dim light, wearing a coarse cloth nightgown over her bony frame, she looked like a proletarian Minerva. Eventually the cat began to show signs of impatience, and so Delfina cut short her lecture.

"If you do as I say, you'll learn the rest," she told him. Onofre asked her what it was he had to do. The main thing, she said, was to spread the word, to sound the trumpet that would awaken the sleeping masses. "You're new to Barcelona," she said finally. "No-one knows you, you're very young, and you appear innocent. You can contribute to the cause and earn some money along the way. Not a lot, because we're very poor, but enough for you to pay your rent. As you can see, we're not the dreamers some people say we are: we understand that people have to live. Well, what do you think?"

"When do I start?" asked Onofre. Although he wasn't particularly enthusiastic about the idea, Delfina's suggestion at least gave him some breathing space.

"Tomorrow morning, you're to appear at Number Four, Calle del Musgo," said Delfina, her voice dropping to a whisper. "Ask for Pablo. He's not my boyfriend, but he knows about you and is expecting you. He'll give you instructions. Be very careful and make sure no-one is following you: remember the police are always on the lookout. As for my father and your week's rent, don't worry about that. I'll see to it. Come on, Beelzebub."

Without another word, she blew out the candle, plunging the

room into darkness. Onofre felt the weight of the cat disappear, and heard the soft thud of its four paws on the floor tiles. He saw the eyes of that fearsome animal glinting in the doorway, until finally the door closed silently.

3

By asking various passersby, Onofre discovered that the address Delfina had given him was in Pueblo Nuevo, relatively close to the city centre. A mule-drawn tram went there, but as he did not have the 20-centavos fare, he had to walk all the way along the tracks. Calle del Musgo was a gloomy, solitary place backing on to the wall of a municipal burial ground for suicides. The street was full of skittish dogs with sparse, patchy coats and sharp teeth that went digging among the tombs at night for something to eat.

It had rained during the night and the sky was overcast; the atmosphere was damp and clammy. None of this affected Onofre Bouvila, who was in excellent spirits. At breakfast that morning Señor Braulio had come over and told him: "My wife and I were talking things over last night, and we decided together, as we always do, to grant you a week's credit." He scratched an ear that was as pink as a carnation. "Times are hard, and you're very young to be out on the street in a world such as ours," he said. "We're also confident that you'll soon find the employment you are so earnestly pursuing. We're convinced that your honesty and dedication will eventually provide you with an honourable future," he concluded emphatically. Onofre had thanked him and glanced at Delfina, who at that moment was crossing the dining room with a bucket full of dirty water, but she either pretended not to see him or actually didn't.

He knocked on the door of Number 4 Calle del Musgo. It was

immediately opened by a skinny individual with a domed forehead and thin, parched lips.

"I'm Onofre Bouvila and I'm looking for someone called Pablo."

"I'm Pablo," the man said. "Come in."

Onofre stepped inside an apparently deserted warehouse. The walls were covered in mould and saltpeter; there were patches of oil on the floor, a few crates, and coils of rope. Pablo took a packet out of one of the crates. "These are the pamphlets you're to distribute," he said, handing the packet to Onofre. "You're familiar with the Idea, aren't you?" It amused Onofre that both Pablo and Delfina called it "the Idea" as though it were the only possible one. He also sensed that with Pablo sincerity was the best policy, and so he said no, he wasn't familiar with it. Pablo looked at him angrily: "Read one of the pamphlets closely," he said. "I don't have the time to instruct you, and besides, the pamphlets explain everything very clearly. You need to know, in case anybody asks you what it's about, do you see?" Onofre nodded. "Have they told you where you're to distribute them?" the anarchist asked. Onofre shook his head. "What, not that either?" Pablo sighed, giving him to understand that the whole weight of making the revolution fell on his shoulders. "Very well, I'll tell you," he added. "Do you know where they're building the World Fair?" Again, Onofre had to admit he didn't. "But my lad," Pablo protested, "what planet are you from?" Still grumbling, he explained how to get to the site, and showed him out. Before he could close the door, Onofre had time to ask:

"What do I do once I've handed out all the pamphlets?"

For the first time, the apostle smiled. "Come back for more," he said almost gently. He told Onofre he should come to the warehouse between five and six in the morning, and not at any other time. "If we happen to bump into each other somewhere, you're to pretend you don't know me," he quickly added. "Don't give anybody this address, or mention me or the person who sent you, even if your life is at stake," he said solemnly. "If anyone asks your name, say it's Gaston: that will be your alias. Now be on your way: the shorter our meetings, the better."

Onofre Bouvila hurried away from that sordid place. When he came to a small square, he sat on a bench, opened the packet, and began reading one of the pamphlets. Children were running about the square, and from an invisible locksmith's nearby came the relentless sound of hammering. This made it hard for him to concentrate properly: he hardly knew how to read, and needed time and silence to understand what was written there. Besides, half the words were incomprehensible to him. The prose was so convoluted that even though he went over it several times, he found it hard to follow. And I'm risking my life for nonsense like this, he said to himself.

Tying up the packet, he set off for where Pablo had indicated. As he walked, he cast a countryman's eye over this area that only a few years before had been cultivated fields. Now, trapped by the advance of industry, it was a barren, black and stinking wasteland, poisoned by the putrid streams emanating from the nearby factories, awaiting its destiny. Absorbed by the thirsty earth, these streams formed a slimy mud that stuck to any passerby's rope sandals and made walking difficult.

At a certain point Onofre must have confused the railway track with a set of tramlines, and lost his way. Since he couldn't see a soul to ask directions from, he climbed a small hillock from where he hoped to be able to spot his goal, or at least discover where he was. The position of the sun, a brief estimate of the time of day, and his country knowledge allowed him to identify the four points of the compass. Now I know where I am, he thought. Over to the east the clouds had cleared, and the sun's rays were filtering through: as they struck the sea, it shimmered with a silver sparkle. Turning his back on the sea, Onofre could make out the hazy silhouette of the city. He could see the belfries and spires of churches and convents, and many factory chimneys. A railway engine was shunting nearby, heading for a siding. The column of smoke it sent up rose only a few feet before the damp, heavy air pushed it back towards the ground. The noise from the locomotive was the only sound that broke the silence.

Onofre resumed his journey. Whenever he saw a mound, he climbed it and scanned the horizon. At last he spotted, on the far side of the railway line where a few moments before he had seen the locomotive, a flat expanse where men, animals and carts were swarming around buildings under construction. That must be the place he was looking for. Or at least there they'll be able to inform me, he told himself. He climbed down from the hillock and headed for the site with the packet of pamphlets under his arm.

The Ciudadela, whose atrocious reputation persists to this day, and whose name is still synonymous with oppression, came into being and disappeared in the following manner: in 1701, Catalonia, jealous of freedoms it saw as under threat, had rallied to the cause of the Habsburg Archduke in the War of the Spanish Succession. When this faction was defeated and the House of Bourbon installed on the throne of Spain, Catalonia was punished severely. The war had been lengthy and cruel, but the aftermath was worse. With the acquiescence of their leaders, the Bourbon soldiers sacked Catalonia, giving full rein to their hatred. After that came the official repression: hundreds of Catalans were executed, and as a punishment and a lesson their heads were stuck on pikes and exhibited at the busiest crossroads in the Principality. Thousands of prisoners were sent as forced labour to distant parts of the peninsula and even to America; they all died in their shackles without ever seeing their beloved homeland again.

Young Catalans were used as comfort women for the troops, resulting in a lack of girls of marriageable age that persists to this day. Many farms were destroyed, and the land sown with salt to make it infertile; fruit trees were uprooted. Attempts were also made to get rid of all livestock, especially the much-prized Pyrenean cow. This only failed because some of the cattle escaped into the mountains, where they survived in a wild state until well into the nineteenth century. This was how they managed to save themselves from the ferocious cavalry charges, the artillery bombardments, and the infantry's bayonets. Castles were pulled down and their stone blocks used to build walls around some of the Catalan villages, virtually turning them into prisons. The monuments and statues adorning avenues and squares were reduced to dust. The walls of palaces and public buildings were whitewashed and covered with obscene drawings and filthy or offensive slogans. Schools were turned into stables, and vice versa; the University of Barcelona, where eminent figures had been both educated and taught, was closed down; the building housing it was demolished stone by stone, and these stones used to block up the aqueducts, canals and irrigation channels supplying the city and surrounding fields with water. The port of Barcelona was filled with blocks of stone; sharks brought especially in tanks from the Caribbean were released into the sea so that the Mediterranean would be infested with them. Fortunately they found it hard to adapt: the ones that did not die due to the climate or from swallowing molluscs, emigrated to other latitudes via the Straits of Gibraltar, in those days in the hands of the English.

The king was informed of all these measures. "Perhaps," he said, "this punishment is not sufficient for the Catalans." Philip the Fifth, the Duke of Anjou, was an enlightened monarch. A French writer has spoken of him as a *roi fou, brave et dévot*. He married an Italian woman, Isabel de Farnese, and died raving. Although he was not naturally bloodthirsty, malicious advisers had blackened the reputation of not only the Catalans but the Sicilians and the Neapolitans, as well as the creoles, Canary islanders, Philippinos and the Indo-Chinese, all of whom were subjects of the Spanish Crown. As a result, he had a huge fortress built in Barcelona where an army of occupation was deployed, ready to pour out and stifle any attempt at revolt. From the start, this fortress was known as the Ciudadela. Inside lived the governor, completely cut off from the inhabitants of the city: a copy of the most rigid Spanish colonial system was introduced. Prisoners accused of sedition were hanged on the flat ground outside the fortress; the dead bodies of executed patriots were left as food for the buzzards.

In the shadow of these fortifications, the inhabitants of Barcelona lived servile lives, weeping with nostalgia and rage. Once or twice they attempted to storm the fortress, but were repulsed with ease. They were always forced to withdraw, leaving the ground littered with casualties. The defenders mocked their attackers; they appeared at the embrasures to urinate on the dead and wounded. The downside to this disgusting behaviour was that they could not leave the castle or mix with the local people, who hated them; prisoners of circumstance, they were not permitted any entertainment. Deprived of female company, the soldiers turned to sodomy and neglected personal hygiene, so that the Ciudadela became a focus for all kinds of disease.

Weary of this situation, both sides petitioned successive monarchs to do away with this symbol of hostility and infamy. Only a few fanatics defended its continued presence. As with all those who possess absolute power, the kings said yes to everything, then put off doing anything about it. By the mid-nineteenth century, the Ciudadela no longer served any purpose; advances in warfare had rendered it obsolete. During a popular uprising in 1848, General

Espartero deemed it more expedient to bombard the city from the top of Montjuich hill than from the old fortress.

Finally, after a century and a half, the Ciudadela's giant walls were demolished. As if to erase all the accumulated suffering, the land it stood on and the buildings were donated to the city of Barcelona. Some of these buildings were with good reason pulled down; others are still standing. The city council decided to turn the site into a public park for everyone's enjoyment. It made a moving contrast to see trees growing and flowers blooming on the esplanade where so many atrocities had been committed, and where until not long before the scaffold had stood. A lake was dug as well, with in its centre a huge fountain known as the Cascada. The park was and still is known as the Ciudadela Park.

At the start or the middle of May 1887, when Onofre Bouvila first approached it, this was where the grounds of the World Fair were being created. The work was already well advanced. The workforce had reached its maximum, that is, four thousand five hundred labourers, an unprecedented number for those days. In addition, there were an unknown but equally large number of mules and donkeys, as well as cranes, steam engines, machinery and wagons. Everything was covered in dust, the noise was deafening, and confusion reigned.

In 1887, Don Francisco de Paula Rius y Taulet was mayor of Barcelona for a second time. Approaching fifty years of age, he had a permanent scowl, a curious bald head, and whiskers so long they covered the lapels of his frock coat. Chroniclers of the city at this period said he had a patrician air. Rius y Taulet was very attentive to the prestige of his city and his administration. In the stormy summer days of 1886, the mayor had faced a difficult dilemma. A few months earlier he had received the visit of a gentleman by the name of Eugenio Serrano de Casanova. "I have grave news to share with you, your excellency," he had told the mayor. Don Eugenio Serrano de Casanova was originally from Galicia, but had settled in Catalonia, where his youthful militancy had been employed in the Carlist cause. With the passage of time, his political fervour had diminished, but not his energy: he was enterprising and a great traveller.

On his travels, he had visited World Fairs in Antwerp, Paris and Vienna, and been dazzled by them. Since he was not a man to let his ideas lie fallow, he drew up plans and asked Barcelona City Council for permission to stage a similar event there. The council offered him Ciudadela Park. "If he wants to get involved in such a messy business, that's his problem," the relevant authorities concluded. Their attitude had been both misguided and dangerous: in reality, none of them had the faintest idea what organising a World Fair implied. These Fairs were a new phenomenon, which they only knew of through the press. Although the idea of a World Fair had originated in France, the first one had been held in London in 1851. Paris came later, in 1855, and was so poorly organised that it opened its doors a fortnight late, and many of the exhibits hadn't even been unpacked on the day of the official inauguration.

Among the illustrious personages who visited the Paris exhibition was Queen Victoria herself, then at the height of her power. *Pas mal, pas mal* she would mutter with a slight twist of the lips as she walked along, doubtless delighted at the signs of incompetence displayed by the French. She was followed by a sepoy who was more than two metres tall, not counting his turban. He carried with him on a crimson silk cushion the Koh-i-noor, at the time the largest diamond in the world – it was as if by this Queen Victoria was saying: "A single one of my possessions is worth more than everything on show here." In this, however, she was mistaken: what was most important was to rival other cities in ideas and progress.

Similar events were subsequently held in Antwerp, Vienna,

Philadelphia and Liverpool. By the time Serrano de Casanova presented his proposal in Barcelona, London had already held its second exhibition in 1862, and Paris in 1867. But although Serrano de Casanova's energy was boundless, his capital was more limited. Barcelona was going through a considerable financial crisis, and the intrepid promoter's repeated requests fell on deaf ears. His initial investment had already been spent, meaning there was a threat the project would be abandoned. Serrano de Casanova went to see mayor Rius y Taulet. In a low voice, as if passing on a secret, he told him: "Your excellency, I have grave news to share with you: much to my regret, I have decided to capitulate."

Work on adapting Ciudadela Park had already begun; in one way or another, the event had already received a great deal of publicity. "Damnation!" exclaimed Rius y Taulet, furiously ringing the gold and crystal bell on his desk. When an orderly appeared, he told him without so much as looking in his direction to take all the necessary steps to summon the dignitaries of Barcelona to an immediate meeting: the bishop, the governor, the Captain-general, the president of the governing body, the university rector, the president of the Athenaeum, and so on. At this, the orderly fainted on the spot, and the mayor himself had to revive him, fanning him with his handkerchief.

When this illustrious group was finally assembled, there was more speechifying than a desire to do anything. They were all happy to give their opinion, but none of them was willing to commit themselves or their institution to the project, still less to offer financial support to Serrano de Casanova's hare-brained scheme. Eventually Rius y Taulet thumped the table with a leather-bound folder and put a stop to all their endless chattering. *Hòstia, la Mare de Déu!* he cried at the top of his voice. This violent exclamation was heard outside in Plaza de San Jaime and became public knowledge, so that nowadays it can be found, together with others of his famous phrases, engraved on the side of the monument to the indefatigable mayor. Hearing this curse, the bishop made the sign of the cross.

A mayor is someone to be taken seriously. Within the hour he had obtained not only their agreement but also the promise of the financial support needed for the project to go ahead. "To abandon it at this stage," he told them, "would be a stain on Barcelona's honour, a confession of weakness." They resolved to press on with the project under the aegis of a Board of Directors. A Board of Trustees was also established, made up of civilian and military authorities, the presidents of different associations, bankers and prominent figures from the business world. This was intended to involve everyone in the project, to make it as much a collective endeavour as possible. A Technical Board was set up, consisting of architects and engineers. As time went by, boards and committees proliferated (committees to co-ordinate with national firms, committees to liaise with potential foreign exhibitors, committees to organise competitions and award prizes, etc.). All of this caused confusion and considerable friction.

Nevertheless, everyone agreed that this organisation was "very modern". However, public opinion was far from unanimous concerning the project's chances of success. *It has to be said*, noted a newspaper of the time, *that the city does not offer sufficient attractions to make the stay of any foreigner visiting for a few days a pleasant one.* In general, everyone thought Barcelona would cut a forlorn figure if it attempted to rival Paris or London. None of them thought of what cities like Antwerp or Liverpool were offering in those years without so much soul-searching. Or if they did, their conclusion was: let others play the fool if they so wish, but we won't. *In Barcelona, apart from its pleasant climate, its excellent situation, its ancient monuments, and a little, very little, initiative of some individuals, we cannot compete with the other European cities of similar size,* says a letter that appeared in a contemporary newspaper. *Everything related to its*

47

administration, the letter continued, *is inferior. The municipal police is in general despicable; security leaves a deal, a great deal, to be desired; a large number of services essential for a city of 250,000 people are either lacking or are badly organised; the narrow streets in the old quarter and the lack of large squares there and in the new city make movement and leisure difficult; we have no decent or varied promenades, and we lack museums, libraries, hospital, hospices, prisons and so on that are worthy of a visit.* This letter took up several pages, and went on to say: *We have spent a great deal on Ciudadela Park, but it is far from being big enough, having no large wood or lengthy promenade, whilst what is meant to be a lake is frankly ridiculous.* In saying this, the author of the letter was doubtless thinking of the famous parks of that day: the Bois de Boulogne and Hyde Park. The letter expands on this criticism: *Ill-conceived ideas and hollow vanity all too often characterise the actions of our local administration. In recent years, Barcelona has become a filthy city. The facades of those houses of any age are usually nothing but repugnant!* Similar letters were frequent in newspapers of the time. Others expressed their reservations more concisely, such as an editorial of 22 September 1866 which began with this headline: IN ECONOMIC TERMS, IS THE WORLD FAIR A BLESSING OR A CURSE?

Despite this, in general there was little opposition to the event. Apparently, the majority of citizens were willing to put up with the risks the venture implied; the rest knew from experience that whatever the authorities decided would go ahead. Centuries of absolute rule had taught people not to waste ink or energy on such matters.

There was a more important factor in public opinion: that the first World Fair in Spain should take place in Barcelona rather than Madrid. This had already been commented on by the newspapers in the national capital. They had come to the sad conclusion that this was inevitable. *Land and sea communications between Barcelona and the rest of the world make it more suitable than any other city in Spain to attract foreign visitors*, they wrote. They seemed satisfied with this, as if it meant the choice of Barcelona to host the fair had been theirs.

However, this argument did not sway the central government. "You're putting it on, so you have to pay for it," they decreed. In those days, Spain's economy was as centralised as everything else: the wealth of Catalonia and all the other regions of the kingdom went directly to the coffers in Madrid. Local councils had to meet their needs by raising local taxes, but for any additional expenditure they had to turn to the Madrid government for a subsidy, a loan, or as in the present case, a curt refusal. This refusal created a great sense of solidarity among the Catalan people and silenced the critics.

"This means," commented Rius y Taulet, "that we can go whistle." No-one disagreed with that. "With Madrid we'll end up fighting, but without Madrid we'll get nowhere at all," said the renowned financier Manuel Girona, at that time president of the Athenaeum. He was well known for never losing his temper: "Let's keep our emotional reactions for a more suitable occasion, and face reality," he said. "We have to do a deal with Madrid. It will be humiliating, but it's worth it." His words brought the discussion to a close.

After High Mass the following Sunday, two delegates from the Board of Trustees set out for Madrid. They travelled in a coach the city council had put at their disposal; the coat of arms of Barcelona was emblazoned on its doors. The two men were carrying all the documents related to the project in enormous folders bound in croco-dile skin, while tied to the back of the coach were several trunks filled with changes of clothes: they expected to be gone for some considerable time, and events were to prove they were not mistaken.

As soon as they reached Madrid, they booked into a hotel, and on the following morning appeared at the Ministry of Public Works. Their arrival caused a great stir: among the clothes they had brought

49

from Barcelona and were now wearing were coats and capes that had once belonged to Joan Fiveller, the city's legendary protector. Over the centuries, the wool of these garments had been reduced to flock, and the silks turned into a kind of cobweb. As the delegates walked across the Ministry carpets, clutching their folders in both hands as if they were holy offerings, they left a trail of brown dust behind them. These two delegates had names that, were it not for the fact they were real, might have seemed invented especially for the occasion: Guitarrí and Guitarró. They were shown into a large room with a high coffered ceiling, where the only furniture was two uncomfortable Renaissance-style chairs, and on the wall a painting some three metres high by nine wide from Zurbarán's studio. This depicted an aged hermit with bluish skin covered in sores and surrounded by bones and skulls. Guitarrí and Guitarró were kept waiting for more than three hours before a half-concealed side door opened and a man appeared. He had a puffy face, muttonchop side whiskers, and was wearing a frock coat smothered in gold and silk braid. The two delegates immediately rose to their feet. One of them, nerves frayed after the long wait, whispered in his companion's ear: "By all that's holy, his look is enough to put the wind up you!" They both bowed deeply. The newcomer, who turned out not to be the minister but an usher, told them curtly that the honourable minister could not receive them that day, but asked them to be so kind as to return to the Ministry at the same time the following morning.

The confusion caused by this man's eye-catching attire was simply the first in a long list of errors: the delegates found themselves in a milieu that was completely alien to them. They did not know what to make of this city full of taverns and convents, street vendors, riffraff, pickpockets, cripples and beggars, in the midst of which existed an even more extraordinary world of glitter and pomp, posturing and privilege, peopled by conspiratorial generals, crooked dukes, miracle-working priests, court advisers, bullfighters, dwarves and court buffoons who all mocked them, their Catalan accent and their odd syntaxis.

Guitarrí and Guitarró spent three months and all their funds in pointless visits to the Ministry, after which they wrote to Barcelona relating what had happened and requesting further instructions. By return of post they received a package from Rius y Taulet containing money, a plaster copy of the Virgin of Montserrat, and a message: *Take heart, one of the two sides has to yield, and thanks be to God it's not going to be ours.* By now the poor delegates rarely left their hotel, where the staff, who had grown accustomed to their presence and were convinced they could not expect any generous gestures from them, no longer bothered to change their towels or sheets or to dust the few sticks of battered furniture in the room they shared to save money. The two men lived in considerable discomfort, cooking breakfast and supper there, using hot water from the bathtub.

What most afflicted them, however, were their morning visits to the Ministry. The swarm of loafers and scroungers in the corridors and antechambers had composed some hurtful verses aimed at them; they heard them being hummed wherever they went. The Ministry employees made them the butt of even crueller jokes: they put pails full of water over the doorways they needed to get through, stretched wires across the floor for them to stumble over, or singed their coat-tails with lighted candles. Some days when they entered the waiting room they found the two chairs occupied by other petitioners who were even earlier risers. Long accustomed to this sort of situation and hardened by a life of being kept waiting, flattery, pleas, submissions and disappointments, they pretended not to even notice the Barcelona delegates, refusing to give up their seats for even a minute during the ritual three hours' wait. Every day, after they had been cooped up in this room, the tiniest details of which they came to know by heart, the concealed door would open, the bewhiskered usher would appear and hand them a silver tray. On it would be a hastily scrawled note in which the minister regretfully informed them that he was unable to receive them that day as he would have wished. The frequency with which he peppered these notes with ribald remarks often rendered them incomprehensible.

This only increased the delegates' anxiety, as they were usually left wondering whether or not they had understood the minister's instructions, and searching for the slightest hint of any change of attitude on his part. Occasionally, after much hesitation and discussion, they replied to these notes with ones of their own. In order to do so they had visited a specialist establishment in Calle Mayor and had cards printed, headed either by accident or design with the crest of Valencia instead of Barcelona as they had requested. To correct this mistake would have meant a month's delay, so they had to make do with them. On these cards they wrote, for example: *We are only too aware of the demands on the time of your excellency, to whom may God grant long life and happiness, and yet with respect we must humbly insist, given the transcendent nature of the mission entrusted to us,* etcetera. The minister would respond the next day with expressions such as "time tighter than a badger's arse" (meaning being short of time), "having his dick in his hands" (overwhelmed with work), "going round shitting a blue streak" (going at full speed), "Saintfuck's day is Monday" (asking them to be patient), "farting my breeches off" (meaning uncertain), and so on. He would sign off by saying: "until the twelfth of never!" or some such expression. *Possibly your excellency would have more time available,* the delegates eventually replied, if *your excellency did not waste so much of it on attempts to be droll.* At night they wrote letters filled with discouragement and longing to their families in Barcelona. Occasionally the ink was smudged where they had been unable to suppress a tear.

Meanwhile, the Board of Directors of the World Fair, presided over by Rius y Taulet, was wasting no time. "Let's defy Madrid with a *fait accompli*," seemed to be their motto. Designs for the buildings, monuments, installations and outbuildings were invited, presented and approved, and the necessary works begun at a speed the available funds would not allow to continue for very long. When the entire Ciudadela Park was turned upside down, the city council invited correspondents to visit it. To entice them, the journalists were offered a banquet whose menu demonstrates the hosts' cosmopolitan vocation: *Potage: Bisque d'écrevises à l'américaine. – Relèves: Loup à la genevoise. – Entrées: Poulard de Mans à la Toulouse, tronches de filet à la Godard. – Légumes: Petits pois au beurre. Rôts: Perdreaux jeunes sur crustades, galantines de dindes trufées. – Entremets: Bisquits Martin decorés. – Ananas et Goteauv. – Dessert assorti. – Vinos: Oporto, Château Iquem, Bordeaux y Champagne Ch. Mumm.*

The after-dinner speeches gave a definite date for the opening (Spring 1887); as a result, appreciative reports of the event appeared in numerous publications. Advertising posters were printed and pasted up in railway stations throughout Europe; invitations were sent to Spanish and overseas corporations and businesses, inviting them to take part in the exhibition; and as was customary at the time, various literary competitions were announced. The response from future exhibitors was lukewarm, but not negligible.

At the end of 1886, the first names of licensed providers of services appeared in the press. *The provision of water-closets and washbasins has been adjudicated (subject to the stated conditions) to Señor Fraxedas y Florit. This perspicacious supplier intends to offer a complete grooming service, providing rooms containing all necessary toilet requisites, white towels, soaps and perfumes. In addition, in each of these facilities there will be a room set aside for the cleaning of footwear, and a suitable number of errand boys will be on hand for the public and exhibitors to take messages and deliver articles bought at the Fair to their homes. We congratulate Señor Fraxedas y Florit for his foresight in seizing this golden opportunity, and having the good sense to avoid it being exploited by foreigners.*

In the end, it was the Minister of Public Works who gave way. He was a corpulent man with such a fierce look he seemed almost inhuman. Behind his back people called him "the African". He had never set foot in Africa, and had no link whatsoever with that continent, but had earned the nickname by his demeanour. When he heard about it, he was far from being offended, and indeed acquired the habit of wearing a ring in his nose. He received the two delegates frostily, but unbeknownst to them, time had worked in their favour; the minister was completely disarmed by their appearance. The countless hours of waiting, the anguish and constant humiliations they had suffered had aged them; being forced to live together day and night, they had come to look as alike as two peas in a pod, and the pair of them now resembled the holy hermit in the painting by Zurbarán's studio they had been staring at for months. Seeing them, the minister suddenly felt exhausted: the whole weight of his power descended on his shoulders. What ought to have been a titanic encounter became a wearisome, melancholy conversation.

4

The World Fair grounds in Ciudadela Park had been fenced off to protect the building works from curious onlookers. However, there were many holes in the fence; and besides, the constant tumultuous comings and goings at the park gates, with people entering and leaving as they wished without any kind of control, meant it was no real obstacle. Onofre Bouvila stuffed five pamphlets down his shirt, hid the rest between two granite slabs by the wall running along the railway tracks, and slipped inside the park. It was only then, when he saw the reigning pandemonium, that it dawned on him how difficult his task would be. Apart from helping his mother around the farm, he had never had any settled work, and had no idea of how complicated direct contact with other people can be. Well, he told himself, I've gone from scattering maize to the hens to spreading revolution in secret. So what? If someone is good at the first, he has to be good at the second, he thought. Spurred on by this idea, he went up to a group of carpenters nailing planks to make the framework for a pavilion. To attract their attention, he called out: "Hey, hello there! God bless you on this fine morning!" and so on. Eventually, one of the carpenters saw him out of the corner of his eye; he raised an eyebrow as if to ask what Onofre wanted.

"I've brought some very interesting pamphlets!" shouted Onofre, taking one of them out to show to the carpenter.

"What's that you say?" the carpenter shouted back; the noise of the hammering he himself was making either made it impossible for him to hear anything at that moment or had permanently deafened him. Onofre was about to repeat what he had said, but just then a cart pulled by three mules forced him to jump out of the way. The muleteer cracked his whip in the air as he pulled on the reins, dug his heels into the ground, and leaned backward as far as he could. "Make way! Make way!" he called out. The back of the cart was piled high with rubble that gave off whitish clouds as the wheels jolted over stones and ruts, producing deep metallic sounds like a heavy door knocker. "Gee up there!" shouted the muleteer.

Onofre fled. For a few moments he toyed with the idea of throwing the pamphlets on a rubbish heap and going to tell Pablo he had handed them all out, but he quickly dismissed the notion: he was afraid the anarchists would be keeping an eye on him, at least during these first days.

"What have you got there, lad?" asked a labourer he had approached; the man was part of a team having a break. One of them kept a lookout: if he saw the foreman coming, he would whistle, and the others would rush back to work.

"It's in case you'd like to start a revolution," Onofre replied, handing him a pamphlet. The labourer screwed it up into a ball, and tossed it onto a pile of waste. "Look my lad, none of us here can read or anything," he told Onofre. "Besides, what do you mean by revolution? That's a very serious matter. Listen", he added, "you'd better clear out of here before the foreman sees you."

Thanks to this warning, Onofre took some time to explore the building site closely. He soon learned to distinguish the foremen. He also saw that they were more concerned with giving orders and making sure they were carried out than watching out for any possible ideological deviations of their workmen. Even so, I'll have to be careful, Onofre said to himself. Each foreman looked after a sector or part of a construction; there were lots of them, and each had their own personality and way of behaving. He also noticed people coming and going around the park wearing dust coats, caps and spectacles. They were inspecting the progress being made, taking measurements with yardsticks and theodolites, examining plans, and giving the foremen instructions. The foremen would listen attentively, and demonstrate immediately they had understood everything. "Don't worry," they appeared to be saying as they bowed, "things will be done exactly as you've said, down to the minutest detail." These important personages were the architects, their assistants and associates. They went round attempting to co-ordinate everything, but apart from this sporadic point of contact, each group of workmen appeared to be acting on their own, oblivious to anyone else. Some were erecting scaffolding, others pulling it down; some were digging ditches, while others were filling them in; some were laying bricks, while others were knocking down walls. All this to the sound of orders, counter-orders, whistles, neighing, braying, the pounding of boilers, the clash of wheels, clink of metal, the crash of stones, slamming of planks and banging of tools. It was as if this was where all the lunatics in the country had been congregated to give free rein to their madness.

By now, work on the World Fair had acquired a momentum of its own that nothing and nobody could halt. There was no shortage of technical know-how to carry it out: at that period, Barcelona could boast 50 architects and 146 master builders, who had at their disposal several hundred kilns, foundries, sawmills and metal workshops. Thanks to the growing unemployment created by the economic recession, there was also a plentiful supply of labourers. The only thing there wasn't an abundance of was money to pay so many people and the suppliers of raw materials. Madrid, according to a phrase invented by a satirical newspaper of the time, had *the purse strings clenched between its teeth.* "Too bad," said Rius y Taulet with a shrug. "We'll get round the problem by not paying." Thanks to this attitude, Barcelona was accumulating massive debts. "Only two things make me really feel like a mayor," he would say: "spending without limits and kicking over the traces". His successors adopted the same slogan.

As yet, Onofre Bouvila was unaware of any of this. While he wandered around the park, trying to get some idea of its dimensions, he had several scares. The worst of these was the sudden appearance of the Civil Guard. However, once he had recovered from the shock, he told himself that in the midst of this colossal uproar they must have more than enough on their hands with brawls, revolts and other serious disturbances, and that if he was careful, his presence would go unnoticed. Reassured, he redoubled his efforts, but by the end of the day had not managed to hand out a single pamphlet.

Exhausted, covered in dust, and not having eaten anything since breakfast, he recovered the bundle he had hidden and walked back to the boarding house. How can it be that something as simple as handing a piece of paper to someone is beyond me? he wondered as he went along. Nay, I'll never admit that, he told himself. Even though it's obvious everything is more complicated than it seemed at first. Before making any move it's important to study how the land lies, he thought. There's no doubt I still have a lot to learn. But I need to do so quickly, he reflected immediately and insistently, because there's not much time. It's true I'm still young, but now's the moment for me to make my way if I want to be rich. Soon it will be too late. And becoming rich was the goal he had set himself.

When his father had emigrated to Cuba, he and his mother had survived great hardships. They often went hungry, and every winter suffered the torment of cold. As soon as he was able to think for himself, Onofre endured these difficulties by convincing himself that someday his father would return laden with money. Then everything will be happiness, he said to himself, and that happiness will never end. His mother had never done or said anything to encourage these fantasies, but she had done nothing to dissuade him either. She simply never talked about it, leaving him free to daydream as he wished. He had never asked himself why, if his father was so wealthy, he didn't every now and then send them some money, but instead allowed his wife and son to live in such misery. When, in all innocence, Onofre had mentioned his fantasies to others, their reaction had been so painful that he too no longer mentioned the topic. From then on, he and his mother shared an obstinate silence.

They had lived this way year after year, until one day Uncle Tonet brought them the news that Joan Bouvila was back from Cuba, and was indeed a rich man. No-one knew how this had reached the ears of the pony and trap driver. Many doubted if it were true, but they were forced to change their minds when a few days later he drove up in his trap with Joan Bouvila on board. Ten years earlier, Uncle Tonet had taken him to the railway station at Bassora on his way to board a ship in Barcelona. Now he was bringing him back. People from all round the valley had gathered in front of the church to see them arrive; they were all gazing up the hill at the road beyond the oak wood. A choir boy was waiting for a signal from the rector to start ringing the church bell.

Onofre was the only one not to recognise his father as the trap appeared round a bend. Despite the fact that a decade of an adventurous life in a harsh climate had changed him physically, everybody else immediately knew who it was. He was wearing a white linen suit that almost glistened in the autumn sun, and a wide-brimmed Panama hat. On his lap he carried a square box covered in leaves. "You must be Onofre," was the first thing he said as he jumped down from the trap. "Yes, señor," he had answered. Joan Bouvila fell on his knees and kissed the dusty ground, refusing to get up again until the rector had given him his blessing. Joan was looking wide-eyed at his son, eyes moist with emotion. "You've grown a lot," he said. "And who do they say you look like?" "Like you, papa," Onofre had replied without hesitation, aware of the curiosity with which all the others were staring at them, and the questions they must be asking themselves.

Joan Bouvila went back to the trap and brought out the square box. "Look what I've got you," he said, removing the covering of leaves to reveal a wire cage. Inside it was a thin monkey slightly bigger than a rabbit, with a very long tail. The monkey appeared to be very annoyed, and bared its teeth with a ferocity that belied its small size. Joan Bouvila opened the cage door and put his hand in; the monkey immediately gripped his fingers. He pulled his hand

59

out and brought the animal up close to Onofre, who was eyeing it warily. "Don't be scared son," his father had said. "Get hold of him, he won't hurt you. He's yours." Onofre had caught hold of the monkey, but at once it scrambled up his arm and sat on his shoulder, lashing his face with its tail. The rector interrupted them: "I've arranged for prayers to be said to thank the Lord God for your safe return," he said. Joan Bouvila bowed slightly, then examined the church facade from top to bottom. The church was made of rough-hewn stone, with a single rectangular nave and a square bell tower. "This church is in need of a proper restoration," Joan Bouvila said out loud. From that moment on, everybody began to call him the *Americano*, and expected him to bring about great changes in the valley. He took off his hat, offered his wife his arm, and together they entered the church. Rows of candles shone in front of the altar: nobody in the village had ever seen such a display.

As he walked back tired and hungry to the boarding house, Onofre had a clear memory of those magical moments. Whenever a carriage passed by, he tried to spy inside it, in case a fleeting glimpse of one of the passengers might fire his imagination. However, the closer he came to the gloomy district where the boarding house stood, the fewer carriages he saw. Not even that could dishearten him.

At daybreak the next morning he was already in the grounds of the Fair. This time, he had left all the pamphlets back at the boarding house: for now he simply wanted to nose around, determined to get to know every inch of what was to be his field of operations. He soon learned that not all those working there were of the same rank. There were skilled workmen and day labourers; between them there was a fundamental difference. The skilled workers had a craft, and were organised according to the hierarchies and customs of the ancient guilds; they were respected by the employers and talked to the foremen almost as equals. They felt the same pride as artists, knew they were indispensable, and were generally uninterested in syndicalist ideas because they earned a decent wage.

The day labourers or peons came from the countryside and were unskilled. They had flocked to the city out of desperation, driven off the land by drought, the ravages of wars and plagues, or simply because there was not enough money in their villages to offer them a livelihood. They dragged with them not only their families but also any distant relatives and crippled dependants they had been unable to leave behind, who they took charge of with the heroic loyalty of the poor.

They lived in shacks made of tin, planks of wood and cardboard on the beach that extended from the World Fair's landing stage to the gasworks. Hundreds of women and children swarmed around this camp that had sprung up in the shadow of the scaffolding and frameworks of what were soon to be palaces and pavilions. Some of these women were married to labourers; others were no more than their unofficial partners; others still were their mothers, unmarried sisters, mothers- or sisters-in-law. Many of them were heavily pregnant.

They spent their day hanging wet washing on lines strung between two poles stuck in the sand, so that the warm sea breeze and radiant sun would air it. They cooked on braziers in the doorways of their shacks, fanning the coals energetically with straw fans, or spent their time darning and sewing. They did all this while looking after the children, who were so filthy it was hard to make out their features. They ran round naked with swollen bellies, and needed no excuse to throw stones at anyone and everyone. If they went anywhere near the women cooking, they ran the risk of receiving a slap or a whack with a frying pan. That drove them away, but they soon came back, attracted by the smell of food. Between the women, squabbles, slanging matches and insults were commonplace, often ending in brawls. Whenever that occurred, the Civil Guard stayed at a safe distance; they didn't intervene unless knives or cut-throat razors were being brandished.

Onofre Bouvila spent days discovering all this. Taking advantage of his inoffensive appearance, and the fact that he wasn't tied to any timetable or any particular sector, he wandered everywhere so that people would grow accustomed to him. He never bothered those who were hard at work, and only asked those resting questions about their jobs. If he saw an opportunity to help someone, he took it. Little by little he became tolerated by all, and appreciated by some.

At the end of the first week, though he hadn't distributed a single pamphlet, on his pillow he found the money promised him by Delfina, which she herself must have put there. Inwardly, he expressed his thanks for the understanding and honesty shown by his taskmasters. I won't let them down, he thought. Not because I have the slightest interest in this revolution I'm supposed to be promoting, but because I want to show I can do this as well as anybody. I'll soon be able to hand out their famous pamphlets: my persistence and discretion are bearing fruit. I've overcome the initial mistrust I probably caused by my clumsiness, and nobody is keeping an eye on me now: they're all obsessed with this crazy Fair.

This was no exaggeration: even in 1886, two years before the opening, one newspaper had warned that *strangers will be constantly coming to Barcelona ready to judge its beauty and signs of progress. In this case,* the newspaper added, *public embellishment, as well as comfort and personal security, are questions that in the present circumstances need to be carefully considered by our authorities.* Hardly a day went by without the newspapers making suggestions: *construct the sewage system for the new part of the city,* one of them proposed; *pull down the barracks that spoil Plaza Catalunya,* suggested another; *place stone benches along the Paseo de Colón; improve the outlying districts such as Poble Sech, which those who wish to take advantage of their stay in Barcelona will have to pass through to reach Montjuich and enjoy the delightful springs that dot the hillside there, etc.* Some were concerned about the attitude of the owners of bars and restaurants, taverns, cafés, boarding houses and so on, whom they exhorted to understand that *the desire for excessive profits is generally counter-productive and rebounds on the perpetrator, since it frightens away the visitor.* This part of the press was less bothered by the impression the city might give than the one its inhabitants could cause. They plainly had doubts about their honesty, abilities and manner.

"I need more pamphlets," said Onofre. The apostle grumbled at him. "It's taken more than three weeks for you to distribute the first packet," he said. "You need to make more of an effort." It was five o'clock in the morning; the sun had risen above the horizon and its rays filtered in through the slats in the warehouse shutters. By the piercing light of the summer dawn, the room seemed smaller, even more dilapidated and dusty. "It wasn't easy at first, but you'll see how things improve from now on," replied Onofre.

It took him only six days to hand out the second packet. Pablo told him: "I'm sorry lad for what I said last time. I know it's hard to get started; sometimes I'm too impatient. It's the heat, the heat and being cooped up in here – it's killing me."

The heat was also making itself felt inside the World Fair grounds. Nerves were easily frayed, and soon there was an outbreak of the dreaded summer diarrhoea, which could kill dozens of children.

"Things will get worse," warned the sceptics. "When all the work here is finished and we're out of a job." The more optimistic thought that once the World Fair was open, Barcelona would once more become a great city, one with work for everybody, improved public services, and all the assistance its citizens needed. Others laughed their heads off at these naive fools.

Onofre Bouvila seized the opportunity to talk about Bakunin, and always ended up handing out a few pamphlets. As he did so, he couldn't help saying to himself: My God, how is it I've become a propagandist for anarchism? A few weeks ago I hadn't even heard of this gibberish, and now I seem like a lifelong convert. It would be laughable if I wasn't risking my neck for it. Well then, he always ended up thinking, I'll try to do it as best I can. After all, it's no more dangerous to do it well as it is to do it badly, and that way I win the trust of both sides. The idea of winning other people's trust without committing himself seemed to him the height of wisdom.

5

"So young man, you're working at the Fair, are you? That's good, very good," Señor Braulio had remarked when Onofre Bouvila handed him his first week's rent. "I'm convinced, and so I said to my wife, who won't have me tell a lie, that this World Fair, unless God decides otherwise, will serve to elevate Barcelona to the position it deserves."

"That's what I think too, Señor Braulio," replied Onofre.

In addition to Señor Braulio and his wife Señora Agata, Delfina and Beelzebub, Onofre had gradually been getting to know the other inhabitants of the little world he was inhabiting. Depending on the day, there were eight, nine or ten lodgers. Only four of them were permanent residents: Onofre, a retired priest called Father Bizancio, a fortune teller by the name of Micaela Castro, and the barber who worked in the lobby, whom everyone simply called Mariano. He was a chubby, florid individual who despite appearing very friendly had a nasty streak. He was also an inveterate talker, and perhaps for that reason was the first guest Onofre became acquainted with.

The barber told him he had learned his trade in the army; after that he had been employed in several Barcelona barber shops until, wishing to improve his situation as he was about to marry a manicurist, he had set up on his own. But the wedding never took place, Mariano told Onofre. "A few days before the ceremony she suddenly burst into tears." He had asked her what the matter was. She confessed that for some time she had been linked to a wealthy gentleman who was smitten with her. He gave her lots of presents, and had promised to install her in an apartment: she had been unable to resist his attentions and flattery, but now felt she could not marry Mariano without making him aware of the situation. Mariano had been dumbfounded. "How long has this been going on?" was all he could think to ask. He wanted to know if it had been days, months or years: to him this seemed the most important question. She did not answer: she was so upset she was hardly aware of what she was being asked, but kept repeating over and over: "I'm so unhappy, so unhappy."

The barber had made strenuous efforts to recover the engagement ring he had given her, but she had refused, and the lawyer he consulted had advised him not to take the matter to court. "You'll be the loser," he had said. Now, all these years later, Mariano was pleased with the way things had turned out. "Women are an endless source of expense," he maintained. On the other hand, he always spoke enthusiastically of his professional life: "One day I was in a barber's shop down in Raval," he told Onofre on another occasion, "when I heard a lot of noise out in the street. I went to the doorway, saying to myself, 'What's going on?' and I saw a cavalry platoon drawn up in front of the shop. All of a sudden, an aide-de-camp jumped off his horse and strode in; I can still hear the thud of his boots and the jangling of his spurs on the floor tiles. Well, he looks at me and says: 'Is the owner in?' I replied: 'He's just gone out.' He asks: 'Is there no-one here who can cut hair?' So I say: 'Yours truly; take a seat, sir.' 'It's not for me', he says, 'it's for General Costa y Gassol.' Can you imagine? No, of course not, you're very young and you won't remember him. You weren't even born then. Well, he was a Carlist general famous for his courage and ferocity. He took Tortosa with only a handful of men, and put half the inhabitants to the sword. Later on, Espartero had him shot by firing squad. He was another great man; if you want my opinion, they were as great as each other, politics apart, which I never get involved with. Where was I? Oh yes, so I see General Costa y Gassol come in, covered with medals from head to toe. He sits in the chair, looks at me, and says: 'Haircut and shave.' Shitting myself, I say: 'At your orders, general sir.' To cut a long story short, I do as he asks, and when I finish, he barks: 'How much do I owe you?' And I say: 'For your lordship there's nothing to pay.' With that he got up and left."

Anecdotes such as this could last for hours, until something or someone put a stop to the flow of his eloquence. As with all barbers of his day, Mariano also pulled teeth, applied potions, mustard plasters and poultices, and brought on abortions. He was always trying to sell the few clients he had health-giving ointments. He himself was very apprehensive; he suffered from gall bladder and liver problems, always went around over-dressed, and avoided Micaela Castro like the plague, because she had foreseen he would soon die a painful death.

This clairvoyant was an elderly woman with one droopy eye. She seldom spoke, unless it was to predict disasters. She firmly believed in her prophetic powers; the fact that what she predicted failed to come about in no way undermined her self-belief – she continued to prophesy catastrophes. "A devastating fire is going to raze Barcelona to the ground, and nobody will emerge unscathed from this terrible conflagration," she would say as she entered what passed for a dining room. Nobody paid her any attention, although they almost all secretly touched wood or crossed their fingers behind their backs. None of them knew how she came to imagine all these horrors, or why. "There will be floods, epidemics, wars, there'll be no bread," she would say, for no apparent reason. She saw her clients in her room, as a special favour from Señor Braulio, who was big-hearted and fond of her. Her clients were of all ages, both sexes, and invariably very poor. They all emerged from these sessions with long faces, and yet were soon back to receive another dose of pessimism and despair. Perhaps they came again because her ominous predictions lent their monotonous lives a certain grandeur, and also because an imminent tragedy made their wretched present more bearable. In any case, nothing that she prophesied ever came to pass, although something different but equally disastrous usually did.

Father Bizancio used to exorcise her from the far end of the dining-room, staring at the tablecloth and muttering under his breath. They never sat together, but since they both lived immersed in the spiritual world, they respected each other, even if they acted in opposing spheres. Father Bizancio regarded Micaela Castro as a worthy opponent, Satan incarnate. For her part, she regarded Father Bizancio as a constant reassurance, because he believed in her powers, even though he attributed them to the Devil.

By now old and infirm, Father Bizancio did not want to die without visiting Rome in order to, as he said, prostrate himself at Saint Peter's feet. He also wanted to see with his own eyes Santiago de Compostela's giant censer, which he mistakenly thought was in the Vatican. Micaela Castro had predicted he would soon undertake the journey to Rome, but that he would die en route, without ever setting eyes on the Holy City.

The neighbouring parishes (the churches of La Presentación, San Ezequiel, Nuestra Señora del Recuerdo, and so on) turned to Father Bizancio whenever they needed another priest for a solemn ceremony or someone extra in the choir or monastery. He was also called on to sing plainsong, antiphonies and verses from the psalms, to be a gospel reader and even as a singing and dancing *seise*, roles almost forgotten nowadays, but which Father Bizancio was familiar with, although not exactly an expert at any of them. Thanks to this and occasionally filling in as a priest, he earned just enough to allow him to live without worries.

The priest, the barber, the fortune teller and Onofre Bouvila himself had rooms on the second floor, which, though no bigger or better than the others, had the priceless advantage of a balcony overlooking the street. This made their rooms bright and cheerful despite the cracks in the ceiling, the uneven floors, patches of damp on the walls, and the drab, ill-assorted pieces of furniture. The view from the balconies on to the dead-end street was depressing, but occasionally luminous. Every day dazzlingly white turtle doves that must have got lost or escaped and nested somewhere nearby came and settled on the wrought-iron railings. Father Bizancio was in the habit of giving them unleavened bits of bread broken from the unconsecrated host, which was no doubt the reason they kept coming back. The other rooms on the first floor, which had no windows or exterior balconies, were occupied by short-term lodgers.

Señor Braulio, his wife Agata and Delfina slept under the roof on the third floor. Señora Agata suffered from a combination of arthritis and gout that kept her imprisoned in her chair in a perpetual doze. She only stirred when she could eat sweets and cakes, but as these were strictly forbidden by her doctor, her husband and daughter only allowed her a small taste of them on special occasions. Although constantly in pain, she never complained, out of weakness rather than stoicism. Occasionally her eyes grew moist, and tears began to roll down her smooth, plump cheeks, but her face remained completely expressionless.

This family tragedy did not seem to affect Señor Braulio in the slightest. He was always good-humoured, ready to argue with anyone about anything. He liked to tell jokes and to be told them; however bad they were, he greeted them with a hearty laugh. An hour later, he would still be chuckling at them – he was the ideal audience. He was always very clean and smartly turned out; Mariano would give him a shave every morning, and sometimes again in the evening. Outside mealtimes, when he was always impeccably dressed, he went around in his underwear so as not to crumple the trousers his daughter very reluctantly pressed for him every day. He was friends with the barber, on good terms with the priest, and treated the clairvoyant with respect, although he rarely sat at her table, because whenever she went into a trance she flung her arms about and threatened to spoil his immaculate attire.

Apart from his spruce appearance, his most noteworthy characteristic was being accident-prone. He would appear one morning with a black eye; the next, with a nasty cut on the chin; on another, a bruised cheekbone; then again, a dislocated finger. He was forever covered in bandages, plasters or dressings. For someone so proud of his appearance, this seemed very odd. Either he's the clumsiest man I've ever met, or something strange is going on here, Onofre reflected whenever he paused to think about it. But it was Delfina who was by far the most enigmatic member of the family. She intrigued Onofre, who felt an inexplicable attraction towards her that grew almost into an obsession.

Onofre was so successful at handing out the pamphlets that he often had to return to Calle del Musgo for fresh supplies. He was always met by Pablo, and from seeing each other so frequently, a kind of camaraderie sprang up between the veteran anarchist and the keen novice. Pablo constantly complained of how the police had been relentlessly pursuing him for years, forcing him to lead this clandestine life. He said he was a man of action, and to be cooped up like this was the worst kind of torture – or so he believed at that moment. He was so dispirited that he envied Onofre the opportunity of being in daily contact with the working masses, but criticised him for not taking full advantage of this priceless opportunity, and scolded him for any real or imaginary reason. As he gradually came to know him, Onofre let Pablo talk; he knew that at bottom he was a poor devil, nothing more than cannon fodder. Pablo was easily offended, argued for the sake of it, and always wanted to be in the right: three unmistakable symptoms of a weak character. He also needed Onofre's company, and above all his acquiescence, to stay in the world of the sane.

Despite these weaknesses, he came to a sad end he didn't deserve. In 1896, after spending several years in the dungeons of Montjuich fortress, his gaolers took it out on him after the Corpus Christi bombing. One morning they dragged him out of his cell blindfolded and bound with leather thongs that cut his wrists to the bone. They had no problem carrying him, because starvation and harsh treatment had reduced his weight to no more than thirty kilos.

When they removed the blindfold he discovered he was only a few steps from the cliff edge. He could see waves breaking against the rocks below, and when they pulled back, the black, razor-sharp reefs. He was left propped against one of the castle merlons, his feet dangling over the abyss. A gust of wind would have been enough to make him lose his balance and finish him off. Tempted as he was to topple over and put an end to all his suffering, he did not want or did not have the courage to do so. I won't die at my own hand, he told himself.

A thin-faced, deathly pale lieutenant pressed the tip of his sabre into his chest. "You're going to sign a confession," he told him, "or I'll kill you on the spot. If you sign, you might go free one of these days." He showed Pablo a declaration he had supposedly dictated, in which Pablo confessed to being one of those responsible for the Corpus Christi tragedy, and to be an Italian called Giacomo Pimentelli. This was completely absurd: he had been in prison for several years, and so could not possibly have participated in an attack like the one he was accused of, which had happened in the street only a few days earlier. Nor was he even remotely Italian, although up to then nobody had been able to discover his real name or origins: whenever he was interrogated, he insisted that Pablo was his only name and that he was a citizen of the world, a brother to all exploited humanity.

Having failed to get him to sign the confession, they returned him to his cell. There they hung him up from the door by his wrists for eight hours. Every now and then a gaoler came in, spat in his face, and savagely tweaked his genitals. Almost every day, Pablo was forced to go through a mock execution: sometimes they put a noose round his neck, at others they laid his head on a block and pretended they were going to chop it off, at others still, they made him stand in front of a firing squad.

Eventually he could bear it no more, and signed the confession, admitting a guilt that was at least partially true, because by now he hated all human beings and would have killed indiscriminately if he'd had the chance. After that they did shoot him, like so many others, in the castle moat, on direct orders from Madrid.

The man who gave this brutal order was Antonio Cánovas del Castillo, then the Spanish prime minister for the fifth time. A few months later, when he was taking the waters with his wife at the Santa Agueda spa, he told her he had bumped into a strange individual who had bowed low in greeting. "I should like to know who he is," the prime minister said. As he spoke, a dark shadow flitted across his face, a sense of foreboding he had no wish to alarm his wife with. Cánovas always wore black; he collected paintings, porcelain, walking sticks and antique coins, was a man of few words, and hated any gold or jewellery that might appear ostentatious. Preoccupied by the domestic and foreign problems Spain was facing, he had given orders that the anarchists should be crushed with an iron fist. We've got more than enough headaches without this pack of rabid dogs adding to them, was his view. Pursuing this tough line seemed to him the only way to avoid the chaos he saw gathering on the horizon.

This time the individual who greeted him in that summer of 1897 was indeed Italian. His name was Angiollilo, and he had written in the spa register that he was a correspondent for *Il Popolo* newspaper. He was young, with ash-blond hair and a somewhat decadent appearance, but exquisite manners. One day soon afterwards, when Cánovas was reading the newspaper in a wicker chair shaded by a tree in the garden of the spa, Angiollilo approached him again. "Die, Cánovas," he said. "Die, you tyrant, you bloodthirsty, pathetic man." Pulling out a revolver, he shot him three times at point blank range, instantly killing him. Furious, Cánovas' wife attacked the assassin with the mother-of-pearl and lace fan hanging from her wrist. "Murderer!" she screamed. "Murderer!" This accusation offended Angiollilo: he protested he was no murderer, but the avenger of his anarchist comrades. "I have no quarrel with you, señora," he added. Men rarely explain themselves, and when they do, they get it wrong.

According to one newspaper, so great were the quantities of materials used daily in the construction work for the World Fair *that almost all the brick-making kilns are running out. The same is true of cement, brought in from several parts of the principality and abroad. The Great Palace of Industry alone consumes 800 quintals of this commodity. In addition, the huge iron-making foundries of La Maritima and Casa Girona are working at full capacity to fulfil their contracts for frameworks and girders, as are numerous carpentry workshops, where many extremely important orders are being completed.* The grounds of the World Fair covered some 380,000 square metres. The first buildings were rising skywards. The ones still preserved from the former Ciudadela were being refurbished. The remaining lengths of wall had been demolished, and new barracks were being built on Calle de Sicilia to erase the final traces of Montjuich's military past.

None of this meant the works were on schedule. In fact, the date originally set for the opening had already passed. A new date was set, *this time not to be postponed*: 8 April 1888. Despite this definite-sounding announcement, there was a renewed attempt to postpone the fair, which came to nothing: Paris was preparing an exhibition for 1889, and to coincide with that would have been suicidal. The Barcelona press's initial enthusiasm had waned, often giving way to criticism. *In our opinion, it might perhaps be better for so much effort and money to be spent on more urgent tasks, rather than be wasted on ostentatious public works built for immediate effect but of only fleeting, if any, utility,* some of them argued, whilst others were even more scathing. *To anyone versed in the matter, it is as clear as day that the Barcelona World Fair, as conceived by its promoters, will either never take place or will do so in such a manner as to heap ridicule on Barcelona in particular, and Catalonia in general, and bring about the irreversible ruin of our municipality.*

Such was the situation when the mayor Rius y Taulet visited the site. He was accompanied by numerous dignitaries, waving their top hats in the air to protect themselves from the dust as they hopped from plank to plank, leaped across trenches, stepped over cables, and kept a safe distance from the mules, who tried to nibble their coat-tails. The dynamic mayor was delighted with the spectacle. "I won't be content," he said, "until we reach the climax."

Onofre Bouvila was making progress as well. By dint of so often explaining what was in his pamphlets, he had come to understand them himself, and realise how justified the revolutionaries were in their demands. Any spark would be enough to light a fire. Sometimes he used logic to explain these ideas, at others demagoguery. Those he managed to convince began to help him spread the message. In early September, storms turned the World Fair site into a quagmire, and there were outbreaks of typhoid fever, as well as delays in paying daily wages due to Madrid's slowness in releasing the scant subsidy the government had finally conceded to the World Fair – all of which gave renewed impetus to his efforts.

Onofre was the first to be surprised at his success. "After all," he told Pablo, "I'm only thirteen." The anarchist rewarded him with one of his rare smiles. "In the early days of Christianity," he said, "children won more converts than adults. Saint Agnes was thirteen like you when she died at sword point; Saint Vitus was a martyr at twelve. Even more astonishing," he went on, "is the case of Saint Cypriacus Quirze, the son of Saint Julita. Aged only three, he so amazed the prefect Alexander with his eloquence that he smashed the little boy hard enough against the platform steps to crush his skull, and his brains spilled out all over the floor and the tribunal table."

"How do you know all these things?" Onofre asked him.

"I read about them. What else can I do shut up in this cage? I kill the hours and days by reading and thinking. Sometimes my thoughts become so powerful I scare myself. At others I'm gripped by irrational anguish: I think I'm in a dream, and I wake up terrified. Or I burst into tears without reason, and that can last for hours without me being able to control it," the apostle said. But Onofre wasn't listening; his own mind was in turmoil.

CHAPTER TWO

1

What's happening to me, Onofre wondered. It can't be what others call love. And yet throughout the summer and a good part of the autumn of 1887 his obsession with Delfina grew and grew. They had not said a word to each other since the night when she came to his room with Beelzebub to suggest he work to spread the Idea. From that moment on, they had barely acknowledged one another with a glance or gesture when they passed by in the corridors. Every Friday he would find the money on his bed, although by now it seemed to him scant reward for his efforts and success: he was worth more than that. That candlelit conversation was all he knew about her; day after day he went round carefully analysing what she had said, repeatedly and systematically trying to glean information from it, to discover hidden meanings. In fact, all this was simply the product of his imagination; nothing he thought he remembered had actually happened; he was building castles in the air from scraps of memory. He was probably experiencing his sexual awakening, but was unaware of that: he still thought everything could be explained rationally.

Now, however, he realised this attitude was getting him nowhere. What am I to do? he wondered. There was only one thing he was sure of: she had told him there was a boyfriend, and this to him was an open wound. All he could think of was destroying his rival, but to do that he needed to find out who he was, where and when they met, what they got up to when they were together. Given the boarding house's unvarying routine and the fact that Delfina's parents were oblivious to her amorous adventures, he concluded that the couple must meet at night.

This in itself was uncommon in those days. Apart from a handful of exceptions, until well into the twentieth century all activity ceased soon after sunset; anything that did not do so could be reliably classified as irregular and suspicious. Popular fantasy saw the night as peopled with phantoms and full of danger; anything carried out by candlelight took on an exciting, mysterious aura. There was also a belief that night was a living being which had the strange power to attract people, and that anyone venturing into it without a specific goal would never return. As a rule, night was equated with death, and dawn with resurrection. Electric light, which put an end to darkness in cities once and for all, was still in its infancy, and was viewed with reservation by many. *Artificial light should not dazzle or flicker; it should be abundant without scalding the eye,* says one 1886 magazine: *Bright lights should never be used unless they are shaded by glass screens, due to the concentration of light in the filament.* On the other hand, another Barcelona magazine from the same year asserts that: *According to the prominent ophthalmologist Professor Chon de Breslau, electric light is preferable to any other for reading and writing, providing it is steady and abundant.*

Onofre himself imagined Delfina engulfed in darkest night, transformed into a being both fearsome and enchanting as she sought out her lover. Her hermetic appearance, lizard-like skin, mop of hair as filthy as a chimney-sweep's brush, her ragged, outlandish clothes that in the daytime made her a laughable monstrosity, under cover of darkness turned her into a ghostlike figure.

Determined to catch the clandestine lovers out, Onofre resolved to stay awake all night. When the last noises in the boarding house died down, and the last lamp was extinguished, he would leave his room and take up his post in the stairwell. If she leaves her room, she'll have to come this way, he thought. She'll pass by without seeing me, and I'll be able to spy on her and find out where she goes and why. He became accustomed to interminable sleepless nights. The church bells of La Presentación, Saint Ezequiel and Nuestra Señora del Recuerdo were exasperatingly slow at marking the passing of the hours.

Nothing disturbed the boarding house's tranquillity. At around two in the morning, Father Bizancio always left his room to go to the toilet. He would return a few minutes later, and almost immediately start snoring again. At three o'clock, Micaela Castro began talking to herself or to the spirits; her muttering went on until daybreak. At four and half past five, the priest visited the toilet again. The barber slept peacefully through the whole night. Onofre registered all these details from his hiding place, so bored that any distraction acquired huge significance. What most concerned him was the cat, the treacherous Beelzebub; the idea that it might be roaming the building chasing mice, or that Delfina might take it with her during her night-time escapades, filled him with terror. As the night wore on, he would dream up a safe way of getting rid of the cat without arousing suspicion. Dawn would find him stiff, weary and in a foul mood, still lost in these conjectures. Before the others woke, he would return to his room, pick up the packet of pamphlets and head for the Fair. I'll go back to the same spot tonight, he would say to himself, and every night of the year if need be. Even so, once he was under the stairs, tiredness would often overcome him; his eyes would close and he would nod off.

One night, he woke with a start when he heard the rustle of fabric. Holding his breath, he made out the sound of footsteps going cautiously downstairs. At last, he thought. Kneeling under the stairs, he sensed a body pass a few centimetres from his face. An intense perfume sent his mind reeling: he would never have thought Delfina would be so coquettish as to take such great pains when she ran to meet a man. She's done it for him, he said to himself. So that's what love is!

Onofre waited a moment or two before starting down the stairs himself; the feet of pursuer and pursued made hardly any noise on the imitation marble steps. It occurred to him that if the figure stopped for any reason they would collide, and so he redoubled his caution. When he noticed the distance between them was growing, he became afraid he might lose her. She knows this place like the palm of her hand, and I'm so stupid I didn't even take the precaution of counting how many steps there are on each flight, he thought. Bewildered, he lost all notion of space and time: he had no idea whether he was already on the first or ground floor or if he had spent a few moments or an hour in this senseless pursuit. Then he heard the hinges of the front door creak. Heavens, she really is getting away from me, he thought, and rushed down the remaining stairs. When he reached the lobby, he tripped, banging his knee on the floor, but even so he limped on after her.

There was no moon, and the street was as dark as the boarding house interior. After Onofre's first few steps out in the open, the perfume faded. A damp wind was blowing from the east. When he reached the first corner, he peered left and right, but couldn't see or hear anything. He walked around for a while until he realised it was useless, and so returned to the boarding house. He took up his post again under the stairs, but the damp had penetrated his bones, and he began to shiver.

All this is pointless, he told himself, as he tried hard not to sneeze and give away his position. He didn't have the strength to continue his vigil, and so went back up to his room and climbed into bed. He felt extremely sorry for himself. She's fooled me, he thought. Right now she's in someone else's arms, and they're laughing at me, while I'm here, in my own bed, and I'm ill.

He must have fallen asleep, because when he opened his eyes again a man he knew from somewhere was examining him closely. "He must have died a few minutes ago," Onofre heard him say. "There's no smell, and his limbs are still flexible," the man went on. The nightlight glinted off his spectacles, and threw a gigantic shadow on the wall. "Ah, now I know who he is," Onofre told himself. "But what's he doing here, and who is he talking to?" As though wanting to clear up any doubt, Onofre's father emerged from the shadows and approached the bespectacled man. "Do you think he'll look alright?" he asked him.

Joan Bouvila was wearing the same white linen suit, but out of regard for the solemnity of the occasion, he had removed his Panama hat. "Don't worry, Señor Bouvila," the man replied. "When we return him to you, it'll be as if you had never lost him." Now I know I'm dreaming, thought Onofre.

This dream brought back an event he had experienced several years earlier. One winter morning, the monkey his father had brought him from Cuba was found dead. His mother, who was always the first to rise, had discovered the body curled up in its cage. She had never been particularly fond of the monkey: she thought it was dirty, wild and vicious, showing no affection for those who fed it. And yet when she saw it dead she couldn't restrain a rush of compassion, and shed a few tears. Coming here to die, so far from its loved ones, she thought. What a lonely death! She was still indignant when her husband came down. "You're to blame for this," she told him. "You shouldn't have taken him out of his native country. Our Lord put him there for a reason. I don't know where so much determination and ambition lead to," she said, somewhat inconsequentially. By this time, Onofre was awake, and heard his parents arguing. "Who knows

79

what would have happened to it if I hadn't brought him with me," the *Americano* protested. "I have an idea!" he exclaimed, once the argument died down. "Onofre," he said, addressing him for the first time, "would you like to get to know Bassora?"

Joan Bouvila often went to Bassora: it was common knowledge that he had invested part of his fortune there, and deposited the rest in the town's banks. Whenever he made the trip he would be gone for three or four days, and on his return never said a word about what he had been doing, what he had seen or the progress of the business affairs he had gone to supervise. Sometimes, though not always, he brought back inexpensive presents: ribbons, sweets, a perfumed soap or an illustrated magazine. At others he reappeared in an excited state. He would never explain why he was so fired up, but at supper time he would be far more talkative than usual. He would tell his wife they would make the next journey together, and that before returning home they would visit Barcelona or Paris. Inevitably, these fervently made promises came to nothing.

After the death of the monkey, however, Onofre, who had just turned twelve, did go with his father to Bassora. As it was early winter, the road was still passable, but it was already growing dark by the time they reached the town. The first thing they did was to go to see a taxidermist whose address a policeman gave them. The taxidermist's professional interest was piqued when they brought him the dead body in a bundle. He had never stuffed a monkey, he said, palpating the animal's lifeless body with expert hands. The walls of his darkened workshop were lined with an assortment of animals, all of them at different stages of the dissection process. Some of them had no eyes; others no antlers; still others were stripped of their plumage. Most of them had a hole in the stomach showing the framework of canes replacing their bones: bits of straw and threads of cotton stuck out on all sides. The taxidermist apologised for the lack of light; he had to keep the shutters tightly closed so that no bluebottles or moths could get in.

When they were leaving, the *Americano* handed him a sum of money as a deposit; the taxidermist gave him a receipt. He also warned them that he wouldn't be able to complete the work before Twelfth Night. "We're in the midst of the hunting season, and it's become fashionable to display trophies in dining rooms, parlours or sitting rooms," he explained. "Bassora is a place for people of refined tastes."

While the taxidermist was dealing with his father, Onofre wanted to see the dead monkey's body one last time. The table it had been left on gave off a potent smell of formaldehyde. Lying on its back with its arms and legs drawn up, it looked smaller; a damp draught was stirring the poor animal's grey whiskers. "Let's go, Onofre," his father said.

By the time they emerged from the taxidermist's, the streets were dark, but the sky was as red as the dome of hell in the illustrations of a religious manual the rector had shown Onofre to inspire a proper fear of God in him. But, as his father explained, in Bassora it was produced by the blast furnaces. "Look, son, this is progress," he had told him. In America he had seen cities where the smoke from the factories never let the sunshine through, he added.

They had gone for a stroll round the town centre, along gaslit streets where groups of workmen were trudging from home to work as the factory sirens announced a change of shift. Along the middle of one street ran a narrow-gauge tram; the hot embers from its locomotive rose into the air, fell onto the passersby and streaked the walls of the buildings black. The pedestrians' faces were also smeared with soot. There were bicycles, a few carriages, and many carts pulled by snorting dray horses.

On the main avenue the lighting was stronger, and the passersby were better dressed. Nearly all of them were men; the hour for going out for an evening stroll had passed, and the women were already indoors. The pavements were narrow, and taken up almost entirely with restaurant and café canopies. The customers' silhouettes were visible through the windows as they enjoyed themselves noisily.

Onofre and his father went into a cheap restaurant. Onofre realised the customers were glancing with amusement at the *Americano*: his white linen suit, Panama hat, and the blanket wrapped round his shoulders to protect him from the cold, caught everybody's eye in that inland town in the midst of winter. For his part, the *Americano* was as unresponsive as if he were blind. They sat down, and, tying a napkin round his neck, he studied the menu with a frown, then ordered noodle soup, baked fish, goose with pears, salad, fruit and cream. Onofre was astounded; he had never tasted such delicacies before.

Now, however, these memories came back as a nightmare from which Onofre woke bathed in sweat. He had no idea where he was, and was overwhelmed by an inexplicable fear. After a few moments, he recognised his room and heard the bells from the La Presentación clock, and these familiar details restored his sense of calm. What troubled him now was not the dream about the taxidermist, but a vague idea that he had been deceived in some way. This idea went round and round in his brain without him being able to work out where it came from or why it persisted for so long. As he went over what had happened that night, it became increasingly hard to shake off. I could swear I saw Delfina sneaking out, he told himself. And yet there's something about all this that doesn't add up; either I'm making a big mistake, or there's more mystery here than meets the eye.

He tried to analyse the facts coolly, but his head was spinning, his temples were throbbing, and he was alternately suffocating from heat or felt an icy cold that made his teeth chatter. When he managed to fall asleep, the taxidermist reappeared, and he relived with painful precision the details of that long-distant journey to Bassora. Whenever he woke up, he was plunged once more into the nocturnal adventure he had just experienced. The two events seemed to be connected in some way. What happened back then, Onofre asked himself. What happened that could give me the key to what took place last night? These questions made it impossible for him to rest. I'll think about it in the morning, when my mind is clearer, he told himself, but his brain stubbornly persisted in that pointless, exhausting search, turning every passing hour into endless torture.

"Don't be afraid, my boy, it's me," said the voice Onofre had been hearing in his dreams. He awoke, or thought he awoke, to see a strange face peering anxiously down at him. Had he not been so weak, he would have cried out. The stranger grimaced and carried on speaking softly, as if talking to a child or a little dog: "Here, drink this infusion. It has quinine in it to lower your fever; it'll do you good." The man brought a steaming cup to Onofre's lips, and the youngster drank thirstily. "Hey, go slower, go slower, my boy, you don't want to choke." By now, Onofre had recognised Father Bizancio's voice. Seeing the young man gradually coming round, the priest added: "You have a high fever, but I don't think it's too serious. You've been working hard and not sleeping much recently, and on top of that you caught a dreadful cold, but there's no need for you to worry. Illnesses are manifestations of God's will; we should accept them patiently, even gratefully, because it's as if God Himself were speaking to us through his microbes to teach us a lesson in humility. I myself, although thankfully I'm in good health, have a few problems that age brings: every night I have to go to the bathroom three or four times to relieve my bladder, which plays me up the whole time. I also find it very hard to digest starchy food, and when the weather changes, my joints ache. So you see."

"What time is it?" Onofre asked.

"About half past five," the priest replied. "Hey, what are you doing?" he added, seeing Onofre attempt to get out of bed.

"I must go to the World Fair."

"Forget the World Fair. It'll have to make do without you," Father Bizancio said. "You're in no state to get up, still less leave the house. Besides, it's not half past five in the morning, but in the afternoon. You've been delirious all day, and talking in your sleep."

"Talking?" Onofre said in alarm. "And what did I say, Father?"

"What people always say in cases like this, my son," the priest replied. "Nothing. At least, nothing I could understand. Now get some sleep."

When eventually Onofre recovered and was able to return to the World Fair site with his bundle of subversive pamphlets, that dusty, deafening world seemed as distant to him as if he were returning from a long voyage rather than a couple of days' absence. I'm wasting my time here like an imbecile, he told himself. He thought of having a serious talk with Pablo, to ask him to give him a more important task, to promote him up the revolutionary ladder. He soon realised, however, that neither Pablo nor the other fanatics would understand how reasonable his request was. The Idea they were promoting was not something undertaken as an opportunity for advancement: it was an ideal for which one had to sacrifice everything, without expecting anything in return or asking for compensation or recognition. This supposed idealism, Onofre reasoned, is what gives them the licence to use people while ignoring their legitimate interests or needs; these fanatics regard everything as justified if it can bring about the revolution.

Telling himself this, Onofre vowed to do whatever he could to break free of the anarchists as soon as the opportunity arose. This hatred and thirst for revenge prevented him from seeing just how far the anarchists' idiosyncratic view of the world had influenced him, how far he was imbued with it. Despite the fact that his subsequent aims were diametrically opposed to theirs, he always shared with them an exaggerated individualism, a taste for direct action, risk, immediate results and simplification. Like them as well, he had an exacerbated instinct for killing. However, he never became aware of any of this. On the contrary, he always regarded them as his sworn enemy. They're riffraff who preach justice but have no hesitation in exposing me to all kinds of risk, and in mercilessly exploiting me, he reflected. Oh, how much fairer the bosses are: they openly exploit their workforce, but pay them for their work, allow them to prosper by the fruit of their labours, and listen, even if reluctantly, to their demands.

This latter thought was uppermost in his mind because the labourers at the World Fair were discontented. They had called for a rise of half a peseta in their daily pay, or for their working day to be reduced by an hour. The Board had turned down this request: "The budgets have already been approved," they argued, "and we're not in a position to modify them." The same response as always. There were rumours of a strike that worried the Board. Things were not going smoothly: the funds were being depleted at a rate that bore no relation to how far the work had advanced. Of the eight million pesetas promised as a subsidy by the Madrid government, only two million had been disbursed. In October 1887, the Barcelona City Council had been authorised to raise a loan of three million pesetas to cover the World Fair's debts.

By this time the Café-Restaurant was almost completed; the Palace of Industry was well advanced, and work had already started on what was to be the Triumphal Arch. In that same month, one of the Barcelona newspapers reported: *The Board of the World Fair has been presented with the project for a building in the form of a church for the display of religious objects from the Catholic faith. The project is in the best taste, the brainchild of Parisian architect M. Emile Juif, of Charlot and Co, who are to meet all the costs themselves.* A few days later, the following article appeared: *We can reveal that the well-known Barcelona industrialist D. Onofre Caba, manufacturer of the patented purified salt sold under the trade name "La Paloma" is preparing a magnificent and curious installation for the coming exhibition in our city. This consists of an exact reproduction, in table salt, some ten handspans high, of the Fountain of Hercules, to be placed on the former Paseo de San Juan.*

At the end of November, the temperatures dropped dramatically. The cold spell lasted only a few days, but it was a foretaste of the bitter winter to come. Still convalescing and weak from fever, Onofre was badly affected by the cold days. For the first time since his arrival in Barcelona six months earlier, he felt homesick for the valley and mountains he had left behind. The perpetual state of agitation Delfina unknowingly produced in him only served to increase his anxiety. I must do something, he told himself, or I'll hang myself from a tree.

He had gone to the site of the World Fair as he did every day, carrying his packet of pamphlets. That November morning, though, he was also carrying a heavy sack. He spent a few hours touring the grounds, chatting to people. They told him about the labourers' demands, the plans for a strike, the tense atmosphere. "This time," they told him, "we'll carry things through. This time we've got the cat by the tail." Onofre agreed with everything, but rather than the strike, he was thinking about Delfina and her cat. Whatever he heard or saw made him think of her. It was as if his thoughts were tied to her by a piece of elastic that stretched and stretched until it suddenly snapped back. Despite this, he kept nodding his agreement. By this time he had acquired what was to become a lifelong habit: saying yes to something whilst deep down he was busily concocting the most ghastly schemes and betrayals.

When the sun was high in the sky and the cold had eased a little, he got together a group of workmen and began to speechify in his usual way. Tired from their physical work, the men appreciated any distraction, and gathered round him. He had to be quick, because the foremen, thinking there might be a mass protest, could call in the Civil Guard.

"But that's not what I want to talk to you about today," Onofre said, without changing his tone of voice, as if the conversation were going to continue in the same vein. "Today I've gathered you here to share a sensational discovery that can change your lives as much or more than the elimination of the state in all its forms, as I was telling you about the other day."

Reaching down, he opened the sack and took out a small bottle filled with a cloudy liquid. He held it up to his audience.

"This scientifically proven hair restorer is guaranteed to obtain results. I'm selling it to you today not for one peseta, not for two reals, not even for one real, but for . . ." And so began Onofre Bouvila's business career. Years later, his mood swings could make Europe's stock markets tremble, but for now he was selling bottles of hair restorer stolen the previous night from Mariano the barber's cubbyhole. Onofre had been listening to the street vendors hawking their wares at Puerta de la Paz, and was now trying to imitate their style.

His words were met with total silence. I've gone too far, he told himself. I've laid it on too thick. I've staked my only way of making a living on a single card, and I've lost. The anarchists won't forgive me for what I've done. The workmen feel insulted, and they'll kick my ribs in, or worse still, hand me over to the Civil Guard. I'll end up in Montjuich castle.

All at once a deep voice roared from the crowd: "I want a bottle!" The speaker was a giant of a man with a flat face and sloping forehead who pushed his way to the front. He flourished the ten centavos the product cost. Onofre took the coin, handed the giant the bottle, and asked if anybody else wanted one. A lot of them did. They jostled and shoved holding up ten-cent pieces, desperate not to miss out. In less than two minutes the sack was empty, and Onofre told the workmen to disperse.

He set an example by rushing off to hide in the narrow, unfrequented alleyway between the western facade of what was intended to be the Martorell Museum and the wall separating the World Fair from Paseo de la Industria. He took all the coins out of his pocket and studied them with delight. As he was doing so, he noticed a shadow looming on the wall, and tried in vain to stuff the money back in his pocket. Turning round, he found himself face to face with the giant who had bought the first bottle. He still had the hair restorer in his hand. "Do you remember me?" asked the giant. His bushy eyebrows and beard gave him a terrifying, ogre-like appearance. He seemed to be hairy all over, his chest hairs merging with the beard under his chin.

"Of course, I remember you," said Onofre. "What is it you want?"

"My name is Efrén, Efrén Castells. I'm from Calella. Not Calella de Palafrugell, but the other one, on the coast. I've only been working here as a day labourer for a month and a half: that's why I'd not seen you before today, nor you me. But I know who you are, and I've followed you to tell you to hand over two pesetas."

"And might I know why I should hand them over?" Onofre said, trying to sound innocently surprised.

"Because thanks to me you earned four. If I hadn't bought your first bottle, you wouldn't have sold anything. You're a good talker, but that's not enough. I know, because my maternal grandfather was a horse-trader. Go on, give me the two pesetas, and we can be partners. You talk, and I'll buy. That will get people going. You'll be able to talk less, you'll get less tired, and not run so much risk. And if there's any trouble, I can defend you: I'm very strong, I can split anybody's skull with one blow."

Onofre studied the giant from head to toe. He liked the look of him: it was obvious he was honest, and was willing to be satisfied with what he was asking for, and just as willing to split his head open if he didn't get it. So Onofre told him it was true he looked very strong. "What I don't understand is why you don't just steal my four pesetas without such long-winded explanations," he told him. "Nobody can see us here, and even if I wanted to, I couldn't report you to the police."

The giant guffawed. "You're very smart," he said, once he had stopped laughing. "What you've just said proves that. I on the other hand am as dumb as I am strong. However hard I think, nothing ever occurs to me. If I robbed you of the four pesetas now, that's all I'd get. But I reckon that you're going to go far, so I want to be your partner and for you to give me half of what you earn."

"Look," Onofre told the giant from Calella, "this is what we'll do: you help me sell the hair restorer, and for every day you work I'll guarantee to give you a peseta, however much I earn. And as for what arrangements we have in the future, we can talk about that when the time comes. Deal?"

The giant reflected on this for a moment, then agreed. "It's a deal," he said. He was so slow, he admitted, that he hadn't really understood what Onofre was proposing, although he was sure that, clever as he was, Onofre must be cheating him. Even so, he found it impossible to refuse. "I know my limitations," he added. They shook hands on it there and then, sealing a pact that was to last decades.

Efrén Castells died in 1943, ennobled as a marquis by General Franco in reward for services to the nation. Despite the physical decline brought on by age and infirmity, he was still a giant when he died, and had to have a coffin specially made. He left a substantial fortune in stocks and shares and properties, as well as a priceless collection of Catalan art. He bequeathed this to the Museum of Modern Art, then located in the Ciudadela's former arsenal. This building, redesigned and refurbished precisely for the 1888 World Fair, was only a few metres from the spot where Castells sealed his first deal with the person to whom he dedicated his life with blind devotion, and in whose shadow he attained wealth, the title of marquis, and an introduction to a life of crime.

2

On his way back to the boarding house that evening, Onofre bought more bottles of hair restorer in a pharmacy and surreptitiously replaced the ones he had stolen from the barber. He was very pleased with himself, but after supper, alone in his room, he racked his brains to think of somewhere he could hide his earnings. He was suddenly assailed by all the concerns that money brings, and nowhere seemed safe enough. In the end, he decided to always keep it on him. Then he considered Efrén Castells. This had been an unexpected turn of events, but what was done was done. Anyway, the giant could be useful to him, and if not, he would find a way to get rid of him.

He was more worried about Pablo: sooner or later the anarchists would get wind of what he was up to under cover of their cause. Onofre wasn't sure how they would react. Perhaps when they found out, he could abandon revolutionary propaganda and devote himself entirely to selling things, but would they accept that? No; he knew too much: they would regard him as a traitor and were bound to use violence against him. Nothing but problems, he said to himself.

It took him a long while to get to sleep; he woke up several times and had troubled dreams. In them he again saw himself back in Bassora with his father, and when he woke, he couldn't help being surprised at the persistence of this memory. Why are those trivial events so important now, he wondered, trying to recall everything that had happened back then.

He and his father had been eating supper when three gentlemen from Bassora had come into the restaurant. When he caught sight of them, Onofre's father had turned pale. These three men were the descendants of the ones who in the early years of the nineteenth century had begun the process of industrialisation in Catalonia. Their titanic efforts had transformed that rural, lethargic land into a prosperous and dynamic place. Unlike them, however, their descendants were no longer from the countryside or small workshops. They had studied in Barcelona, travelled to Manchester to learn about the latest advances in the textile industry, and had been in Paris during its years of splendour.

In the City of Light they had enjoyed both the most noble and the most depraved experiences. They had visited the *Palais de la Science et de l'Industrie* (where they could admire open-mouthed the most extraordinary inventions and the most refined, complex technology, and where the bronze banner over the entrance invited them to *Enrichissez-vous*). They had been to the *Salon des Refusés* (where Pissarro, Manet, Fantin-Latour and other artists exhibited their disturbing, sensual canvases, painted in the style then becoming known as "Impressionism"). The most curious and zealous among them had even been to La Salpetrière to see the young Doctor Charcot performing experiments in hypnosis, as well as going to the Quartier Latin to hear Friedrich Engels forecast the imminent arrival of the proletarian uprising. They had drunk champagne in the most fashionable restaurants and cafés, and absinthe in the roughest dives. They had squandered their money on the useless pursuit of the most celebrated courtesans, those *grandes horizontales* that some were already identifying Paris with. They had watched the sun set from the Seine aboard the brand-new *bateaux-mouches* (the *Géant* and the *Céleste*), and from the towers of Notre Dame had been intoxicated by the air and light of that magical city. More often than not, their parents had been obliged to tear them away from it with promises and threats.

Now there was nothing left of that Paris: its very grandeur had aroused the envy and greed of other nations; boundless pride had sown the seeds of war; injustice and blindness had given rise to hatred and discord. Old and ill, Napoleon III was living in exile in England following the humiliating defeat at Sedan, while Paris was struggling to recover from the tragic days of the Commune. The memory of that lost Paris lived on in these representatives of Catalonia's *haute bourgeoisie*, the fortunate inheritors of the Second Empire's *chic exquis*.

"Good Lord, Bouvila, fancy seeing you here, what a small world!" roared one of the three gentlemen who had entered the Bassora restaurant as Onofre and his father were busy with their meal. "Is your family all well?" The other two men had come across to the table and slapped the *Americano* on the back. For his part, Joan Bouvila was casting embarrassed glances at them and his son, whom they were now surveying. "And who is this young man? Your son? How he's grown! What's your name, boy?"

"Onofre Bouvila, at your service," he replied.

When his father stood up to greet them, his chair toppled over.

They all laughed, and Onofre realised that these fine gentlemen considered his father as little more than a figure of fun.

"My son and I came to carry out a painful obligation," Onofre's father explained, but the three gentlemen from Bassora were no longer paying him any attention.

"That's good, very good," they said. "We don't want to interrupt your meal. We're only here to have a little something and carry on talking about business affairs. Then we'll go home and put up with our families for a while. Apart from him," the speaker added, pointing to one of his companions. "He's single, and has no ties, so he'll be out on a spree." The butt of this joke blushed slightly. His features were a strange mixture of youthful vigour and decadence, as though he were still suffering from the effects of the alcohol and drugs consumed years earlier in sleazy Parisian haunts, and his body was still sluggish from the soft caresses of some *demi-mondaine.*

The others were already leaving. "Enjoy your meal," they told Joan and his son. Onofre's father had carried on eating in silence; for some inexplicable reason, his mood had soured. When the pair of them left the restaurant an icy wind was blowing, and there was a layer of hoar frost on the pavement that crackled and split under their feet. Onofre's father wrapped the blanket tighter round his shoulders. "Those nincompoops," he muttered. "They think I'm going to kowtow to them because I'm from the countryside and I'm in their territory. They think they can look down on me. Bah, they're city swells who can't tell a pear tree from a tomato plant! Never trust people from the city, Onofre," he had added out loud, addressing him directly for the first time since the three strangers had butted in on their meal. "They're nothing, but they think they're God's gift." His teeth were chattering from the cold or from anger, and he was striding out so purposefully that Onofre had to run to catch up with him.

"Who were they, father?" he asked. The *Americano* shrugged. "Nobody," he said. "Provincial fops. Men with money. They're called Baldrich, Vilagrán and Tapera; I've done business with them on occasion." As he spoke he was looking round in search of the inn where they had reserved a room for the night. At that late hour the only people in the street were women on their own, with gaunt faces and greyish complexions, who swayed their hips and shivered under the gas lamps' pale halo. When he saw them, Joan Bouvila took his son by the arm and made him cross the street. Eventually they came across a puffy-faced nightwatchman who told them how to get to the inn.

They were very tired by the time they arrived. It wasn't the same to walk down darkened streets as walking in the countryside. At the inn they gradually recovered from the bone-chilling cold: the pipe from the stove in the lobby went up from the ground floor to the rooms above, giving off heat and a yellowish smoke that seeped out from the joists and left an acid taste on the tongue. From downstairs or a nearby house came the sound of a piano and muffled voices. They heard a train whistle in the distance, and in the street outside the clatter of horses' hooves on the cobbles.

They had both climbed into the double bed, and Onofre's father had put out the lamp. Before falling asleep, he had told his son: "Listen, Onofre, it's time you knew that there are women who do terrible things for money. Another time when we come I'll take you to one of those places, but for now don't tell your mother anything of this. Go to sleep and don't think anymore about what you've seen and heard tonight."

More than a year had passed since then, but what Onofre had seen and heard that night was still on his mind. He could recall with complete clarity the laughing faces of the three gentlemen, and felt pursued by those fearsome, anonymous women his father had mentioned and who now, in his drowsy state, sometimes took on a disturbing likeness to Delfina.

The next morning found him exhausted and despairing, but he slung the sack over his shoulder and returned to the World Fair site. He couldn't give up now. What's done is done, he repeated to himself. Besides, if he didn't give Efrén Castells the promised peseta he ran the risk of receiving what could be a mortal blow. Despite all this, when he arrived at his usual spot and started selling hair restorer as he had done the previous day, his good humour returned. The expectation of earning money and the feeling that he was finally acting on his own behalf lifted his spirits.

Business was so brisk in the days that followed that he became increasingly concerned about where to hide the proceeds. Keeping it on him meant he lived in a constant state of apprehension: in the neighbourhood where he lived there were many thieves and footpads. The idea of opening a bank account never even occurred to him; he thought banks only accepted money that had been honestly earned, which he didn't consider his to have been. Anyway, it made no difference: since he was a minor, no bank would have accepted his application. In the end he resorted to the classic solution: hiding the money in a mattress. Not his own, however, but Father Bizancio's. The priest was as poor as a church mouse, he would never suspect he was sleeping on a fortune. And any idea that Delfina might beat the mattress was preposterous and could be completely ruled out. Besides, the priest left the boarding house very early every morning, meaning it was easy to slip into his room.

With that problem solved, there remained the anarchists. The day finally came when Pablo confronted Onofre in a state of great agitation and knocked him to the ground without warning. As Onofre lay there, the apostle leaped on him, trying to punch him in the face and kick his ribs. "You swindler, traitor, Judas!" he shouted. Onofre protected himself from the blows without attempting to return them. "Calm down, Pablo, calm down! What's wrong? Have you completely lost your head?" he said.

"You know exactly what's wrong with me, you snake in the grass; you leave me speechless," Pablo retorted. "Tell me what you've been up to these past few days, why don't you? Selling hair restorer, is it? Is that what we're paying you for?"

Onofre let him unburden himself, and then began to explain. After a while they both ended up laughing heartily. Irrespective of their personal ideologies, they both shared a conviction: they had a very low opinion of society and its members. To them, any deceit was morally justified by the stupidity of the victim. They both adopted the law of the wolf.

Eventually, Onofre managed to convince Pablo that the sale of hair restorer was simply a ruse to throw the police off the scent, a decoy for his real activities. Over the past few months he had handed out more pamphlets than anybody else: wasn't that sufficient proof of his loyalty to the Idea, he asked. In the end, who ran all the risks?

Pablo finished by apologising for his earlier violence. "Having to live in hiding is driving me mad," he said once more. He found it degrading to have to keep an eye on what other people did. All he wanted to do was plant bombs, but he wasn't permitted to. Onofre had already heard enough of his lamentations, and was no longer listening: at that moment, his mind was on other matters.

Since the night when Onofre had followed a perfume and footsteps out into the street, only to be fooled by the darkness, he had counted and recounted the number of steps on the boarding house staircase and calculated the angle of each landing. He had memorised obstacles in the way and made the descent many times with his eyes shut. If Delfina goes past again, I'll let her get ahead, then follow her without any fear of losing her a second time, he told himself. Provided, that is, she doesn't have that damned cat with her, he thought with a shudder. He had once asked Efrén Castells how he could go about killing a cat. "It's very easy," the giant responded. "You wring its neck until it dies. That's all there is to it." Onofre never again asked his advice about anything.

Finally, one night shortly before Christmas, he again heard the rustle of fabrics on the second-floor landing, and the muffled sound of footsteps coming downstairs. Holding his breath, he told himself: It's now or never. He let the perfume waft past him, waited as long as seemed to him necessary, then set off. He reached the foot of the stairs just as the unknown figure was opening the front door. That night there was a moon, and the figure of a woman stood out in the doorframe. This lasted for a split second, but that was enough for Onofre to realise it wasn't Delfina he was following.

This discovery led him to make doubly sure he didn't lose sight of the woman, whose dim outline he could make out in the moonlight, or more clearly when she passed in front of a religious niche where there was always a wax candle burning, placed there by some pious person in honour of the Virgin Mary or a saint. In those days, beyond the main thoroughfares, this was the only lighting in Barcelona.

It was a bitterly cold night during that terrible winter of 1887. The mysterious woman was striding along the deserted streets. Not even the unsteady steps of a night owl or the thud of a nightwatchman's staff on the pavement signalled anyone else's presence. A woman has to be mad to be out alone at this time of night, Onofre thought.

By now they were entering a strange part of the city: a hollow which in those days separated the side of the mountain from the railway line at El Morrot. It was no more than half a kilometre round, and lay to the south of the old city wall. The only approach to it was along a ravine about two hundred metres long by two or three wide that was in fact an enormous heap of coal imported from England or Belgium in big cargo boats and piled up in the hollow waiting to be transported to the factories in or around Barcelona. This coal tip was kept far from the centre of the city due to the great risk of combustion. Out here, next to the sea, it was easier to stifle any outbreak of fire, at least if it was on the surface. If on the other hand a fire began inside the mountain of coal, it would not become visible until it had reached catastrophic proportions. First there appeared thin columns of milky, acrid smoke that were highly toxic; soon, these emissions merged to form a cloud covering everything, until finally proper flames appeared. By then it was too late to try to fight the raging fire. The flames could reach up to twenty or thirty metres in the air, casting a red glow in the sky that on clear nights could be seen from Tarragona and Mallorca. Ships moored in the docks would set sail and anchor out to sea, preferring the swell to the heat and noxious fumes any such fire gave off. These fortunately rare conflagrations could last for several weeks and cost a fortune: to the loss of the imported coal had to be added the paralysis of all industrial activity.

This meant that the vicinity of the coal dump was not a safe place to live, and explained why the most infamous slum neighbourhood in Barcelona had grown up at the far end of the ravine. There were cabarets offering lewd, tawdry shows; filthy, riotous taverns; the occasional cheap opium den where three shared a room (the better ones were in the upper part of the city, in Vallcarca); and sinister brothels. Only the dregs of Barcelona came here, as well as sailors who had recently disembarked, many of whom never set sail again. The regular inhabitants were prostitutes, pimps, criminals, smugglers and delinquents. A thug could be hired for a few centavos, and a murderer for not much more. The police never entered the area except in broad daylight, and then only to negotiate or propose an exchange.

It was almost an independent state, with IOUs that circulated as though they were real banknotes. It also had its own codes of behaviour; extremely efficient summary justice was dispatched, and it wasn't unusual to find a hanged man swinging from the lintel of a place of entertainment.

When Onofre saw where the mysterious woman was leading him, he asked himself: If this isn't Delfina, why do I care who it is, and why am I venturing into this tunnel of coal where a villain could leap out, kill me, and bury me without anyone knowing or even finding out? Even he had heard stories of people who had died violent deaths there, and if they weren't left on display as a public warning, were buried in the coal mountain, where they would remain undiscovered until a crane loaded the coal onto a barge, railway wagon or cart. Sometimes, as he went to shovel coal into a locomotive's boiler, a stoker would catch sight of a boot, clawed fingers or a skull with a few tufts of hair still stuck to it.

Onofre was tempted to give up his pursuit, but in the end, he did not turn back; he soon found himself on the edge of the notorious slum. As often happens in the poorest urban areas, the streets formed a precise rectangle. Drunkards surrounded by their own stinking excrement lay on the street's dry, cracked mud. The sounds of singing and guitars being plucked drifted out from taverns. The songs were bawdy, but above all gave an overwhelming sense of melancholy and anguish. How did I come to live this life? the singers seemed to be saying in their liquor-soaked, croaking voices: This isn't what I dreamed of as a child. There was also the noise of castanets and flamenco foot-stamping, shouts, glasses being smashed, furniture overturned, people running, brawls.

The mystery woman strode determinedly along the streets of the slum. Concealed in a doorway, Onofre saw her enter a hovel; its wooden door swung closed behind her. He decided to remain outside and wait to see what happened next. A cold, damp and salty wind was blowing from the nearby Mediterranean; he covered his nose and mouth with the scarf he had brought with him.

He did not have long to wait: within a few minutes, the woman reappeared, the din from inside swelling as she pushed open the door. For the first time, Onofre was able to see her face. Even though it was against the light and only a momentary glimpse, he was able to recognise the brazen woman's features. "It can't be?" he muttered. "I'm seeing things." The woman was sniffing some white powder from a small envelope. Then she closed her eyes, opened her mouth wide, stuck out her tongue, and shook her shoulders and hips. Her whole body juddered. Howling like a satisfied dog, she headed for the nearest tavern, which had a window looking out onto the street.

The heat from a stove inside made the air condense on the glass panes. This and the grime made it hard for Onofre to make out what was going on, but did allow him to peer in without being seen. The customers were all villainous-looking: some were playing cards, their sleeves stuffed with aces, and with knives at the ready to slit the throat of any cheat. Others were dancing with glassy-eyed, skinny whores, to the tunes a blind man was playing on a concertina. At his feet lay a dog that appeared to be asleep, but every so often snapped at the dancers' ankles.

In a corner, the woman Onofre had followed was arguing with a handsome young buck with ringlets and a swarthy complexion. She was waving her arms about dramatically, while he frowned at her. Then Onofre saw him slap her. She grabbed the man by the hair and tugged as hard as she could, but couldn't get a firm grip because it was so greasy. The man punched her in the mouth; she stumbled backwards and fell onto a card table, knocking over bottles and glasses, and scattering the pack of cards. The lowlife advanced on her, a deadly glint in his eye and a curved shearer's knife in his hand. Tears were streaming down the woman's cheeks, but the other customers simply laughed at both of them. The owner of the den brought the confrontation to a swift end. He ordered the woman to get out at once: it was obvious to everyone she was to blame for the argument.

Concealed in the doorway, Onofre saw her stagger out. A trickle of blood oozed from the corner of her mouth, turning violet where it mixed with her face powder. Feeling to make sure none of her teeth had come loose, she took off her wig, mopped the sweat from her brow with a spotted handkerchief, replaced the wig, and set off back the way she had come. The wind had dropped and the air was still, dry and crystal clear, but so cold it hurt the chest to breathe. Onofre caught up with her just as she was entering the coal tip.

"Hey, Señor Braulio!" he shouted. "Wait a moment! It's me, Onofre Bouvila, your lodger; you've nothing to fear from me."

"Oh, my boy," said the boarding house owner, his cheeks still moist with tears, "I've been hit in the mouth, and they would have stuck me like a pig if I hadn't managed to take to my heels. The scum!"

"But why on earth do you come to this dreadful place to let yourself be punched, Señor Braulio? And dressed as a woman! That can't be normal," Onofre said.

Señor Braulio shrugged and set off again. Dark clouds had blotted out the moon, and they couldn't see a thing. It was impossible to avoid tripping over the coal and scraping their knees, hands or faces. In the end, Onofre and Señor Braulio had to link arms to support one another.

"Ah," Señor Braulio suddenly exclaimed, "have you noticed, Onofre? It's starting to snow. It's been years since it snowed in Barcelona!"

Behind them the hubbub grew louder, as inhabitants and customers of the depraved slum poured out into the street with torches and lanterns to gawp at this unheard-of spectacle.

3

That was Barcelona's coldest winter in living memory. It snowed without stopping for several days and nights, until the city was covered in more than a metre of snow. Traffic came to a standstill; all business activity and even the most essential public services were halted. Temperatures fell several degrees below zero, which may not be a lot in other regions, but is in a city where no precautions against this kind of weather had ever been taken, and people's constitutions were unprepared for it. Sadly, many succumbed.

Onofre had been toughened by life in the countryside and so was immune to the rigours of winter. One morning when he opened his balcony door to look out at all the white-roofed buildings, he found the frozen body of one of the turtle doves perched on the rail. When he tried to pick it up, it fell to the street and smashed, as if made of porcelain. As water froze it burst pipes and tubes; none came out of taps or public fountains. A system for supplying potable water was organised, with tankers positioned in different neighbourhoods at specific times. The drivers announced their arrival by blowing on brass horns, and people formed laborious queues in the street, despite being chilled to the bone.

This service was so slow that the police often had to step in to prevent brawls or full-scale riots. Occasionally someone in a queue froze stiff with cold and had to be lifted from the ground by throwing hot water over their feet or simply by tugging at them. Many of the city's inhabitants chose instead to collect water by bringing bucketfuls of snow into their homes and waiting for it to melt. Others did the same with the icicles hanging from their eaves. However inconvenient all this was, it did create a sense of shared adventure, which brought the people of Barcelona together: there was always an anecdote they could recount.

For those working out in the open, the cold was almost unbearable. The workers at the World Fair site suffered most, because it was close to the sea and was a flat, open expanse. Whereas in other similar places such as the docks, work had been temporarily suspended, at the World Fair it continued at increasing speed. After the labourers' demands went unanswered, they resolved to call a strike. When Onofre told Pablo this, he grew angry. "This strike makes no sense," he insisted. Onofre asked him to explain why.

"Look lad, there are two kinds of strike: one aimed at obtaining a specific benefit; the other aimed at shaking the established order, to contribute to its eventual destruction. The first sort is very harmful to workers, because basically it reinforces the unjust situation prevailing in society. That's simple enough to understand: there are no two ways about it. Striking is the only weapon the proletariat has, and it's stupid to waste it on mere details. Besides, this strike has no organisation, no base, no leaders, and no specific aims. It'll be a complete failure and our cause will have taken a huge step backwards."

Onofre disagreed: he thought Pablo's ire came from the fact that the strikers had not turned to the anarchists at all; they hadn't asked them for advice or invited them to join their collective action, much less play a leading role. As it was, Onofre quickly learned that a strike is indeed a double-edged sword that the workers needed to use very carefully, something which the bosses could benefit greatly from if they exploited it properly.

For the moment, all Onofre did was follow events closely, trying not to miss any aspect of what was going on, or to run any risk if things turned ugly. As Pablo had foreseen, the strike achieved nothing. One morning Onofre arrived at Ciudadela Park and found almost all the workers gathered in the central part of the future World Fair, in the former Plaza de Armas, opposite the Palace of Industry. As yet, this was nothing more than a vast wooden framework occupying 70,000 square metres and 26 metres high. That morning, covered in snow, empty and abandoned, it looked like the skeleton of some antediluvian creature.

The assembled workers did not speak to one another. To ward off the icy cold, they stamped their feet or slapped their sides. From the air, the gathering resembled a restless sea of caps. The Civil Guard had taken up strategic positions: on the surrounding flat roofs the unmistakable outline of their capes and three-cornered hats stood out against the clear morning sky. A cavalry detachment was patrolling the park's perimeter.

"If they charge, remember they can only use their sabres on the right-hand side of their horses," some veterans of previous skirmishes warned the inexperienced. "They can't harm you on the left. And if they catch you, throw yourselves to the ground and cover your heads. Horses never trample bodies lying flat. It's safer than running away."

Others said horses were very stupid animals that scared easily if you waved a handkerchief in front of their eyes. If you did that, they reared and with a bit of luck unseated their rider. Hearing this, everybody thought: let someone else give it a try. Finally the order to set off was given, though nobody knew where it came from. The crowd began to move very slowly, dragging their feet. Onofre, who was walking at some distance from them, was struck by the fact that, as soon as the march began, the group, originally more than a thousand strong, had shrunk to only two or three hundred: all the others had melted away. The remaining strikers left the park through the gate between the Winter Garden and the Café-Restaurant and headed down Calle de la Princesa, aiming for Plaza de San Jaume. They did not look very threatening, but rather as if they all wanted an end to what they realised was a pointless gesture; only pride and solidarity kept them united. The shops on Calle de la Princesa had not pulled down their shutters; people were leaning out of windows to watch the demonstration go by. The cavalry platoon followed the workers at walking pace, more concerned about the cold than any possible disturbance.

Onofre kept up with the march for a while, then turned into a side street, hoping to get beyond the demonstrators and rejoin them further along the route. In a nearby small square he ran headfirst into a mounted company of Civil Guardsmen hauling three small-calibre artillery guns on carriages. When he rejoined the workers, he realised that if things got out of hand, the demonstration would end in a bloodbath.

Luckily, nothing serious occurred. Once they reached the cross-roads at Calle Montcada, the marchers halted by common accord. They seemed to think it was all the same to stop there as to carry on marching until Judgement Day. One of the workers climbed up the bars on a window and declared the demonstration had been a success. Another man climbed up and said it had been a complete failure, due to the lack of organisation and class consciousness. He encouraged the strikers to return to work at once. "Maybe that way we can avoid reprisals," he concluded. Both speakers were listened to very closely and respectfully. As Onofre later learned thanks to Efrén Castells, the first speaker was a police provocateur; the second, an honourable labourer with trade union sympathies. This man lost his job because of the strike, and was never seen again in Ciudadela Park. The result of the workers' action was that by midday all of them had returned to work; none of their demands were met, and the local press did not even mention the incident.

"It couldn't have turned out any differently," Pablo muttered, a gleam of satisfaction in his tiny, feverish eyes. "Now it'll take years before they can think of any further collective action. I don't even know if it's worth you continuing to hand out pamphlets."

Alarmed at the thought he might lose this source of income, Onofre tried to change the conversation by telling Pablo what he had seen when he left the marchers. "Of course, what did you expect?" Pablo said. "They're not going to let a handful of workers have their own way and create a disastrous precedent. They let them get on with their march if they can, while a squad of police takes care of public order and directs the traffic. As a result, people say: "I don't know what they're complaining about, we've got such a tolerant government." But if things get out of hand, the cavalry charges. And if that's not enough, bring in the artillery!"

"Why go on trying then?" asked Onofre. "They have the weapons. Nothing will ever change. Let's devote ourselves to something more profitable."

"Don't say that, my boy, don't ever say that," Pablo replied, his eyes fixed on a distant, imaginary horizon, broader and brighter than the one offered by the damp, cracked walls of the basement he was forced to live in. "It's true that all we have to use against their weapons are our numbers. Our numbers and the courage that comes from despair. But one day we shall triumph. It will cost us a lot of suffering and blood, but the price we have to pay will be small because it will enable us to purchase a future for our children, a future in which everybody will have the same opportunities, a future where there'll be no more hunger, no more tyranny, no more war. It's possible I won't live to see it – nor even you, Onofre, my lad, although you're very young. It will take many years, and there are countless things that need to be done first: to destroy everything that exists now is only a first step. We must put a stop to oppression and to a state that not only makes this possible but encourages it; abolish the police and the army, private property and money. Get rid of the Church and education as it exists now . . . what else? There's at least fifty years work ahead of us, believe you me."

The cold that claimed so many victims in Barcelona that winter did not spare the boarding house. Micaela Castro the fortune teller fell gravely ill. Father Bizancio brought a doctor to examine her: a young man in a white coat with red stains on it. He took some dirty, slightly rusty implements out of his bag and used them to tap and prod his patient with. They all realised that this so-called doctor didn't know the first thing about medicine, and that the stains were made by tomatoes, but they pretended not to notice. Despite his obvious incompetence, the doctor was very adamant about his diagnosis: Micaela Castro did not have long to live. "Old age and other complications are taking her," he said. He prescribed a sedative and went on his way.

The permanent residents got together with Señor Braulio in the entrance hall, where Señora Agata was sitting, feet in a basin. Mariano was in favour of getting the sick woman out of the boarding house as swiftly as possible. The doctor had said that the clairvoyant's illness was not contagious, but the barber was very apprehensive.

"Let's take her to the poorhouse," he proposed. "They'll look after her there until she dies."

Señor Braulio agreed with him; as usual Señora Agata said nothing, nor made any sign to show she had grasped the reason for the meeting. Onofre declared he would go along with the majority. Only Father Bizancio was against the idea: as a priest, he had visited several public hospitals and the conditions there seemed to him deplorable. Even if they could find a free bed, he said, to abandon this poor woman to her fate in an unknown place, looked after by strangers and surrounded by more people in their final days, would be a cruelty unworthy of Christians. Micaela Castro's illness did not require any special care and wouldn't cause any inconvenience.

"That poor old woman has lived here for years," he said. "This is her home. It's only right to let her die here, surrounded by us, who are her family in a certain sense, all she has in this world. Bear in mind," he added, looking at each of them in turn, "this woman has made a pact with the Devil. She can expect to be condemned to an eternity of torments. Faced with that dreadful perspective, the least we can do is to try to make what is left of her life on this earth as less painful as possible."

The barber was about to protest, but was interrupted by Señora Agata. "Father Bizancio is right," she said in a voice as gravelly as a miner's. None of them, apart from her husband, had ever heard her speak; her laconic utterance settled the matter. Onofre immediately realised this, and was quick to signal his agreement. In the end, the barber also agreed: he had no choice. Father Bizancio promised to attend to the sick woman so that she would not be a burden on any of the others. The conclave dispersed amicably. At supper time, Micaela Castro's absence fell like a pall of melancholy on the lodgers, who would never again be entertained by her trances.

The year 1887 limped to a close. For one reason or another, it seemed to everybody to be longer than the previous ones, perhaps because it had not brought any good luck. "Let's hope the next one is a little better," people in Barcelona wished one another. It's also likely that the bitter cold of the final weeks helped give a poor impression of the year as a whole. Where the snow had not been cleared, it turned to ice and caused many falls and broken bones. "This is like the North Pole," quipped some wags. Plaza Cataluña, which was in the process of being dug up, was full of holes, mounds of earth and trenches, and looked as desolate as the tundra. One newspaper published a startling report: in one of these holes several large eggs had been discovered. When analysed in a laboratory, they had turned out to be penguin eggs. The news was almost certainly false, and the newspaper in question had meant to publish it as a Yuletide joke, but it had been mislaid and was published at a later date. But this in itself indicates to what extent the cold was part of life in the city, especially for those lacking the means to protect themselves from its ravages.

On the beach, where homeless workers lived with their families, the situation became desperate. One night, rather than die a lingering death, the women picked up their children and began a march. The men preferred not to follow them, correctly judging that their presence would alter the tenor of the demonstration. The women and children crossed the iron bridge linking the beach with Ciudadela Park and walked through the half-built pavilions until they came to the Fine Arts Palace. This building, which no longer exists, was on the right of the Salón de San Juan if one entered the grounds of the Fair through the Triumphal Arch, in the apex formed by the Salón and Calle del Comercio; in other words outside the park itself, although still part of the grounds. The Fine Arts Palace was 88 metres long by 41 metres wide and 35 metres high, not counting its four domed towers crowned by statues of Fame. Inside the palace, as well as the rooms and galleries intended to display works of art, there was a magnificent hall measuring 50 by 30 metres, where the Fair's most solemn events were to take place.

It was here that the women and children chose to spend the night. The Civil Guard officer patrolling the park informed the relevant authorities. "Pretend you haven't noticed," he was informed.

"But they're building fires in the middle of the hall," the officer said, "and smoke is pouring out of the windows."

"So what? We're not going to start shooting and have the news appear in the foreign press only four months before the opening of the Fair. You carry on as usual, and we'll see," he was told unofficially.

"Very well," the officer replied, "but I want a written order to that effect. If it's not in my hands within half an hour, I'll do whatever is necessary to clear the Palace: I'll organise a bloodbath and won't accept any responsibility. And bear in mind we have a machine-gun on the Café-Restaurant roof, ready to mow them down as they come out."

In the end, the city authorities were forced to dispatch a councillor who, braving the cold and slipping flat on his back several times on the ice, arrived with the order minutes before the Civil Guard officer carried out his threat. The next day an agreement was reached, whereby the workers' families (but not their menfolk) were permitted to occupy the new barracks on Calle Sicilia for a fortnight. There they could light fires and do whatever they thought fit. Negotiating with the women was no easy matter. Efrén Castells had sold them a lot of bottles of hair restorer, and some of them had grown beards, so that the official sent to the Fine Arts Palace by the mayor was confronted by a committee of bearded women. This came as such a great shock that he conceded all their demands, and it was only thanks to his connections in high places that he wasn't dismissed.

All this was a result of Efrén Castells' mad passion for women. He was a real satyr: he used the excuse of selling hair restorer to worm his way into their shacks when their partners were at work on the World Fair site and caused mayhem. He was huge, well-built and had a manly look about him that pleased nearly all women; he was a jovial sort who knew how to flatter and was happy to spend money, and as a result had considerable success in affairs of the heart. Onofre disapproved of his partner's weakness. "One of these days, we're going to have a serious problem thanks to you," he would warn him.

"Don't worry," replied Efrén Castells. "I know what women are like: they cheat on their husbands at the drop of a hat, but they'd prefer to be flayed alive than let down any lover who sweet-talks them. Why should that be? Search me, my boy! I reckon they like to suffer. If you want a woman to protect you, mistreat her and betray her; there's no better system. I'm a mug; otherwise, knowing them as I do, I could easily live off them. But what can I do, it's not in my nature? I'm one of those who lose their head and let themselves be squeezed like a lemon."

Efrén spent the pesetas he earned from Onofre Bouvila on buying gifts for his conquests. "It seems you have to be lavish as well as unprincipled," Onofre concluded. "People are only there for what you can get out of them. That's the way human beings are: malleable material." These and other reflections occupied Onofre Bouvila during his interminable vigils under the stairs at the boarding house, spying on Delfina. He was chilled to the bone, and it was only his youth and rugged health that prevented him falling seriously ill.

Señor Braulio had not been out on any more nocturnal adventures: he was waiting for spring to dress up again in his finery. Onofre had not told him he kept watch every night on the stairs to see if he could catch Delfina in flagrante with her boyfriend. He imagined Señor Braulio knew nothing of his daughter's trysts, just as she was unaware of his.

One such night, on the stroke of two o'clock, he heard a voice that roused him from these ruminations. It was Micaela Castro, calling for water. Father Bizancio, who was meant to be looking after her, was sleeping like a log, or possibly had become hard of hearing in his old age. Minutes went by, and nobody answered her call. The clairvoyant went on pleading for water in such a weak voice it was hard to tell where it came from. Onofre went down to the kitchen, took a glass out of the cupboard, filled it with water and brought it up to her. The room gave off a revolting smell, like seaweed drying in the sun. Onofre felt for the medium's icy hand and forced the glass between her fingers. He heard the avid gulps as she drank, and recovered the empty glass. The dying woman whispered something incomprehensible. Onofre leaned closer to the bed. "May God bless you, my boy," he thought he heard, and said to himself: Bah, that's all it was. Yet it set in train an idea of his own.

By mid-January, the good weather had returned, and the city came out of hibernation. As the ice melted in the World Fair grounds, the foremen discovered balustrades and pedestals they had been searching for in vain for weeks. Huge puddles also appeared that were not only a nuisance, but dangerous, because they could and did lead to small landslips. This meant that as some buildings settled, wide cracks appeared. One entire building collapsed, leading to the death of a bricklayer, buried beneath the rubble. There was no time to recover his body: the debris was simply levelled, and the building reconstructed. This never came out in public, and so visitors to the World Fair never knew they were treading on a dead body. Yet not everything that happened in the exhibition grounds was so tragic. There were also comical events, such as the following:

With the thaw, a group of gypsies appeared on the beach. The workers' wives came out to the doors of their shacks to block their entrance, as it was believed that gypsy women stole breastfeeding babies. In fact, this group only wanted to make some money repairing pots and pans, clipping dogs' fur, telling fortunes and making a bear dance.

The workers, who had no long-haired dogs or kitchen utensils or any wish to know what the future might hold, were only interested in seeing the bear dance. As a result, the Civil Guard was called to expel the gypsies, who had installed themselves in Plaza de Armas and were playing their tambourines. The Civil Guard officer, who had been promoted as a result of the incident at the Fine Arts Palace, confronted the man who appeared to be the gypsies' leader. He ordered them all to leave at once. The gypsy replied that they weren't doing anyone any harm. "I'm not going to argue with you," said the officer. "I'm just going to say this: I'm going for a piss. If, by the time I return, you're still here, I'll shoot the bear, send the men to do forced labour and shave off the women's hair. It's up to you." As if by magic, bear and gypsies vanished into thin air.

But the amusing part came two or three days later, when another group appeared, as picturesque as the previous one. At the head was a gentleman sporting a green frock coat and a velvet top hat of the same colour. He had a jet-black waxed moustache. He was followed by four men carrying a trestle on which stood a large object covered by a tarpaulin. As soon as they saw this procession entering the park, the Civil Guard charged them and began beating them with their rifle butts.

It turned out that the man in the frock coat was the first exhibitor for the World Fair, a certain Gunther van Elkeserio, together with four workmen who had accompanied him from Mainz. This poor man had brought an electric spindle of his own invention and was wandering around, asking in German and English where he could register, and where he could leave his invention until the Fair opened its doors.

To avoid last-minute congestion, the authorities had encouraged exhibitors to bring whatever they were displaying to Barcelona well ahead of time. This meant freeing up several warehouses where all the exhibits could be stored until the pavilions were finished. This was a much more complicated operation than seemed at first sight. Not only had these objects to be protected from the elements, the damp (some of them were sophisticated machinery, works of art or simply fragile articles) as well as from the ravages of rats, cockroaches, termites and so on, they also had to be stored in such a way that when the time came they could be identified and found without trouble.

The authorities had thought of this and published an exhaustive classification of every single object in the world. To avoid any problem, each one was given a number, letter or a combination of the two. A copy of these lists soon came into Onofre Bouvila's possession. He studied it closely: he had never imagined the existence of so many things that could be bought and sold. This discovery made his mind whirl for several days, until finally he and Efrén Castells overcame a thousand obstacles and managed to get into one of the warehouses. When they lit the oil lamp they had brought with them, they discovered crates and packages of all sizes stacked from floor to ceiling. Some were so big they could have contained a coach and horses; others so small they would have fitted into a pocket. There was something in every one of them. Onofre consulted his list by the flickering lamp Efrén Castells was holding aloft. The list was headed: *Mechanical apparatuses used in medicine, surgery or orthopaedics; chairs, beds, etc.; bandages for the reduction of hernias, varicose veins, etc.; apparatuses for use by patients: crutches, special footwear, spectacles, ear trumpets, wooden legs, etc.; synthetic and mechanical prostheses: teeth, eyes, artificial noses, etc.; jointed artificial limbs; other non-specified mechanical orthopaedic apparatuses; equipment for forced and extraordinary feeding; straitjackets, etc.* "Good God!" exclaimed Efrén Castells. Urged on by Onofre, the giant used his great strength to open one of the biggest crates. Inside it was a calender paper press.

The kind-hearted giant had won over the urchins on the beach, the offspring of the women he seduced. He used them to exchange love letters and arrange rendezvous. He and Onofre now began to organise and train these youngsters. At night, the youngsters stole into the warehouses, broke open the crates and took the contents back to the pair. According to what they might be, they either sold them or raffled them off. The youngsters were given a certain sum for each article.

Whatever Efrén gained in this way lasted no time at all; Onofre Bouvila on the other hand never spent any of it. By this time he had accumulated a small fortune in Father Bizancio's mattress. "I don't understand what you want so much money for," the giant would say to his partner. "I could be forgiven for saving, because I'm stupid and have to think about the future; but I can't see why you, who are so clever, need to save." The truth was that Onofre did not spend because he didn't know what to buy and had no-one to teach him nor any reason to do so.

After a long time spying on her, Onofre concluded that Delfina only left the boarding house for barely an hour each morning to do the shopping. Thinking that would be a good opportunity to approach her, one day he abandoned his business activities and followed her to the market. Delfina left with two big wicker baskets, accompanied by her cat. She walked purposefully, but with an absent air, as if she were daydreaming. Because of this, she regularly stepped into filthy puddles with her bare feet, or in piles of rubbish. The children playing in the alleys watched her go by with caution: they would have mocked and thrown stones at her but the cat scared them off.

The market traders had no great love for her either. She never gossiped with them and was very demanding when it came to the weight and freshness of her purchases. She bargained ferociously. She always bought things that were going off, and claimed she should be given a discount. If a stallholder said a cabbage wasn't rotten, but was still fresh, Delfina would retort that it wasn't true, that the cabbage stank, was riddled with worms, and that she wasn't going to pay an exorbitant price for such garbage. If the vendor argued back and tempers became frayed, Delfina would grab Beelzebub and plonk him on the counter, where the cat would arch its back, fur standing on end, and extend its claws. This strategy always worked: chastened, the stallholder would invariably give in. "Here," she would say, "take the cabbage and pay me whatever you like, but don't come back to my stall, because I've no intention of ever serving you again, do you hear me?" Delfina would shrug and return the next day with the same attitude. The stallholders would turn livid with rage when they saw her; they had turned to a witch who wandered round the market to put the evil eye on her, and above all on the cat.

Onofre had no difficulty learning all this, because when the market women were no longer being molested by her and the malevolent animal, they didn't spare their comments.

On the way back from the market, Onofre went up to Delfina.

"I was out for a walk," he told her, "and by chance saw you coming. Can I help?"

"I can manage perfectly well on my own," she replied, quickening her step as if to show that the overflowing baskets were not slowing her down.

"I didn't say you couldn't manage, I was only trying to be friendly."

"Why?" asked Delfina.

"There's no 'why' about it," Onofre replied. "People are friendly for no reason. If there is a reason, it's no longer being friendly, it's being self-interested."

"You're a smooth talker," she interrupted him. "Clear off or I'll set the cat on you."

Onofre had to get rid of Beelzebub. He dreamed up many good schemes, but they all presented insuperable difficulties. In the end he hit upon one he thought might work: he would coat the boarding house roof with oil. When Beelzebub climbed on the roof, as all cats do, it would slip and fall off. Falling from the fourth floor down to the street was bound to kill it, Onofre reasoned. He nearly killed himself carrying out his plan. When he had coated all the tiles with grease, he went back to his room and lay on his bed. That night, nothing happened. The following one, when he had become so bored with waiting that he fell asleep (the San Ezequiel church clock had chimed two) he was woken by a sudden noise: he could hear moans and curses coming from his balcony. He was terrified Beelzebub had fallen on a late-night passerby. That would really be bad luck, he told himself. Opening the balcony window, he stepped out. What he saw in the moonlight gave him a terrible fright: a man was dangling from the railing, calling for help as he scrabbled desperately to find a foothold in the brickwork. "Please," he begged when he saw Onofre, "give me a hand or I'm a goner."

Onofro seized him by the wrists, pulled him up and dragged him into the bedroom. As soon as the man tried to stand up, his feet slipped and he sat down abruptly. "I've bashed my arse in twenty places," he moaned again. Lighting a candle, Onofre warned him to be quiet. "Now tell me what you were doing hanging from my balcony," he urged him.

"How should I know," the man replied. "Some lousy wretch must have greased the roof. Luckily I grabbed onto the railing, or that would have been it."

"But what were you doing on the roof at this time of night?" Onofre asked.

"What's that to you?" came the reply.

"Nothing at all," said Onofre, "but perhaps the owners of the boarding house and the police would like to know."

"Whoa there," said the man. "I'm not a thief and I wasn't doing anything wrong. My name is Sisinio. I'm the boyfriend of a girl who lives here."

"Delfina!"

"Yes, that's her name. Her parents are very strict and won't let her have anything to do with men. We see each other at night, up on the roof."

"How remarkable!" said Onofre. "And how do you get up there?"

"I use a ladder. I put it behind the house, where the ground rises and it's not so high. I'm a house painter."

Sisinio looked about thirty-five. He was narrow-chested, with thinning hair and a receding chin. He had two teeth missing and spoke with a lisp. So this is my rival, Onofre thought dejectedly.

"And what do you do up on the roof?"

"That's private."

"Don't be afraid. I'm one of you. My name is Gaston. Pablo can vouch for me."

"Oh, that's right," said Sisinio, smiling for the first time. He told Onofre that in fact they didn't get up to a great deal. They talked about this and that, now and then gave each other a kiss. It was difficult to do much more than that up there. Sisinio had suggested a thousand times they go somewhere more comfortable, but Delfina always refused. "Afterwards, you won't love me anymore," she would tell him. This had been going on for two years. Onofre asked why they didn't get married.

"That's a different story," said Sisinio. "In fact, I'm already married. I have two daughters. I haven't told Delfina yet: I don't have the courage to upset her. The poor thing has such high hopes. If my wife kicked the bucket, everything would be fine, but she's as strong as an ox."

"And what does *she* say?" Onofre asked. "Your wife, I mean."

"Nothing. She thinks I work at night. Before I get home, I splash paint on myself, to pretend I've been on a job."

"Don't move from here," Onofre said. "I'll go and fetch Delfina.

If she goes up on the roof to meet you, she's bound to slip and kill herself."

He went out into the corridor just as Father Bizancio was going into the bathroom. The fortune teller was moaning with pain. All I need now, Onofre thought, is to bump into Señor Braulio dressed as a can-can dancer. What kind of a place have I ended up in?

No sooner had Onofre knocked softly at Delfina's bedroom door and identified himself than he heard her whisper, "Go away or I'll set the cat on you."

"I only came to tell you that Sisinio has had an accident," Onofre said.

The bedroom door opened in a flash. Four eyes gleamed in the door frame. The cat hissed, Onofre jumped back, but the maid said: "Don't be afraid, he won't touch you. What's happened?"

"Your boyfriend fell off the roof. He's in my bedroom. Come on, but don't bring Beelzebub."

As the two of them started down the stairs, Onofre took hold of Delfina's arm. She didn't pull away, and said nothing. He realised she was trembling.

Sisinio lay stretched out on the bed. By candlelight he looked like a corpse, although his eyes were darting about and he was trying to smile.

"I'll leave you to it," Onofre told Delfina. "Try to make sure he doesn't die in my room; I don't want trouble. I'll be back at first light."

He went down to street level and hesitated a while in the doorway, unsure which way to head. All of a sudden he heard a loud meow: a small body brushed his shoulder, and crashed to the ground. Onofre picked up an iron bar and pushed Beelzebub's dead body into an open drain. And so, in a single night, Delfina lost both her pillars of support.

4

As a novice, His Excellency the Right Reverend Bishop of Barcelona had travelled to Rome. During a stay of several days in Milan, he saw His Imperial Highness Archduke Ferdinand of Austria (the same man who was to die tragically years later in Sarajevo) inspect the guard. This image stayed with the illustrious prelate to the end of his days.

At this moment, the men working on the Fair were pausing in their tasks, straightening up, and doffing their caps as he passed by. The bells from Ciudadela Church were ringing, and the trumpets of the cavalry platoon accompanying the entourage blared out. His Excellency the Bishop and the honourable mayor were driven side by side under the Triumphal Arch. They were followed by a swarm of dignitaries. Behind them came the diplomatic corps, nearly all of them rather bored. Close beside the ordinary came a deacon carrying the stoup, a silver bowl filled with holy water. The bishop had his crosier in his left hand, and with his right he was shaking the aspergillum, occasionally dipping it into the bowl. Whenever he managed to sprinkle one of the workers, the man immediately crossed himself. It was a sad sight to see how the bishop's cape was becoming covered in dust. The Palace of Industry, where the official ceremony was to take place, was still missing most of its outer walls, but this fact was hidden by tarpaulins that made it look like a marquee.

A chapel had been erected in a prominent position, containing a recently restored gilded silver statue of Saint Lucia dating from at least the eighteenth century. The municipal band was waiting to the left of the central nave; when the procession entered they struck up a march. The bishop blessed the site. He and the mayor gave speeches, at the end of which there were loud cheers for His Majesty the King and Her Majesty the Queen Regent.

The two Madrid representatives who had travelled back and forth from Barcelona so often that they could reel off from memory the names of all the towns en route, were in tears. They saw themselves as, if not the progenitors of the event, then at least its midwives. In fact, their contribution had been disastrous: the central government had not come up with either enough funds to save the municipality of Barcelona from ruin, or so little that the Catalans could claim all the credit for themselves. The two government emissaries seemed unaware of this, or if they did know, they were overcome with emotion anyway. The end of the religious act was signalled by another peal of bells, and work restarted at once. It was 1 March 1888, a month and seven days before the official opening.

Onofre Bouvila's business ventures had diversified and grown spectacularly, especially after taking on the child thieves and later when they came across a consignment described as *betel, Peruvian leaves, haschish and other plants for smoking or chewing* intended for the Palace of Agriculture (situated, like the Fine Arts Palace, outside the park itself, by the north wall of the Fair between Calles Roger de Flor and Sicilia on the main road to San Martin and France). They sold the goods at a high price thanks to the efforts of a master stucco plasterer as affable as he was prone to falling from scaffolding and ladders.

Onofre's success worried Pablo, who was gradually realising that his apprentice, however considerate he was towards him, was playing him for a fool. Pablo did not know how to react. He knew the prestige Onofre enjoyed among the World Fair workers. Nor did he dare reveal to his fellow believers the quandary his weakness had left him in. The only information he had from the outside world was whatever Onofre chose to share with him. Pablo was a puppet in his hands.

Since Pablo had often explained that the very first thing that needed to be demolished in Catalonia was El Liceo opera house, Onofre decided to go and see for himself. "El Liceo is a symbol, like the king in Madrid or the Pope in Rome," Pablo had told him. "Thank God here in Catalonia we don't have a king or a pope, but we do have El Liceo." Onofre paid what seemed to him an exorbitant amount, and was shown to the entrance for the poor. He had to go down a side alley full of cabbage stalks, whilst the rich descended from their carriages at the main entrance on Las Ramblas. The ladies had to be almost lifted out: their gowns were so long that when they had already disappeared through the glass front door, their trains were still sliding from their coaches, as though a reptile were going to the opera.

Onofre had to climb countless flights of stairs until he arrived panting at a level where the only seating was a long, lice-infested iron bench, already occupied by music lovers who had been there for days. They slept draped over the parapet like mats spread out to air, ate hunks of bread with garlic, and drank wine out of a skin. They carried stubs of candles so that they could read the scores and librettos in the dark theatre. Some of them had lost their health and their sight in El Liceo.

The rest of the opera house down below was quite different. Onofre was dazzled by the luxury: the silks, muslins and velvets, the sequined capes, jewels, the constant popping of champagne corks, the comings and goings of waiters and the constant hum of conversation produced when rich people gather together: all this enchanted him. That is how I want to be, he told himself, even if it means I have to put up with this never-ending insipid music. He had the misfortune to be attending the premiere of *Triphon and Cascanti*, a grandiloquent mythological opera performed only once in El Liceo, and on a few other occasions in the rest of the world.

*

The next morning at breakfast, Delfina came up to him. Not even her ugliness could hide the effects of not having slept or her anxiety. She asked him if by any chance he had seen Beelzebub. "No, why would I have?" Onofre replied. "He's been missing for days," Delfina said dejectedly. "It's no great loss," he replied.

Efrén Castells was waiting for him at the entrance to the Fair. "Things don't look good," the giant said as soon as he saw him. "For the past few days I've noticed two individuals who seem to be keeping an eye on you. At first I thought they were just curious, but they're too insistent. I know they don't work here. And they've been asking questions."

"They must be policemen."

"I don't think so; it's not their style," said Efrén Castells.

"What then?"

"I don't know, my lad, but I don't like it. Maybe we ought to take a holiday: everything here is almost finished anyway."

It was true. Onofre scanned the huge enterprise he had followed almost from the outset. The first time he had entered the park a year earlier, it had looked like a battlefield. Now it resembled the backdrop for a fairy story. Everything was garish, heterogeneous, and out of proportion. When the Technical Board presented their first plan to the mayor, he tore it up with his own hands. "What you've brought me is a flea market," he exclaimed. "What I want is a cyclorama." Two and a half years later, some concessions had been made to common sense, but the mayor's wishes had been more than fulfilled.

Onofre and the giant from Calella sat on limestone blocks in front of a thatched hut erected by the Philippines Tobacco Company. A half-naked native was shivering as he squatted in the hut doorway, rolling cigars. He had been brought expressly from Batangas and told not to move until the World Fair was over. The only thing he had been taught was to say *au revoir* to the visitors. Whenever the sky became overcast, he would peer up at it apprehensively, fearing a whirlwind might sweep him and the hut up into the air and deposit them back in Batangas, like spinning tops.

"There's no point to any of this," Onofre said. "It doesn't mean a thing. And it's the same with us: our desires, our work – they mean nothing." "Bah," replied Efrén Castells, "don't take it so much to heart, lad. You're very smart, you're bound to make sense of it all."

Back at the boarding house later that day, Onofre entered the fortune teller's room without knocking. The dying woman was lying in bed with her eyes closed, blankets up to her chin. Onofre could see just how old Macaela Castro was thanks to the light of a candle flickering in a cheap holder attached to the bedhead.

"Is that you, Onofre?" the fortune teller asked.

"Carry on sleeping," Onofre said, "I only came to see if you needed anything."

"I don't need anything, but you do," whispered Micaela. "It's obvious you're drowning in a sea of confusion."

"How do you know that?" asked Onofre in astonishment, because the old woman hadn't even opened her eyes.

"No-one comes to see me unless they're confused, my boy. You don't have to be a fortune teller to know that. Tell me what's wrong."

"Can you read my future for me, Micaela?" Onofre asked.

"Oh, my boy, I don't have much strength left. I'm not part of this world anymore. What time is it?"

"About half past one," Onofre replied.

"I don't have long left," said Micaela. "I'm going to die at twenty past four. That's what I've been told. They're waiting for me, you see. I'll soon be with them. I've heard their voices all my life; now I'll add mine to their chorus, and somebody in this world will hear me. We spirits have our cycles too. I'm going to take the place of a

124

weary spirit. I'll take his place and he will finally be able to rest in the peace of the Lord. I know Father Bizancio says the Devil is waiting for me, but that's not true. He's a good man, but he's very ignorant. Give me my cards, and let's not waste more time. You'll find them on the third shelf in the little cupboard."

Onofre did as he was told. In the cupboard were a stack of black clothes, various other belongings, and a few rice paper boxes tied up with silk ribbon. On the shelf she had mentioned he saw an old prayer book, a rosary with white beads, and a rotten spikenard bracelet. He also found the pack of cards; he took it and handed it to the medium, who had opened her eyes.

"Bring up a chair, my boy, and sit beside me," she said. "But first help me sit up ... yes, like that, that's right, thanks. Things must be done properly so we won't seem like fools: I don't want them to laugh when they see me coming."

Smoothing the bedspread, she laid out nine cards in a circle, face down.

"The circle of knowledge," she said. "Also known as the mirror of Solomon. This is the centre of the heavens and these are the four constellations, with their elements." Spinning her hand round in the air, index finger extended, she plunged it down onto a card. "The house of dispositions, or the eastern corner," she said, turning it over. "I see you will have a long life, you will be rich, will marry a very beautiful woman, have three children. Perhaps you will travel and enjoy good health."

"That's fine, Micaela," said Onofre, getting up from his chair. "Don't tire yourself. That's all I wanted to know."

"Wait Onofre, don't go. What I've just told you is pure rubbish. Don't go, there's more ... Now I see an abandoned mausoleum, in the moonlight. That means a fortune and death. A king; kings mean death as well, but also power, that's their nature. Now I see blood; blood means money as well as blood. And now, what's this I see? Three women. Bring a chair over, Onofre, and sit at the top of the bed."

"I'm here, Micaela."

"Then listen carefully to what I'm about to say, my boy. I see three women. One is in the house of reversals, setbacks and sorrow. She will make you rich. The next is in the house of legacies, which is also the dwelling of children. She will bring you fame. The third and last is in the house of love and true knowledge. She will make you happy. In the fourth house there is a man. Beware of him: he is in the house of poisonings and tragic ends."

"I don't understand a word of what you're telling me, Micaela," said Onofre, perturbed by her predictions.

"Ah, my boy, that's the way with oracles: they're accurate but vague. Do you think if that weren't the case, I'd be dying here in this filthy boarding house? Just hark my words and remember. When what I've foretold happens, you'll know it at once. Not that it will do you much good. At best, it can be reassuring. But let's return to the cards; let them speak. I see three women."

"You've already said that, Micaela."

"I haven't finished yet. One will make you rich, another will bring you fame, the third will make you happy. The one who makes you happy will bring you bad luck; the one bringing you fame will enslave you; the one who makes you rich will curse you. Of the three, this last one is the most dangerous, because she's a saint, a famous saint. God will hear her curse you and, as punishment, He will create a man. He's the man the cards speak of, a devil of a man. He has no idea God placed him on this earth to carry out His vengeance."

"How will I recognise him?" Onofre asked.

"I don't know; but these things are always obvious. In any case, whether you recognise him or not the result will be the same. It's already decided that he will be the one who destroys you. It's pointless for you to go against him. His weapons are different from yours. There will be violence and death. Both of you will be devoured by the dragon. But don't be afraid: dragons look fierce, but all they do is roar and belch flames from their mouth. It's the goat you must fear: they are the symbol of treachery and deceit. Now don't make me work anymore, I'm very tired," Micaela concluded.

The cards slid from the bedspread and scattered across the floor. Micaela's head fell back on her pillow, and she closed her eyes. Thinking she had died, Onofre unhooked the candle holder and brought the flame up to her face. It wavered: she was still breathing. Onofre picked up the cards and put the pack away in the cupboard, though not without first carefully shuffling them so that no-one else would know what the future held for him. He tiptoed out of the dying fortune teller's room and went back to his own. He lay down on his bed trying to make sense of what he had just been told.

Delfina continued going to the market every day. Seeing her arrive without the cat, the stallholders unleashed all their rancour stored up over the years when she had terrorised them. They refused to serve her or kept her waiting for ages; they called her ragamuffin, scarecrow or simply didn't talk to her at all. They short-changed her, and if she protested, laughed in her face. One of them threw a rotten egg at her back, which she didn't even bother to wipe off.

Onofre had not seen or heard anything more of Sisinio, but it seemed to him that the painter and Delfina had not met again since the night Beelzebub died.

Micaela Castro passed away the night she read him the cards. When Father Bizancio entered her room at daybreak, he was confronted by her dead body. He closed her eyes, snuffed out the candle, then went to inform Señor Braulio and the other lodgers. Micaela was buried the next day, and a prayer for the dead was said for her in San Ezequiel church.

A search in her wardrobe revealed a few personal documents. According to them, her name wasn't really Micaela Castro, but Pastora López Marrero, and at her death she was sixty-four years old. There was no way they could trace any relatives, and what she had bequeathed did not justify a more thorough search. Delfina changed the deceased's sheets for an equally grubby pair, and that same day her room was taken by a young philosophy student. Nobody told him that somebody had died in the bed a few hours earlier. Some time later this student went mad, but for other reasons.

Close to the World Fair park entrance on Paseo de la Aduana stood a small pavilion covered inside and out with tiles, called the Pavilion of Nitrogenated Waters. It had been completed by the end of January, but by mid-March was still empty. Onofre Bouvila and Efrén Castells had got hold of a key, and this was where they kept their stolen goods. The day before, the child thieves had made off with a collection of timepieces. Onofre and Efrén had no idea what to do with so many of them. There were normal pocket watches, but also clocks for towers and public buildings, repeater watches, ones with second hands, pocket and marine chronometers, pendulums, astral watches, chronometers for astronomical and scientific observation, water clocks, hourglasses, regulators, complex timepieces indicating the main elements of the solar and lunar cycles, electric clocks, special watches for gnomonic measurements, equinoctial as well as polar clocks, horizontal, azimuth, right ascension and declination ones, meridional and septentrional ones, pedometers and meters for construction, industry, locomotion and the sciences, devices to regulate the movements of light sources in general, apparatuses to detect, fix and specify natural phenomena, and implements for monetary and price calculations, as well as every conceivable spare part. All of them had been listed. "I've no idea what we can do with all this stuff," the giant said. "Apart from going crazy from so much ticking and chiming."

5

In the run-up to the opening of the World Fair, the authorities had promised to rid Barcelona of "undesirables". *For some time now city officials have been making strenuous efforts to rid us of that plague of tramps, delinquents and vagabonds who, unable to pursue their criminal activities in smaller towns, are seeking temporary refuge in the confusion of more populous cities. Even if the authorities have not succeeded in cutting out all these social cancers that eat away at the foundations of this refined capital, they have made great strides in this extremely arduous task,* a newspaper of the time reported. To reinforce this, there were police roundups every night.

"Don't come back here for a while; the group is disbanding temporarily," Pablo said. Onofre asked what he was thinking of doing, and where he would hide. The apostle shrugged: he didn't seem very concerned at this turn of events. "Rest assured, we'll be back all the stronger," he added, somewhat unconvincingly.

"What about the pamphlets?" Onofre asked. Pablo twisted his mouth derisively. "No more pamphlets," he said. Onofre asked what would happen to his weekly payments. "You'll have to do without them," Pablo responded, a hint of malicious glee in his voice. "Sometimes circumstances call for sacrifices. Besides, this is a political struggle; we don't guarantee anybody wages."

Onofre wanted to ask more, but the apostle dismissed him with a wave of the hand. As Onofre went to open the door, Pablo caught him up. "Wait," he said, "it's possible we may never meet again. Our struggle is a long one," he added in a rush. It was obvious this wasn't what he really wanted to say, and that his mind was on something more important, but he was either too timid or tongue-tied to come out with it. As a result, he resorted to well-worn rhetoric: "What matters is, we must never give up the fight. Those fools the socialists reckon the revolution will solve everything. They think the exploitation of man by man only happens once, that as soon as society is free of those in power now, everything will be alright. But we anarchists know that wherever there is a relationship of any kind, the strong are bound to exploit the weak. This struggle, this terrible combat is mankind's inexorable destiny," he exclaimed, flinging his arms round Onofre. "This could be the last time we meet," he said, his voice choking with emotion. "Goodbye, and may good fortune be with you."

One of the victims of the nightly police raids was Señor Braulio. He had gone out dressed in all his finery to be roughed up by some handsome young thug, but this particular night it was the police who gave him a beating. Then they demanded bail money to release him. "Whatever you want," he told them. "As long as my wife, who is ill, and my daughter, who is still very young, don't find out about this." Having no money on him, he sent a boy to the boarding house with a message to ask the barber Mariano for the amount the authorities were demanding. "Tell him I'll repay him just as soon as I can," he said.

Back at the boarding house, Mariano claimed he didn't have the money. "I don't have any cash," he said, though this was obviously untrue. The boy ran back to the police station and told Señor Braulio exactly what the barber had said. Seeing no way out of the inevitable scandal, Señor Braulio took advantage of a momentary lapse by his guards to plunge his pointed hair comb into his heart. The whalebone stays of his corset deflected the prongs, so that he only suffered a few surface wounds, but these bled copiously. His skirt and petticoats were ruined, and a puddle formed on the police station floor. Snatching the comb from him, the guards kicked him in the groin and kidneys. "Let's see if we can beat some sense into you, you old whore," they shouted.

Lying on a narrow bench, still in pain and covered in blood, Señor Braulio sent the messenger back to the boarding house. "There's a lad there by the name of Bouvila, Onofre Bouvila," he told the boy. "Be discreet when you ask for him. I don't think he has a penny, but he'll know how to help."

It's either him or I'm done for, Señor Braulio told himself once the messenger had left. He began to wonder what he could use to attempt suicide again. All because I'm not right in the head, he thought.

At the boarding house, Onofre Bouvila listened to the boy's message and thought this must be his lucky day. "Tell Señor Braulio that I personally will go to the police station with the money before dawn," he told the messenger. "Tell him to be patient, and not to try any more stupid tricks." As soon as the boy had left, Onofre went upstairs and knocked on Delfina's door. "I don't see why I should open for you," she said when he identified himself. Onofre couldn't help but smile at this sour reply.

"You'd better open the door, Delfina," he said softly. "Your father is in a tight spot. The police have arrested him and he's attempted suicide, so you can see how serious it is."

The door opened a crack, and Delfina appeared, blocking the way into her bedroom. She was wearing the same shabby nightdress he had seen her in twice before: when she had appeared in his bedroom to offer him work, and again when he had gone to take her to see the injured Sisinio. All of a sudden Onofre heard Señora Agata's mournful voice from the adjoining room.

"Delfina, the washbasin," came the voice.

Delfina waved her hand impatiently. "Don't bother me, I have to take my mother her water."

Onofre stood his ground. He could glimpse fear in the maid's eyes, and that emboldened him still further. "Let her wait," he growled. "You and I have more urgent matters to attend to."

Delfina bit her bottom lip before replying. "I don't understand what you mean," she said at last.

"Didn't I tell you your father's in danger? What's wrong with you? Are you dumb or something?"

Delfina blinked several times, as if this unexpected series of questions made it impossible for her to judge the situation as a whole. "Oh yes, my father," she murmured finally. "What can I do for him?"

"Nothing," sneered Onofre. "I'm the only one who can help him now; his life depends on me."

The colour drained from Delfina's face and she lowered her eyes. The San Ezequiel church bell rang several times. "What time is it?" asked Onofre. "Half past three," said Delfina, adding: "If you really can help him, why don't you do so? What are you waiting for? What do you want from me?"

Her sick mother continued to wail from the next room: "Delfina, what's going on? Why don't you come? Whose voice is that, daughter, who are you talking to?"

Delfina tried to squeeze past Onofre into the corridor, but he seized her by the shoulders and pulled her violently towards him. There was more brutality than passion in this; as long as she hadn't moved, he had also remained still, but when she tried to escape it was the signal for action. Through the stiff fabric of her nightdress, he could feel Delfina's bony body pressed against him. She didn't struggle, but simply pleaded, "Please let go of me: it's cruel to keep my mother waiting. She could have an attack if I don't see to her."

Onofre ignored this. "You know what you have to do if you want to see your father alive," he said, pushing her inside the room. He kicked the door shut and fumbled with the buttons on her nightgown.

"For the love of God, Onofre, don't do this to me," she protested. He gave a low laugh and said heartlessly: "There's no point resisting; your cat isn't here to defend you now. Beelzebub is dead; he fell off the roof and splattered on the ground. I myself washed his disgusting remains down the drain. Oh, the devil take it!" he exclaimed, unable to unbutton her nightgown; this was the first time he had ever had to fight with female attire, and his excitement only made matters worse.

Seeing his embarrassment, Delfina flopped back on her bed, pulled the nightgown up to her waist, and said: "Come on then."

By the time Onofre got up again, the San Ezequiel church clock was striking four. "The sun will be up soon," he said. "I promised Señor Braulio I'd be at the police station with the money before daybreak, and I intend to keep my word. Business is business," he added, looking down at Delfina, who stared back impassively. "I don't know why you went to such great lengths," she said, as if talking to herself. "I'm not worth all that effort."

The pale light of dawn stole all the colour from her body; her skin looked deathly grey against the crumpled sheets. How skinny she is, thought Onofre, mentally comparing her body to those of the workmen's wives he had seen frolicking almost naked in the sea to ward off the summer heat. How odd, he thought, how different she looks to me now. Raising his voice, he told her: "Cover yourself." Delfina pulled up the edge of the sheet, her stiff, dishevelled hair creating a halo round her face. "Do you have to go already?" she asked. He didn't reply, but finished dressing as quickly as he could. Señora Agata was no longer calling out, and silence reigned in her bedroom. Onofre went over to the door, but Delfina's voice made him pause.

"Wait," he heard her say. "Don't go yet. Don't leave me like this. What's going to happen now?" She waited a few moments for Onofre to reply, but he hadn't even understood what she meant. She covered her face with her left hand. "What will I tell Sisinio?" she asked eventually.

Hearing his name, Onofre guffawed: "You don't have to worry about him," he said. "He has a wife and children. He's been deceiving you all this time; if you're expecting anything from that two-faced scoundrel you're very much mistaken."

Delfina stared at Onofre. "One day I'll tell you something," she said, her voice calmer. "One day I'll tell you a secret. Now go."

Onofre went down to the first floor, hid until Father Bizancio went into the bathroom, and then took the money he needed from his mattress. He used it to get Señor Braulio out of jail, and brought him back to the boarding house in a hackney cab; the older man was very weak from losing so much blood. When they arrived, Delfina was writhing with stomach cramps. She had been vomiting, and was losing blood. Worried that Onofre had made her pregnant, she had applied a homemade purgative that had left her at death's door.

"Daughter!" cried Señor Braulio. "What's happened to you?"

"And you, father, dressed like that . . . and covered in blood!"

"Covered in blood and shame, Delfina my love, as you can see. But what have you done?" he asked.

"The same, father. I'm exactly the same as you," Delfina replied.

"Whatever happens, your poor mother mustn't hear about this," insisted her father.

When they went in to see her, Señora Agata was much worse. Alarmed by the moans and sighs from the third floor, Father Bizancio went up in his nightshirt to see if there was anything he could do to help. Señor Braulio hid in a wardrobe so the priest wouldn't see him dolled up as a woman. Onofre sent Father Bizancio for the doctor friend who had attended Micaela Castro. Once the priest had left, Delfina took Onofre to one side.

"Leave the boarding house and don't come back," she told him. "Don't stop even to gather your things. You have been warned. I won't say anything more; it's your choice."

Without pausing to consider exactly what her threat meant, Onofre understood that Delfina wasn't making it in vain, and fled. The sky was streaked red; the birds were chirruping. Men and women were heading for work, many of them carrying small children in their arms so they could sleep a little longer, at least until they reached the factory gates. There their parents woke them up, and they parted: the adults went to the more dangerous places and the hardest work, the children to less burdensome tasks.

When Onofre reached Ciudadela Park, he saw the tethered hot-air balloon rising above the treetops and flagpoles. Engineers were making sure it was working properly, and that the mooring ropes were securely fastened. Nobody wanted the balloon to break free in the middle of the Fair and drift away on the wind, its basket filled with terrified tourists. Looking after the "*touristas*", as they were called, was the chief concern in Barcelona at that moment. The newspapers mentioned nothing else. *When they return to their country, each and every visitor will become an apostle who will spread the news of all that they have seen, heard, and learned.*

The tethered balloon worked perfectly, except when the treacherous wind known as *vent de garbi* blew and turned it on its side. Twice that morning, the engineer in charge had been left hanging onto a rope with one foot on the ground, obviously in distress. But these were only small details, the sort of last-minute hitches that always occur.

The entrance to the World Fair was through the Triumphal Arch.

This arch, still to be admired today, was made of bare brick in the Mudejar style. The sides of the arch featured the coats of arms of the Spanish provinces, with Barcelona's at the keystone. There were also two friezes on the sides. These were bas-reliefs showing Spain's support for the Barcelona World Fair (in memory of the original disputes) and Barcelona welcoming foreign nations.

The Triumphal Arch led to the Salón de San Juan, a broad tree-lined avenue paved with mosaics and adorned with elaborate gas lamps and eight bronze statues. Come on in, they seemed to be saying. On the Salón de San Juan stood the Palace of Justice, which still exists, the Fine Arts Palace and the palaces of Agriculture and Science, which are no longer there. Two pillars marked the entrance to the actual park. At the top of each pillar was a stone sculpture. One represented Commerce; the other Industry, as though the message they were transmitting was: *we get things done.* More inclined to spiritual imagery, the Madrid government looked askance at this, and this was possibly yet another factor dissuading it from providing greater material assistance. Both pillars can still be admired today.

Going over in his mind images of what had taken place a few hours earlier, Onofre wondered: How come Efrén, who is such an ass, can attract women so easily, whereas I, who am much cleverer, have to go to such extremes? He never came up with a satisfactory answer. Nor was he able to find Efrén Castells anywhere that morning, despite visiting all their agreed meeting places. Onofre ended up walking down to the beach. A team of workmen were raking the sand to erase the last traces of the camp that had stood there for more than two years. Now part of the beach had been built on; two pavilions related to maritime affairs: one for shipbuilding and the other for the Transatlantic Company. Another part was used to exhibit stud stallions, whose neighing could be heard whenever the crash of waves subsided. A pier with a luxury restaurant thrust out into the sea. The sun sparkled on the water, blinding Onofre. He had no idea what had happened to the women and children who until a short while before had lived on the beach. A warm, tangy spring breeze was blowing.

That night he went back to the boarding house. The lobby was empty, and so was the dining room. He saw Mariano's head poke out of his cubbyhole. "What are you doing here?" the barber asked. "You gave me a fright."

"What's happened, Mariano?" said Onofre. "Where is everyone?"

The barber could barely string his words together. He seemed frightened, as white as if he'd had a bag of flour poured over him.

"The Civil Guard came and took away Señor Braulio, Señora Agata and Delfina," he said. "They were all carried out on stretchers: Señora Agata because she was very ill, on her deathbed I reckon. Señor Braulio and his daughter because they were both losing blood. It's dark now, so you probably didn't see them, but there are pools of the stuff in the entrance. It must be congealing already. I don't know whether they were taking them to jail, the hospital or straight to be buried. Just recalling the scene makes me want to retch, even though in my line of business I've seen more than enough."

"Why did they take them away?"

"How should I know? As you'll understand, they didn't come and explain anything to me. But I've heard rumours. They say that frightful girl belonged to a gang of criminals, the ones they call anarchists. I'm not saying it's true, it's what I've heard. You know what women are like. Apparently she had relations or dealings – I've no idea what kind – with someone else in the gang. A house painter and anarchist. The painter was denounced to the police, and the girl was hauled in with the rest."

"Didn't they ask after me, Mariano?" Onofre wanted to know.

"Yes, now you come to mention it, I think they were asking about you," said the barber, a hint of satisfaction in his voice. "They searched every room, yours most thoroughly of all. They asked us what time you usually came back. I said at nightfall. I didn't tell them that something was going on between you and Delfina, because to be honest I don't know. I've seen and noticed things, but officially as it were, I know nothing. Father Bizancio told them you didn't live here anymore, that you'd left the boarding house some days ago. Because he wears a cassock, they believed his lies, and not my true version. That's why they haven't left anyone on guard."

Onofre took to his heels. As he fled, he reflected that it must have been Delfina who went to the police out of spite, to avenge herself on Sisinio and him. She must have denounced the entire organisation. She had told him to get out of the boarding house as quickly as he could. "Pack your things and don't come back," she had warned him, to prevent him falling into the hands of the Civil Guard. And now Sisinio was in jail, as well as Pablo and Delfina herself.

She wanted to save me, even though in fact I'm the one who caused all this chaos. What a mess, he thought. Still, I have to disappear from Barcelona. After a while, things will calm down, he told himself. The anarchists will be released from prison if they haven't been shot first. He too would be able to get back to business; maybe he could get the child thieves together again, or even convince the anarchists it would be better to devote themselves to lucrative schemes, that the revolution they dreamed of was impossible.

For the moment, though, he had to flee. First, however, he needed to recover the money that was still back at the boarding house in Father Bizancio's mattress. Returning there was risky: he was sure the treacherous barber Mariano would have informed the police he had been there as soon as his back was turned. And yet there was no way he was going to give up on the money.

Fortunately he knew what to do: he found a ladder at the Fair, and carried it across town to the boarding house. He had to cross half Barcelona with it on his shoulder, but that didn't attract anybody's attention. Then, after dark, he propped the ladder against the back wall, as Sisinio had explained. He climbed up onto the roof where for two years Delfina and the housepainter had canoodled. He had used the skylight to climb out onto the roof to grease it, and remembered where it was. The third floor of the boarding house was empty: all its occupants were in jail. If there were any guards lurking, they would be down in the lobby, expecting him to come in by the front door, not the roof.

The darkness worked in his favour: Onofre knew better than anyone all the nooks and crannies on the stairs, and could find his way without a problem. He went down to the second floor and pushed open the door to Father Bizancio's room. He listened to the old man's breathing as he slept, crawled under the bed, and waited. As the clock on La Presentación church struck three, the priest got out of bed and left the room. It wouldn't take him more than two minutes to return, but it wouldn't take him any less either; Onofre had that long to act. Pushing his hand into the mattress, he discovered the money had vanished. The straw stuffing disintegrated between his fingers as he groped around. He soon realised there was no mistake: the money wasn't there.

Hearing Father Bizancio on his way back from the bathroom, Onofre's first thought was to jump on him and throttle him until he found out what had happened to the money, but he decided against it. If the police were inside the boarding house and heard a suspicious noise, they would soon appear, pistols at the ready. There was nothing for it but to wait for a better opportunity. He had to spend another hour suffocating under the bed until the priest went to the bathroom once more. Then Onofre crawled stiffly out, gained the corridor, the stairs, the roof, and finally the street.

Day was breaking when he saw Father Bizancio pass by on the way to say his prayers. Checking that nobody was following him, Onofre caught up with the priest.

"Onofre, what a pleasure to see you, my boy!" exclaimed Father Bizancio. "I thought I'd never see you again!" As he said this, his eyes brimmed with tears. "Have you heard about all the terrible things that have happened? I was just going to church to say a Mass for poor Señora Agata, who's the one who needs it most. Later on I'll say others for Señor Braulio and for Delfina. One thing at a time."

"That's very good, Father, but tell me where my money is," said Onofre.

"What money, my son?" asked the priest.

There was nothing about his attitude that suggested he wasn't being sincere. Maybe Delfina herself hid the money before she went to the police, Onofre thought. Or perhaps the police came across it during their search. It was even possible that Father Bizancio had found the money by chance and given it to charity without realising what he was doing. After all, how could anyone suspect the money was mine? I was really stupid not to have spent it as soon as I got it, like Efrén Castells did.

As he was heading to the Fair to see if he could save at least part of what the child thieves had stolen, Onofre had to stand back to allow a colourful procession to pass by: fighting bulls were being taken from the station to the ring where they would be killed during the celebrations by the famous matadors of the day: Frascuelo, Guerrita, Lagartijo, Mazantini, Espartero and Cara-Ancha. The beasts tossed their heads, tried to gore curious onlookers, and stopped to myopically examine the bases of some of the street lamps. As the bulls went past, some clown or other would untie his neckerchief and taunt them. The herdsmen goaded the lead animals with their pikes and, if possible, bashed these clowns as well.

When Onofre reached Ciudadela Park, he went straight to the pavilion where they had kept all the timepieces. It was empty. That's the last straw, he told himself. As he was leaving the building, two men came up on either side of him, and grabbed his arms. Onofre noticed one of them was extraordinarily good-looking. He decided there was no point resisting, and meekly let himself be led away.

Before leaving the park, Onofre cast a glance over his shoulder. The pavilions had all been finished overnight, and now gleamed in the sunlight. Through tree branches stirring in the breeze could be seen kiosks and statues, awnings and parasols, and tiny Moorish domes on stalls and booths. In Plaza de Armas, opposite the former Arsenal, engineers specially brought in from England were testing the Magic Fountain. Even Onofre's kidnappers gaped open-mouthed at this for a moment. The jets and arches of water changed shape and colour without any obvious mechanism: everything was done by electricity. That's how life should always be, Onofre thought as he was being frogmarched away, possibly to his death. Where's Efrén, he wondered. After all he's cost me, where is he when I need him? He had no way of knowing that the faithful Efrén was following them at a distance in the shadows.

"Get into the carriage," the men ordered Onofre when they reached a berline. The blinds were down over the windows, making it impossible to tell if there was anyone inside or not. Up on the driver's seat sat an elderly coachman, smoking a pipe.

"I'm not getting in there," said Onofre.

One of his kidnappers opened the carriage door, the other pushed him: "Get in and shut up," he said. Onofre did as he was told. There was only one man seated inside. He looked to be around fifty, but could have been younger; he had a prominent belly and jowls, but was narrow-shouldered, with sharp cheekbones. He had a flat, high forehead that ended in a right angle, topped by a mop of dark hair that was growing grey only at the temples and was cut like a bristly lawn. He was clean-shaven from ear to ear, but sported a bushy, twirled moustache that made him look like a French field marshal.

This was Don Humbert Figa i Morera, for whom Onofre was to work for many years.

In those days, a monarch's entourage was huge, for both practical and symbolic reasons. The latter were more important: since the king was God's representative on earth, it was unseemly for him to do anything at all for himself, not even lift a spoon to his mouth. In addition, from time immemorial, Spanish monarchs had never dismissed anyone who had served them, if only for a short time: every service afforded the royal house carried with it a position for life. There had even been instances when monarchs, despite being grown men, had gone off to war taking with them their former wet nurse and nanny. The reason was that the king could not possibly stoop to saying, "I no longer need this," since that might imply on the one hand a need to save money, and on the other an admittance of having needed something at some point. This applied to everyone, whether chamberlain, butler or sommelier, and meant that the monarch was at the centre of a labyrinth, a throng of people who often prevented his generals from speaking to him in times of war, and his ministers in times of peace. It was also why their majesties seldom left the court.

In 1888, His Majesty Don Alfonso XIII (RIP) was two and a half years old when he came to Barcelona accompanied by his mother Doña María Cristina, the Queen Regent, his sisters, and their retinue.

Their arrival brought the city to a standstill. The former residence of the governor of the Ciudadela had been refurbished for their majesties (which in addition meant they were already inside the grounds of the Fair, thus obviating the awkward question of the entrance fee of one peseta, or twenty-five for a season ticket) and so had the Arsenal, but the chamberlains and purveyors, masters of the hunt and equerries, grooms and stewards, gentlemen at arms, pantrymen, chandlers and upholsterers, almsmen, chambermaids, maids of honour, ladies-in-waiting and dowagers all had to be found accommodation.

The arrival of foreign monarchs, nobles and dignitaries complicated matters still further. This gave rise to all kinds of anecdotes, such as a Saxon burgrave being forced to share a bed for the night with an artiste newly arrived from Paris, as the poster for the Equestrian Circus proudly proclaimed, while announcing underneath his act of trained cats. Or that of the swindler who passed himself off as the Great Mogul and managed thanks to his good looks to dine out for free in several taverns and cafés.

The people of Barcelona went to great lengths to welcome the visitors to the Fair, for which, as usual, they received scant recompense. In general their guests were arrogant, wrinkling their noses at the slightest inconvenience, and went round complaining, "how dreadful, what a place, what unpleasant people", and so on. They obviously thought disdain was the done thing.

The Barcelona World Fair opened as scheduled on 8 April, 1888. The inauguration took place as follows: at half past four in the afternoon, His Majesty the King and his entourage made their entrance into the great hall of the Fine Arts Palace. The king mounted the throne; since his legs did not reach the ground, they rested on a pile of cushions. Alongside him were the Princess of Asturias, Doña María de las Mercedes and the Infanta Doña María Teresa.

Next to the Queen Regent, dressed in mourning, sat the Duchess of Edinburgh, dressed in deep mourning. After them came, in the following order: the Dukes of Genoa and Edinburgh, Prince Rupprecht of Bavaria, and George, Prince of Wales. Behind them followed the prime minister, Don Práxedes Mareo Sagasta, and the ministers of War, Development, and the Navy, the royal gentlemen at arms, those Spanish grandees who had accepted the invitation (flanked by halberdiers, as was the privilege of their rank, or barefoot, if they chose to demonstrate their noble prerogative in that manner), local authorities in morning coats, the diplomatic and consular corps, special envoys, generals, admirals, vice-admirals, the Board of Directors, as well as a host of dignitaries. Stationed throughout the room were lackeys in knee breeches carrying the emblems of the noble visitors: a brass key or chain, ribbon, riding crop, stag's antler, claw, crossbow or bell.

All in all, five thousand people were present. The speeches concluded, the royal children were led away by their tutors. The adults visited some of the pavilions, commencing with that of Austria, the birthplace of Her Majesty the Queen Regent. In the French pavilion they were greeted by a piano piece by Chopin, and in the Governor's Palace they were served a meal known as "luncheon" by the English. The Queen had already finished her "luncheon" as the last of the guests were entering the Austrian pavilion. Huge crowds watched the illustrious visitors pass by.

That evening there was a gala performance in El Liceo, which the Queen Regent attended wearing her coronet. The opera performed was *Lohengrin* – by the time the curtain went up on the second act, some guests were still eating "luncheon".

All things considered, the opening was a solemn, well-organised affair, and the Fair's exhibits proved worthy of these eminent visitors. Some of the buildings were unfinished; others completed much earlier were already showing signs of disrepair. The press wrote of "wide cracks" and "great confusion", but the most important thing was that people enjoyed the Fair. In hindsight, the austere design of the installations, with their carved floral wooden crowns, black crepe drapes and canopies, made them look rather funereal, but they represented the taste of the time, and its concept of elegance.

Sixty-eight warships from different nations were anchored in the port, with nineteen thousand seamen and five hundred and thirty-eight cannon. Although nowadays this might seem threatening, back then the people of Barcelona viewed it as an unmistakable gesture of courtesy and friendship. This was before the First World War, at a time when weaponry still had something decorative about it. In a poem written specially for the occasion, Federico Rahola neatly encapsulates this spirit:

> *May cannons never cease*
> *In their thund'rous roar*
> *As mighty monsters of war*
> *Pay humble homage to peace*

Melchor de Palau expresses the same thought in his *Hymn for the Opening of the World Fair*, one of whose verses begins:

> *And thunder without harm, ye horrid cannon fire*

The World Fair remained open until 9 December 1888. The closing ceremony was a much simpler affair than the inauguration: a *Te Deum* in the cathedral and a brief event in the Palace of Industry. The Fair had lasted two hundred and forty-five days and been visited by more than two million people. It had cost five million, six hundred and twenty-four thousand six hundred and fifty-seven pesetas and fifty-six centavos. Some of the installations could be put to a new use, but the accumulated debt was huge, and burdened Barcelona City Council for many years. The Fair also left a memory of days of splendour, and the feeling that when it so wished, Barcelona could once more be a cosmopolitan city.

CHAPTER THREE

1

Little is known about Don Humbert Figa i Morera. He was born in Barcelona, where his parents kept a modest dried fruits store in the Raval district. He studied under the aegis of some missionary monks who due to the vicissitudes of politics in far-off lands had been left stranded in Barcelona, where they undertook teaching so as not to be too much of a burden. After that he studied law at university. He married late, at the age of thirty-two. Professionally, he met with great success: by the age of forty he headed one of the most famous legal practices in the city. This fame was more like notoriety: even though by the mid-nineteenth century nobody in their right mind questioned the equality of everyone before the law, the reality was very different. Respectable people, well-to-do individuals, enjoyed a protection denied to reprobates. The latter were unaware of their rights, and had they been aware of them, would not have known how to defend them; even if they had done so, it is doubtful whether the judiciary would have recognised them; they were always likely to lose.

In this respect, judges had only a few guidelines, but these were clear. The age was dominated by a faith in science: it was thought that every event or phenomenon must have a precise cause. If that cause could be identified, an unchanging law could be formulated for all similar cases, and with a mere handful of these immutable laws, the future could be infallibly predicted. The same applied to human behaviour: reasons for it were sought that could thereafter be formulated as laws. There were theories to suit all tastes: some maintained that genetic inheritance was the determining factor for everything that an individual did throughout his life; others that it was the context into which a person was born; others that it was down to education, and so on. Still others brought up the question of free will, but their arguments fell on deaf ears: such a theory, they were told, will get us nowhere. Determinism was in vogue, and this made things much simpler, especially for those called upon to judge human behaviour. These judges did not hold justice in contempt, but applied it in their own harsh way. They had no truck with subtleties: one glance at a prisoner was enough for them to know what they thought of him. If an educated person from a known, well-off family committed a crime, they told themselves there must have been a powerful reason for him to behave the way he did, and they were very understanding. If the perpetrator of a crime was a reprobate, they didn't bother to look for any motive for his behaviour or speculate in any way. They thought not only that the character passed down from parents to child inclined them to lawlessness, but that these inclinations could not be curbed by the dictates of religion, civic conscience or culture.

In this they were of one mind with the sociologists. If the accused alleged mitigating circumstances, their response was sarcastic. "The accused can plead whatever he likes," they would tell them. "If he thinks he's so smart, that's enough, off to jail with him." In prison attempts were made to rehabilitate the inmates, but the results were not always encouraging.

Don Humbert Figa i Morera, of humble origin himself, had a different, more practical view of things. "The problem for poor people who break the law," he was wont to say, "is that they don't have a good lawyer to get them out of trouble." This was true: no attorney was willing to waste his talents on a lowlife: they all wanted to work for worthy, aristocratic families. Since there were few of these, the lawyers making money were few and far between as well. The poor are a huge market, the problem lies in how to exploit it, Don Humbert Figa i Morera said to himself. But since I'm a nobody, with no connections to respectable people, it would be just as difficult for me to make my way in the upper echelons as it would among the dregs of society.

As a result, he had begun to seek out the poor and needy, to offer them his help and knowledge. He had special business cards printed with Gothic lettering that was easier to read than the usual typefaces. "If you get into trouble, remember me," he would say, and hand people his card. He was usually met with mistrust; they didn't want to know, laughed at him or sent him packing. Later on, when they did indeed find themselves in trouble, some of them would remember him and fish out his card. What the devil, they would think. It's worth a try. If as is likely I end up in the clink, I won't pay him and that will be that.

They brought him the most hopeless cases, which he willingly accepted. He treated his clients with respect. He didn't laugh at them or condescend towards them, and worked very diligently on their behalf. At first, thinking he must be doing this out of altruism, judges and prosecutors tried to dissuade him. "Don't waste your time, esteemed colleague, these people are rotten by nature, born criminals, prison fodder."

Don Humbert Figa i Morera would listen to these arguments respectfully, but pay no attention to them; deep down, he agreed, but he was only interested in his fee. He had been educated by mission-aries, who had taught him to be patient, to always say yes. They had also taught him the art of persuasion, and against all expectation, he won the majority of his cases. He was second to none at knowing all the intricacies of the legal process, and always came up with some loophole or other he could employ. The indignant judges and magistrates had to concede he was right; the prosecutors threw their penal codes and gowns to the floor, tears welling in their eyes. "Things can't go on like this," they would say. "We're being obliged to make a mockery of the law." And the law was generous in guarantees and gaps because it had not been created for the benefit of the dregs of society. The authorities were caught unawares when a colleague put the law's resources at the service of the worst kind of offender. The judgments they handed down showed their bewilderment: "You've caught us with our pants down," they said, "but we have to acquit, and so we shall." The acquitted criminals couldn't get over their astonishment either, asking Don Humbert Figa i Morera with real superstitious curiosity, "Why are you helping us, your honour?" as if they were dealing with a saint. "For money," came his reply, "so you pay my fees." Faithful to their typical ethical code, they paid up punctually to the last peseta, and never questioned them. This was how Don Humbert Figa i Morera became rich. Then, one winter's night years later, he received a strange visit.

His office was in Calle San Pedro, in the lower part of the city; besides him, there were two clerks, a secretary and an office boy. That night everyone had left apart from the young lad and Don Humbert, who was going over the final details for a case due to be heard the following morning. There was a knock at the front door. That's odd, he thought. Who can it be at this time of night? He told the office boy to go down and see, but to make sure first that whoever was knocking was well-intentioned – something that was very hard to determine, as normally it was only the roughest sort who came calling.

On this occasion, however, there was no problem: standing in the street were three distinguished-looking gentlemen, plus a figure who looked bizarre, but not threatening. The three gentlemen were wearing masks, something not that uncommon in Barcelona in those days.

"Have you come with good intentions?" the boy asked the three masked visitors.

They said they had, and pushed him aside with the tips of their swordsticks. The three masked men sat down around a long table at the centre of one of the office reception rooms. The fourth person remained standing; despite the passage of the years, Don Humbert had no trouble recognising him. He was one of the missionaries who had taken charge of his education. It was thanks to their generosity that he had been able to get on in life; perhaps he had returned to ask a favour, which Don Humbert couldn't deny him. As he later learned, the monk's vocation had taken him to Ethiopia and the Sudan. He had made many converts there, but, as the years went by, he had ended up converting to the pagan religion he had at first opposed. He had been sent back to Barcelona by the dervishes to preach witchcraft. He was dressed in ordinary attire, but in his right hand carried a stick topped with a human skull. Pebbles rattled inside whenever he shook it.

"To what do I owe the honour of your visit?" Don Humbert Figa i Morera asked his mystery guests. They glanced at one another from behind their masks.

"We have been following your work with great interest," one of them said. "Now we have a proposition to put to you. We're businessmen, and our conduct is beyond reproach: that's precisely why we need your help."

"If it's within my power . . ." Don Humbert said.

"You'll soon see that it is," said one of the masks. "As I've just told you, we are well known in Barcelona, and we value our reputations highly. You on the other hand have won well-deserved repute among the dregs of society. In short, we want somebody to carry out a disagreeable task – and we want you to be our go-between. It goes without saying that cost is no object."

"Ah," Don Humbert exclaimed, "but that's immoral."

At this point the apostate missionary intervened. "Morality can be divided into two categories: individual and social," he said. As regards the former, he continued, Don Humbert could have a clear conscience. He would not be agreeing to commit an immoral act, but simply acting in his professional capacity. As far as social morality was concerned, there was no problem either: the important thing was to maintain social order, the smooth functioning of the mechanism. "You, my son, have saved many criminals from justified incarceration," the renegade missionary said. "It is therefore only right and proper that you now lead others towards punishment and the scaffold. That will help keep the balance."

The men in masks had heaped money on the table. Don Humbert Figa i Morera accepted the assignment, and everything went like clockwork. After that he was inundated with similar requests: every night masked gentlemen and a considerable number of ladies passed through his office; there were so many carriages they created a logjam outside. Real criminals, who had nothing to hide, came there during working hours, in broad daylight without any disguise.

"You wouldn't believe," Don Humbert told his wife, "how well things are going for me."

So well that he needed to employ more people: not only clerks and secretaries, but agents who could operate freely in Barcelona's underworld. He recruited these agents wherever he could, without worrying about their pasts.

"I've been told you know what's what," he said to Onofre Bouvila when the two of them were ensconced in the berline, "that you know your way around. You'll work for me."

"What kind of work?"

"Doing what I say," replied Don Humbert Figa i Morera, "and not asking ill-advised questions. The police are on to you. Without my protection, you'd already be in jail. This is the choice you have: either you work for me, or face twenty years inside."

Onofre worked for Don Humbert from 1888 to 1898, the year Spain lost its last colonies.

Initially, Onofre was put under the command of the extraordinarily handsome man who had abducted him in Ciudadela Park. This was Odón Mostaza, originally from Zamora, aged twenty-two at the time. Onofre was given a cut-throat razor, a blackjack and a pair of knitted gloves. He was told only to use the blackjack when necessary, the razor only in desperate situations, and in both cases to put the gloves on first so as not to leave fingerprints. "What's most important is for you not to be identified," Odón Mostaza told him. "Because if you are, then I could be as well, and if they identify me, they could identify the person who gives me orders, and so on like links in a chain until they reach the chief, Don Humbert Figa i Morera."

It was an open secret in Barcelona that Don Humbert had dealings with the criminal underworld, but since the authorities and many leading figures in politics and business were implicated to a greater or lesser degree, nothing ever came of it. Respectable people kept their distance, even though publicly they hailed him as a great man. Don Humbert was oblivious to the ambivalence of their feelings. He was pleased to think he belonged to the lay aristocracy, and Odón Mostaza and the rest indirectly enjoyed this conceited view. If they happened to be near Paseo de Gracia at midday, they would say to each other, "Let's go and see Don Humbert ride past." Every day without fail he would parade there, mounted on the back of a fine-looking Jerez mare. He would wave a gloved hand at other riders or raise his emerald-green velvet top hat to the ladies passing by in open carriages.

Odón Mostaza and his gang would secretly admire Don Humbert from a distance, so as not to threaten his prestige. "You ought to be very proud, my lad," Odón told Onofre Bouvila, "very proud to have the most elegant man in Barcelona as your employer. The most powerful one as well."

This was an exaggeration: Don Humbert Figa i Morera remained a nobody, and even in his own line of work he had a more powerful rival: Don Alexandre Canals i Formiga. Don Alexandre was never seen showing off on Paseo de Gracia, despite living close by: he had a three-storey Mudejar-style mansion built near Calle Diputación, only a few metres from that famous avenue. The office he died in was on Calle Platería; his entire life took place between these two buildings. The only exception was an occasional visit to a carrousel on a patch of waste ground near his home, where he took his little, slightly backward, son. Don Alexandre had had three more children, but they all died in a tragic outbreak of the plague in 1879.

At first, Onofre Bouvila was given only menial tasks, and he was never allowed to act on his own. He would go down to the port with Odón Mostaza to watch goods being unloaded, or they would wait outside the door of a house, without being told why, until somebody said to them, "Alright, it's fine, you can go now." Then they would have to report to someone Odón Mostaza called Margarito, whose real name was Arnau Puncella.

Puncella had begun working for Don Humber Figa i Morera some years earlier. He was one of the first clerks the lawyer had taken on; he had prospered in his shadow until gradually becoming one of his most trusted collaborators. By now he supervised all contact with the criminals and all the shady deals. He was short and ugly-looking, with pebble glasses and a jet-black toupee; he had very long, far from clean fingernails; the clothes he wore were scruffy and grease-stained; he was married and it was said he had lots of children, though no-one could be sure because he was very secretive and never opened up to anyone.

He was also very meticulous, mistrustful and perceptive: it didn't take him long to notice Onofre's remarkable ability to retain dates, names and figures. "It's essential to be careful in our line of business," he would tell his children, whom he insisted keep their wits about them. "Any mistake could easily lead to a catastrophe." This was what had first alerted him to Onofre Bouvila's talents, but he soon came to see other aspects that disturbed him. Onofre was unaware of the interest he aroused. He tried to pass unnoticed, not yet realising that intelligence is as hard to hide as the lack of it; he seriously believed no-one had picked him out. For the first time ever, he was living his own life.

Odón Mostaza was a very good-looking thug. Dissolute and sociable, he was well known in every place of entertainment in and around Barcelona. Since he was not only handsome but liked a good time and spent his money lavishly, he was welcome everywhere. Thanks to Odón Mostaza, Onofre began to find despite himself that for the first time in his life he had a circle of friends. He had moved to a guest house rather more salubrious than the one run by Señor Braulio and Señora Agata. There, seeing that he had a steady income, they treated him like a prince.

Almost every night, he went out to Barcelona's low dives with Odón Mostaza and his gang. He found lots of women willing to take his money in return for offering him their charms and a few moments of pleasure. This seemed to him both fair and easy: it fitted in well with his way of life. When he occasionally recalled Delfina, he reflected: All that needless effort and suffering, when it can be so simple. He considered himself cured forever of the pangs of love.

With the arrival of summer, they all went to the famous marquees, where he particularly admired the chandeliers, carpets, the garlands of paper flowers, the crush of people, the sweating orchestras, the scent of perfume and the typical dances: the candle waltz, the *ball de rams*. Groups of exuberant young girls also went arm-in-arm to these marquees. They burst into laughter at everything they saw; if anybody said anything to one of them, they would all have a fit of the giggles. Among them, the fish-girls were the liveliest and most mischievous, the housemaids the most naive and the seamstresses the trickiest and most dangerous.

Onofre and Odón would also go to the bullring in Barceloneta. Afterwards they would have a drink of beer or red wine with soda in the nearby bars, where there would be heated debates until dawn. On another occasion Onofre went on a whim to visit the World Fair that was proving so popular. The whole of Barcelona was in festive mood: people had been encouraged to paint their house fronts; carriage owners to paint and clean their carriages; and everyone to dress their servants smartly. The city council had employed a hundred municipal guards to attend to the foreign visitors, and had obliged them to learn French in a few months. Now these guards wandered around Barcelona like souls in torment, muttering incomprehensible phrases. Children followed and pestered them, imitating their guttural sounds and calling them *gargalluts*. Onofre went to the Fair alone and paid the entrance fee: he was amused to be going in through the main door like a respectable patron. He let himself be swept along by the crowd, had refreshments in the Castell dels Tres Dragons Café-Restaurant (more than 170 men had helped build it, and he knew almost every one of them by their first names). After that he visited the Museo Martorell, the Monserrat diorama, the Horchatería Valenciana, the Café Turco, the American Soda Water, and the Seville pavilion, built in the Moorish style. He had his photograph taken (unfortunately, this has been lost) and went into the Palace of Industry.

In it he saw the stand where Baldrich, Vilagrán and Tapera, the three gentlemen from Bassora, were exhibiting their machinery. This brought back unpleasant memories that made his blood boil. He suddenly found himself gasping for air, and the people all around him seemed unbearable. He pushed his way out of the Palace as quickly as he could. As he strode away from the park, the Fair seemed to him like a joke in bad taste: he could not disassociate it from the trouble and hardships he had suffered there only a few months earlier. He never went back, and he didn't want to know anything more about it.

On the other hand, the nightlife in old Barcelona, that marginal side of the city unaffected by the pomp of the World Fair, filled him with all the enthusiasm of a provincial. He went whenever he could, on his own or with his associates, to a place called L'Empori de la Patacada. This was a ramshackle, evil-smelling dive in a semi-basement on Calle Huerto de la Bomba. By day it was gloomy, lifeless and cramped; it was only after midnight that it came to life, thanks to a rough but generous clientele. It seemed to thrive on its defects and grew visibly larger. There was always room for another couple; there was always a table for everyone. At the door there were always two youths carrying lanterns to light the way, and shotguns to scare off any attackers. This was necessary because the place was not only the haunt of crooks, who knew how to defend themselves, but also of debauched young men from good families as well as a few young ladies accompanied by a friend, a beau or even their husbands. These ladies usually covered their faces with a thick veil, and came for the thrill it gave them to escape their everyday routine with a *frisson* of danger. The next day they recounted what they had seen, exaggerating the dramas they had witnessed.

There was not only dancing at L'Empori de la Patacada, but also *tableaux vivants*. These had been very popular in the eighteenth century, but by the end of the nineteenth had disappeared almost completely. Stationary scenes depicted by real people, they could be "contemporary" (their majesties the King and Queen of Romania receiving the Spanish ambassador; Grand Duke Nicholas in lancer's uniform with his illustrious wife, etc.) or "historical", also known as "didactic" (the suicide of the Numantians; the death of Admiral Churruca at Trafalgar), but usually they were "biblical" or "mythological". These were the most popular, because all or nearly all the characters were naked. For people in the nineteenth century, to be naked meant to wear tight-fitting flesh-coloured leotards. This wasn't because people back then were more prudish than they are today, but because they rightly thought that what was most pleasing was the human form, and that to be able to see the skin in all its hairiness was more distasteful than erotic. Over the centuries, customs in this respect had varied. As is well known, in the eighteenth century, nudity was not regarded as important in any way: people would appear naked in public without hesitation, and without it diminishing their dignity in the slightest. Men and women took baths in the company of visitors, changed clothes in front of their servants, urinated and defecated on the public highway. There is ample testimony to this in the diaries and correspondence of the period. *Dîner chez les M****, the Duchess of C*** wrote in her journal, *madame de G***, comme d'habitude, préside la table à poil.* And in a later entry: *Bal chez le prince de V*** – presque tout le monde nu, sauf l'abbé R*** déguisé en papillon; on a beaucoup rigolé.*

At L'Empori de la Patacada an orchestra of four musicians led the dancing. The waltz had by this time been accepted by every social class; the pasodoble and the chotis were reserved for the lower classes; the tango had yet to make its mark. At society events, the rigodon, mazurka, the lancers and the minuet were still in vogue. The polka and the java might be all the rage throughout Europe, but not in Catalonia. Traditional dances such as the sardana and the jota were banned in places like L'Empori de la Patacada. Too hot for the torrid summer months, it had its moment of glory on autumn nights, when storms swept the streets and the cold drove people indoors. With the return of spring, it lost most of its clientele to café terraces and open-air dancing.

In the midst of all this boisterous fun, Onofre Bouvila did his best to have a good time. Although he occasionally succeeded, despite his best efforts he usually remained anxious and ill at ease. He never managed to fully enjoy the entertainment offered, could never quite lose his head with all the brouhaha. Odón Mostaza, who had grown very fond of him and even felt somewhat responsible for his well-being, was concerned when he saw him always looking so serious. "Come on lad, why don't you forget about your worries for a while?" he would tell him. "Why not have some fun? Just take a look at those girls, aren't they enough to drive you crazy?" Onofre usually replied with a gentle smile: "Don't try to force me, Odón. I find it too tiring to have fun." Odón would laugh at this paradox, not realising Onofre was telling the truth. To be distracted from his thoughts even for a few minutes would have required a huge amount of energy. It would have taken a superhuman effort to escape for even a moment from the memory of that horrible morning when a strange individual had turned up at his parents' house.

Uncle Tonet had brought him from Bassora in his trap: he was wearing a threadbare frock coat, starched shirt front, a pair of spectacles and a top hat, and was carrying a bulky leather briefcase. He approached the house, trying not to get his shoes wet in the puddles, skirted round the piles of dirty, heaped-up snow, seemingly afraid of everything: a bird flapping its wings on a branch scared him half to death. Presenting himself in an extremely roundabout way, he then skipped over to warm himself at the embers still burning in the hearth. A late February sun lit half the room; its cold rays picked out the shapes of objects as precisely as if drawn by a sharpened pencil.

This man had begun by saying he was speaking on behalf of the people who had sent him: the gentlemen Baldrich, Vilagrán and Tapera. He explained that he was merely a clerk in a Bassora legal practice, and begged them not to take personally what he was about to say. "I deeply regret having been given this unpleasant task, but carrying out orders is my profession," he had said. "You will judge for yourselves," he added, with a compassionate gesture directed at none of them in particular. Onofre's father had waved his hand impatiently: Please get on with it, he seemed to be saying. The legal clerk cleared his throat, and Onofre's mother said she had to go and feed the hens. "The boy can go with me, so we'll leave you two in peace," she said, looking her husband in the eye.

"There's no need for you to go," he said. "Better for you to stay and hear what this gentleman has come to tell me." The clerk was rubbing his hands and coughing all the time, as if smoke from the fire was catching in his throat. In an almost inaudible voice, he told Onofre's father that his clients had decided to present a claim for fraud against him. "That's a very serious accusation," said the *Americano*. "Please explain what you mean."

Flustered, the visitor had embarked on a confused explanation. Apparently Joan Bouvila had given everyone in Bassora to understand that he had returned from Cuba a very rich man. He had gone to see all the industrialists and financiers in the town in his tropical attire and convinced them he was looking for a safe investment for his fortune. With this pretext he had obtained advances, loans and even donations. As time went by and his promised investments showed little sign of materialising, Messrs Baldrich, Vilagrán and Tapera, whose company had lent most to Bouvila, decided to make enquiries. They had done this with proper care and discretion, the clerk insisted. These enquiries proved what everyone already suspected: that Joan Bouvila didn't have a penny. There was no doubt this was a case of fraud, said the clerk, immediately turning pale and adding that this definite assertion did not imply any moral judgment. He quickly added that he was simply the mere instrument of someone else's decision: "This being the case, I am absolved from any responsibility for the harm this may be causing you."

Onofre's mother broke the silence following these words: "Joan, what on earth is this man talking about?" Now it was Onofre's father's turn to clear his throat; eventually he confessed that what the clerk had said was nothing but the truth. He had lied to everyone: in Cuba, where even the slow-witted became rich, he had been unable to earn the minimum needed to lead a comfortable life. He admitted shamefacedly that what little he did manage to save at the outset, at a time when he was still full of hope, was stolen from him by a Colombian adventuress. After that he had taken out loans that he had ploughed at once in business ventures – ventures that had invariably turned out to be swindles. In the end he had been forced to take on the most disgusting jobs. "There's no spittoon in Havana I haven't cleaned, boot I haven't polished or latrine I haven't unblocked, with or without tools," he told them. During his years in Cuba he had seen starving emigrants arrive who a few months later would throw coins into puddles in the street for him, laughing as they watched him plunging his arm in up to the elbow. He had eaten banana skins, fish bones, rotten vegetables and other things it wouldn't be polite to mention. In the end, he had told himself, "That's enough, Joan, that's enough."

"I had a little money," he went on, "that I got in an ignominious way: some English sailors paid me to obtain the most degrading pleasures for them. I used that money, the fruits of their vileness, to buy the suit I stand up in, a monkey at death's door and a return ticket in the bilges of a cargo boat."

Before Joan left, he had scrounged a little more money, knowing he had no intention of returning it, and one night prepared to embark in the midst of a downpour. He had stripped off and smeared his body and face with pitch so that his creditors wouldn't recognise him if he bumped into them. "In this undignified manner," Joan Bouvila continued, "I walked the streets of that promised land which for me had been nothing more than a yoke, a shackle, humiliation."

Once the ship had set sail, he had not washed or put his clothes back on, but remained in his hiding place until they were outside Spanish territorial waters. After that he had lived from the meagre amount he possessed and by cheating others. He had always known that sooner or later the truth would out; the painful confession he had just made relieved him of a great burden. Deep down, he admitted, he was glad this catalogue of deceit was coming to an end. And, he finally confessed, he hadn't done any of this because he was disreputable or greedy, but simply out of a sense of false pride. "The truth is," he said, "I did it all for my son." He had wanted Onofre to get a glimpse of what life could be if he had not had the misfortune of having the useless father God had given him.

In the end, the affair had no grave consequences: convinced they would not recover the money swiftly, Baldrich, Vilagrán and Tapera had withdrawn their lawsuit. Instead they had obliged Onofre's father to work for them, deducting a percentage of his wages to repay what he owed them.

Onofre found it impossible to forget his father's words. He drank heavily and was a regular client at several brothels. He also spent a lot of money on extravagant clothes. However, he never ran up debts and avoided gambling like the plague. He had stopped growing and was never going to be tall. He did, however, have broad shoulders and a barrel chest; he was strong and by no means disagreeable to look at. Although reserved by nature, he was amiable and seemed quite open: thugs, prostitutes, pimps, drug traffickers, policemen and informers thought highly of him, and almost everyone wanted to be his friend. Despite himself they all instinctively recognised his innate leadership qualities. Even Odón Mostaza, who was meant to give him orders, had fallen under his spell. He allowed Onofre to take the lead, to decide what should be done and what avoided; and agreed he should be the one to talk things over when necessary with Arnau Puncella, alias Margarito.

This confirmed the latter's suspicions: That lad will make a name for himself, he thought. He's only been with us a year and he's already cock of the walk. If I'm not careful, the moment I'm not looking he'll trample over me. I ought to destroy him, but I don't know how. Right now, he's too insignificant, he'd slip between my fingers like a flea, but it could be that soon it'll be too late for me.

He tried to win Onofre Bouvila's trust. Whenever they talked together, he brought up the question of clothes, and always praised the suits Onofre had just had made – like every slovenly dressed person, he was very aware of other people's elegance. Onofre didn't even notice that the other man looked a fright, but believed in good faith that the pair of them shared a taste for well-cut clothes, and even asked his advice on where to buy ties, boots and so on.

Onofre had turned into a real dandy. At the guest house he always went round in a patterned ankle-length kimono. Sometimes he felt prey to a vague anxiety; in the hot, clammy summer nights when he couldn't get to sleep, he would wrap the kimono round his shoulders and go out onto the balcony to smoke a cigarette. What's the matter with me, he wondered. But even though he believed he had very clear ideas, he could find no convincing answer to this question. In fact, as is often the case, he lacked any self-awareness; he only saw the reflection of his personality and actions in other people, and from that formed an entirely erroneous opinion of himself. But this

163

view could not resist close inspection, and only aroused his sense of dissatisfaction and unease.

It was at moments like these that the memory of his father returned to haunt him. Onofre believed he hated the *Americano* for betraying the fantasies his son had created while he was in Cuba, for not having fulfilled expectations that had only existed in his own imagination, but which he had always regarded as justified. He had accused his father of stealing his birthright, and saw this as the reason he had run away from home. He was the one who forced me to come here: he's the one really responsible for everything I do, Onofre told himself.

And yet this hatred was only superficial: deep down he continued to feel the admiration his father had always inspired in him. Without any valid reason, without even being aware of it, Onofre still believed his father was not a failure, but the victim of a vast conspiracy. This vague conspiracy that had unjustly robbed his father of the fortune and fame he deserved was what now gave Onofre the right to seek his revenge, to seize without scruple what was rightfully his.

These random, absurd thoughts conflicted with his nature and the nature of the things around him. He no longer had money worries, he had quit the sordid world of the first boarding house, and as the months went by, the memory of Delfina was slowly fading. He had friends, he was successful, and when he managed to forget his resentment at the world, he felt full of life, almost happy.

During those summer nights when his anxiety drove him out onto the balcony, he could hear familiar sounds from the street: the clash of plates and soup bowls, the clink of glasses, laughter, voices and arguments, the chirping of caged goldfinches and canaries, a piano in the distance, the warbling of a young woman learning to sing, a dog that wouldn't stop barking, the harangue of drunks leaning on lamp posts, blind beggars crying out for alms for the love of God. I could spend the whole night out here, he thought with melancholy, unable to prise himself away from his observatory. Or spend the whole summer here, lulled by the sounds of this anonymous city.

Then he would become anxious once more. Flattery from the riffraff around him was not enough to erase the harm done to him, the humiliation whose memory continued to persecute him, the stigma he imagined imprinted on his brow. I have to do better, he told himself, I can't stay where I am. If I don't do something quickly, my life is doomed, I'll simply become yet another criminal.

However fascinated he was by the easy lives of underworld villains and loose women, reason told him that these marginal beings were living on borrowed time. Society tolerated them because they were useful, or because it seemed too costly to completely get rid of them. It kept them discreetly at a distance, using them for its own ends, but always reserving the ways and means of eradicating them whenever they so wished. The lowlifes, however, believed they had turned the world upside down just because they carried a knife in their belt and because a few impressionable young girls pretended to swoon when they looked at them.

But Onofre lacked the willpower to quit this merry brotherhood of boastful men and brazen women, to leave behind a life that suited him perfectly. So, day after day, he kept postponing the decision to make a radical change to his way of life. He didn't yet know that these radical changes only come about when driven by emotion. Since Onofre had resolved never to fall in love or to lose his head over any woman, he could see no pressing reason to want to transform himself. And he would have gone on in the same way for years, losing sight of his ambitions, as happened to so many others, and would have ended up like them, stabbed by a rival, in jail or on the scaffold, or turned into a drunken professional thug, if Arnau Puncella had not crossed his path. Eventually, Onofre was forced to change to survive.

2

In those years the hidden strings controlling political life in Barcelona were pulled by Don Alexandre Canals i Formiga. He was a stern-looking man of few words and gestures, with a high forehead and a black goatee beard. He dressed with extreme care, and always wore exquisite perfume. Every morning a barber, a manicurist and a masseuse came to his office, which he seldom left. These were the only pleasures he allowed himself; the rest of his working day, which extended well into the night, was devoted to taking the most important decisions and putting in train measures of great consequence for the city. He rigged election results, bought and sold votes, could make or break political careers. Completely unscrupulous, he devoted all his time and energy to these affairs, which meant that over the years he had accumulated limitless power. However, he made little use of it, preferring to hoard it the way a miser hoards coins. Politicians and influential citizens in Barcelona feared and respected him, and didn't hesitate to turn to him. It was also said he was the only one who, when the time came, would be able to divert and halt the trade union storm that the most far-sighted could see brewing on the horizon. He himself kept his own counsel about this.

He did not hesitate to use violence to achieve his aims. For this he could count on a gang of crooks and gunmen led by one Joan Sicart. He was a man with a troubled past: his family was from Barcelona, but he was born and raised in Cuba, where his parents, like Onofre's father, had gone to seek their fortune. Both of them had succumbed to fever when Joan Sicart was very little, leaving him completely abandoned. Attracted to violence and discipline early on, he had wanted to join the army, but a slight pulmonary infection saw him rejected for the military academy. He returned to Spain and lived for a while in Cádiz, where he spent some time in jail. He finally ended up back in Barcelona, commanding Don Alexandre Canals i Formiga's private army, which he ruled with an iron fist. He was bony, with sharp features and small, sunken eyes, which gave him an Oriental look, as well as oddly straw-coloured hair.

It was inevitable that this much-feared organisation would occasionally clash with Don Humbert Figa i Morera's. In the past, any friction between them had been resolved without too much difficulty. Both Don Humbert Figa i Morera and Arnau Puncella (alias Margarito), his adviser and lieutenant, were moderate men who always sought a compromise. At some moment they had tried to open negotiations with Don Alexandre Canals i Formiga to reach a definitive agreement, but the latter knew he was in a more powerful position and refused to consider any proposal. Don Humbert's side had to yield, because the imbalance between their forces was obvious. Don Alexandre not only had more men, but they were much better organised. They could form squads like the militia, with one person in command; they had experience of strike-breaking and disrupting meetings. Don Humbert's men on the other hand were a gang of hooligans only fit for tavern brawls. But Barcelona was too small and insufficiently rich to have room for both these groups, which kept on growing. Sooner or later there was bound to be a battle between them. Nobody wanted to admit this, but everybody knew it.

The interview with Onofre Bouvila took place in the late afternoon one Friday in March. The sky was clear, the sunlight was fading against the curtains; the trees outside in the square were showing the first signs of spring. Don Humbert pushed back the curtains with the edge of his hand, looked down at the square and leaned his forehead on the windowpane. I don't know whether I'm acting correctly, he thought. Time flies and nothing changes, he told himself.

I feel sad and I don't know why. He recalled the World Fair, then thought of Onofre Bouvila, and somehow the two images merged in his mind: the great event and the provincial lad trying to make his way by whatever means possible. By now the Fair had closed its doors; almost nothing remained of that colossal effort, apart from the odd building that was too big to be of any use, some statues and a mountain of debt that the city council did not know how to pay off. The whole of society is based on these four pillars, he thought. Ignorance, laziness, injustice and foolishness.

The previous evening Arnau Puncella had paid him a visit, and what he had to say had left him feeling very uneasy: things could not carry on as they were.

"We have to strike the first blow," Arnau Puncella had told him. "Either that or resign ourselves to being inexorably crushed."

"We all knew this had to happen," Dom Humbert had replied. "But I didn't think it would be so soon." Arnau's plan seemed to him mad; he could see no possibility of it succeeding. "What brought you to dream up such a crazy idea?"

Puncella told him it wasn't a question of succeeding, but of re-asserting themselves. "Strike first," he explained, "and then immediately renew negotiations. Let him see we're not helpless, that we won't be intimidated. That's language he will understand, even if he refuses to be reasonable. We're bound to lose some men," he had said. "That's inevitable."

"Won't we be at risk?" asked Don Humbert.

"No," his lieutenant had reassured him, "there's no fear of that. I've thought it through and planned the operation down to the smallest detail. Besides, I've been keeping an eye on the boy for some time now: he's very talented and will carry it out to perfection. It's just a shame we have to sacrifice him."

Normally, Puncella was a kind-hearted fellow, but at that moment he was blinded by fear and envy. After his talk with Don Humbert, he called Onofre into his office and told him he was going to entrust him with a very important task. "Let's see how you get on," Margarito told him. At that moment Don Humbert Figa i Morera entered through a tall, narrow double door. "Arnau Puncella tells me you're very talented," he said. "Let's see how you get on," he added, unaware he was repeating what the other man had just said. Then the pair of them explained the plan in great detail. Onofre Bouvila listened to them open-mouthed. He doesn't understand a thing, thought Arnau Puncella, studying his face. Everything we're telling him is as foreign to him as life on the moon. "Above all," he said, "don't breathe a word about this."

On his own once more, Onofre Bouvila spent several hours going over the plan in his mind, and then went to find Odón Mostaza. When they were together, Onofre said: "Listen carefully, this is what we're going to do." He had decided to ignore the plan put to him in Arnau Puncella's office, and adopt one of his own. He was determined to make his mark. I've had enough of taking orders, he said to himself.

For some time, he had been aware of Don Alexandre Canals i Formiga, Joan Sicart and their formidable army of thugs. He had even considered offering Joan Sicart his services. He was not disloyal by nature, but knew where the real power lay, and was in no position to support lost causes. He knew that Joan Sicart was key to Don Alexandre Canals i Formiga; that he was at the centre of the entire organisation.

This was the basis for his plan, and he had thought through everything before he went to see Odón Mostaza. "Our weakness is so obvious," he told him, "that nobody will take us seriously. That's our advantage. We need to add speed and daring." He thought but didn't say: and brutality. He had concluded that if they followed his strategy they had a reasonable chance of success.

Onofre Bouvila carried things out exactly as planned. Barcelona had never seen anything like it: for as long as the struggle lasted, the entire city appeared to hold its breath. Perhaps if the two sides had been more evenly matched, Onofre would not have had to act in such a cruel fashion.

The war began that same night. Some of Sicart's men were gathered in a bar on Calle del Arco de San Silvestre, near Plaza Santa Catalina. Several hooligans led by Odón Mostaza came in, apparently looking for trouble. As this was not uncommon, nobody paid them any attention. Odón Mostaza was well known in this milieu: the women said he was the best-looking and strongest man in all Barcelona. Sicart's men laughed at them: There's more of us and we're better trained, seemed to be their attitude. Odón Mostaza's thugs responded to this affront with one of their own: they pulled out knives and slashed at those of Sicart's band who were nearest. Then they ran out of the bar without giving the others time to react. A carriage was waiting for them in Plaza Santa Catalina, and they sped off in it.

Reports of this encounter spread swiftly through the Barcelona underworld. Less than two hours later came the reprisal: twelve men armed with shotguns burst into L'Empori de la Patacada and began shooting in the middle of a *tableau vivant* entitled *The Sultan's Slave Girl*. They left two dead and six wounded, but neither Onofre Bouvila nor Odón Mostaza were among them. The attackers ran from the bar; when they found themselves outside in the dark, lonely street they realised their mistake too late. Two closed carriages came galloping towards them. They were caught in a crossfire: their enemies fired at them from the windows with American revolvers. They could have wiped out all twelve of Sicart's men, but made do with passing by twice: one died on the spot and two more a few days later.

Joan Sicart was nonplussed. I don't understand what they're after, he said to himself, or how far they're willing to go. What's their motive, and what's their aim? He was puzzling this over when one of his men came to tell him a woman wished to see him. She was unwilling to say who she was, but claimed she had the solution that was escaping him. Out of curiosity he had her brought to his office. He had never seen her before, but since he was not immune to feminine charms, he received her politely. Speaking through a veil, she said in a hoarse voice: "I've been sent by Onofre Bouvila."

Joan Sicart responded that he had no idea who Onofre Bouvila was, but the woman pretended not to have heard him, and went on: "He wants to see you. He is worried as well; he doesn't understand either why there is all this killing." She spoke as an ambassador might talk to a head of government on behalf of another head of government; this left Joan Sicart speechless. The woman added: "If you want to put a stop to this absurd situation, go and see him or receive him here, on your own ground. He won't refuse to come if you offer him guarantees." Joan Sicart shrugged. "Tell him to come if he wants to, but on his own and unarmed." "Do I have your word that he will leave here safe and sound?" the woman asked. Through the veil covering her face, Joan Sicart could glimpse anxiety in her penetrating eyes. She could be his lover or his mother, he thought. The unease his power caused in this beautiful woman emboldened him: "You have nothing to fear," he told her.

They agreed on a time for the meeting, and Onofre Bouvila turned up punctually. When Joan Sicart saw him, he pulled a face. "Now I know who you are," he said. "Odón Mostaza's whelp. I've heard about you; what have you come to offer?" He said this in an offhand manner, but Onofre did not react. "I don't need any recruits, spies or traitors," Sicart sneered. Eventually exasperated by Onofre Bouvila's continuing nonchalance, he shouted: "What do you want, why have you come here?" Hearing the shouting in the outer office, his men didn't know whether they should intervene or stay where they were. "If he needs us, he'll call," they decided.

"If you don't want to hear what I have to say, why did you make me come here?" said Onofre Bouvila finally, once Sicart had exhausted his anger. "I'm in danger here, and I'm risking my position."

Joan Sicart had to concede that he was right. It irritated him to have to talk to such a callow youth as an equal, but he couldn't help being impressed by the calm and authority the youngster showed. In a flash his attitude changed from scorn to one of respect.

"Alright then, what do you have to say?" he asked Onofre. The latter knew he had won. He's backing down, he thought. Out loud he said the war that had just broken out made no sense. There must have been a misunderstanding somewhere. Nobody knew how it had started, but now it was real and threatened to snowball and bury them all. "I can see it worries you," he said, "and I'm even more concerned, because I could be the next victim. Don't you think we ought to put a stop to this unwanted mess?"

"Hey," Joan Sicart protested when he heard this. "We didn't attack first, you did."

"That's not the point now," Onofre Bouvila replied. "The thing is to put a stop to revenge attacks." Lowering his voice, he added confidentially: "This war isn't in our interest: what do we get out of it? There are fewer of us, and we aren't as well prepared as you; we're nothing in comparison. I'm telling you this so you don't doubt my intentions. There's no subterfuge behind this, I've simply come to give you the chance to make peace."

Joan Sicart instinctively mistrusted Onofre, but despite this wanted to believe he was being sincere: he too was repelled by this senseless fighting. His men were being gunned down, all lucrative activity had come to a halt, and the tension in the city was harming business. Their conversation came to no conclusion, but they agreed to meet again once they had both thought it over. Convinced by Onofre that he was holding all the winning cards, Sicart did not realise he was on the slippery slope to destruction: he was digging his own grave.

That night the armed skirmishes would have continued, but for the fact that it rained from sunset to dawn the next morning. Only two small groups ran into one another in a dark alleyway. They fired the pistols and shotguns they always now carried with them through a curtain of rain. The flashes from their guns lit up the streams of water pouring from the rooftops. Their feet stuck deep in the mud, the two gangs kept on shooting until their ammunition ran out. Thanks to the downpour, nobody was injured on either side.

There were two further incidents: a sixteen-year-old boy who was part of Don Humbert Figa i Morera's gang died when he fell off a wall he had climbed to escape from real or imagined pursuers; he was unlucky enough to slip and smash his head on the ground. That same terrible night, somebody threw a dead mastiff through the window of a brothel that Odón Mostaza, Onofre and their associates were known to frequent. No-one could understand the meaning of that macabre gift. In fact, as a precaution, none of them had gone to the brothel that evening. As it was, the poor girls spent a sleepless night, terrified at the thought of a bloody attack. At three in the morning they all said the rosary.

The next day, the mystery woman paid Joan Sicart another visit. She told him Onofre Bouvila wanted to see him again, but for security reasons he didn't want to come to Sicart's office. "It's not you he mistrusts, but your men. He's afraid you don't have complete control over them. He refuses to put his head in the lion's mouth. He says you should choose a neutral meeting place. He'll go there on his own, but you can take whatever escort you wish."

Stung by this attitude, Sicart arranged for them to meet in the cathedral cloister. His men surrounded the cathedral and stood guard in all the side chapels, while the reverend bishop turned a blind eye to the presence of armed men in that holy place. Sicart also kept a watch on all Don Humbert's gang, and so knew Onofre really was coming alone. He couldn't help but admire his daring.

"There's still time to make peace," Onofre began. He spoke in a quiet, steady voice, as if to fit in with the solemnity of the place they were meeting in. Following the previous night's rainfall the rosebushes in the cloisters had bloomed, and the recently washed stonework was glowing like alabaster. "By tomorrow it could be too late. The authorities can't just sit doing nothing in a situation like this. Sooner or later the disruption to public order will force them to intervene. They'll either sort things out or use force: they'll probably declare a state of emergency and bring in the army to occupy the city. That would be the end for you and me: our bosses would escape, but we would be gallows meat. We'd end up in the mass graves at Montjuich. The authorities are worried that the trade union conflict is gathering pace, and won't waste this chance to show their decisiveness and power. You know I'm right. And it's possible your own boss may have something to do with this."

Joan Sicart was increasingly suspicious, but despite himself, Onofre Bouvila's words struck home.

"I've no reason to suspect my boss, Don Alexandre Canals i Formiga," he replied haughtily.

"That's your affair," said Onofre. "As far as I'm concerned, I trust no-one; I wouldn't put my hand to the flame for either of them."

At the same time as Onofre Bouvila was sowing the seeds of doubt in Sicart's mind, the mystery woman managed to get to see Canals i Formiga himself by concocting a confused sob story. Don Alexandre took the bait and had her brought to his office. Before she entered, he sprayed himself with the perfume he kept in the desk drawer next to his revolver. The woman refused to uncover her face, but without preamble told him she knew from a reliable source that Joan Sicart was about to betray him. "When the shooting starts again, he'll go over to the enemy. At the crucial moment he'll leave you defenceless," she said, her voice quavering.

Don Alexandre laughed. "What you say is impossible, madam. Where did you get such nonsense?" She burst into tears. "I suffer on your behalf. If anything were to happen to you . . ." she blurted out. Flattered by her concern, he tried to calm her down. "There's no reason to worry," he told her, offering her a glass of liqueur. She sipped it nervously and returned to the question troubling her. She said Joan Sicart had already met twice with Don Alexandre's enemies; once in his own headquarters and at that very moment they were meeting again in the cathedral cloister. "Make enquiries and you'll see I'm not lying," she said. "If Humbert Figa i Morera's men couldn't count on Sicart's complicity, why would they start a war they knew they were bound to lose?" she argued. "Think about what I'm saying, Alexandre. Sicart is in league with Humbert Figa i Morera."

Don Alexandre did not want to discuss such serious accusations with a stranger. "Be on your way now, I've got more important things to think of than this tittle-tattle of yours," he said, but once she had gone, he sent a message to the cathedral to ask for confirmation that Joan Sicart was there. I don't believe a word of what that crazy woman told me, he said to himself. But it's always wise to take precautions, especially at a time like this.

In reality the mystery woman's visit had affected him more than he was willing to admit. Who would have said that I, who lead such a monastic life, could have caused such an attractive woman to be secretly concerned about my safety, he said to himself. My word, there's something immoral in this, he thought. Be that as it may, I can't completely discount the information she brought. It's obvious she's exaggerating, and she is probably mistaken, but what if she isn't?

Word came back from the cathedral confirming Sicart's presence in the cloister. Don Alexandre sent for him and tried to press him for information in a roundabout way. Sicart was aware what he was trying to do, and this only served to confirm the suspicions Onofre had planted in his mind. Even so, he pretended not to notice anything in his chief's attitude, so as not to give himself away. Maybe he's planning to replace me with somebody else and doesn't know how to get rid of me, he thought. Sicart had a deputy by the name of Boix, a dim-witted man with bestial instincts who for some time now had envied Sicart his position. Perhaps now Don Alexandre had his eye on Boix: perhaps they had secretly come to an agreement.

As the two men talked, they each noticed the other's reticence beneath their apparent camaraderie. However, they agreed it would be wisest to launch a pre-emptive attack against Don Humbert Figa i Morera's men. Sicart said goodbye to his boss, promising he would wipe their enemy out. But when he was alone, he began to think: What if this is part of the same plan? As long as he's facing an enemy, even one as insignificant as Don Humbert, he'll still need me. But if I eliminate his rival's gang, what's to stop him eliminating me? No, he told himself, I have to make a pact with Onofre Bouvila. I need peace as much as he does, and he seems like a reasonable man. I'll go and see him, and between the two of us we'll make sure things return to normal.

Once Sicart had left, Don Alexandre Canals i Formiga collapsed into his leather armchair, let his arms droop over the sides and almost burst into tears. My most faithful servant is abandoning me, he said to himself. What will become of me? He feared for his own life, but was much more concerned about what might happen to his son. This boy was twelve years old; he had been born with a curvature of the spine that made it difficult for him to walk. When he was little, he hadn't been able to take part in games or any mischief, but he was passionate about studying and had shown an extraordinary facility for mathematics and mental arithmetic. He was a sad, friendless boy. Since the couple's other children had died almost simultaneously in the '79 epidemic, Don Alexandre felt a boundless affection and infinite compassion for his remaining child. The same could not be said of his wife: after the tragedy she developed an understandable though unjustified resentment towards her son.

Don Alexandre said to himself: If those ruthless thugs are planning something big, they might try to attack my son; they know that would be a mortal blow for me. Yes, they're sure to try that if I don't stay one step ahead of them. The next day, he dispatched his son, Nicolau Canals i Rataplán, together with his mother, a governess and a maid, to France, where Don Alexandre had friends and substantial capital.

When he heard of their departure, Joan Sicart was convinced he was being betrayed. He had a message sent to Onofre Bouvila: "Joan Sicart wants to see you urgently." "This time," Onofre replied, "just the two of us." "As you wish," Sicart responded. "You say where." Onofre Bouvila pretended to think this over, though he already had everything planned. "In San Severo church, half an hour before seven o'clock Mass." "The church will be shut at that time of day," came Sicart's reply. "I'll make sure it's open," said Onofre.

The whole of that day was spent passing these messages back and forth. There was no fighting, but the streets of Barcelona were deserted; none of its inhabitants was willing to risk leaving their homes unless absolutely necessary.

Before daybreak the next morning, Sicart's men had taken up position in the adjoining streets, the arcades and in an olive oil store next to the church, as well as in some palace ruins. They were hoping to see Onofre arrive, but he had been too clever for them: he had spent the night inside the church. At the agreed time, he himself opened the doors. Three of Sicart's minions rushed into the building, weapons at the ready, in case Onofre had laid a trap for their boss. The only people they found were Onofre, standing unarmed and serene by the door, and a poor chaplain quaking with fear as he prayed on his knees in front of the altar. Though he feared for his life, he was even more afraid the church would be profaned. The three gunmen were taken aback. "As you can see, there was no need for all your precautions," Onofre gently told them. They didn't notice that his brow was covered in sweat; they grabbed hold of the chaplain, dragged him out into the street and took him to see Joan Sicart. "No sign of anyone," they told him, "but we've brought you this chaplain so that he can confirm it."

Sicart confronted him.

"Do you know who I am?" he asked.

"Yes, sir," the chaplain replied in a faint whisper.

"So you know what will happen if you lie to me?"

"Yes, sir."

"Tell me the truth then: who is inside the church?"

"Only that lad."

"Do you swear to God?"

"I swear to God and all the saints."

"What about Odón Mostaza?"

"He's waiting in Plaza del Rey with the rest of the gang."

"Why in Plaza del Rey?"

"Onofre Bouvila told them to wait there."

"Alright, you can go," said Joan Sicart, turning away from him.

This dialogue increased his fears rather than reassuring him. He had been awake the entire night, turning things over in his mind, and was unsure what to do. He was faced with a crucial decision: on the one hand, he wanted to reach an agreement with Onofre Bouvila and maintain the status quo; on the other, it wasn't in his nature to negotiate. He was a warrior, and the chance to win a victory over an enemy blinded him to reason. What's to prevent me sending my men to Plaza del Rey and have them wipe out Odón Mostaza and every last one of his men? I could personally deal with this Bouvila, who's waiting for me like a lemon. In only a few minutes we would have driven our enemies from the city, and Barcelona would be ours. But he wasn't entirely convinced by this, and the doubt paralysed him.

His deputy urged him to take action. "Let's go: what are you waiting for?" he said. This was Boix, the man whose loyalty Sicart was also unsure of. Everything that during the night had seemed so clear to him was now a nightmarish confusion. "As soon as you see me enter the church, leave three men at the door. Take the rest and go to Plaza del Rey," Sicart told him. "That's where Odón Mostaza and his men are. Kill every last one of them. Remember that above all: no survivors. I'll join you soon afterwards."

3

The sun had already risen by the time Joan Sicart entered San Severo church. It'll be easy for me to do away with him, he was thinking. That way we'll resolve this dangerous, stupid situation once and for all. As soon as he's within range, I'll shoot him. Of course, I gave him my word and until now he has kept his, but since when have questions of honour bothered me? I've always been a rogue, and yet now I'm worried about scruples? Bah!

For a few moments, the church's gloomy baroque interior prevented him making out anything clearly. He heard Onofre Bouvila's voice calling to him from the altar. "Come up, Sicart, I'm here. You've nothing to be afraid of." Sicart shuddered. It's like killing my own son, he thought. Once he had become accustomed to the darkness, he advanced between two rows of pews. He kept his left hand in his trouser pocket, where he carried a hidden weapon. This was a small pistol, the sort that can only be used point-blank and fire a single shot. They were manufactured in Czechoslovakia and at the time were almost unheard of in Spain. Sicart guessed Onofre Bouvila would be unaware that this kind of pistol existed, and so would not notice he had one in his pocket, ready to kill him once he was close enough.

Another pistol identical to the one Sicart was carrying, though made of silver and encrusted with diamonds and sapphires, had been given by Emperor Franz Josef to his wife, Empress Isabel. So as not to offend her, because one does not give firearms to a lady, especially one of noble birth, he instructed the armourers to make it in the shape of a key. "No-one need see it," the emperor told her. "Carry it in your bag, just in case. There are lots of assassination attempts these days, and I'm apprehensive for you and the children." The Empress didn't deign to respond to this show of concern; she did not love her husband, and treated him with unconcealed disdain, even at official ceremonies and receptions.

Be that as it may, she was carrying the pistol in her bag as he had suggested on that fateful morning of 10 September 1898, when, as she was about to board a steamship at the Mont Blanc quay in Geneva, she was assassinated by Luigi Lucheni.

He had been lying in wait for two days outside the gates of the hotel where she was staying, but they had never coincided. Since he didn't have enough money to buy a dagger (they cost twelve Swiss francs), he had made one of his own with a brass needle and hilt. The previous day the Empress had gone to visit Baroness Rothschild, whose property was full of exotic birds and porcupines brought from Java.

Empress Elisabeth was sixty-one when she died, but had kept her slender figure and a very beautiful face; she embodied all that remained of elegance and noble dignity in Europe. She enjoyed writing elegiac poetry. Her son had committed suicide; her brother-in-law, Emperor Maximilian of Mexico, had been shot by firing squad; her sister had died in a Parisian fire; her cousin, King Ludwig II of Bavaria, had spent his last years vegetating in an asylum.

Luigi Lucheni, the man who killed her, was born in Paris but grew up in Parma. He also killed himself twelve years later in Geneva, where he was serving a life sentence. If Empress Sissi, as her subjects liked to call her, had made use of the pistol the Emperor had given her, she could doubtless have repelled her assailant. The fact was that Lucheni wasted several seconds before dealing the fatal blow: as both the Empress and her companion Countess Sztaray were carrying parasols to shield their faces from the sun, he had to poke his head beneath each to identify his victim. Dazzled as he was, he could have made a mistake that would have left him looking ridiculous in the eyes of History. He peered into the shade of their parasols and muttered, *scusate, signora*. Doubtless the Empress had forgotten she had a pistol in her bag, or possibly remembered, but decided to ignore it: she was, as she herself often said, tired of life. *I am so weary of the burden of life,* she had written shortly before to her daughter, *that I often feel in physical pain and think I would prefer to be dead.*

Sicart extended the hand not holding the pistol, ready to shake Onofre Bouvila's. But the latter, when Sicart was only a few steps away, and without bothering to look what the other man was doing with his concealed hand, raised his arms to the sky, went down on his knees, and cried:

"Sicart, for pity's sake, don't kill me! I'm too young to die, and I'm unarmed."

Sicart hesitated a few seconds – the last of his life. A man emerged out of the darkness, leaped on him and strangled him. Blood poured from his nose and mouth. Everything happened so quickly Sicart didn't even have time to pull the gun from his pocket, let alone use it (as was the case with the unfortunate Empress Sissi several years later).

The murderer was Efrén Castells, the giant from Calella. Onofre had kept him in the shadows all these months, without anybody even knowing he existed, so that he could turn to him when he was most needed. Joan Sicart's lifeless body lay at the altar: a tremendous sacrilege, but the deed was done. Onofre and Efrén raced down the main nave, closed the front doors to the church and bolted them. The men Sicart had left on guard out in the street suspected something might be happening to their boss and tried to get in, but to no avail.

While all this was happening, the rest of Sicart's men had headed for Plaza del Rey. The three others caught up with Boix and told him what was going on: "The church door is shut and bolted, and Sicart hasn't come out," they said. Boix didn't pay them much attention: for some time now he really had been coveting Sicart's position, and wasn't exactly upset to learn he had fallen victim to a lethal trap. Blinded by his ambition, he rushed with all his gang straight into Plaza del Rey. He hadn't sent any scouts out in advance or taken any other precautions – something that would never have happened if Sicart rather than Boix had been in charge.

Boix himself realised too late how reckless he had been: the square was empty; Odón Mostaza's men had vanished. His own followers turned towards him: What are we doing here, they seemed to be asking. With no visible enemy, Boix himself was at a loss. All at once Odón Mostaza's men, who had split up and climbed onto the rooftops, began to rake the square with fire. This was the start of a battle that lasted almost two hours: despite being more numerous, ~~~ ~as always at a disadvantage. Their defeat was due to the ~~~ they were so disciplined: with Sicart gone and Boix ~~~nd in fact, he was one of the first to fall) in the eyes of his men, none of them knew what to do. Mostaza's thugs on the other hand were in their element amongst all this confusion: it was second nature to them. In the end, Boix's men threw down their weapons and fled. Odón Mostaza let them escape – it would have been impossible for him to regroup and pursue them.

As yet, Don Alexandre Canals i Formiga knew nothing about this crushing defeat that dealt such a tremendous blow to his empire. In fact, he was in an excellent mood: his masseuse had just left, and his valet was helping him knot his tie. He knew his son was safe and sound in Paris, and he had managed to get rid of his wife, with whom he didn't really get on. Sunlight was streaming in through his office window when a fresh visit by the mysterious lady was announced. He received her just as soon as he had perfumed his beard.

On this occasion he made so bold as to take her by the waist when offering her a seat, leading her to a cherry-coloured velvet sofa. She resisted his advances only half-heartedly, her eyes on the window the whole time. When Don Alexandre engaged her in conversation, she was evasive and somewhat incoherent. A short while later, when Don Alexandre was trying to paw her, she saw a light flashing from a nearby roof. Onofre Bouvila and Efrén Castells were signalling to her with a mirror: it's all over, now it's your turn.

At this, she removed her veil and whipped off her hat and wig to be able to act more freely. Don Alexandre Canals i Formiga's jaw dropped. From between her false breasts, the mystery woman drew a dagger. She closed her eyes for a few seconds.

"May God forgive me for what I am about to do," was the last thing Don Alexandre heard before he fell dead on the sofa. At the last, he thought of his son: Thank heavens I got him away from here. Of himself, he could only reflect sarcastically: And I thought I was making a conquest!

The mystery woman was Señor Braulio, Onofre Bouvila's former landlord. Onofre had gone to seek him out in La Carbonera, down by the coal heaps. Señor Braulio still frequented the area, trying to drown his sorrows and loneliness with the constant use of drugs, and allowing himself to be roughed up by closet homosexuals keen to show how macho they were by punching transvestites. After his second arrest – this time as an alleged member of an anarchist cell when Delfina denounced him to the police – he had been released because it wasn't hard for him to prove his innocence and to demonstrate to the police and the prosecutor that his passions lay elsewhere.

A free man once more, he had tried to resume running the boarding house, but was greeted by a desolate panorama. His wife had died in hospital, and Delfina was about to be tried, together with her accomplices. The charges against them could not have been more serious: if she were not condemned to death, she would spend the rest of her days in prison. I'll never see my daughter again, Señor Braulio said to himself.

While he had been under arrest, nobody had been looking after the boarding house. Everywhere was covered in dust, and there were rotting food remains all over the kitchen. Señor Braulio tried to clean things up, but was too downhearted. With the help of Father Bizancio and the barber he placed advertisements in the newspapers, and it wasn't long before he found somebody willing to take on the property.

With the money from the sale, Señor Braulio sank into the depths of La Carbonera, degrading himself to the point where he could feel death fluttering around his haggard cheeks. This was what he had gone looking for, but now it was staring him in the face his courage failed him yet again. One night, as he was coming out of a low dive, he unexpectedly bumped into Onofre Bouvila. Flinging himself impulsively into his arms, he exclaimed: "Please help me, don't let me die here." Onofre replied: "Come with me, Señor Braulio, you don't belong in a place like this." Ever since then Señor Braulio had done whatever Onofre told him to do, without questioning if it was good or bad.

Now, in Don Alexandre's office, he finished taking off his gown and hid it behind the sofa where the man he had just killed was lying. In his underclothes, he went over to the window and with the mirror on his powder compact signalled to the rooftop where Onofre Bouvila and Efrén Castells were awaiting the outcome. When he had explained what Señor Braulio was to do, Onofre had insisted he lock the door and not open it until he himself came to fetch him. Señor Braulio suddenly realised that because he had been so nervous, he had forgotten to do this. He heard hurried footsteps and shouts in the corridor outside: Don Alexandre's men were coming to the aid of their boss. When one of them tried the door, Señor Braulio almost fainted, but nothing happened: Don Alexandre himself had taken care to lock the door so that the woman he was hoping to seduce could not escape. Without meaning to, he had saved his murderer's life.

They're all the same, the swine, Señor Braulio thought when he saw the door was locked, but having to spend so long in the company of his victim's dead body set his nerves jangling. When Onofre Bouvila and Efrén Castells finally burst in, they found him on the verge of suicide, about to jump out of the window. He had hung a heavy bronze vase round his neck in case the rope wasn't long enough.

Onofre and Efrén Castells seized all the papers they found on Don Alexandre Canals i Formiga's desk.

"With these we can make half of Barcelona dance to our tune," the giant said. "They're all here. No-one can escape us now."

That same afternoon, the pair of them presented themselves at Arnau Puncella's office. "Job done," they told him, showing him all the documents they had taken from Don Alexandre Canals i Formiga.

Arnau Puncella glanced at them and couldn't avoid a whistle of appreciation: "No-one can escape us now," he commented. Hearing his own expression repeated, Efrén Castells guffawed.

It was only now that Arnau Puncella acknowledged the presence of the giant; until that moment he had been pretending he hadn't noticed him. Turning to Onofre Bouvila and trying to restore his authority, he asked who this person was. Onofre replied softly that the giant's name was Efrén Castells. "He's my friend and right-hand man," he said. "He was the one who killed Joan Sicart."

Arnau Puncella, alias Margarito, began to tremble, suddenly realising something awful was about to happen to him. If they're not worried about me knowing that, it's because they're going to kill me, he thought. Even as this flashed through his mind, Efrén Castells lifted him under the arms and carried him aloft through the office, as though he were a baby.

"What kind of joke is this?" shouted Arnau Puncella, desperately kicking his legs. He knew this was no joke, however, and added in a high-pitched squeal: "Where are you taking me?"

"To where you deserve," Onofre Bouvila said. "You plotted all this to get rid of me. You wanted Sicart's men to kill me. And I always return favours." He opened the balcony door, and the giant from Calella heaved Arnau Puncella over the rail.

It was on that same balcony that, a few days earlier, Don Humbert Figa i Morera had stood, reflecting on the meaning of life. Now the door to his office was flung open and Onofre Bouvila and Efrén Castells strolled in. They had come to report on the success of their operation, they told him. Canals i Formiga's gang had been broken up; his deputies, Sicart and Boix, were dead, as was Don Alexandre himself. They had discovered all his papers, which were now in Onofre's possession. The losses in the gun battle had been minimal:

four dead and half a dozen wounded. To this total had to be added the regrettable loss of Arnau Puncella, who had just suffered an inexplicable accident.

Don Humbert Figa i Morera didn't know what to do or say: he had never thought Arnau Puncella's plan could lead to such a bloody outcome. He had also just heard his deputy's anguished cry, and understood that things were going to be very different from now on. Well, he said to himself, there's nothing to be done; I'll just have to get used to it. Right now, I have to focus on coming out of this alive. He asked for some additional unimportant information, which Onofre supplied in a few words: he knew Don Humbert wasn't really listening.

By answering Don Humbert, Onofre was demonstrating that his intentions were honest and that he was still willing to follow the other man's orders. Odón Mostaza and his men admired and loved Don Humbert, and would never have betrayed him, not even for Onofre Bouvila. Aware of this, he had no thought of making any move of that kind.

Eventually Don Humbert realised this, and the two men embarked on a lengthy discussion. Doubts flooded Don Humbert's mind. He told himself: The entire city is mine now, but I'm not ready to wield so much power overnight, especially since I've just lost my most faithful lieutenant, whose body is still lying sprawled on the pavement below. What am I to do?

Onofre Bouvila immediately sought to resolve these doubts: he knew exactly what should be done. Without a hint of arrogance, but with an aplomb that belied his age and position, and which Don Humbert was obliged to accept, he told him he had to take over the dead man's organisation, "but not integrate it into our own". He used the word "our" with deliberate insolence. Don Humbert would have dearly loved to whip him with the riding crop he always kept at hand, but was dissuaded from doing so by the fear Onofre inspired in him, as well as the threatening presence of Efrén Castells. Besides, what this audacious youngster was saying made sense. It's true it's best not to mix the two things up, he decided. I am who I am, and Canals, may God have mercy on him, was Canals.

The problem now, following Arnau Puncella's death, was to decide who to put in charge of Canals' affairs. When Onofre Bouvila immediately said he knew the perfect man, Don Humbert Figa i Morera couldn't hide his astonishment. "You don't mean Odón Mostaza or this brute here, do you?" he said. Onofre Bouvila was not offended. "No, no, of course not. Each to his own. The man I mean is expert at this sort of thing and is loyal to the death. In fact, he's waiting in the outer office. With your permission I'd like to call him in for you to meet him," he said.

Permission granted, Onofre showed Señor Braulio into the office. His former landlord was so obsessed with the idea that he had killed somebody with his own bare hands that his mind was in a complete muddle. He could no longer separate the two facets of his character, and one minute spoke with the manly restraint of property magnate, and the next in a falsetto, as if he were about to take out a pair of castanets and burst into song.

"I'm a person of extremes," he told Don Humbert when they were introduced. "When I'm not overcome by desire, all I can think of is suicide. This time luckily it wasn't serious, but you should have seen the previous attempt: I was covered in blood."

Don Humbert Figa i Morera scratched his head: he could not imagine how this grotesque figure could be relied on for such an important role.

4

By the time summer arrived, things in Barcelona had returned to normal. Nobody even recalled the shootouts and pitched battles that had held the city in suspense a few months earlier. Although at first they were reluctant, little by little everybody in the organisation accepted Señor Braulio in place of Canals i Formiga. The former landlord always acted with exquisite tact; he was very conservative, never went too far and kept the accounts scrupulously. Onofre Bouvila had forbidden him from returning to his escapades; there was no way he was to carry on with his nonsense in La Carbonera, he told him. "We're respectable now. If you need to kick over the traces or to have some fun, pay for it and do it at home. We earn more than enough for that. But in public, you are to behave," he told him.

Señor Braulio moved into a large apartment on Ronda de San Pablo, above the business offices. Some nights, his neighbours heard singing coming from the apartment, the strumming of guitars, the sound of quarrelling and furniture being smashed. The next day, he would turn up to meetings with Barcelona's leading citizens with his head bandaged, a black eye or other injuries. The only thing gnawing away at him was the thought that his daughter Delfina was still in prison. He was powerful enough by now to obtain her release: that kind of favour was what he specialised in; but Onofre Bouvila had expressly forbidden it. "It's not something we can permit ourselves yet," he would tell him. "That sort of manoeuvre would get us talked about and stir up the past. There'll be plenty of time to take care of Delfina in the future, when we're more secure."

Poor Señor Braulio adored his daughter, but was too weak to disobey Onofre. He secretly sent her packages of food and preserves, as well as the finest bed linen and underwear. Rather than thank

189

him, Delfina tore the clothes to shreds with her teeth and returned them unworn.

Odón Mostaza now worked for Señor Braulio as Joan Sicart's replacement. He did not have his murdered predecessor's leadership qualities or talent, but knew how to make himself loved by his men. And since he was enormously physically attractive, Señor Braulio was head over heels in love with him.

Onofre Bouvila himself had taken Odón Mostaza's place. He also carried out the functions that Arnau Puncella had been responsible for. Don Humbert Figa i Morera gave his blessing to all these changes. He was happy, in the best of all possible worlds; without deliberately setting out to do so, he was now at the pinnacle of Barcelona's underworld; at the centre of every intrigue. He had never dreamed of reaching such heights. Don Humbert was a man riddled with contradictions: a perfect mixture of shrewdness and stupidity, calculated histrionics and genuine innocence. He blithely undertook the most arduous tasks completely unaware of any consequences. As a result, everything worked out splendidly, and he claimed all the credit. He was very self-confident, but above all else, he was vain: he lived only to be seen. Whatever urgent business he was grappling with, he never failed to appear at midday on Paseo de Gracia dressed up to the nines and riding his famous dapple-grey mare. He had paid a fortune for this horse from Jerez, and it was well trained: it trotted the length of the avenue between Calle Caspe and Calle Valencia, pirouetting in between the tilburys. This display never ended well: the mare was weak in the legs, and at some moment each morning it came a cropper, crashing to the ground and sending its rider flying. Both of them would rise to their feet in an instant: the mare neighing and Don Humbert brushing manure off his frock coat. Invariably, a street urchin would rush from the pavement in between the carriage wheels and horses' hooves to retrieve Don Humbert's top hat and riding crop, returning them to him when he was back in the saddle. Unperturbed, he would reward the boy's efforts with a coin he held up to glint in the midday sun, thus converting the accident into a ceremony of vassalage.

This was exactly how the haute bourgeoisie interpreted it; utterly devoid of any sense of humour, they bestowed their broadest smiles on him. This, they all said, was the mark of a true gentleman. Because he was so dim, Don Humbert thought these displays of deference meant they accepted him. Nothing was further from the truth: since the Barcelona upper classes lacked the aristocracy's complex, rigid heraldic system, they had to be more rigorous in practice. They admired Don Humbert Figa i Morera's wealth, and above all his way of spending it, but considered him personally to be a social climber and parvenu. In their heart of hearts, none of them ever considered him their equal. Don Humbert, however, did not notice this; as with all true vanity, his was an end in itself. He didn't preen in order to bolster his prestige, still less to seduce his female audience, among whom, unbeknownst to him, he was held in high esteem: all the married women and numerous young ladies of marriageable age sighed as he rode past.

Things went no better for him in his private life. His wife considered herself the height of beauty, intelligence and distinction, convinced that nothing was good enough for her and that she had married beneath her. She kicked him around, and when they saw this, their servants were equally rude. He put up with all this ill-treatment without a word: nobody had ever seen him lose his temper – it was as if he lived in his own world. Accustomed to having no-one listen to him, he wandered round his house emitting unintelligible grunts, not in the hope of receiving a reply, but simply for the pleasure of hearing his own voice. On other occasions, he imagined he had said out loud something he had merely thought. This total breakdown of communication didn't have the slightest impact on him. Work absorbed all his energy; his limited social success satisfied his self-esteem; and his daughter, whom he idolised, fulfilled all his need for love.

Back then, summer holidays were very different from what they are today. When the hot weather began, only well-to-do families imitated the royal couple and transferred their households up into the less humid climate of the mountains. They preferred not to stray too far from Barcelona, holidaying in Sarriá, Pedralbes or La Bonanova, nowadays all swallowed up by the city. The rest of Barcelona's inhabitants combated the heat with fans and pitchers of cool water. Sea bathing was becoming popular with the French-influenced younger generation, and this created a huge scandal. Since hardly anybody could swim, each year the number of drownings was correspondingly high; in their homilies, parish priests would often quote this statistic as proof of God's wrath.

Don Humberto Figa i Morera, who had come on to the scene too late to acquire a summer property in a well-established resort, had to have one built for him to the north of the city centre, in an area known as La Budallera. He had bought an uneven plot of land covered with magnolias and pine and chestnut trees, and had an unpretentious chalet constructed there. As is often the case with lawyers, he had bought the plot without much forethought, so that now he had to spend time, effort and money trying to resolve centuries-old land disputes. The plain fact was, he had been swindled: the property was gloomy, damp and mosquito-infested. So out of favour was the area that his only neighbours were a few hermits who lived in dank caves, ate roots and bark, wandered the hills showing their private parts, and over the years had lost the use of speech and reason.

"Only an imbecile like you could have thought of buying land in a rubbish tip like this," his wife told him every day, often several times. She would have liked to have gone to take the waters at Ocata or Montgat, rubbing shoulders with the most snobbish members of the emerging bourgeoisie. For once, however, her husband had put his foot down.

"Neither you nor our daughter knows how to swim," he had said. "You could be swept away by any current. I've also heard it said that there are octopuses and lampreys on the seabed that sting bathers and rip them to shreds while their families and friends look on in horror."

"That's their fault," his wife retorted, "for bathing naked. Exposing their flesh rouses the appetite of creatures that can only distinguish humans from animals by their clothes," she added, grimacing as if secretly pleased at the misfortunes befalling people who ignored the dress etiquette. She was convinced no creature would dare sink its teeth into her; she still wore old-fashioned crinolines, an embroidered two-metre-long train and any amount of jewels at all times of the day and night.

It was to this summer residence that Onofre Bouvila came to visit Don Alexandre in August 1891.

He had galloped up the mountain, only to discover he was lost in the woods. His horse was in a lather and panting for breath. This animal is going to die under me and leave me stranded here, Onofre fretted. It's curious that I'm the one who can't find his way in the hills; I've become a city dweller. Eventually he spied a house surrounded by a leafy garden and a low, dark stone wall. A column of smoke was rising from the chimney. He dismounted and, leading the horse by the reins, approached on foot, leaning over the wall to see if anybody could help.

The garden appeared to be empty: birds were singing, flies and wasps buzzing, butterflies fluttering by. Dazzled by the midday sun, through the trees Onofre glimpsed a young girl go by. She was wearing a lacy, white short-sleeved organdie dress, adorned with scarlet velvet ribbons. Two sets of corkscrew coppery curls poked out from under a bonnet embroidered with cloth flowers. The curls and bonnet meant Onofre could only see parts of her face: the bridge of her nose, a rosy cheek, the gentle slope of her brow, the oval of her chin.

Onofre Bouvila stood rooted to the spot; by the time he reacted, the vision had gone. Who can that have been, he wondered. She didn't look like a country girl, but all alone out here ... how mysterious! At that moment a young lad appeared. Onofre signalled to him, and when he came over, asked if this was the place he was looking for. When the boy confirmed it was, Onofre handed him the reins and asked to be announced.

Don Humbert Figa i Morera had strictly forbidden any of his men to visit his summer residence; he had no wish to be disturbed there on any account. Nor did he want his family to be involved in his affairs. Onofre took it upon himself to disobey that order: he intended to see how far Don Humbert would tolerate his insubordination.

A maidservant led him to a hexagonal room on the first floor, which had several doors leading off it. The only light filtered in through an opaque skylight, giving the room a pleasantly cool feel. The mother-of-pearl stuccoed chimney breast glowed in this half-light; on the mantelpiece stood a tall mirror in a gilt frame, a bronze candelabra and an Empire-style clock in a glass dome. The few pieces of furniture in the room were a painted wooden corner table supporting an alabaster Venus emerging from her seashell, a Moorish pedestal table and a pile of satin cushions.

Onofre Bouvila was enchanted by what he saw. What simplicity, he thought, what refined elegance. A sharp click behind his back made him wheel round. From force of habit his hand went to his trouser pocket, where he now always kept the pistol he had snatched months earlier from Joan Sicart. One of the doors had opened without warning: there stood the same girl he had glimpsed a few minutes ago in the garden. She had removed her bonnet and was reading what looked like a black prayer book. The unexpected presence of a stranger in the room brought her to a standstill in the doorway. Onofre opened his mouth to say something, but no sound came out; perhaps less inhibited, the girl closed her book, made a graceful curtsy down to the floor and murmured something Onofre didn't catch.

"I beg your pardon," he said. "What was that?"

His intense gaze made the young girl lower her eyes and stare at the arabesques on the floor tiles.

"Hail Mary full of grace," she said at last in a whisper.

"Ah!" exclaimed Onofre. "Conceived without sin."

She curtsied once more without looking him in the face. "I didn't know there was anybody in here," she said, blushing. "The maid didn't warn me . . ."

"No, don't say that," he interrupted her hastily. "On the contrary, it's I who should apologise if I gave you a fright . . ."

Before he could finish his sentence, she had vanished, closing the door behind her. Left to his own devices, Onofre began to pace around the room. Animal, idiot, dimwit, he said to himself, not caring whether he was muttering under his breath or speaking out loud. Why did you let her go? Now God only knows if you'll get another chance to see her. Never before, even in far more difficult situations, had Onofre hesitated: he had always known what to do. Either that, or I won't live to tell the tale, he moaned. Oh, he groaned, sinking onto the pile of soft cushions. And I thought I was safe forever from this kind of turmoil.

Bah, what am I saying, he asked himself, still in that penitent pose. She's a slip of a girl: if I spoke to her of love, what would she understand? She'd be terrified, or worse still laugh at me. After all, I'm nothing more than a donkey, a country bumpkin who's become a paid gunman for crooks. He struggled to tear from his heart the arrow fate had wounded him with. He struggled in vain against the wave of emotion sweeping over him: it was as useless as someone building sand ramparts to hold back the sea.

Enraged, he picked up the alabaster Venus and flung it with all his might at the mirror over the fireplace. The statue fell to the floor and smashed; the mirror cracked, hung there for a fraction of a second, then crashed down. Six or eight large pieces splintered and sent shards of glass scattering to every corner of the room. All that remained in the mirror frame was a mess of quicksilver and mortar. Again Onofre heard a sound behind his back: this time a stifled cry. The girl had returned; she was staring in horror at the mirror that no longer reflected anything, as if the room and its occupants had ceased to exist. This image helped her understand what he had wanted to say to her; she saw what lay behind his vandalism. She let him pull her towards him and felt the impassioned man's heart beating wildly.

"No-one has ever kissed me," she said, with what little breath she could muster.

"Nor will they as long as I live," said Onofre Bouvila, "if they don't want me to blow their brains out." Saying this, he kissed her on the mouth, then added: "And yours as well."

Her whole body arched backwards: her copper-coloured hair fell loose down beyond her waist. Her arms hung limp by her sides, her fingers brushing the cool floor tiles. Her knees folded, and she lay draped across Onofre's arm. Her half-open lips let out a prolonged sigh. "Yes," she said, sealing her future in that instant.

Glancing up, Onofre blinked in surprise: somebody else had entered the room. It was Don Humbert Figa i Morera, who had just come in, accompanied by two other gentlemen. One of them was a man by the name of Cosme Valbuena, an architect by profession. Dreadfully bored, Don Humbert had decided to build an extension to the house, using the structure of an old henhouse and dovecote that ran alongside it. Unfortunately, to do so was to encroach on the adjacent property. Building on a foot or two of his neighbour's land had led to a dispute with the owner, who as it happened was also Don Humbert's friend and occasional business associate. Too caught up in far more important affairs to bother about such a trifling matter, Don Humbert had sent for a lawyer who was young but had a very good reputation, particularly when it came to boundary issues. He now stood alongside the other two men.

The three of them had spent the day going round the house, garden and surrounding fields. The lawyer took measurements with a rope and made architectural suggestions the architect didn't even deign to listen to. He in turn suggested possible legal ways of winning the lawsuit. The three men got into heated arguments, and thoroughly enjoyed themselves. Then they sat at table and ate with enviable appetites.

Don Humbert's wife made no fuss about having these hangers-on around the house: her daughter would soon be of marriageable age, and both the lawyer and the architect were bachelors; both appeared to have a brilliant future ahead of them. At the very least they offered access to their respective professional circles, something that couldn't be said of her lackadaisical husband. He always replied to her machinations with typical good humour: "My dear, what ideas you have: our daughter has only just turned ten."

But now he didn't know what to think. He wasn't so stupid as to fail to grasp the meaning of his daughter's languid swoon or his subordinate's steely, hungry look. He also realised that the best thing for him to do was to pretend he hadn't noticed what was going on: "Well, well," was his only comment. "I see you two have been introduced and are getting on splendidly. That's what I like to see, yes indeed."

The two of them were so flustered it took them some time to

disentangle themselves, recover their balance and composure. Even Onofre Bouvila, who until a few moments before had looked down on Don Humbert, now saw him as the father of the woman he loved, and was ready to show him the utmost respect. His anger quickly evaporated and he looked contrite. The lawyer and the architect meanwhile were walking round the room, assessing the damage.

"The important thing," the lawyer insisted, "is for no-one to cut themselves on the broken glass."

Onofre Bouvila rode back to Barcelona with the sun on his back. Crickets were chirruping in the undergrowth; the early evening sky was filled with stars. What's to become of me now, he was thinking as he stared up at this map of the heavens. He realised that as long as Don Humbert Figa i Morera's daughter reciprocated his love, it would be impossible for him to betray her father.

Before the summer was out, the architect and the lawyer had both asked Don Humbert Figa i Morera for her hand. Their rivalry and the need for her to choose allowed her first of all to stall, and then to absolutely refuse to marry either of them. Sometimes her refusals were forceful, at others forlorn, and they were often accompanied by tears and tantrums. Because she was so delicate, she hurt herself when she banged her forehead against the wall or punched furniture with her fists, so that she was soon covered in bandages. Her attitude and the veiled threat that worse things might happen to her if her wishes were ignored led her father to quickly change his mind.

Her mother, however, knew instinctively that this insuperable resistance was not so much due to her daughter's rejection of the two suitors, whom she barely even seemed to have noticed, but for some other, more urgent reason. She recalled the broken mirror and the smashed alabaster statue, and the fact that these accidents had coincided with the highly irregular visit of one of her husband's subordinates to their La Budallera residence, and drew her own conclusions. When she questioned Don Humbert, he eventually admitted he had indeed burst in on their daughter and that young man. Even though he underplayed the scene as he described it to his wife, it might, he admitted, lead one to think their daughter felt some affection towards the youngster.

"And who was that youngster?" his wife demanded. Don Humbert gave her a garbled explanation she didn't bother to listen to; she wasn't interested in what her husband might say, but what he was trying to hide. His hesitation led her to conclude that Onofre Bouvila was the least suitable candidate for her daughter's hand. Very well, she said to herself, we'll do without the lawyer and the architect, but let's make sure our girl is safe from that clodhopper. Once she has forgotten him we can find her a suitable husband. She's still very young and can afford to waste half a dozen opportunities. At her insistence, Don Humbert sent their daughter to a boarding school run by nuns.

The girl didn't oppose this, as it meant she was free of any suitors. All things considered, it's the best that could happen to us, she told herself. When Onofre recovered from his indignation, this was also how he came to see it. She'll be mine some day, he thought. For now I'll just have to be patient.

He used every conceivable means to get hundreds of letters to her. This had one great merit: before then he had barely been able to sign his signature, and so it could be said he learned to write fluently thanks to his love letters. She replied less frequently, struggling to avoid the nuns' censorship. *Above all*, she wrote in one of these missives, *I give thanks to God through His son Jesus Christ, because the Lord, whom my spirit worships, is witness to how you are constantly in my thoughts, as I plead with Him in my prayers, if it be His will, to find at last a blessed day when I can reach you, because my heart yearns to see you.* Such language, based on Saint Paul, was highly unusual for a young girl in love, but could be explained by a fear that her letters might fall into the hands of the nuns or her parents, or out of a sincere religious devotion. Later, after her marriage, she was always very devout. Those who knew and dealt with her as a grown woman offered conflicting verdicts: "serene" and "bemused" were the two adjectives most often used to describe her. Others thought she ended up seeking solace in religion because she was so unhappy at the hands of Onofre Bouvila.

Barcelona meanwhile was preparing to cross the threshold between the nineteenth and twentieth centuries, carrying with it more headaches than hopes. "I think that all we've achieved with so much effort is going to vanish overnight," the city's leading lights would mutter in the sombre quiet of their circles, clubs and salons. The economic recession was dragging on and on. One after another, the luxury shops on Calle Fernando began to close; big department stores began to take their place on Las Ramblas and Paseo de Gracia. They were a novelty that the inhabitants of Barcelona welcomed only up to a certain point. DEPARTMENT STORES: ALADDIN'S LAMP OR ALI BABA'S CAVE? was the striking headline in one of the newspapers of the time.

The Madrid government's economic policies didn't help. Deaf to the arguments and pleas of Catalans based in Madrid to argue their cause, as well as a few Spaniards who were prescient or were paid to be so, the government abolished all or nearly all the protectionist measures shielding national industry. No longer having to face tariffs, foreign products that were better, cheaper and easier to use than Spanish ones eventually led to the collapse of an already weak market. The closure of factories and mass, unforeseeable layoffs added to the afflictions already plaguing the working classes.

In addition, there were wars in Cuba and Melilla. Every week hundreds of young men, some of them still adolescents, were shipped off to fight in America and Africa. Heart-rending scenes took place on the quays and at the railway station in Barcelona. The Civil Guard repeatedly had to charge mothers trying to prevent the troops being transported by clinging on to the ships' mooring ropes or blocking the passage of locomotives. Very few of these young men who left for the front overseas ever came back, and those who did were either maimed or gravely ill.

All this only increased popular unrest. The workers' associations that the deceased Canals i Formiga had been so concerned about were flourishing, above all those of the anarchists. Some were followers of Foscarini, others of De Weerd or of leaders who had appeared subsequently. From time to time, these groups banded together to call and hold general strikes that never got anywhere. Infuriated by all these failures and wasted effort, and seeing that the situation was only worsening, some decided to take direct action. Inspired by their Italian, French and above all Russian colleagues, they sought to *cut off however many heads the hydra has, the more the merrier,* as one of them put it.

This was the beginning of the dark decades of terror: no public event, parade, procession or spectacle was safe from the sudden explosion of a bomb. Deafened, blinded by the smoke, survivors would search among the victims for family and friends. Others fled in all directions, wild-eyed and with their clothes covered in blood, not even pausing to check if they were mortally wounded or had emerged unscathed. Wherever the upper classes met, the anarchists made them feel the weight of their anger and despair.

Every time something of this sort happened, Onofre Bouvila couldn't help recalling Pablo and his anarchist theories, which he himself had reluctantly helped to spread. Sometimes he wondered if it hadn't been Pablo himself who threw the bomb at Martínez Campos or in El Liceo, the tragic echoes of which still resound faintly in the boxes and corridors of that famous opera house on gala occasions. But Onofre never shared his thoughts with anyone: due to his present position, he wished to conceal the fact that in the past he had been linked to the anarchists. On the contrary, he let it be understood by his beloved and those he had professional relations with that he was from a good family whom reversals of fortune had obliged to undertake work of a dubious nature, as he was doing on Don Humbert Figa i Morera's behalf. Nobody remembered anymore the part he had played during the violent days that had put an end to the life and criminal empire of Canals i Formiga. Whenever the opportunity arose, Onofre would condemn violence and declare himself in favour of repressing the anarchists with an iron fist. He did not hesitate to call them "rabid dogs" or praise the bloodthirsty policy the government adopted in an attempt to restore order.

Naturally, this attitude was favourably received by the members of the haute bourgeoisie with whom he had dealings. With their wealth and lives under threat, they had called a truce in their centuries-old quarrel with Madrid. They argued that however damaging the Madrid government's attitude was to Catalonia's commercial interests, losing their armed protection in this struggle would have been worse. Later, in private, they lamented having to accept such a compromise. "It's sad," they said to one another, "that we have to throw ourselves into the arms of a tin-pot general when Catalonia has provided the Spanish army with their fiercest lions." By this they were referring to General Prim, the hero of Mexico and Morocco, and General Weyler, who at that time was keeping the Cuban rebels at bay. What worried the most timorous ones above all was that the Catalan separatists, who were gaining strength, could win elections and incense the Madrid government, to whose benevolence they felt they owed their lives.

In this climate, Señor Braulio's affairs prospered. In private, Onofre Bouvila gleefully rubbed his hands. Years later he was heard to say: "I always thought Spain's greatest problem was that its wealth was in the hands of a bunch of uneducated, gutless cowards." For its part, the Madrid government did no more than reap the rewards this situation offered and attempt to deal with Catalonia's internal problems as if they were yet another colonial headache. It dispatched military troglodytes to the principality, men who spoke only the language of bayonets and wanted to impose peace by running through half the population.

Ah, Onofre thought when he saw what was going on around him, what splendid times for someone with a bit of imagination, enough money and a lot of daring. I have more than enough of the first and last of these, but where can I get the money? There must be a way for me to get my hands on it, because destiny offers occasions like this just once in a lifetime, and sometimes not even that. Having a beloved only served to fuel his ambition; never being able to see her left his energies intact. He no longer went out on sprees with Odón Mostaza and his gang, preferring not to be seen in public with hoodlums. Señor Braulio and Efrén Castells helped provide him with a few small pleasures in private.

Around this time the newspapers announced that the Sargon comet was nearing the Earth. It was said to be more than 50,000 kilometres in diameter. There was no lack of prophets predicting the end of the world: the current disturbances and disquiet were no more than its prelude and a warning. This naturally caused great concern, but in the end, nothing came of it.

CHAPTER FOUR

1

The traveller arriving for the first time in Barcelona soon realises where the old city ends and the new one begins. Winding streets give way to broader straight ones, with wider pavements. Tall plane trees offer welcome shade, and the buildings are grander. Some visitors are bewildered, thinking they have been magically transported to another city. Consciously or not, the inhabitants of Barcelona encourage this ambiguity: when they go from one part to the other, their physical appearance, attitude and attire seem to undergo a change. The city wasn't always divided in this way: it has its explanation, its history and its legend.

During its many centuries of existence, Barcelona's city walls never prevented conquest or looting. They did, however, stifle its growth. Whilst the population inside the walls grew until life became unbearable, outside them lay vegetable gardens and empty fields. At sunset and during public celebrations, the inhabitants of the surrounding villages would climb to the top of the hills (which today are El Putxet, Gracia, San José de la Montaña, etc.) to observe (sometimes through brass telescopes) the people of Barcelona. Febrile, disciplined and punctilious, the city dwellers would come and go, greet one another, get lost in the maze of narrow streets, bump into one another again and greet each other a second time, take an interest in their health and affairs, then say goodbye until the next occasion. The villagers enjoyed this spectacle tremendously: some of the more dim-witted threw stones to try to hit somebody inside the city, despite the fact that distance and the walls made this impossible.

Such crowded conditions made Barcelona unhygienic: any illness soon became an epidemic, and there was no way of isolating the sick. The city gates would be closed to prevent the plague spreading, and the villagers outside put up barricades and used brute force to drive back any fugitives from the city, while tripling the price of their produce. The overcrowding also undermined decency. *Accommodated in a hostel that had been enthusiastically recommended to me,* one traveller noted in his journal, *I discovered I had to share a room at most six metres square with as many others, that's to say, five people and myself. Two of these others turned out to be a newly wedded couple on their honeymoon who, as soon as they had retired to bed and the light had gone off, enlivened the night with a profusion of panting, cries and giggles. All this at an exorbitant price, thank you very much!* Father Campuzano wrote more succinctly: *It's a rare inhabitant of Barcelona who, before reaching adulthood, has not graphically learned of how he or she was engendered.* There was a consequent relaxation of morals, frequent outbreaks of venereal disease, abuse of minors, and other mistreatment. In some cases, like that of Jacinto or Jacinta Peus, the cramped conditions gave rise to grave psychological disturbances: *As a result of so often seeing my parents and my brothers and sisters, my uncles and aunts, my grandfathers and grandmothers, my male and female cousins and the household servants going around with no clothes on, I ended up not knowing which were men and which were women, nor to which of the two genders I was meant to belong.*

The housing problem was desperate; most of a family's income went on paying the astronomical price of somewhere to live. A few easily understood figures are relevant here. In the mid-nineteenth century, the surface area of Barcelona was 427 hectares. At the same date, Paris occupied 7,802 hectares; Berlin 6,310; and London 31,685.

Even such an apparently small city as Florence covered 4,226 hectares, that is, ten times more than Barcelona. The population density per hectare is also revealing: 291 in Paris, 189 in Berlin, 128 in London, but 700 in Barcelona.

Why weren't the walls torn down? Because the Madrid government would not allow it. Weak strategic excuses were advanced to keep the city asphyxiated and to prevent Barcelona growing in size and power. The kings, queens and regents who followed one another on the Spanish throne claimed they had more pressing problems to deal with, while the governments were dilatory, if not sarcastic: "If Barcelona wants more land," they would say, "let them burn down more convents." This was an allusion to the convents set on fire by mobs during the bloody disturbances that took place in those turbulent decades, and to the fact that the sites of the convents had been turned into communal spaces: squares, markets and such like.

Finally the walls were demolished. "Now at last we'll be able to breathe," the inhabitants told themselves. But little had changed in reality: with or without walls, the city was still overcrowded. People lived unbearably promiscuous, indecent lives crammed into tiny rooms. Families were forced to share with their animals. Now the walls had gone, they could clearly see the valley outside the city, stretching as far as the Collserola mountain range; the sight only made their own wretched conditions all the more obvious. "Good Lord," the city dwellers said. "All that empty countryside and here we are like rats in a den." Is it right, they asked themselves, for lettuces to have more space than we do? All eyes turned to the mayor.

This mayor was not the same one who years later carried out the plan to hold the World Fair. This man was a short, pot-bellied fellow, who was very religious and went to Mass every day to take Holy Communion. During those minutes of reflection he tried not to think of municipal problems, preferring to concentrate his attention on the miracle of transubstantiation. And yet he could not keep his mind off the overwhelming dilemma. "Something has to be done," he told himself. "But what?" He had studied the expansion of other European cities: Paris, London, Vienna, Rome, Saint Petersburg. The plans were good, but costly. Besides, Barcelona was a special case. Whenever someone praised for example the plan for Paris, the mayor always replied that it was a good one, "but it doesn't take into account Barcelona's idiosyncracies". He said the same of the plan for Vienna, and so on. He was convinced Barcelona had to come up with and complete its own plan, avoiding any imitation.

One day shortly after receiving communion he had a vision: he was sitting in the mayor's chair in his office when a mace bearer came in to announce a visitor. The mayor wondered if it could be a councillor or delegate. "He says," said the usher, interrupting his thoughts, "that he is a gentleman from Olot." At that, the visitor entered, and the mace bearer withdrew.

The mayor was dumbstruck. The visitor gave off rays of light, his head surrounded by a halo. In amazement, the mayor noted that the apparition's skin was shiny, as though he had been silver-plated. His shoulder-length hair was made up of strands of silver. His tunic also gave off a dull glow, as if everything about the visitor was of supernatural origin. The mayor was careful not to ask for any explanation, but merely enquired as to what he owed such an honour. "We have become aware," said the visitor, "that for some time now you have been distracted when you receive the Host." "It's my attention rather than my devotion that is wavering," replied the mayor by way of an excuse. "It's the urban development plan that's making my life a misery. I've no idea what to do."

"Tomorrow at cockcrow," said the visitor, "you're to be at the old western gate. There you will see the chosen one – but don't tell him that I appeared before you." The mayor woke with a start: he was in the church, kneeling on the prayer stool, and still had the holy wafer on his tongue. He had dreamed all this in the blink of an eye.

The next day at the appointed hour, the mayor was on the spot where, by chance, years later the Triumphal Arch was to be built at the entrance to the World Fair. People, beasts of burden and carts were already on the move. So as not to be recognised, the mayor wore a simple cape and a wide-brimmed hat. He was carrying a clay pot in which he had put a goat's cheese, dousing it with oil and sprinkling it with thyme as he had seen his grandparents do as a boy in their farmhouse. He spent the whole day at his post. In the city, passersby commented on the tense atmosphere caused by the mayor's disappearance – he had been searched for in vain ever since he had not turned up that morning at the church where he infallibly attended Mass. What was most shocking, they all agreed, was that not a centavo was missing from the public coffers.

At dusk, as the sun became a huge red disk, the mayor saw a strange being approaching him. The left half of the apparition's face was smooth and hairless, the result of being scalded with boiling water when he was a child; the other half, however, was wrinkled and had half a moustache and an extraordinarily long half beard, because he had just walked the pilgrims' way to Santiago or was about to do so. He was called, or so he said, Abraham Schlagober, which in German means "whipped cream". He said that despite the name, he was not Jewish, but from an ancient Christian family; that he was fulfilling a vow he had made as a pilgrim, and that he was a builder. The mayor immediately took him to the city hall, showed him the maps of Barcelona and its environs and gave him everything necessary to draw up a master plan. "This will be the City of God that Saint John tells us of," declared Abraham Schlagober. "The new Jerusalem." Since Jerusalem had been destroyed, never to rise again since the Lord had said that no stone would be left upon another stone, a new city was called upon to take its place as the centre of Christendom. Barcelona was on the same latitude as Jerusalem and was a Mediterranean city: everything pointed to it becoming the chosen city. The two of them read the words of the Apocalypse: *And I saw the Holy City, the new Jerusalem, being sent down by God from heaven, all clothed in readiness, like a bride who has adorned herself to meet her husband. And I heard a loud voice crying aloud from the throne: this is the dwelling of God's tabernacle pitched among men. He will make His dwelling place among them, and they will be His own people and He will be among them, their own God. He will wipe every tear from their eyes, and there will be no more death or mourning, or cries of distress, no more sorrow.*

The city plan was completed in less than six months, after which Abraham Schlagober disappeared without trace. Some say he never in fact existed and that it was the mayor himself who drew up the plans. Others that he did exist, but that his name was not what he had said it was, and that he wasn't a pilgrim or builder, but an adventurer who, noticing the mayor's troubled state of mind, decided to take advantage of him. He succeeded in cleverly translating onto paper his protector's visions, and for as long as the work continued, was able to live at the city's expense, something that was hardly unusual. When the project was completed, the mayor was delighted, and submitted it to the city council for approval.

Today that original proposal no longer exists: either it was deliberately destroyed or it is irretrievably buried in the depths of the municipal archives. Only partial, unreliable sketches that were part of the outline report have come down to us. All the measurements were in pes, parasangas, codos and stades, which would doubtless have confused the workmen if the work had gone ahead. From what today is known as Tibidabo down to the Mediterranean, a navigable canal was planned, with twelve narrower and shallower canals branching off to right and left (one for each of the tribes of Israel). These flowed into an equal number of artificial lakes, on the shores of which would be built neighbourhoods or semi-religious, semi-administrative clusters, to be governed by a deputy mayor and a Levite. Nowhere is it stated where the water feeding this canal and its tributaries would come from, although there are veiled references to wells situated in what today are Vallvidrera, La Floresta, San Cugat and Las Planas. In the centre of the old city (which according to the plan was to be razed to the ground, apart from the cathedral, Santa María del Mar, el Pino and San Pedro de las Puellas) five bridges were to be built across the canal, representing the five theological virtues. The city hall and the buildings housing the provincial governing body and the civilian government were to be replaced by three basilicas representing the soul's three faculties. There was a Market of Temperance and a Market of the Fear of God and suchlike. Other aspects of the plan remain unknown and are unlikely ever to surface.

The city council didn't know what to make of all this, but in the end decided to welcome the project. They gave it the municipality's unanimous, unconditional backing. However, the city cabinet pointed out the need to comply with all the stipulated regulations: the project they had all approved had to be signed off by the Interior Ministry, which was in charge of all the city councils in Spain. The mayor was incandescent. "How is it possible that even God's will has to be submitted to Madrid?" he protested. "That's the law," responded the relieved councillors. Whilst they pretended to share the mayor's anger, deep down they wanted to pass the hot potato to Madrid, and for Madrid to rescue them. Whenever they get the chance, they do us down, they thought. This time they would be doing us a favour for once if they rejected the scheme.

Madrid's reply was not long in coming: "His Excellency the

Minister acknowledges receipt of the so-called Expansion Plan for the City of Barcelona, but he will not consider it as it does not meet the requirements of the relevant legislation." The law in effect required that three alternative proposals be submitted, with the minister retaining the right to choose the one he preferred.

The mayor almost blew his top. The councillors managed to calm him down. "Let's organise a competition, then send Madrid our project plus two others; the minister cannot help but choose ours, he is bound to see it's the best," they told him. The mayor could see no objection to this: he believed his scheme had been inspired by God and that there was not and could never be a better one. He therefore allowed a competition to be held, and waited impatiently for the projects to be presented, judged and pre-selected according to the timetable established by the competition rules. He even agreed to present his own proposal together with the others, convinced it would be selected, as indeed it was.

As a result of this, the mayor's scheme, previously seen by only a few people, went round from hand to hand, and its details were passed on by word of mouth. It was the talk of all the elite gatherings in the city. Finally the three chosen projects were sent to Madrid. There the minister kept them as long as he could without offering any explanation. The mayor was in despair. "Is there any news from Madrid?" he would ask in the middle of the night, waking up with a start. His aide-de-camp had to enter his bedroom and calm him, as the mayor had no partner.

At long last, the minister sent his reply. It exploded like a bomb: His Excellency the Minister of the Interior had decided not to select any of the three projects put forward, since in his view none of them was of sufficient merit. Instead, he preferred and gave his stamp of approval to a fourth project that had either not been entered for the competition or had done so but been rejected by the jury. Now it reappeared, sanctioned by a ministerial decree. This was what later came to be known as the Cerdá Plan.

The mayor preferred to take this lightly: *I am convinced*, he wrote to the minister, *that your excellency was having his little joke at our expense by pretending to give his seal of approval to a project that not only was not one of those presented to your excellency, but which from the outset is sure to meet with the disapproval of all the inhabitants of Barcelona.* This time, the minister's reply was brutal. *The inhabitants of Barcelona, my friend, can consider themselves fortunate if the Cerdá Plan is one day carried out exactly as I have sanctioned it,* he wrote to the mayor. *And as far as you yourself are concerned, my esteemed mayor, permit me to remind you that it is not incumbent upon you to decide when a minister is or is not making a joke. Content yourself with carrying out my instructions to the letter, and do not oblige me to remind you on whom in the last instance your position depends.*

The mayor called a full council meeting once more. "We've had a slap in the face," he told them. "It serves us right for having submitted to Madrid's dictates rather than proceeding on our own account, as our position allows and our honour dictates. Now due to our lack of determination, Barcelona's honour has been offended: let that be a lesson to us all." This was met with a round of applause. The mayor called for silence and went on, his voice echoing round the Salón de Ciento council chamber.

"Now it is our turn to respond," he said. "What I am about to propose may seem rather drastic, but I beg you not to jump to conclusions. Consider it closely and you will see there is no other way. What I suggest is the following: since Madrid will not heed our arguments but is attempting arrogantly and disdainfully to impose its will, each one of us, as representatives of the people of Barcelona, should challenge the civil servant who corresponds to his rank and kill them in a duel, or die in the defence of our rights and dignity. Here and now I publicly throw down my gauntlet to the floor of this historic chamber and challenge His Excellency the Minister of the Interior to a duel, so that once and for all he and his wretched bureaucrats will understand that from this moment on, when a Catalan is denied justice in any government office, he will seize it with his fist on the field of honour."

With that he threw to the floor a grey kid glove he had bought the previous day in Can Comella and had kept vigil over through the night before the altar in Santa Lucía church. The councillors cheered him to the rafters and gave him a never-ending ovation. Those who had gloves imitated his gesture; those who didn't threw down their hats, starched shirt fronts and even shoes. The poor mayor wept with emotion. He had no inkling that the councillors who so fervently welcomed his idea had not the slightest intention of following his example. Some had already sent letters to Madrid expressing their support for the minister, deploring the mayor's inappropriate tone, and even expressing serious doubts as to his mental well-being. Blithely ignorant of any of this, the mayor sent a letter with his challenge to Madrid. The minister tore it up and returned it in a sealed envelope, on the back of which he had handwritten: *Keep your tomfoolery to yourself.*

The city councillors suggested to the mayor that he shouldn't insist, that there was nothing more they could do, that he should take a holiday. He eventually realised he had been left on his own. He resigned, moved to Madrid and tried to drum up interest in the matter at the national parliament. A handful of members pretended to listen to him out of political expediency: some thought it was a way of winning the Catalans' sympathies, others were hoping for economic reward for their support. When they realised that the ex-mayor was merely a crackpot acting entirely on his own behalf, they indignantly refused to have anything more to do with him. The ex-mayor turned to bribing the most venal among them, wasting his substantial personal fortune on these efforts.

Three years later, ruined and heartbroken, he returned to Barcelona. He climbed Montjuich hill and looked down at the outline of the new streets, the trenches where the trains, drains and aqueducts would run. How is it possible that a simple bureaucratic obstacle can deny the express will of God, he thought. He was so distraught he flung himself from the hilltop and killed himself.

His soul went straight to hell, where it was explained to him that the figure he had seen in his dream had in fact been Satan himself. "Oh, fateful tempter," exclaimed the ex-mayor, filled with remorse at having been so naive, "how you deceived me by saying you were an angel." "Hold on a minute there," Satan objected. "I never said what I was, because as you know we devils can assume whatever guise we wish in order to tempt mortals, apart from that of a saint or angel, far less that of God our Lord or the Holy Mother. That is why I said I was a 'gentleman from Olot', the closest thing I know to being a celestial being. The rest was the result of your vanity and pig-headedness, for which Barcelona and you will suffer the terrible consequences for all eternity." Saying this, he roared with loud, terrifying laughter.

The years that followed were to prove that out of everyone involved in this legend, with the exception of the Devil, who always gets his own way, the mayor was the only one in the right. Despite all its good points, the plan imposed by the Ministry was excessively functional, the product of an exaggerated rationalism. It didn't provide for any open spaces where public events could be held, or monuments symbolising the greatness that every nation seeks, rightly or wrongly, to attribute to themselves. It included no gardens or shady parks to encourage romance and crime; no avenues lined with statues; no bridges or viaducts. Instead, it was a featureless rectangular grid that disconcerted outsiders and locals alike, designed to ease the flow of traffic and the efficient performance of the most prosaic activities. If it had been implemented as initially conceived, the plan would at least have resulted in a city that was pleasing to look at, comfortable and hygienic. As the scheme finally turned out, it didn't even possess these qualities.

Nor could it have been any other way: the inhabitants of Barcelona did not reject the plan as vehemently as the visionary ex-mayor had prophesied, but nor did they take it to their hearts. It did not capture their imagination or awaken any ancestral feeling. They were reluctant to buy plots, were cold and unimaginative when it came to building, and slow to occupy the space they had desired and claimed for centuries: they did so only gradually, driven by demographic pressures rather than fantasy.

Thanks to this general indifference and the connivance of those who could perhaps have prevented it (the same people who behind the back of the demented mayor had sent letters to the minister to protect their privileges) the land ended up in the hands of speculators. They distorted the original scheme and turned the pleasant, healthy new quarter into a noisy, pestilential place as crowded as the old Barcelona that the Cerdá Plan was intended to replace. Lacking a dominant principle (such as the one that a love of God and the Devil's trickery had inspired in the unfortunate ex-mayor) Barcelona was left without a nerve centre (the only possible exception being Paseo de Gracia, which, despite being so bourgeois and pretentious, did at least function for strictly commercial purposes), a focal point where public celebrations, riots, mass meetings, coronations and lynchings could take place. Successive waves of the city's expansion were carried out haphazardly, the sole aim being to find somewhere to put those there was no room for in the already finished sectors, and to maximise their profit out of the operation. The new neighbourhoods ended by segregating social classes and different age groups once and for all. The decay of everything old became the only indicator of progress.

2

Uncle Tonet had aged; he had grown so long-sighted he could hardly see. Even so, he still drove his trap almost every day from Sant Climent to Bassora, and from Bassora to Sant Climent. One day his mare, who was more than eighteen years old, was found dead in the stable. She had never so much as folded her legs to lie down and rest, but now lay there with her legs in the air, limbs all stiff, as if she were trotting in the Antipodes. Instead of retiring as he should have done, Uncle Tonet bought another mare. The new horse didn't know the route: however intelligent a mare may be, it will take her several years to learn such a long and complicated path. Between her mistakes and her driver's poor eyesight, they got lost several times, once with serious consequences. This was when night overtook them and Uncle Tonet had no idea where they were. Earlier in his life, he had found his way by the stars, but now he was ploughing through a fog that grew thicker by the day. Wolves were howling, and he had to whip the terrified mare to urge her forward.

Eventually he spied some bonfires and he urged the horse towards them. He was hoping it would be shepherds, even though the rocky terrain was unsuitable for any livestock. In fact it was a bandit camp: Cornet and his men. These bandits were survivors from the last Carlist wars; rather than lay down their arms, give themselves up to the victors and throw themselves on the mercy of an amnesty, they had chosen to head for the mountains. "If we surrender they'll put us to the sword," Cornet told his men, whose trust and even devotion he had succeeded in winning in the course of that bloody conflict. "I suggest we become bandits. We've escaped death by a miracle up to now; we can allow ourselves the luxury of risking our lives for next to nothing." Convinced by this argument, he and his men went on to display extraordinary recklessness. They evaded all the armed squads sent to hunt them down, and acquired a reputation throughout the region as a band of romantic outlaws. The local farmers and shepherds tolerated them. Weary after several centuries of warmongering being waged around them, they didn't protect them, but nor did they denounce them or shoot them down when they had the chance. The bandits, who had counted on living only a short while and dying with dignity, weapons in hand, ended up growing old in the hills, completely forgotten by the authorities.

When Uncle Tonet stumbled upon their camp, all he found was a group of frail old men who could barely raise their blunderbusses. "I thought you'd disappeared years ago," he told them. "That you were nothing more than a legend." They gave him supper and allowed him to spend the night with them. They said very little to him: they weren't used to talking to strangers and had long since exhausted all conversation among themselves. They knew Uncle Tonet by sight: they had spied on his comings and goings thousands of times, but had never attacked him because they knew he carried essential goods for the country folk.

The next morning they set him on the right track and gave him a hunk of bread and some sausage. Before he left, they took him to see the small burial ground containing the remains of the bandits who had died of sickness in the mountains. There were almost as many of them as there were survivors. On the tombs there were always fresh wild flowers as well as a profusion of crosses: Cornet and his gang were all great believers.

This had happened some time ago: by now the new mare knew the route, and Uncle Tonet was almost blind.

"And yet," he was saying as he finished telling this tale to the traveller who had hired him that afternoon in Bassora, "and yet, as I say, your voice is familiar to me. In fact, not exactly that, but the tone of voice."

The traveller said nothing, and in the end Uncle Tonet couldn't help chuckling. "Of course! You're Onofre Bouvila! Don't tell me it isn't you!" Onofre didn't confirm or deny it, and Uncle Tonet laughed out loud once more. "That shows I'm right. I thought I knew your voice, but your angry silence has convinced me: you're just as crazy as your father, whom I knew well. When he left for Cuba I took him to Bassora in this very same trap. I don't know how old he was back then, but he can't have been much older than you are now, and he gave himself the same airs as you. As if the rest of us were spouting drivel like snot from our noses. When he came back from Cuba I took him home again. The whole village was gathered in front of the church. It's as if I were seeing it right now with these poor useless eyes of mine: your father was sitting exactly where you are now, his back ramrod straight. He was wearing a white drill suit and a straw hat, one of those they call a Panama hat. He didn't say a word over the entire journey. He pretended he was rich, though he didn't have a centavo – but you know that, don't you? Do you know what he brought instead of money?"

"A monkey," replied Onofre.

"A sick monkey, that's right: I see you have a good memory," said Uncle Tonet, using the whip on the mare, which had stopped to eat weeds on the wayside. "Whoa there, *Persa*, don't eat now, it's not good for you." He cracked the whip in the air. "*Persa*," he explained. "that's her name. That was what she was called when I bought her. What were we talking about? Oh yes, your father's conceitedness: he was a cretin, if you want my opinion. Hey, youngster, would you hit an almost blind old man? Well, I can see plainly enough that you would, so alright, I'll hold my tongue, even though that doesn't change what I think in the slightest. I know that's how you people are: you don't like to be told what you don't want to hear. All you want to hear is what you like, even if you know that what you hear isn't what people are really thinking. Bah, that's plain stupid. But don't imagine it shocks or even surprises me: I learned years ago to judge human vanity. I've dealt with lots of people and have had time to reflect on it. Every time I've made this journey alone I've used the time to think. Now I know how things are. I also know I can't change them, whatever I do. I can't and I don't have the time to change things. I'm not even sure I'd want to, even if I did have the power and the leisure to do so. There are people who only see what they want to see. Not me. I could have been like that, but I'm not."

Uncle Tonet carried on like this, with the incoherence that old and slow-witted people sometimes take for wisdom. Onofre Bouvila wasn't listening to him: he was resigned to hearing him drone on, but wasn't paying him any attention. Instead, he was staring at the road he had taken in the opposite direction eight years earlier.

He had set out one spring morning, shortly after sunrise. The previous day he had announced to his parents his plan to go to Bassora and see Baldrich, Vilagrán and Tapera. He was sure they would give him a job in one of their businesses, allowing him to help pay off the debts his father had contracted.

His father had protested: he was the one responsible for the family's difficult situation, and wouldn't allow his son to sacrifice himself . . . Onofre silenced him. His father had long since lost what little authority he once had, so he said nothing. Onofre told his mother he would stay in Bassora however long it took him to save the money they needed. "A few months," he told her. "At most a year." He would write to them straightaway, he promised. "I'll keep you informed of what's happening through Uncle Tonet." In fact, he was already planning to go to Barcelona and never return. He had thought at the time he would never see his parents again or set foot in the house where he was born and had lived until that day.

That day, when he climbed up onto the trap, his father had handed him the bundle containing his clothes; he took it and carefully placed it on the floor. His mother wrapped a scarf round his neck, and since nobody said anything, Uncle Tonet clambered up into the driver's seat and said: "If you're ready, let's go." In response, Onofre had simply nodded, in case his voice betrayed his emotion. Uncle Tonet cracked his whip and the mare set off, digging her hooves into the icy mud. "It's going to be a tough journey," Uncle Tonet told him. His father waved his Panama hat; his mother called out something Onofre didn't catch. He began to look at the road ahead, and didn't see his parents vanishing in the distance.

The trap crossed the river path, the one to the enchanted cavern, the one to go bird-hunting and the one to go fishing, which wasn't the same as the river one, the one to go picking mushrooms in autumn; Onofre had never imagined there could be so many of them. When the valley disappeared in the early morning mist, Onofre could still see the church tower. They passed a couple of flocks of sheep: the shepherds bid him farewell, raising their crooks and laughing. Their faces were muffled in scarves; they wore sheepskin jackets and red woollen caps. The shepherds had known him since the day he was born. Now I'll never meet anybody who knows me the way they do, Onofre said to himself.

On the remainder of their journey they passed many abandoned farmhouses. The cold and rain had left doors and windows hanging open; inside they could see empty rooms piled high with dead leaves. Birds flew out of some of the roofs. These were the homes of people who had gone to Bassora to look for work in factories; they had *let the fire in their hearth go out*, as the expression was in those days.

Eight years had gone by, during which time Onofre Bouvila had done many things. He had met many people, most of them eccentric and nearly all of them wicked. He had ended the lives of some of them, without really knowing why; with others he had formed more or less stable alliances. Now the trees, the colour of the sky seen through the foliage, the whisper of the breeze in the woods and the smell of nature all seemed so familiar to him he felt he had never left the valley, and that everything else was a dream. Even Don Humbert Figa i Morera's daughter, for whom he felt such a passionate desire, now seemed to him a fleeting vision, a lightning flash in his imagination. He had to struggle to recall her features.

"What am I complaining about?" Uncle Tonet said, interrupting Onofre's daydreaming. "Am I complaining about the mist that's closing in around us? No sir. Am I complaining about the weather? No sir. About the poor state of the road? No, sir, I'm not complaining about that either. So what am I complaining about? Human stupidity, of which, as we were saying, your father is a prime example. Why am I so much against him? Out of envy? Yes sir, I'm so against him out of pure envy."

Night had fallen by the time they came to a halt outside the church. Uncle Tonet asked if his parents had been informed of his visit. "No," Onofre said. "Ah, you want to give them a surprise," the old man replied. "No," Onofre responded, "I simply didn't tell them." "Say hello from me," said Uncle Tonet. "I haven't heard anything about them in years, although at one time your father and I were good friends. Have I told you already that I took him to Cuba when he had the mad idea of emigrating there?" Onofre left Uncle Tonet in the village square, groping his way to the tavern, and headed for his parents' house.

His mother was at the front door and was the first to see him arrive. She had gone there by chance to watch the sunset, something she hadn't done for years. After Onofre had left, she had got into the unconscious habit of standing in the doorway at dusk every day, because that was when the trap arrived, if it came. After some time, without mentioning it to her husband, she no longer went to the door: it had dawned on her that Onofre was not coming back. Now that he had, she didn't want him to think she indulged in such an absurd habit. "I'll go and heat up supper," she said. "Where's father?" asked Onofre. She pointed inside the house.

Onofre's first impression was that he had aged a lot. Time hadn't stood still for his mother either, but he was too young to realise his mother could change as well. His father was still wearing his drill suit, which by now was threadbare and frayed, yellowing from so many washes and shapeless after all the darning and patches. He was sitting staring at the table: when he raised his eyes, they brimmed with tears. His expression didn't change, as if nothing untoward had happened. He waited for his son to break the silence. It was obvious the boy must have a powerful reason for coming home, but when Onofre said nothing, he asked a bland question: "How was the journey?"

Onofre replied, "Fine." Silence fell again, while his mother watched them closely.

"You're very well dressed," his father said.

"I'm not giving you any money," Onofre cut in. His father turned pale. "I hadn't any intention of asking you for any, my boy," he muttered, in order to say something. "In that case, keep quiet," Onofre snapped. His father understood that in his son's eyes he had become nothing more than ridiculous. He jumped up and said: "I'll go into the yard to look for eggs," and went out, taking with him a low stool. He didn't say why he needed it.

Left on his own with his mother, Onofre looked all round the room. He already knew it was bound to seem smaller than he remembered, but was surprised to see how poor and ramshackle it was. He saw his old bed, next to his parents': it was still made, as though it had been slept in the night before. His mother anticipated his comment: "When you left, we felt very lonely," she said apologetically. Onofre dropped into a chair, weary from the jolting journey; the bare wood jolted him again. "So I have a brother?" His mother lowered her eyes: "If we'd known where to write to you . . ." she said eventually. "Where is he?" Onofre asked, as if to say, let's get this farce over with once and for all. His mother said he would soon be back.

"He's a great help," she said after a long pause. "You know what farm work is like. Your father's no good at it: he's never been a farmer, not even as a young man. I suppose that's why he went to Cuba. He's suffered a lot," she insisted, as though talking to herself. "He thinks he's the one to blame for you leaving. When he saw the months go by and there was no word from you, he made enquiries. He was told you weren't in Bassora, but they thought you were in Barcelona. He borrowed some money and went to look for you. It was the first time he'd borrowed any in years. He spent almost a month in Barcelona, searching everywhere for you and asking everybody for news of you. In the end he had to come back. I felt so sorry for him: for the first time I saw what defeat meant to him. It was then we had the boy; you'll see him any moment now. He's different from you: he's also very quiet, but he's not headstrong like you. He takes more after his father."

"What does he do?" asked Onofre Bouvila.

"Things could have been worse," she said. Onofre knew she was referring to his father and was no longer thinking of his brother. "Those three gentlemen from Bassora who were about to send him to jail – do you remember? Well, they gave him a job so that he could make a living. I think they behaved well, when it came down to it. They gave him a suitcase and sent him off to visit villages and farmhouses to sell this new thing called insurance. His situation was passed on by word of mouth throughout the region; everybody knows him. People come out when they see him arrive in his white suit. Some of them laugh at him, but every so often he sells a policy. Thanks to that and what we earn from the land and our hens, we get by well enough." She stood up and went to peer into the darkness outside. "It's strange he's not back yet," she said, without explaining who she was referring to. The mist had cleared and bats could be seen circling in the moonlight. "It's his health that worries me now. He's getting on, and the life he leads isn't good for him. He has to walk kilometres in the heat and cold; he gets tired, drinks too much and eats only a little and badly. On top of all that, one day four or five years ago he lost his hat. A gust of wind blew it off into a wheat field; he was looking for it until nightfall. I've tried to convince him he should buy a cap, but he won't listen . . . Ah, here he comes."

"I went to get some onions and mint," his father announced as he came in. He was no longer carrying the stool.

"I was telling Onofre about the hat," said his mother. His father laid what he had brought on the table, then sat down, pleased to have something he could talk about. "It was an irreparable loss," he said. "I can't find anything like it in Bassora or Barcelona. An authentic Panama hat."

"I told him about Joan as well," his mother said. His father turned red to the roots of his hair.

"Do you remember," he said, "when you and I went to Bassora to have the monkey stuffed? You'd never been in a big town, and everything seemed to you . . ."

Onofre was staring at the boy who had appeared in the doorway but didn't dare enter. He was the one who said: "Come in and draw nearer to the light so I can see you. What's your name?"

"Joan Bouvila i Mont, if it please God and yourself, sir."

"Don't call me sir," said Onofre. "I'm your brother. You knew that, didn't you?" The boy nodded. "Don't ever lie to me," Onofre warned him.

"Why don't you all sit down?" the mother said. "We'll have supper. Onofre, you say grace."

The four of them ate in silence. When the meal was over, Onofre said: "You don't think I've come back to stay, do you?" None of them answered; the truth was, it hadn't even occurred to them. One look at him was enough to see that was the last thing he would do.

"I've come for you to sign some papers for me," he said to his father. He took a document out of his pocket and left it folded on the table. The older man stretched out his hand, but in the end didn't pick it up. He stopped and lowered his gaze. "It's a mortgage on this house and your land," Onofre said. "I need funds to invest and this is the only way I can get them. Don't worry: you can carry on living in the house and working the land. You would only be evicted if things went badly for me, but they won't."

"Of course your father will sign, won't you Joan?" his mother said hurriedly.

The father signed the contract Onofre had laid on the table without so much as reading it. As soon as he had done so, he got up from his chair and left the room. Onofre watched him go, then glanced towards his mother. She nodded. Onofre went out into the fields to look for his father. He finally found him sitting under a fig tree on a three-legged milking stool – the one he had taken with him earlier that evening. Onofre leaned against the tree trunk, looking at the back of his father's neck, his slumped shoulders. His father began to speak without him asking:

"My whole life I thought . . ." he began, pointing vaguely into the distance, but in fact intending to encompass everything illuminated by the moon. ". . . I thought that everything we can see had always been like this, exactly as it is now, that all this was the result of unchanging natural cycles, seasons that come and go from year to year. It took me many years to realise how wrong I was. I know now that every inch of these fields and woods has been worked on with pick and shovel, hour upon hour and month after month; that my parents and before them my grandparents and great-grandparents, whom I never knew, and generation upon generation before them fought against Nature so that we can live here now. Nature isn't wise as they say, it's stupid, clumsy and above all cruel. But successive generations have gradually altered this Nature: the course of rivers, the flow of their waters, the rainfall and the outlines of the mountains. They've domesticated animals and changed the system of trees and cereals and plants in general. Now what was once destructive is productive. And the result of that huge effort over many generations is what we have in front of us now. Before I could never see that: I thought cities were the important thing, and that the countryside was nothing. Nowadays I think the opposite is true.

"The thing is that working on the land takes an awfully long time; it has to be done little by little, step by step, exactly at the right time, not too early or too late, which means it looks as though in fact nothing much has changed. It's not the same in any city in the world: there the exact opposite is normal. We see at once how big and high it is, and the infinite number of bricks required to raise it from the ground. But we're wrong about that as well: any city can be built in only a few years. That's why people in the country are so different: more silent and more accepting. If I'd understood these things earlier on, maybe my life would have been different, but it was written that wasn't how it was to be. Either these things are in your blood from birth, or you have to learn them the hard way over many years and mistakes."

"Don't you worry, father," Onofre told him. "Everything will turn out just as I said, and I'll repay you in no time."

"Don't think I'm concerned about the mortgage, son," his father said. "In reality, before today I didn't even know this place could be mortgaged. If I had known I'd probably have done so many years ago to try my hand at some business venture or other. If I'd done that, it wouldn't be ours now. But with you it'll be different, I'm sure of that."

"It cannot fail," said Onofre.

"Don't think about it anymore; go to bed," his father said. "You've a long journey ahead of you tomorrow. Wouldn't it be better to stay a day or two?"

"It's already settled," Onofre said.

The following day Onofre set out for Barcelona once more. As he passed through Bassora he had the contract signed by a notary. He had spent the night in his old bed; Joan slept with his parents. In a calmer mood, he contemplated the countryside as he rode back in the trap. Last time, he told himself, I thought I was saying goodbye to these fields forever; now I know I'll never be free of them. Anyway, it's no matter. But if I am to see them often, let's put them to use. That was his entire philosophy in those days: to buy and sell, buy and sell.

3

Though the plans for Barcelona's Ensanche, the controversial city expansion project, appeared to have been pulled out of the Minister of the Interior's hat one fine day, work initially followed a more or less logical course. First to be built on were the areas in the valley – divided into lots – that naturally enjoyed the best water supply, for example those alongside a stream, irrigation canal or riverbank (like the present-day Calle Bruch, navigable until quite recently as far as Calle Aragón) or close to potable water wells or underground springs. Similarly, those plots close to quarries, as this greatly reduced building costs. An area was also seen as desirable if it was on a tram line, or if the train passed through it, and so on.

Wherever for one of these reasons buildings were constructed, the price of land immediately shot up, because in the western world no people is more gregarious than the Catalans when it comes to choosing somewhere to live. Wherever one of them goes, that's where all the others want to go as well. "Anywhere at all," was the slogan, "but all together." Because of this, property speculation always followed the same pattern: somebody bought as many plots of land as he could in what he thought was a likely-looking area and built one apartment block or at most two on one of those plots. He waited for all these properties to be sold and occupied by their new owners, and then put the remaining plots up for sale at a price far higher than he had paid for them. The new proprietors, who had been obliged to come up with a much greater sum than their original valuation, made up for the loss by splitting each plot into two halves, building on one half and selling the other at the price they had paid for the two halves put together. Naturally enough, the person buying this second half did exactly the same, that is dividing it in half; and so on and so on. As a result, the first block constructed in an area was of a more than adequate size; the next one was smaller, until eventually the final buildings were so tiny there was only one apartment per floor, and that was miserable and dark, built of the poorest quality materials and lacking any ventilation, conveniences or services.

These shoeboxes (which can still be seen today) cost twenty-five, thirty or even thirty-five times more than the original outlay for the spacious, sunny and hygienic dwellings built at the start of the building boom. It could be said – and in fact, somebody did – that *the smaller and uglier the house, the more expensive it is.* What in fact happened was the following: the owners of those privileged residences, *residences of the first batch* as they were sometimes known, hastened to sell them once the circle was closed. This meant that, as the minimum price was set according to the highest values – that is, of the smallest, nastiest dwellings – the price of the larger and better ones rose forty, forty-five and even fifty times. Once all the houses of the first batch had been sold, those of the second wave came on the market – those built on half a plot; and so on, until they were all sold. Sometimes this process didn't stop when all the apartments in an area had been sold, but instead a second round of reselling began, and even a third and a fourth. As long as there was someone willing to buy, there was someone willing to sell. And vice versa.

To understand this phenomenon, this fever, it should be remembered that not only were the people of Barcelona an eminently mercantile race, but for centuries they had been accustomed to living as tightly packed as lice. They couldn't give a damn about homes as such and wouldn't have budged an inch for all the comforts of a harem; but the chance to make a profit from one day to the next was like a siren song to them. Not only the well-off indulged in this unbridled speculation – those who lived comfortably and even had a surplus to "put to work" as was said in those days – but also many in less favourable circumstances, who risked their all in an attempt to become rich. The former bought and sold land, properties and apartments (they also bought and sold purchasing options, pre-emption and cancellation rights, established leases and emphyteusis, exchanged and hypothecated rights and obligations, charges and transfers). And yet invariably they themselves lived in rented houses or apartments, since anyone who "sat on his own capital" was held to be a fool. Let someone else keep all their money tied up, they said to themselves. I'll pay by the month and put my money to work.

The less affluent, on the other hand, occasionally found themselves in dire straits, forced to sell their homes at the worst moment and take to the streets with their families, servants and possessions and start a door-to-door search for somewhere to spend the night or to temporarily leave a sick relative or infant and their nurse. It brought tears to the eyes to see them roaming the streets of Barcelona on winter nights or in heavy rain, with their goods and chattels piled up on handcarts together with their freezing children, still muttering under their breath: "I invested so much, I'll make so much and can reinvest so much." The more sensible among them tried not to sell if the situation was unfavourable for personal reasons, preferring to pass up the opportunity for the sake of their family's health or dignity. Often, however, they were not allowed to do this, because that would have broken the speculative circle the whole city was gripped by. As a result, some families changed domicile seven or eight times a year.

None of this meant that everyone who invested money in this way became equally rich or that it was a safe game to play. As with any lucrative investment, there were risks involved. For things to turn out as hoped, the first building constructed in a new area had not only to be sold at a good price, but the new owners or renters had to lend it an air of distinction that made the area attractive to others. Certain very well-reputed families could increase property values if they moved in, whereas others could lower the status of an entire neighbourhood. One such case was a family whose name or nickname was Gatúnez, apparently originally from La Mancha. It was never clear what this sizeable family did or did not do, but it was plain that not long after them moving in, the demand for the homes nearby fell to zero. Since the owners of these properties who wanted to sell them could not prevent the person who sold to the Gatúnez family from doing so, or succeed in annulling the transfer, they had to turn to the painful recourse of bribing the Gatúnezes to leave or purchasing the property they had just bought at whatever price the Gatúnez family demanded. The opposite happened with some elderly couples with a foreign-sounding name, especially former consuls in Barcelona from one of the great powers.

It could also happen that one of the reasons that had privileged the growth of a particular district over another disappeared all of a sudden: the supply of water from a well could dry up, or the railway company that had announced the imminent construction of a branch line to such and such a destination could subsequently change their mind and leave that already developed area completely isolated. In such cases, entire fortunes were lost.

Since some of the factors involved were fortuitous and others not, obtaining rapid, reliable information was of crucial importance. There was nothing to be done about the fortuitous ones, although, blinded by greed, some people attempted to penetrate the mysteries of nature and usually ended up in the clutch of fake dowsers or other unscrupulous shysters who tricked them and led them to financial ruin. Nor was there any shortage of swindlers who claimed to have a friend or relative who worked in one of the public service companies, the city hall or the regional parliament. These fraudsters were paid extortionate sums of money for all kinds of cock-and-bull stories.

It was into this turbulent, uncertain market that Onofre Bouvila cautiously ventured in September 1897. With the money he obtained from mortgaging his parents' land, he was only able to buy a medium-sized plot in an area that apparently offered no great attraction or possibility of development. As soon as he owned it, he put it up for sale.

"I've no idea who'll buy such an out-of-the way place from you," said Don Humbert Figa i Morera, whom he had been polite enough to ask for advice. Don Humbert gave him plenty, all of which Onofre ignored. "We'll see," he replied.

Six weeks went by and only one possible purchaser came forward. He offered the same amount that Onofre had been obliged to pay for the land in the first place. Onofre pulled a face.

"My good sir," he said to the potential purchaser, "you are doubtless having fun at my expense. My plot is currently worth four times its original value and the price is going up day by day. If you don't have a more interesting offer, I beg you not to waste my time."

Perplexed by so self-assured a response, the potential purchaser raised his offer slightly. Furious, Onofre had Efrén Castells throw him out. This left the potential buyer thinking that perhaps what Onofre Bouvila had told him was true. Maybe for some unknown reason that nondescript piece of land *is* worth that much, he thought. To clear the matter up, he made some discreet enquiries, and it wasn't long before he heard a rumour that kept him awake at night: the firm of Herederos de Ramón Morfem had not only bought the plot of land adjacent to the one Onofre Bouvila was selling, but they were intending to transfer their main business there within the year. Good heavens, the potential buyer said to himself. That rogue knows it and that's why he's refusing to sell at the price I offered him. And yet if the news is true, that land will soon be worth not four but twenty times what it is today. Should I make him a fresh offer? Of course, if the rumour isn't confirmed, if Herederos de Ramón Morfem isn't going to move, what will the land be worth? Nothing, a few pesetas. Oh, what a dreadful game of chance property speculation is, the poor purchaser kept telling himself.

He was not mistaken. If the rumour he had heard about Herederos de Ramón Morfem were true, then this meant that the entire city was going to change, because at the end of the nineteenth century there could be no more prominent institution, nothing more solemn and respectable than a high-class confectioners. It was no easy matter to become one of their customers: to join the list of clients could take a lifetime of persistence, a substantial investment and many contacts. Even when one belonged to this select group, a good *tortell* had to be ordered a week in advance; a month for a tray of assorted pastries, a *coca* for St John's Eve in June three months or more; and a Christmas *turrón* no later than 12 January. Although no self-respecting confectioner had tables or chairs, nor served hot chocolate, tea or refreshments, they all had very spacious and elegant foyers, usually in the Pompeian style. The heat in these foyers was stifling due to the proximity of the ovens, and the atmosphere was heavy and cloying. It was here after Mass on Sunday mornings that the high society of each neighbourhood would gather. They chatted for a while, getting ready for their family lunch, which usually went on for four or six hours.

Well, if Herederos de Ramón Morfem quits Calle del Carmen, the potential purchaser told himself, Calle del Carmen and the entire neighbourhood will go down the drain, and the Pla de la Boquería will cease to be what it is now: the focal point of Barcelona. But if it's not true, if Herederos de Ramón Morfem doesn't move, then everything will stay the same . . . And the worst of it is, he groaned, there's nothing I can do to confirm or dismiss these persistent rumours, because if word gets out, then I can forget about my purchase. What a calamity!

In the end his greed outweighed his common sense, and he paid Onofre's asking price. As soon as the deal was struck, he hastened to the confectioners on Calle del Carmen and asked to speak to the proprietors, who received him in a very friendly way. They were the heirs of the legendary Ramón Morfem: Don César and Don Pompeyo Morfem. They wrinkled their flour-dusted brows when they heard the unfortunate purchaser's query. "What? Transfer our business? No, not on any account. The rumours you have heard, dear sir, are completely unfounded," they told him. "We have never had any intention of moving from here, still less to the neighbourhood you mention; there is nowhere uglier or more uncongenial in the Ensanche, or less suitable for a confectioners. Our father would be spinning in his grave," they concluded.

The purchaser then returned to Onofre Bouvila in an attempt to cancel the sale. His hair was dishevelled, and a trickle of saliva was dribbling from his lower lip. "You circulated those wretched false rumours; now you owe me compensation." Onofre Bouvila let him blow off steam and then turfed him out. That was the end of the matter, because no-one could prove he was behind the rumours, even though everybody was convinced he was. The Herederos de Ramón Morfem Affair became notorious; for a while there was a popular expression: *to be caught like the Herederos de Ramón Morfem fellow*, meaning someone who thought they were smarter than all the rest, buying something at a high price that wasn't worth it, or was worth very little.

"You need to be careful," Don Humbert Figa i Morera warned Onofre. "If you acquire a bad reputation, nobody will want to do business with you."

"That remains to be seen," Onofre replied.

With the profit from that shady deal, Onofre Bouvila bought more plots in a different neighbourhood. Let's see what he does now, the experts in the sector said to themselves. After a few weeks, seeing that nothing was happening, they lost interest in the matter. "Maybe this time he's genuine," they said to one another. The plots of land were in an unappealing district far from the city centre, at what is nowadays the corner of Calles Rosellón and Gerona. Who wants to go and live there, people asked themselves.

One fine day several carts arrived, transporting lengths of metal that the sun glinted off so powerfully that they could be seen by the men at work on the nearby Sagrada Familia cathedral. They were tramway rails. A team of workmen began to dig trenches in the stony ground of Calle Rosellón. On the same corner, another smaller team began to build a rectangular pavilion with a barrel-shaped roof: the shed where the mules pulling the trams could rest.

"This time there's no doubt," people said, "the area's on the up." In three or four days they had taken all the plots off Onofre Bouvila's hands for whatever was his asking price. "This time," Don Humbert Figa i Morera said, "you've had more luck than you deserve, you scoundrel." Onofre said nothing, but laughed up his sleeve: a few days later, the same workmen who had laid the tram tracks dug them up, loaded them back onto the carts and took them away.

On this occasion the merchant and financial groups in the city had to admit the ruse was impressive. When the purchasers came to them in tears, they responded with a sly grin. "You should have asked the tramway company if they were serious about it," they told them. "Why would it occur to us it wasn't for real?" the dupes complained. "We saw the rails and the shed and thought . . ." "Well, you shouldn't have thought," came the reply. "Now, in exchange for a fortune, you've been sold land that's no use even as a rubbish dump, and a half-built shed you'll have to pay to knock down."

This operation, which everybody called the Tram Rails Affair to distinguish it from the other one, the Herederos de Ramón Morfem Affair, was followed by many others. Even though by now everybody was forewarned, Onofre invariably managed to sell the plots of land he bought, in no time at all and at a huge profit. He always came up with some scheme to fool people. He created great expectations in the minds of his purchasers, but these expectations were soon dashed; they were no more than mirages he himself had created.

In little more than two years Onofre became extremely rich. At the same time, he did irreparable damage to the city. The victims of his ruses found themselves the owners of worthless plots of land they had paid huge sums for, and now they had to do something with them. Normally those plots would have been used for cheap housing to be occupied by poor immigrants and their progeny. However, since the initial cost had been so high, they had to be made into luxury residences. It was a very *sui generis* kind of luxury: many of them had no running water, or so little that it only came out of a tap when the other homes had theirs turned off. Others were built on strangely shaped plots and had so many corridors and tiny bedrooms they ended up looking like rabbit warrens.

In order to recoup some of their lost capital, the owners skimped on their construction: the materials were cheap, and the cement was mixed with so much sand and salt that quite a few buildings collapsed only a few months after they had been inaugurated. Land that had originally been designated for gardens or leisure parks, coach houses, schools and hospitals was also built on.

To compensate for the disaster, great emphasis was placed on the facades of these new buildings. Stucco, plaster and ceramics were used to create dragonflies and cauliflowers decorating the walls from the sixth floor down to street level. Grotesque caryatids held up balconies, while sphinxes and dragons peered down from galleries and flat roofs. The Ensanche was populated by mythological beasts that at night, under the street lamps' greenish glow, were truly frightening. Beside ground-floor entrances appeared slender, effeminate angels covering their faces with their wings, more suited to a mausoleum than a family home, or busty, mannish women in helmets and breastplates, imitating the then fashionable Valkyries. The facades were painted in bright or pastel colours. All of this in an attempt to recuperate the money Onofre Bouvila had swindled them out of.

So, from pure necessity, the city grew at breakneck speed. Every day thousands of tons of earth were dug out and taken by endless lines of carts to be dumped behind Montjuich or into the sea. Mixed in with this earth were the remains of more ancient cities, Phoenician or Roman ruins, the skeletons of Barcelona's inhabitants from previous eras, reminders of less tumultuous times.

4

By the summer of 1899, Onofre Bouvila was a mature adult. He was twenty-six years old and possessed a considerable fortune, and yet cracks were already appearing in his burgeoning empire. The electoral chicanery he carried out thanks to Señor Braulio either bore no fruit or cost a huge effort. Following the disasters of 1898, the mood in Spain had changed; a new generation of politicians was raising the banner of reform. They roused popular enthusiasm by claiming they would replace the old social order. Onofre understood that for the moment it would be useless, if not counter-productive, to fight them. He preferred to disassociate himself from the past and give the impression he shared these new trends and ideals.

To this end he persuaded Señor Braulio to retire, as he had become a symbol of corruption. This meant he also separated him from Odón Mostaza, with whom he was still blindly in love. Señor Braulio burst into tears and immediately thought of ways to end his life. He eventually desisted, concerned as he was for the safety of the man he loved.

Odón Mostaza was not very bright, and had not learned how to adapt to their new way of life. He was still a thug, reaching for his revolver at the slightest excuse. Women continued to lose their heads over him, and on several occasions venal officials had to be bribed to cover up scandals. Bodies had to be made to disappear, and justice's palm to be greased. Onofre Bouvila frequently had to bring him to order. "You can't carry on like this, Odón," he would tell him. "We're businessmen now." The thug always promised to mend his ways, but soon went back to his old habits. He oiled his hair, wore loud clothes and, even though he ate and drank freely, he never put on weight. He sometimes won a fortune gambling and would invite anybody he met to join him in what were legendary celebrations. On other occasions he lost everything, racked up huge debts and had to turn to Señor Braulio for help. He showered Odón with reproaches, but found it impossible to deny him anything, and covered up all his misdemeanours. What he most feared was that, without his protection, Onofre Bouvila would unleash his anger on his beloved.

On this occasion, Onofre Bouvila went up to La Budallera in a closed carriage despite the heat. He was wearing a black woollen double-breasted suit made for him by a well-known tailor who had his shop on Gran Vía, between Calles Muntaner and Casanova. Onofre had been there several times over the summer for fittings and was now trying it out for the first time, a gardenia in his lapel. He felt ridiculous, but he was going to ask Don Humbert Figa i Morera for his daughter's hand. He had bought a ring in a jewellers on Las Ramblas.

He had only seen Margarita a few times, when she had left her boarding school to spend the summer with her parents at La Budallera. As Onofre was not allowed inside the house, he was obliged to talk to her briefly out in the countryside when there was an excursion, but then they were always surrounded by other people. She regaled him with trivial details of life at school. Accustomed as he was to the salacious gossip of the whores he visited, this foolish chatter seemed to him the language of true love. For his part, he was unable to think of what to say to her. At first he had tried to interest her in his real estate investments, but he had quickly seen she wasn't following a word. They had parted each time with some relief, while swearing to be faithful to one another.

Now he was a rich man and she had left the nuns' boarding school to be presented in Barcelona society that autumn. As Don Humbert's daughter, there was little chance of her being accepted, yet it was always possible that an eligible young man would be dazzled by her charms, succeed in overcoming his family's objections, and marry her: that would legitimise Margarita's position and indirectly that of her parents as well. Fearing her beauty would lead her to triumph among any smart company, Onofre Bouvila was desperate to avoid this danger by being the first to ask for her hand.

"If she sets foot in El Liceo, I'm a goner," he confided to Efrén Castells. The giant from Calella had changed over the intervening years: he no longer chased skirt like a rudderless ship. He had married a young seamstress who was very gentle but strong-willed; they had two children and he had become domesticated and responsible. Even though he would have done anything Onofre asked of him without hesitation, he preferred more serious, legitimate activities. He had followed Onofre's lead and done some property deals; had been shrewd enough to save and reinvest wisely, so that now he was comfortably well-off.

"Talk to Don Humbert," he said to Onofre. "He owes you a lot. He'll listen to you, and if, as I think, he is a man of honour, he will admit his daughter's hand should be yours rather than anybody else's."

Onofre was shown into a small reception room and asked to be so kind as to wait. "Don Humbert is in a meeting," said the butler, who didn't know him. Onofre felt he was suffocating in the small room. It's as hot in here as in Barcelona, he thought, and I'm parched. They could at least have offered me a drink. Why are they being so inconsiderate, today of all days? After what seemed to him a lengthy wait, he left the reception room and went down a corridor with whitewashed walls. As he was passing a closed door, he heard voices and recognised Don Humbert's among them. He stopped to listen. Eventually, fascinated by what he heard and almost forgetting his reason for coming, he flung open the door and entered what turned out to be Don Humbert's study.

The lawyer was with two other men. One was a North American by the name of Garnett, an obese, sweaty man who had betrayed his country by serving Spanish interests in the Philippines during the recent wars, until the outcome had made it advisable for him to make himself scarce for a while. The other was a lean Spaniard with a tanned complexion and a greying moustache, whom the others called simply Osorio. Both he and Garnett were wearing striped suits with white shirts, celluloid collars and no tie, as was the custom in the colonies, and rope sandals. They had their hats laid on their knees – two Panama hats that immediately reminded Onofre of his father, and of the fact that he still had not redeemed the mortgage on his parents' house and land. His sudden appearance led the three men to fall silent; they all turned to look at him. His black suit, the gardenia in his buttonhole and the eye-catching jeweller's box seemed out of place in Don Humbert's study.

After Don Humbert had introduced Onofre to the others, Garnett continued with his story of how on the eve of the naval battle fought in the Philippines in May of the previous year, he had met with Admiral Dewey, the commander of the enemy fleet. He made him an offer on behalf of the Spanish government: a hundred and fifty thousand pesetas if he allowed the Spanish ships to sink the American ones. Their interview took place in a bar of what was then the British colony of Singapore. At first Admiral Dewey had thought he was crazy. "You know perfectly well," he said, "that the Spanish warships are so puny that mine can send them to the bottom of the sea without even coming in range of their guns."

Garnett had nodded and replied: "You know that, and so do I, but Spanish naval experts have assured His Majesty's government that the exact opposite is the case. If the Spanish navy is sunk, just think how devastated they'll be."

"There's nothing I can do about that," was Dewey's answer.

"That is how we lost our last colonies," Don Humbert said when the North American had finished. "And now our ports are over-flowing with returnees . . ." This was true – every day, ships arrived in Spain bringing survivors of the wars in Cuba and the Philippines. They had fought for several years in the malaria-infested jungles and despite being very young, they already looked old. Nearly all of them were ill with tertian fevers. Their families were reluctant to take them in for fear of contagion; nor could they find work or any means of survival. There were so many of them they even had to queue up to beg. People refused to give them a centavo: "You allowed your country's honour to be trampled underfoot, and you have the gall to come and ask for compassion," they would say. Many of the returnees allowed themselves to die of starvation on street corners, lacking the will to go on.

Now any investment in Spain's ex-colonies had to go through middlemen like Garnett, who was a US citizen. The man they called Osorio turned out to be none other than General Osorio y Clemente, the former governor of Luzón and one of the biggest landowners in the Philippine archipelago. Don Humbert Figa i Morera was trying to reconcile the two men's interests and provide the necessary legal guarantees.

Once they had left and Onofre was alone with the lawyer, he outlined the reason for his visit. Inevitably he was extremely nervous, while Don Humbert himself was embarrassed. He had previously spoken to Onofre about the matter, and without committing himself had let it be understood he already considered him as his son-in-law. Now it seemed as though he was trying to find the gentlest way of going back on his word.

"It's my wife," he finally confessed. "It's humanly impossible to get her to give way. I argued until I was hoarse, but her mind is made up, and in these matters, as you yourself will see when you have children, it's the women who rule the roost. I don't know what I can tell you: you'll have to accept it and look elsewhere. Believe me, I'm truly sorry."

"And her?" asked Onofre. "What does she say?"

"Who? Margarita?" said Don Humbert. "Bah, she'll do what her mother tells her to, however much she may regret it. Women suffer a lot for love, but they never compromise their future. I trust you understand."

Onofre didn't say a word, but picked up the jeweller's box and left the house, slamming every door on the way. If they reckon anybody is going to fall head over heels for a silly little girl like her, they have another think coming, he muttered to himself rancorously. You'll come looking for me one of these days, begging me on your knees to forgive you, but I won't, because the most haggard whore in La Carbonera is worth a thousand times more than the lot of you.

But as the carriage rattled over the cobblestones his irritation subsided, and by the time they reached Barcelona he was sunk in a deep gloom. He shut himself in his house and refused to see anyone for a fortnight, attended by a maid he had taken on three years earlier and to whom he paid a ridiculous wage to ensure her devotion. Eventually he agreed to see Efrén Castells. Worried at finding his partner in such an unheard-of state, the giant had made enquiries and was anxious to tell Onofre what he had discovered.

*

Don Humbert Figa i Morera's wife was no fool: she was well aware that no young man from a good family would make the mistake of marrying her daughter Margarita. Yet nor was she willing to hand her over to a pariah like Onofre Bouvila without a struggle. Turning this over in her mind day and night, she finally came up with the ideal candidate for her daughter's hand. On the face of it, her choice made no sense. This candidate was none other than Nicolau Canals i Rataplán, the son of the Don Alexandre Canals i Formiga that Señor Braulio had stabbed to death in his office eight years earlier, on Onofre's orders.

Following his father's demise, Nicolau and his mother had continued to live in Paris, where Don Alexandre, like many other Catalan capitalists of the time, had "put his money to work" in French companies. These stocks and shares, which amounted to a small fortune, were to pass in their entirety into the hands of Nicolau Canals as soon as he came of age. Until then, his mother had administered them prudently and had even increased their value thanks to some sensible, well-judged investments. Mother and son lived quiet lives in a spacious, comfortable town house on Rue de Rivoli.

Nicolau, who was now eighteen or nineteen years old, was a sad young man: despite the passing of the years he had never recovered from the death of his father, whose memory he venerated. He had never got on with his mother, by contrast, although neither of them was to blame. Losing her two eldest children had been a blow the poor woman had never recovered from. She unjustifiably blamed her husband for their deaths and ceased to feel any affection for him. She extended this coldness to her only surviving child. Despite being aware that she was treating him unfairly, she could not help herself. Added to this, Nicolau Canals i Rataplán's physical defect, the problem with his spine that had meant he grew up misshapen, seemed to her a constant reproach for her lack of warmth. From his early childhood, she had done her best to see as little as possible of him, entrusting his care to a stream of nurses, nannies and governesses.

When he came of age, she was reduced by circumstances to living in isolation, her only company a boy she had never loved and on whom she now depended legally and financially, since even the bread they ate was his by law. Nicolau was painfully aware of how much she suffered from his presence and had no illusions about her feelings towards him, and so tried his utmost to avoid any communication with her. Prevented by his physical defect from making friends among his classmates, he lived in almost total solitude. All he had in the world was Paris.

When his mother and he first fled there, Paris had seemed a hostile city to him, its inhabitants little more than wild animals. Then without meaning to, he had gradually become accustomed to everything, and had developed a real passion for the city. Now it was his only joy: to wander along its streets, sit in its squares, roam its districts and gardens, observe people, the light, the houses and the river. Occasionally, on one of his walks, he would suddenly stop on a corner without knowing why, and peer all around him as if seeing everything he knew inch by inch for the very first time. This sensation filled him with such intense emotion he could not prevent tears welling in his eyes. If it were raining, he would close his umbrella so that the Paris rain would soak him. Seeing this anonymous, crippled figure sobbing in the rain tugged at the heartstrings of passersby, unaware that in fact they were tears of joy. On other occasions, a feeling of terror quickly replaced his sense of happiness. Oh, he thought, what would become of me if one day I didn't have Paris, if for some reason or other we had to leave? He was aware that it wasn't his home, and this produced an almost physical sense of rootlessness in him. Between a mother who could not help rejecting him and an adopted city he could lay no claim to, his life was one of constant anxiety. Little did he know how well-founded were these fears.

Don Humbert Figa i Morera's wife wrote Don Alexandre Canals i Formiga's widow a long, rambling letter. Despite the apparent circumlocutions, she soon got to the point. *Forgive me, dear friend, for being so bold as to address you in such an unceremonious manner, but I am sure that your maternal heart will instantly be able to place itself in my position; that it will understand the reason for my rashness when it reads these clumsy phrases, inspired only by the deepest feelings.* She went on to directly outline her plan, in short, that her daughter Margarita Figa i Clarença should marry Nicolau Canals i Rataplán. She was quick to point out that both of them were only children, and therefore the sole heirs to their respective family fortunes. Both, she then insinuated, were as good as banished from Barcelona high society. Then again, what hopes could Nicolau Canals entertain in this regard in Paris, where he would always be a foreigner and a social outcast? *This union, which in my maternal breast I celebrate in anticipation,* she wrote, *would cement the prolonged sharing of interests and aims that has always united our two lineages.* She concluded by saying that *although Margarita and Nicolau have not yet had the opportunity to meet and to get to know one another, I have no doubt that as they are both young, intelligent, physically appealing and dutiful children, it will not take them long mutually to profess the respect and affection upon which true conjugal happiness depends.*

By some means or other she found out Don Alexandre Canals i Formiga's widow's address and sent her the letter. Once she had dispatched it, she informed her husband of what she had done and showed him an almost exact copy of it. Don Humbert could not believe his eyes.

"Damnation, woman! How could you!" he finally managed to

splutter. "To offer our daughter as if she were for sale . . . It's beyond me! Such audacity! And to offer her hand in marriage to the son of my former rival, someone for whose death more than one person claims I am in some way responsible. How shameful! And in what evil moment did it occur to you to say that the poor wretch was 'physically appealing'? Haven't you heard he was born a monster? A half-wit? Reading it makes me want to die of shame."

"Calm down, Humbert," his wife replied, without turning a hair. She was dimly aware of how foolish she had been, but trusted to her good fortune.

Meanwhile, Canals' widow had received the letter in Paris and was reading it thoughtfully in her Rue de Rivoli residence. What an insult, she thought. That scrounger doesn't know the meaning of the word dignity. Under normal circumstances she would have torn the letter into a thousand pieces. She was about to turn forty and all that remained of her former beauty was a serene harmony that could be quickly undermined by bitter remorse. When she weighed up her life, it appeared to her like a rosary of dashed hopes. *Une vie manquée*, she murmured, dropping the letter onto a nearby table and wearily fanning herself with an ostrich feather. As she did so, her bracelets tinkled, and she could hear the constant sound of carriages out in the street. "*Anaïs, sois gentille: ferme les volets et apporte-moi mon châle en soie brodée*," she said to her maid, a black woman from Martinique who always wore a yellow kerchief round her head.

A year earlier the widow had met a poet of obscure origins by the name of Casimir. He was only twenty-two, and had dragged her to the bohemian haunts of Montparnasse, where his ilk met to read their verses and drink absinthe; she had even gone with him to the funeral of the poet Stéphane Mallarmé. Yet she was very conscious of the difference in their ages and financial circumstances, and refused to yield to his advances. He sent her flowers stolen from cemeteries and passionate love sonnets. In the eyes of the world it was an anomalous situation that gave rise to a lot of malicious gossip. So what, she thought. I've been unhappy all my life and now that fate has left this gift on my doorstep, am I supposed to reject it because of what people say? Besides, this isn't Barcelona, she told herself in an attempt to overcome her own resistance. This is Paris, and I'm nobody here, which means I'm free.

All the same, she did nothing, held back by her son's presence: she saw him as the obstacle blocking her path to happiness. If she had openly explained the situation to him, he would have understood and accepted it. He would doubtless have supported his mother in her decision, pleased to at last be able to show her his affection and solidarity as an adult; however, the years of distance and repeated reproaches meant any possibility of sincere communication between them was closed.

Therefore she guiltily considered how she could rid herself of this awkward witness, and reflected on the contents of the letter she had just received. On the one hand, the offer was tempting, but on the other, everything in her told her she should reject it: she suspected that behind this unexpected marriage proposal lay a perverse plot. After all, she told herself, who could possibly want my poor Nicolau for a son-in-law? He's a nonentity, a cripple and a simpleton. What could anybody see in him apart from money? Yes, that must be the reason. And if that's the case, then Nicolau's life would be in danger. If that scoundrel was responsible for the death of my husband, may he rest in peace, there's no reason why he couldn't now also be plotting the death of his heir. It may be that it's some sort of vendetta, one of those repeated acts of revenge that have been carried out ritually in Istanbul for centuries.

This idea occurred to her because at a reception she had met the ambassador to France of Abdul the Red Sultan, the decrepit ruler presiding over the definitive ruin of the once fabulous Ottoman empire, which for decades had already been known as "the sick man of Europe". This ambassador, a follower of Enver Bey and therefore of the "Young Turks", never wasted an opportunity to discredit the state he was meant to serve, and from which he received splendid remuneration. In fact, he was a living example of the moral collapse that he and his fellow revolutionaries claimed to wish to remedy.

She shivered and drew the Manila shawl her servant had brought tighter round her shoulders. She pulled the bell cord, and when Anaïs answered her call, asked if her son was at home. "*Oui madame*," came the reply. "*Alors, dis-lui que je veux lui parler; vas vite,*" she told her. She wanted to be friendly towards him, to discuss the matter as equals, and yet she couldn't hide a look of dismay when she saw him come into the parlour.

"What's this?" she said, in a strained voice. "You're in your *robe de chambre* at this time of day?"

Nicolau hastily apologised: he was not going out and had decided to spend the evening reading. But if she had something else in mind . . . "No, no, that's fine," she said. "Go on, off you go, I've got a dreadful headache. I don't want to be disturbed until morning."

She locked herself in the study, where she composed and tore up drafts of a letter until the small hours, before she finally hit upon a tone she deemed appropriate. *Your letter, dear friend, produced in me a mixture of gratitude and confusion which you will be the first to comprehend,* she wrote. *I have always been of the opinion that in matrimonial affairs it is for those directly involved to decide, guided above all by their feelings, and that it is not for us, their mothers, to impose our opinion, however unselfish our wishes may be. Etc.*

When Don Humbert Figa i Morera's wife read this, she realised she had carried the day. However evasive, the letter established a common language and opened the way for dialogue and negotiation. She showed it to her husband, feeling genuinely proud of herself. He didn't understand a thing.

"It says here, a wedding, on no account," was all he could find to say.

"Oh, Humbert! Don't be such a dolt," she chided him. "The mere fact that she replied implies a yes, even though her reply says no. It's women's wiles."

Nicolau Canals i Rataplán's mother presented him with a *fait accompli*. He hadn't seen any of this coming, and put up only a feeble defence.

"Bah!" she interrupted him, tapping her foot nervously on the parquet floor. "What do you know about life? I, on the other hand, have years of experience; I've suffered a lot, I'm your mother and I know what's good for you," she said. Then she added, feigning conviction: "And what's good for you is to go to Barcelona and get married to that girl. There's nothing to stop you being happy."

"But do you know who these people are, mama?" Nicolau stuttered. "They're the ones who had papa killed."

"That's just gossip," she cut in. "Besides, the girl wasn't involved. She must have been a child back then. And what's done is done. That was many years ago; we can't always live with the burdens of the past, can we?"

Nicolau Canals i Rataplán went out for a walk and only returned to their residence on Rue de Rivoli at dusk. He went straight in to see his mother.

"I don't want to get married, mama. Not to that girl, whom I'm sure is admirable, and not to anybody else. Nor do I want to go and live in Barcelona. What I want is to stay here with you. We're happy here in Paris aren't we, mama?"

She didn't have the courage to tell him that no, she wasn't happy, and that it was his fault, that he was in the way. "That has nothing to do with the matter under discussion," was all she said. "You're too old to be clinging to your mother's skirts," she added. Nicolau finally glimpsed the truth and spread his arms in what he intended as a gesture of acquiescence.

"If it's living with me that upsets you," he said, "I can go and find an attic in Montparnasse."

After prolonged debate, they reached an agreement: Nicolau Canals i Rataplán would go to Barcelona and make the acquaintance of Margarita Figa i Clarença. It was only then, when they knew all the facts, that they would make a final decision. He could choose to return to Paris if he so wished. This represented a great concession on his mother's part, but she didn't feel strong enough to demand anything more. This move, which she saw as cruel but necessary, had led her to realise how close she was to her son despite everything. She was keen to be free of him, but now as he was about to leave, she was again filled with the direst forebodings.

Meanwhile, all of this had come to the ears of Onofre Bouvila. From his self-imposed reclusion he was busily thinking up a strategy to head off this disastrous turn of events.

5

First, he found out where Osorio, the ex-governor of Luzón, and his American agent Garnett were staying. He learned the North American had a suite in the Hotel Colón, in those days situated in Plaza Catalunya, beside Paseo de Gracia. Onofre was also told that he took all his meals at the hotel and only ventured out in an enclosed cab that came to pick him up twice a week – on Tuesdays and Thursdays – and left him at the front door of an opium den in

Vallcarca, where he spent the night. The next morning, the same cab took him from the opium den and deposited him back at the hotel.

This famous opium den, the last of these notorious establishments in Barcelona, was the haunt of gentlemen and a good number of society women, as well as dressmakers and their apprentices. It was not then known that opium and its by-products could lead to addiction: its use was neither penalised nor frowned upon. Many of the young women ended up in prostitution to procure a pleasure that their modest incomes did not allow them to acquire often enough. In general, the men in charge of opium dens also managed clandestine brothels where it wasn't hard to find underage girls.

Garnett spent the rest of his time shut in his hotel suite reading the adventures of Sherlock Holmes. These were as yet unknown in Spain, but were very popular in Britain and the United States, from where he had them sent by American Express.

For his part, Osorio y Clemente had rented an apartment on Calle Escudellers, which was fashionable at the time. He lived there with only a Filipino servant and a Pomeranian for company. He attended Mass every morning in San Justo y Pastor church, and in the afternoons went to play a game of cards at a bullfighting *aficionados'* club frequented in the main by retired military men like him, top officials posted to Barcelona, and high-ranking police officers.

Onofre Bouvila decided to approach Garnett. He went to see him in his hotel and immediately explained his plan. "Osorio is finished," he said. "He's old and the tropical climate is unforgiving. If something unfortunate were to happen to him, you could see to it that the properties Osorio owns, rather than passing on to his heirs, fall into my hands, for example."

The North American screwed up his eyes. He was sipping a mixture of lemonade, rum and soda water.

"Legally it's more complicated than it seems," he said eventually.

"I know," Onofre said, showing him a sheaf of documents. "I've got hold of a copy of the contracts you two signed with the lawyer Figa i Morera."

"We would need Don Humbert's co-operation," Garnett said, glancing at the contracts.

"I'll take care of that," Onofre said.

"And who will take care of Osorio?" Garnett asked.

"Me as well."

The North American said he preferred not to say any more on the subject. "Come and see me in three or four days," he said. "I have to think it over."

At the end of the fourth day, the two men met again. On this occasion, the North American revealed his reservations. "If something happens to Osorio ... how did you put it? 'Something unfortunate' – that's right, if something unfortunate happens to him, doesn't everything point to me being involved in his misfortune?"

Onofre Bouvila smiled. "If you hadn't raised that objection," he said, "I myself would have cancelled our agreement. Now I can see you're a prudent man who has weighed up all the eventualities. Let me explain my plan."

Once he had finished, Garnett declared himself satisfied. "Now let's talk percentages." They soon came to an agreement about that as well.

"Naturally," said Onofre Bouvila as he got up to go, "there is not, nor ever will be, any written record of what we've discussed."

"I've dealt with people like you before," Garnett said, "and I know a handshake is enough."

The two men shook hands.

"As for silence . . ." said Onofre.

"I know what it's worth," Garnett said. "I won't say a word to a soul."

Efrén Castells meanwhile, loyal as ever to Onofre, had once more turned on his charms as a seducer behind his wife's back. He had won over a young maidservant in Don Humbert's household and thanks to her knew everything going on behind closed doors. In this way he and Onofre could closely follow the tortuous path leading to Don Humbert's daughter's wedding to Nicolau Canals i Rataplán. As Don Humbert had predicted, the mother's will had triumphed over her daughter's feelings. Margarita tried to rebel, but could do little faced with her mother's intrigues. Instead of abruptly announcing things as the Parisian widow had done with her son, she gradually wrung concessions from her daughter.

In this she had an advantage: she was aware of the relationship between her and Onofre, whereas her daughter thought she knew nothing about it. This meant Margarita could not use that as a reason for her aversion to her mother's plans; she was frightened that in doing so she would harm Onofre. As a result, she was unable to raise any serious objection in response to all her mother's ambiguous hints. Therefore she first accepted that her parents and Canals i Formiga's widow should correspond with one another, an exchange that gradually became a series of matrimonial concessions; then, committed to the marriage in writing, she had no choice but to consent to the betrothal. Step by step she allowed her fate to be sealed.

"Bah, don't start with your qualms now," her mother would say whenever she attempted to refuse to do something. "This doesn't commit us in any way, and it's only polite we answer."

"Oh, mama, you said the same the last time, and the one before that, and the one before that. So, without committing myself, as you say, I'm already on the steps of the altar."

"Nonsense, child," her mother retorted. "Anybody listening to you would think we were still in the Middle Ages. You have the last word, you silly goose: nobody is going to force you to do anything you don't want to. But I see no reason to reject out of hand all the kindness shown us by that charming woman and her son, an intelligent, honest and rich young man."

"And hunch-backed."

"Don't say that until you've seen him. You know how people like to exaggerate the defects of others. Besides, physical beauty becomes wearisome over time. Beauty of the soul, on the other hand . . . what can I say? . . . I suppose you appreciate it more each day. But don't make me go on talking, because all this commotion exhausts me!" She walked along the corridor ringing a little bell to call a maid, then asked for a bowl with water and vinegar, and some linen cloths she could press against her brow and temples. "You're going to be the death of me, all of you! So ungrateful, dear God!" Margarita could think of no way to get round her.

Efrén Castells was able to inform Onofre of all these arguments.

"Fine," Onofre Bouvila finally said to him one day. "Now is the time to take action."

On the chosen night they found the garden gate open. The porter, the gardener and the gamekeeper had been bribed; the dogs had been muzzled. Efrén Castells was carrying a five-metre-long ladder; every few strides he had to stop to stuff a handkerchief in his mouth to stifle his laughter. "What on earth is wrong with you?" asked Onofre Bouvila. The giant replied that this absurd situation reminded him of the good old days: "When you and I went round stealing clocks and other things from the World Fair's warehouses. Remember?" "Bah, who thinks about that anymore," Onofre retorted. Eleven years had passed since then, and here was Efrén raking up the past. Roused by their voices, the dogs began to bark, and Don Humbert appeared on the first-floor balcony in a silk dressing gown. "What's going on down there?" he shouted. The porter came out of his lodge and doffed his cap. "Nothing, señor, the dogs must have seen an owl."

After Don Humbert returned inside, Onofre and Efrén Castells renewed their approach to the house. "To me it seems like yesterday," the giant said. The maid was waiting for them, her white apron and cap standing out against the ivy on the front wall. Pointing to a window, she raised her hands to her cheek to mimic someone fast asleep. Efrén Castells leaned the ladder against the wall and checked it was firmly set. "You two wait for me here," Onofre said. "Don't move until I come down." The giant from Calella held the ladder while Onofre climbed up. He was not as agile as he had once been: he didn't want to look down in case he felt giddy. Damnation, he thought. It seems like yesterday to me too. He was roused from these reflections when he felt a blow to his hip: his revolver butt had banged into a rung of the ladder. He took it out of his pocket and whistled. When he saw Efrén Castells raise his head, he dropped the gun and the giant caught it in mid-air.

Onofre soon reached the window, but found it was shut. Neither the heat nor the health recommendations that often appeared in the newspapers in those days had induced Margarita to sleep with the window open. He had to knock several times before her drowsy, bewildered face appeared. "Onofre!" she exclaimed. "It's you! What does this mean?" He gestured impatiently. "Open the window and let me in," he said. "I have to talk to you." At this, the giant and the maid hissed at them from down below. "Hey, you two, keep your voices down!" they warned them. "With all that noise you're going to wake the whole house."

Margarita opened the window an inch or two and brought her mouth down to the gap. Her loose hair fell round her shoulders, its coppery colour contrasting with the white skin of her throat. The heat had made some curls stick to her brow. Onofre couldn't remember ever having seen her look so beautiful.

"Let me in!" he said, his voice thick with desire. Margarita blinked in alarm. "I can't do that," she whispered. Now that they were face to face they both found it hard to know what to say. Onofre could feel his blood start to boil the way it had when he had smashed the mirror with the alabaster statue. "Is it true you're going to marry a hunchback?" he asked with such venom it terrified her. For the first time, she understood the enormity of what her mother was proposing. "Good Lord!" she murmured. "What can I do? I don't know how to avoid it." Onofre smiled. "Leave that to me – just tell me you love me." Margarita clasped her hands together and raised them above her head, as if imploring the heavens to come to her aid. Closing her eyes, she flung her head back, just as she had done years earlier when Onofre had held her in his arms for the first time. "Oh yes, oh yes!" she said in a hoarse voice that seemed to come from deep within her breast. "Yes, my love, my life, the man I love!"

Onofre let go of the ladder and thrust his arms in through the narrow opening. His fingers tore at her nightdress and exposed her bare white shoulders. His movement was so violent he risked losing his balance. Seeing this danger, Margarita grabbed him and pulled him towards her: out of sheer desperation she succeeded in bringing him sprawling headfirst into the room. Without knowing how, the pair found themselves entwined on her bedroom floor. She could feel his panting breath on her bare shoulders and, swooning but with no regrets, gave herself to him.

Whilst they spent the rest of the night consummating their long-repressed love, the train in which Nicolau Canals i Rataplán was travelling to Barcelona arrived at Port Bou. There all the passengers had to disembark, as the gauge of the tracks in France was different from that in Spain. Nicolau asked how long it would be before this manoeuvre was completed and the other train set off. He was told it would take half an hour, maybe more, and so he decided to stroll along the platform to stretch his legs and work the stiffness out of his joints. From Paris to the border he had been forced to share his sleeping compartment with a fellow who at first said he was a travelling salesman, and then a consular agent. He had pestered Nicolau first with his chatter and later with his snores. No matter, Nicolau told himself. I wouldn't have been able to sleep anyway.

Leaving the station behind, he came out onto an esplanade, from which he could see the Mediterranean bathed in the sharp, unrelenting dawn light. He was setting foot in Catalonia for the first time in years, and he felt foreign: all he could clearly recall of Barcelona was the memory of his father, of afternoons when he left his office and took Nicolau for turns on a merry-go-round lit by paper lanterns and pulled by an aged horse. It was a small, shabby contraption that still seemed to him the most beautiful thing in the world. As he gazed out at that clear, limpid dawn, he felt he was nearing the end of his days, that he would never return to the misty, rainy Paris he had come to love so much. He shivered, then shrugged. Inclined as he was to hypochondria, he was used to gloomy thoughts and sudden fits of melancholy, and had learned not to lend them much importance. The sun was high in the sky by the time the train left for Barcelona.

Efrén Castells was staring anxiously up at the window. The household will soon start to stir. We'll be discovered in the most compromising situation possible. What are we to do? he was thinking. He had spent the night keeping watch in the garden with the maid and had been unable to control himself. "It's the scent of the jasmines," he whispered to her, "and the smoothness of your skin." Now the maid was naked and in tears behind a bush, so distressed she could not struggle back into her uniform. Her tears were well-founded: as a result of this moment of madness she would become pregnant and lose her job. When this happened she went to ask Efrén for help; he was so worried that the tale might reach his wife's ears that he turned to

Onofre Bouvila. "Pay her what's necessary and tell her to keep quiet," was his advice. The giant did as he suggested, and in due course a boy was born. Years later this boy, who had inherited his father's size and strength, came to play for FC Barcelona, founded in the year he was conceived, alongside Zamora, Samitier and Alcántara.

When Efrén tried to give Onofre back the revolver he had thrown down to him, he refused to take it. "From now on," he said, "I've no intention of carrying a weapon. Others can do it for me."

Nicolau Canals i Rataplán installed himself in a large, airy room at the Gran Hotel de Aragón. He took breakfast on the balcony, looking down at the colourful bustle on Las Ramblas. Breathing in the aroma from the flower stalls and listening to the different birds singing in their cages had restored his good spirits. He put the forebodings he had experienced at Port Bou down to a lack of sleep. I'll spend a few pleasant days here, then I'll return to Paris, he said to himself. A change is as good as a rest; I'll appreciate Paris all the more and it's likely my absence will lead mama to welcome me with affection.

This last conjecture was not far from the truth. By now, his mother regretted having let him leave. A few days after his departure she had gone in search of Casimir and taken him to her home on Rue de Rivoli. "You'll be fine here," she told him, "I'll take care of you, and you'll be able to devote yourself to writing." At midnight she woke with a start and saw he was no longer beside her. Throwing a peignoir on over her nightdress, she left her bedroom to look for him. She found him standing at the window in the parlour, apparently staring fascinated up at the stars.

"*Qu'avez-vous, mon cher ami?*" she asked. When Casimir made no reply, she stole up to him and took his hand in hers. The young poet's hand was burning: she instantly realised that in the space of a few days she had lost her son and her lover.

The next day she wrote to Nicolau: *Come back to Paris. What we are doing is madness. You should know, Nicolau my child,* she added, *that for some time now I've had a lover by the name of Casimir. I never dared tell you about him because I was afraid you wouldn't understand; in this too I have been unjust towards you. I wanted to force you to accept a marriage proposal that you found as repugnant as I did, but I did so out of selfishness, because I thought that with you gone I would recover my freedom. Now Casimir is dying of consumption and I'm going to be left completely alone. The years are weighing on me, and I need you at my side.*

This letter, which in any other circumstances would have delighted Nicolau, reached him too late. Don Humbert Figa i Morera's family had returned from their La Budallera summer home when he wrote to tell them of his arrival in Barcelona. He sent a note to Don Humbert's wife with his respects and accompanied it with a bouquet of flowers.

"There's no denying the boy is well educated," she said. The following day they sent Nicolau an invitation to join them that evening in Don Humbert's box during the interval, to share refreshments. It took Nicolau some time to realise this was an invitation to the Gran Teatro del Liceo, where there was an opening night they presumed he was bound to be attending. He had to send a bellboy to purchase a stalls seat, and get the hotel to iron his dress suit as quickly as possible. Because of his misshapen figure it had taken a great deal of effort to make this suit, and however well it was ironed, he always looked a fright in it.

When he arrived at El Liceo he found it cordoned off by three lines of police. He wondered whether there had been another bombing similar to the one committed five years earlier in the same opera house by Santiago Salvador, an attack he had heard a lot about from the Catalans who occasionally turned up at his Rue de Rivoli home when visiting Paris. In fact, on this occasion it was because there was a state visit by Prince Nicolas I of Montenegro, who had deigned to grace with his presence this opening night that marked the culmination of Barcelona's Fiestas de la Merced. Nicolau reached his seat just as the gas lights were being dimmed and darkness gradually filled the magnificent auditorium. That evening saw the premiere of *Otello* by Giuseppe Verdi. In Paris in recent years, Nicolau had become an enthusiastic follower of Claude Debussy, whom he considered the greatest musician in history apart from Beethoven. He had devotedly attended the first performances of all his works, apart from *Pelléas et Mélisande*, when an unfortunate head cold had obliged him to remain in bed. He had complained so much that his mother had gone out and bought him the musical score. Following this had helped him recover.

Now Verdi's music seemed to him noisy and bombastic. I shouldn't have come, he thought, but when the lights came up he went to fulfil the social obligation he had tacitly agreed to. Completely ignorant of anything to do with Barcelona social life, he had to ask in the corridors which was the Figa i Morera family's box. As he made his way there, he became increasingly hot and bothered. What the devil am I doing, going to eat from the hand of my father's murderers, he asked himself. He was hoping the box would be full of people and that his presence would go unnoticed. But in it he found only Don Humbert, his wife Margarita and a liveried waiter carrying a tray with cakes and *petits fours*. Nicolau was unaware that Don Humbert had sent out many invitations and received an equal number of excuses. Now there were just the four of them: Nicolau stammered the customary polite phrases.

"Coming as you do from Paris, this must seem very provincial to you," Don Humbert's wife said, taking the tray from the servant and offering it to him.

"No madame, not at all, quite the contrary in fact," Nicolau replied, thankful for this show of friendship from his hostess.

The waiter served champagne, and they toasted Nicolau's pleasant stay in Barcelona. "A stay which we hope will be as happy as it is prolonged," said Don Humbert's wife, her eyes twinkling. The husband is a cheap self-made man, Nicolau thought, she is a pretentious fishwife, and the daughter an apprentice *cocotte* whom her parents are trying to sell to the highest bidder. At that moment the gong for the resumption of the opera sounded, and he used that as an excuse to try to escape. Don Humbert took him by the arm.

"Out of the question," he said. "You must stay in our box. As you can see, we have more than enough room, and you'll be a thousand times more comfortable here than in a stall seat. Come now, I won't hear of any objection: it's already settled."

Nicolau was forced to accept, taking a seat immediately behind Margarita. When the lights went down again and the curtain was raised, silhouetted against the glow from the footlights he could see the curve of her shoulders, exposed by her evening gown. Margarita's hair was done up in a thick chignon, held in place by a diadem with small, regularly shaped pearls, leaving visible the nape of her neck and a small area of her back. Nicolau fixed his gaze on her shoulders and let himself drift along to the music; the champagne had brought on an agreeable sense of lethargy.

After his return to the hotel, he took the table and wicker chair he usually had breakfast on out onto the balcony, picked up writing materials, lit the lamp and breathed in the warm air of Las Ramblas. From time to time, the rumble of the last cabs broke the silence. *Tonight,* he wrote, *while we were listening to Verdi's* Otello *in your distinguished parents' box, I was tempted to lean forward and kiss your shoulder. I know that would have been an unforgivable act, and therefore I restrained myself. It could also have been the only way for you perhaps to come to love me some day, although for that to happen I would need to be a different man, one who allowed himself to be carried away by impulse rather than being intimidated; not one who is so cowardly as to confess his guilt by letter. But I am not ashamed to confess the whole truth: it was only with extreme reluctance that I accepted the proposal for us to be linked by marriage, a proposal formulated I am sure without your consent. When I did so, little could I suspect that tonight as we were listening to Verdi's* Otello *I should fall in love with you, completely against my will.* He paused, raised the pen to his lips, thought for a moment, then went on: *This complicates matters a great deal for the future.*

Putting down the pen, he got to his feet, picked up the lamp and went into his bedroom. Standing in front of the mirror, he raised the lamp as high as he could: the looking glass reflected his image, still dressed in his evening clothes. For the first time in his life he was envious of those who had no visible physical defects. Rather than feeling sorry for himself, he was angry. "Take a look at yourself," he muttered, speaking to the figure he could see in the mirror, "you look as if you've just wet yourself . . ." He went back onto the balcony and picked up the pen once more. *I know now,* he wrote, *that I'll never return to Paris.*

By the time he had finished putting down the jumble of ideas and feelings careering round his brain, the letter ran to several pages. Day was dawning, and Nicolau had to put on his dressing gown to ward off the damp morning chill. Street sellers were already setting up their stalls on Las Ramblas when at a quarter to eight he finally finished and folded up the letter without rereading it, then put it in an envelope. A chambermaid came in with his breakfast.

"Would you like to have it on the balcony as usual?" she asked.

"Don't go to any trouble," he replied. "You can leave it where it is. I'll deal with it. But could you please have this letter sent to the address on the envelope and make sure it is delivered directly to the person indicated?"

"A letter has arrived for you as well, sir," said the maid, pointing to the tray.

Nicolau picked it up, thinking it would be from his mother. A glance was enough for him to realise that in fact it came from Margarita. "You may go," he told the maid. "What about your letter, sir?" she asked. "I'll bring it down to the desk myself," said Nicolau. Margarita's letter was as long as his. She wasn't able to sleep last night either, he thought. She began by excusing herself for being so bold as to write to him. She confessed to having had some doubts about him and his intentions, but that night, in the box at El Liceo, he had seemed to her *an educated, sensitive and generous person.* That was why she now dared beg him for help, she wrote. *For years now I have been in love with a man, and he has loved me in return,* the letter said. *He is of humble origin,* she went on, *but I have given him my heart in secret, as well as something else I cannot mention.* The situation that her mother, *doubtless inspired by the best of intentions,* had created for everyone involved was a mistake, one which Nicolau must have found extremely disagreeable. *If you don't help me in this difficult moment, my whole life will be at an end. I do not possess the strength to fight destiny all alone.* She ended by writing: *Dear friend, will you do this for me?*

Nicolau tore up the letter he had spent the entire night writing, and immediately composed another, shorter one. In it he thanked Margarita for her sincerity and begged her to consider him from that moment on *as a loyal, selfless friend. I forbid you to use with me any tone of entreaty, which I in no way feel I deserve,* he added. *It is I who must beg you to abandon your resigned, fatalistic attitude. We all have a sacred duty to be happy, even if to achieve it we are sometimes forced to do violence to the circumstances we find ourselves in,* he concluded.

Rereading his letter, he found it presumptuous and insincere. Further attempts produced no better results. He freshened up, put on a suit and went down to the hotel lobby. "Make sure," he told the receptionist, "that a box of chocolates and my card is sent to this address." Nicolau scrawled a few polite phrases in which he thanked the Figa i Morera family for their kindness the previous evening in their box at El Liceo.

He called for a carriage and had himself driven to San Gervasio cemetery. This was some way out of the city, and by the time he arrived mid-morning, the atmosphere was close and stifling. When he got there, he had to ask which was his father's tomb. For security reasons, he had not attended his funeral. In fact, he and his mother had chosen not to leave Paris, where they had arrived a few days earlier. It occurred to him now that he didn't even know who had organised it. Perhaps it was the murderers themselves who had arranged the burial rites. He gave a tip to the gravedigger who showed him the way. The man began taking bites out of a greasy roll, making little effort to hide the fact. Nicolau had not eaten any breakfast, and he felt a stab of hunger. He almost offered the gravedigger money to share the crude lunch he was busily devouring, but was immediately ashamed of having such a grotesque idea in a place like this, outside his father's tomb, which he was visiting for the first time. "Forgive me, papa, there's nothing I can do to avoid it," he muttered in front of the mausoleum, on the door of which was written in bronze lettering: CANALS FAMILY. "I'm desperately in love," he added, a lump in this throat. The gravedigger was still standing beside him.

"How many people can fit in here?" he asked, pointing to the mausoleum.

"As many as necessary," came the answer. For some reason, his reply reassured Nicolau. He was convinced the premonition he had experienced a few days earlier in Port Bou would soon be realised – the same premonition that the voice of reason had dismissed back then.

"Make sure there are always flowers here," he told the man. "I'll be visiting from time to time."

He climbed into the hire carriage waiting for him on a patch of level ground. There had been no rain for a fortnight, and his shoes sank into a layer of dust whitened by the sun. Back at the hotel, he was handed another letter. This one was indeed from his mother: it was the letter telling him about Casimir and his illness, the letter in which she begged him to return to Paris. *Circumstances dictate that for the moment I must postpone my return indefinitely,* he replied that same day. He expressed his sincerest wishes for Casimir's swift and complete recovery, even though he had not had the pleasure of meeting him. *I trust I will soon be able to make amends for that shortcoming. Like you, I think he should be offered all the care his illness requires, without concern for the cost,* he added. *You may dispose of all my assets as you see fit, mama: they are yours as well,* he concluded the letter, *but do not ask me to return to Paris now. I shall soon be twenty years old, and it's time for me to lead an independent life.*

That same afternoon, Don Humbert Figa i Morera paid him a visit in his hotel.

"I have come to see you, dear friend, as both lawyer and father," he said without more ado. "If your intentions towards my daughter are serious – and I have no reason to doubt it – there are many matters we need to discuss regarding your position and your means."

Nicolau looked at Don Humbert offhandedly. He was thinking: Doubtless these scoundrels noticed the effect their daughter has on me, and now they want to raise the price of the merchandise. While he would readily have made his contempt plain to Don Humbert, he knew this would mean losing Margarita forever. It's only through the complicity of these despicable, money-grabbing parents that I can see a glimmer of hope, he reflected. Yet he couldn't accept that either. The same weakness of character that prevented him from renouncing his impossible love and leaving for Paris straightaway now prevented him from seizing this opportunity thanks to what he saw as reprehensible subterfuge. If I loved her as she deserves, I wouldn't hesitate to sell my soul to the Devil, he thought. The stark choice stunned him so much he decided to respond evasively to everything, to gain time. It was not hard for him to feign a naivety that had been genuine until the previous day.

"I thought my mother and your wife had settled all these matters," he said. In any case, he couldn't deal with this until he had held a series of meetings with his bankers in Barcelona. Don Humbert quickly changed tack: in fact, he had simply come to the hotel to greet him as he was passing nearby, he insisted: "I wished to thank you personally for the chocolates you were kind enough to send, and to make sure you have everything you need."

While the two men were talking, Onofre Bouvila, who was aware of all his rival's movements, was about to put his plan into action. Two days before, he had received a coded message from Garnett, the former governor of Luzón's North American agent: "Everything ready, awaiting instructions." Onofre Bouvila rang a little bell, and a secretary appeared.

"You rang, sir?" the secretary asked.

"Yes," Onofre said. "I want you to search for Odón Mostaza and have him brought here."

The following morning, Nicolau Canals was awakened by a noise; he did not need to be told that what he heard was gunfire. Then came hasty footsteps and shouts. The commotion lasted only a few seconds. Jumping out of bed, Nicolau threw on his dressing gown and foolishly went out onto the balcony. A man standing on the adjacent one told him what had happened.

"The anarchists have killed a policeman," he said. "They're carrying away his body on a stretcher right now."

Nicolau rushed downstairs and out into the street, but all he could see was a throng of curious onlookers gathered around a pool of blood. Everyone was talking at once; he could glean nothing very clear from their confused, fragmentary reports. This incident made a great impression on him; for the first time he felt part of the life of the city. That same afternoon he went to a tailor on Calle Ancha by the name of Tenebrós and ordered several suits. Next he visited Roberto Mas's shop on Calle Llibretería, where he bought dozens of shirts and other items of clothing. Everything suggested he was fitting himself out to spend the winter in the city.

On his return to the hotel, he found an invitation waiting for him: the Figa i Morera family requested his presence at dinner on the following Saturday at their home, now situated in Calle Caspe. I ought not to go, he thought yet again. This is the last opportunity I have to clearly and unequivocally show my rejection of their dubious proposal. But then he remembered Margarita's shoulders and feared he would die of sadness. He replied at once to say he would be delighted. As a gift he sent them a goldfinch in a gilded cage. He had been told it was a very rare and precious species: it came from Japan and sang exotic tunes filled with nostalgia.

6

In that same week, Osorio, the former governor of Luzón and a disgrace to the military establishment, received a package in the post. Inside was a dead turtle, its shell painted crimson. When he saw the turtle, the ex-governor's Filipino manservant turned pale. Osorio shrugged the incident off in front of his servant, but that same afternoon mentioned it to Inspector Marqués, one of the police officers who frequented the bullfighting club. "Among the tribes of Malaya," he told him, "this signifies vengeance."

"It's possible somebody bears you a grudge from your period in office over there," the inspector said.

"Stuff and nonsense, my friend," the former governor retorted. "My record is beyond reproach. It's true that in fulfilling my duties I necessarily created a handful of enemies, but I can assure you that none of the people I upset has the money to pay for the journey to Barcelona."

"Be that as it may," Inspector Marqués said, "the fact is, we cannot take action simply on the basis that you received something unpleasant in the post."

A few days later, the ex-governor received a second package. This time it was a plucked chicken with a black ribbon tied round its neck.

"The sign of the *piñong*," his manservant said with a shudder. "We're as good as dead, general sir. Resistance is useless."

"I talked to my superiors about that dratted turtle affair," Inspector Marqués said, "and as I told you, they were reluctant to get involved. They suggested you look on the bright side. Of course, now, with the chicken on top of the turtle . . . I'm not so sure."

"My dear friend," the ex-governor cut in. "Last time I didn't want to lend too much importance to what I took to be a joke in bad taste, but with the hen, this is no longer funny. I beg you to ask your superiors to show the interest and attention that my person, if not the case, merits."

When the inspector came back with his superiors' reply, he found Osorio staring wild-eyed and quaking in his boots. "Anyone would think you've been visited by all the souls in purgatory," he said.

"This is no laughing matter: things have become extremely serious," the ex-governor said. That morning he had received the third and last package. In it was a dead pig dressed up in an aubergine-coloured satin tunic. The parcel was so heavy it had to be carried in a handcart to his home on Calle Escuders. He had protested at having to pay extra, arguing that the postage covered delivery to his address. "Yes, but not the use of a handcart," he was told. When he saw the pig he no longer had any desire to continue arguing. He paid what they were asking and closed all his shutters and windows. He took his service revolver out of a trunk, loaded it and stuck it into his waistband in the colonial style. Then he boxed the ears of his manservant, who had wetted his uniform. "Be brave," he had told him. "You're a dead man, your honour," his servant had replied, and although he tried to hide it, Osorio was frightened as well. He knew from experience that the Malays were a kind, happy and extraordinarily generous people, but they could also be violent and cruel. During his time as governor he had presided over ceremonies that the government back in Madrid had chosen to tolerate so as not to lose the tribal chiefs' goodwill. During these ceremonies he had witnessed atrocious acts of cannibalism; he now recalled how the warriors covered in war paint would belch savagely at the end of these abject feasts. He imagined those same warriors hidden behind the plane trees on Las Ramblas, or in the porches of the elegant houses on Calle Escuders, their fearsome krises clenched between their teeth. He conveyed his fears to Inspector Marqués, who promised to relay the ex-governor's exact words to his superiors. He didn't dare tell him his superiors never paid him the slightest attention; he had led everybody at the club to believe he was held in much higher esteem than was in fact the case.

Nicolau Canals could neither eat nor sleep, and constantly felt an indistinct pain that no medicines or entertainment could alleviate. That Saturday he arrived at Don Humbert's house feeling extremely weak. A liveried servant opened the carriage door and helped him down, but the cane caught between Nicolau's legs, he stumbled on the carriage step, and eventually the servant had to carry him bodily to the door, returning to pick up his top hat. Nicolau handed it, the cane and his pair of gloves, to a maid in the vestibule. This girl was none other than the one Efrén Castells had seduced, who was already suffering the first symptoms of pregnancy. All this has happened to me thanks to a wretch like him, she thought as she took Nicolau's things. Everyone is staring at me as if I'm some weird creature, thought Nicolau, noticing the way the maid was glaring at him, as though he were a fairground freak.

He was the first to arrive: his Northern European punctuality had not yet been contaminated by Spanish tardiness. Not even the lady of the house was ready: she was still in her bedroom, shouting contradictory orders at her maids, dressmaker and hairdresser, constantly insulting them for no apparent reason.

Don Humbert did the honours in a drawing room that engulfed the two men. He excused his wife light-heartedly: "You know how women are about these things." Nicolau asked anxiously if Margarita would also be late. "Oh no," said Don Humbert. "This afternoon she felt a little indisposed, and doesn't know whether she'll come down for dinner or not. She begged me to apologise to you." Despite realising he was committing the most unpardonable breach of etiquette, Nicolau buried his face in his hands and burst into tears. Seeing this, and at a loss as to how to react, Don Humbert chose to ignore it. "Come with me," he said. "We have plenty of time and I want to show you something I'm sure will interest you."

He led Nicolau to his study and there showed him a mechanical telephone he had just had installed. It was a very rudimentary apparatus comprising of a wire and two mouthpieces at either end, that only allowed one to communicate with someone in the room on the far side. A pane of glass from each window had been removed and replaced by a thin pine wood board, with the wire running through the centre. The board transmitted the sound to the other end. When a greater distance was involved and the wire had to turn a corner, it was necessary to avoid it coming into contact with any solid objects that would prevent the transmission of the sound. In these cases, the wire was suspended from another wire.

By the time they returned to the drawing room, the lady of the house had made an appearance. She was wearing a long dress, a profuse amount of jewellery and an overpowering wallflower perfume. Despite putting on weight, she still preserved the striking beauty that had allowed her to make her way in life. As soon as she saw Nicolau Canals she was all sweetness and light, attempting to enfold him in the snares of seduction, calling him "my son" and demonstrating a theatrical, cloying tenderness. All this humiliation, Nicolau thought, and I won't even see her tonight. He fought to keep the tears from his eyes a second time.

The arrival of other guests rescued him from this embarrassing situation. On this occasion, Don Humbert had made sure some people did accept his invitation. "He's young and has always lived abroad," he had told his wife. "He won't know the difference." These guests were a corrupt city councillor – for whom Don Humbert had secured the only post he could occupy without problems, given his lack of ability – together with his wife; a ruined self-styled marquis whose gambling debts Don Humbert had purchased years earlier in an inspired moment and who ever since had proved useful for adding glamour to such events, accompanied by his spouse, Doña Eulalia "Titi" de Rosales; Father Valltorta, an alcoholic priest with bushy eyebrows; and a professor of medicine whom Don Humbert recompensed in exchange for fake opinions and prescriptions, and his wife. Such was the sad circle to which he had been reduced by Barcelona high society.

Nicolau Canals gave monosyllabic answers to whatever was said to him; nothing he had to add interested them anyway, so his lack of response was not seen as discourteous. Soon the others began to talk among themselves and left him in peace. His hostess occasionally urged him to eat more, but he left the exquisite dishes he was served untouched on his plate.

After dinner they all went back into the drawing room, where there was a grand piano. Don Humbert's wife, aware of Nicolau's musical passion, insisted he play for them, and he agreed to play a few pieces, knowing that none of them would pay him any attention anyway. Reluctantly, he played several Chopin études he knew by heart. When he finished, the other guests applauded rapturously. As he turned round to acknowledge applause he knew was insincere, the blood ran cold in his veins. She had come in. Margarita was wearing a simple organdie gown with a broad scarlet belt round her waist. Her only adornment was a wrought-silver brooch at her neckline, with a flower attached. Her coppery hair was done up in a braid. Coming over to the piano, she murmured an apology for not having been able to join them for dinner; she had felt faint in mid-afternoon and had not been strong enough to come down until now. He believed her every word without question.

"I was listening to you play," she said. "I didn't know you were an artist."

"Nothing more than an amateur," he said, blushing. "Is there any piece in particular you'd like to hear?"

Margarita leaned over the piano as though to leaf through the sheet music. Nicolau could feel the warmth of her body against his back, and her bare arm brushed his cheek. His mouth immediately went dry from a desire to kiss it. "Didn't you receive my letter?" he heard her whisper in his ear. "For the love of God, tell me: didn't they give you the letter I sent to the hotel?" Out of the corner of his eye,

Nicolau could see her beseeching face; he pretended to concentrate his attention on the keyboard. "Yes," he said at last. "Well then," she asked, "what's your answer? Can I count on your generosity?" He made a superhuman effort to respond: "I've lost control of myself," he replied. "I can't sleep or eat and I feel ill all the time. When I don't see you I get a terrible pain in my chest. I can't breathe. I feel I'm suffocating and am about to die." "Well then?" she insisted. "What is your answer?" Good heavens, Nicolau thought. She hasn't heard a word of what I've just said.

As he was leaving Mass at San Justo y Pastor church, retired General Osorio y Clemente was hit by three bullets from a revolver fired from a closed carriage. He had just stepped down from the church stairs and fell dead on the flagstones of the square. Somebody threw a bunch of white flowers out of the carriage window; they landed a few metres from his body. Afterwards, eyewitnesses recalled the most striking aspect of the shooting: as soon as he heard the first shot, the deceased's Filipino manservant ran to the far end of the square. There he did something very odd: kneeling down, he took a curved stick about thirty centimetres long out of his pocket and pushed it into a hole in the ground. In this way he succeeded in lifting a manhole cover that gave access to the city's sewers. He disappeared down it, never to be seen again. The police later claimed that this behaviour proved he was complicit and had helped plan the crime. Others said he had started plotting his escape the day his master received the dead turtle. He had discovered and memorised the exact position of all the manhole covers in the part of the city where the two of them usually strolled, and always carried the curved stick with him.

A few days prior to this incident, Señor Braulio had felt suddenly uneasy, without being able to explain it. I have a terrible foreboding,

273

he said to himself, peering into his mirror. Over the years he had grown obese; now when he dressed as a woman he looked like an elderly matron. He had also grown a short Teutonic-style moustache which made him look more comical than sensual as a transvestite. Even those who in days gone by had laughed at his antics now censured him. Others saw signs of senility in his conduct – what in those days was called a "softening of the brain". Some attributed this to the blows he had received during his nights of revelry.

Everybody remembered the case of the Danish boxer Andersen, much in the news following his recent visit to Barcelona. For years this boxer had challenged the French, German and British champions. He had always lost: without exception they had given him a tremendous hiding. Now he was being dragged from city to city: in Barcelona he was exhibited in a cane and canvas booth erected at Puerta de la Paz. The advertising posters claimed his was a case worthy of scientific study, but in fact unscrupulous managers were exploiting his misfortune. He had returned to childhood, shaking a rattle in his enormous paws and drinking milk from a baby bottle. For a few pesetas, spectators could go in and see him and ask him questions. For a few more, they could have a pretend boxing match with him. He was still a powerful man, broad-chested, with colossal biceps, but he could move only very slowly, his legs barely supporting the weight of his body, and he was almost blind, despite being only twenty-four years old.

Of course, Señor Braulio was nothing like Andersen; he was in excellent health. The passage of time had deprived him of his looks, and he had aged since Onofre Bouvila had forced retirement on him. At the same time, his little manias, his cowardice and his abrupt mood swings had also become more accentuated. At present he was mainly concerned about Odón Mostaza. With no work or money, the thug was leading an increasingly dissolute life. When Señor Braulio reprimanded him over this, he replied insultingly: "You're a fine one to talk. You've spent your life peddling your arse in La Carbonera, and now you come preaching to me." "That's how I lost my wife and daughter," Señor Braulio replied. "Two poor innocents who had to pay for my madness."

Odón Mostaza never listened to him. One day he heard that Onofre Bouvila wanted to see him; he flew to his office. The two friends embraced warmly clapping each other on the back. "It's been years since we last met," said Odón Mostaza. "It's impossible now you've become such a bourgeois. Oh, those were the days," he exclaimed. "Do you remember how we took on Joan Sicart?"

Onofre smiled and let him reminisce. When Odón finally fell silent, he said: "Time to get back in the ring, Odón. We can't rest on our laurels. I need you." Odón's face lit up with a wolfish smile. "Thank God," he said. "My old pistol was getting rusty. What's this about?" Onofre Bouvila lowered his voice so that nobody could hear what they were plotting, not even their respective bodyguards stationed on the street corners. "An easy job, I've got it all planned, you're going to like it," Onofre told him.

On the appointed day, Odón Mostaza went out very early. He hailed a carriage and told the driver to head for the city outskirts. When they reached a certain spot, he levelled his gun at the coachman and told him to get down. One of his men sprang out from behind a bush and bound the coachman hand and foot, thrust a rag in his mouth and gagged him. Then they blindfolded him and knocked him unconscious. The miscreant who had appeared from behind the bush donned the driver's cape and climbed up on his perch. Odón Mostaza got back inside and drew the curtains, then removed the false beard and tinted glasses he had worn so that later on, if the worst came to the worst, the coachman wouldn't be able to identify him.

As Onofre Bouvila had instructed, he bought a bunch of lilies on

Las Ramblas. Inside the closed carriage, they gave off such an intense perfume he thought he would be sick. He checked his revolver was in good working order. The church clock was striking the hour when the carriage entered the square. As this was a weekday, only a few worshippers were coming out of Mass. Pulling back the curtain a little, Odón poked the gun barrel out. When he saw the ex-governor and his manservant appear, he calmly took aim. He allowed Osorio to descend the steps, then fired three times. The Filipino was the only one who reacted instantaneously. As the carriage set off again, Odón Mostaza remembered the flowers. He knocked on the roof for the driver to slow down, picked the bunch of flowers up from the seat and threw it as hard as he could out of the window. By now he could hear loud shouts and stampeding footsteps, as everyone tried to escape.

A few days later the police arrested him when he was coming out of a brothel in the early morning. Knowing he had a watertight alibi, he made no attempt to resist. He was so polite with the police officers they soon realised he was making fun of them. "Laugh all you like," the sergeant told him. "This time you're going to pay for everything you've done." Odón replied by puckering his lips and blowing him kisses, as if he were a whore rather than a police sergeant. This only exasperated the officer still further. The other policemen, who were aware of Odón's reputation, did not take their eye off him. They kept their guns levelled, and had their batons ready just in case. Some of them were very young: they had heard of Odón Mostaza even before they joined the force. Now here they were, taking him to court in handcuffs.

When the judge asked him where he had been on such and such a day at such and such a time, Odón Mostaza didn't turn a hair. He simply repeated the pack of lies he had agreed with Onofre Bouvila, the alibi they had prepared precisely for questions like these. The judge repeated the questions time and again, and the court clerk wrote down the always identical replies, which the judge then read, perplexed. "Are you making fun of me as well?" he said at length.

"Your honour should keep these tricks for cheap crooks, socialists, anarchists and queers," the thug said. "I am Odón Mostaza, a professional with many years' experience; I'm not saying another word."

A short while later, seeing that the interrogation was beginning again as if he were deaf or an idiot, Odón added: "Is your honour trying to make a name for himself at my expense? You should know that many others have tried to do so in the past. They all wanted to be the judge who put Odón Mostaza behind bars. They all dreamed of seeing their name and picture in the newspapers. They all made fools of themselves."

This judge went by the name of Acisclo Salgado Fonseca Pintojo y Gamuza. He was thirty-two or thirty-three years old, with round shoulders, a bull neck, bushy beard and a pale complexion. He spoke slowly and raised his eyebrows whenever he was spoken to, as if everything surprised him. "Tell the court where you were on such and such a day at such and such time," he repeated. Odón Mostaza flew off the handle.

"Let's put a stop to this grotesque comedy!" he shouted in the courtroom, not caring if other prisoners could hear him or not. "What do you want from me? Is it money? Because your honour should know right now that I've no intention of giving you any. I know the story: I give you a hundred today, and tomorrow you'll be asking for a thousand. You can't touch me: you have no proof or witnesses, and I have the perfect alibi. Besides, everybody knows the ex-governor Osorio was killed by Filipinos."

The judge raised his eyebrows in bewilderment. "What ex-governor?" he asked. "What Filipinos?" It took Odón Mostaza some time to take in the fact that he was not being accused of the murder of the ex-governor, but that of a young man called Nicolau Canals i Rataplán, of whom he had never heard.

On the morning of the day in question, a man swathed in a cape, wearing a wide-brimmed hat that shielded his face, had run past the desk at the Gran Hotel de Aragon so quickly the clerk couldn't stop him. By the time the clerk had sent several hotel employees and two policemen who were patrolling the busy area of Las Ramblas after him, the intruder had vanished somewhere on the upper floors. He was never found. Some said he had climbed down the outside of the hotel, and that beneath his cape he was carrying a length of rope with a grappling hook he used for the descent. Others, alleging that no passerby had seen anything of the sort, insisted he had bought off the hotel staff.

The only trace of his fleeting presence was the dead body of Nicolau Canals i Rataplán, who had been stabbed three times, each thrust dealing a mortal wound. Nicolau was buried the following day in the family mausoleum, next to the remains of his father, also the victim of murder. His mother did not attend the funeral: the last remaining child of that branch of the Canals family was gone.

The judge held up the hat and cape. While Odón was in the brothel, the police had searched his home. They had found these items of clothing, together with a switchblade, on which could still be seen traces of blood, even though it had been cleaned. Completely at a loss, Odón continued to deny the charges, obstinately repeating the story of the turtle, the hen and the pig. As the judge said in his summing-up, "The accused was clearly deranged." Odón was forced to put on the hat and cape and parade in front of the hotel receptionist, whom the judge had ordered to appear in court. The clothes fitted perfectly, while the receptionist confirmed Odón was the person he had seen rush past the front desk.

Odón promised one of the court officials money if he got a

message to Señor Braulio. *I don't understand any of what's going on*, he wrote, *but there's something fishy about this*. Señor Braulio went to see Onofre Bouvila. "We'll get him the best defence lawyer in Spain," Onofre assured him. "Wouldn't it be better to resolve this mess privately?" Señor Braulio said. "Before it reaches the higher court?"

The lawyer who undertook Odón's defence was called Hermógenes Palleja or Pallejá. He said he came from Seville and had just joined the legal association in Barcelona, where he wanted to open an office, although in the end he did not do so. Most of the witnesses called by this defence lawyer failed to appear. They were loose women, who disappeared the moment the police came looking for them. Since they had no identity papers and were known only by nicknames, they simply had to change domicile and names to erase all traces of their past.

The three women who did appear in court created a lamentable impression. They said their names were the Sow, the Farter and Romualda the Gobbler. In the courtroom they lifted their skirts, winked at the public, used filthy language and burst out laughing at the slightest excuse. They said, "Yes, darling; no, my love," to the prosecuting counsel; the presiding judge had to call them to order several times. All three stated they had been with the accused on the morning in question, but when cross-examined by the prosecution and even the defence lawyer they contradicted themselves, and ended up confessing they were unsure about the date, time and the person involved.

Odón Mostaza, who had never set eyes on these trollops in his life, but could tell that their testimony was harming him, asked to speak to his lawyer. Palleja or Pallejá claimed to have other urgent clients to attend to, and did not go to visit him in his cell at the Palace of Justice, where he had been transferred for the trial. This Palace of Justice, inaugurated in the previous decade, was built on what had been the grounds of the World Fair, where Odón Mostaza had first met Onofre Bouvila. He was the one on whom the thug was now pinning his hopes of salvation.

However, Onofre showed no sign of being concerned: whenever Señor Braulio went to consult him, at his wits' end after attending the sessions of the trial among the public crowding into the courtroom, Onofre came up with all kinds of excuses not to see him, or if he did do so, turned the conversation to other matters.

The public prosecutor had called for the maximum penalty, and in the end the court condemned Odón Mostaza to death. "Be patient," his lawyer told him, "we'll appeal." He did so, but failed to file the appeal within the allotted time, or made such a hash of the paperwork that the Appeals Court threw the case out.

Alone in his cell, Odón Mostaza grew desperate. He stopped eating and could hardly sleep. Whenever he did manage to drift off, he had terrible nightmares and woke up screaming. The prison guards forced him to be quiet, laughed at his fears and every so often went into his cell and beat him savagely.

In the end Odón underwent a conversion. He realised that by being punished for a crime he had not committed he was in fact paying for the many crimes for which he had escaped justice. He saw the hand of the Almighty in this, and from being a boastful disbeliever, became pious and humble. He asked repeatedly to see the prison chaplain, and confessed his innumerable crimes to him. The memory of his former life, of the quagmire of vice he had wallowed in for so many years, made him weep disconsolately. Despite having received absolution from the father confessor, he did not dare appear in the presence of his Maker. "Trust in His infinite mercy," his confessor said. Odón now always wore a purple habit, with a grey rope hanging round his neck.

Señor Braulio went to see Onofre Bouvila once more. When

admitted to his office, he fell to his knees on the carpet and spread out his arms in a cross. "What is this farce?" Onofre asked. "I'm not moving from here until you listen to me," Señor Braulio replied. Onofre rang a bell; when his secretary appeared, he told him he was not to be disturbed. Once the secretary had closed the door behind him, he lit a cigar, leaned back in his chair and said: "Tell me what this is all about."

"You know why I'm here," Señor Braulio said. "He's a wicked man, but he's also your friend. He was always at your side in difficult moments. You've never known anyone more loyal. And I," he said, his voice cracking, "have never known anyone more handsome."

"I don't know where all this is leading," Onofre Bouvila said.

"I can understand you wanted to teach him a lesson. I'm sure he's learned it once and for all. I'll vouch for him in future," Señor Braulio said.

"What do you want me to do?" Onofre replied. "I've brought in the best lawyers in Spain. I've moved mountains. I'm willing to beg His Majesty for clemency . . ."

"Onofre, don't try to hoodwink me," Señor Braulio cut in. "I've known you for years. You were a snotty kid when you arrived penniless at my boarding house. I know you're behind this. Because you're evil, because there is nothing and nobody you wouldn't sacrifice to get what you want, and also because deep down you've always been envious of Odón. But this time you've gone too far, and you're going to have to put things right whether you want to or not. Look at me: I'm on my knees imploring you to save the life of that wretch. My heart is like that of Our Lady of Sorrows, pierced by seven daggers. Do it for him, or for me."

When Onofre did not respond, Señor Braulio lowered his arms and clambered to his feet. "Well then," he said, "you've asked for it. Listen: in recent days I've been making enquiries: I know that you and Garnett, with Don Humbert's aid, have been doctoring all the representation contracts Osorio signed, so that now all his possessions in the Philippines practically belong to you. I also know that persons in your pay have recently bought a turtle, a hen and a pig, and that they sent heavy packages through the post. None of this will acquit Odón of the crime he is supposed to have committed. On the contrary, an investigation into Osorio's death will make plain his guilt. And yet nobody can be killed twice, and Odón is as good as dead as it is. He could take others with him in his downfall, though. You know what I mean by that," he concluded.

Onofre did not stop smiling or puffing contentedly on his cigar.

"Don't take it that way, Señor Braulio," he said at last. "I've already told you I've done everything humanly possible for my friend Odón. Regrettably, my efforts have not brought about the desired result. However, while I was trying to set one prisoner free, by pure chance I've managed to secure the freedom of another. In this drawer here I have the signed pardon for your daughter Delfina. It cost me a great deal in contacts and money, because the authorities were refusing to grant it to her, alleging she was a threat to law and order – something I personally agree with. But now, fortunately, it's been settled. Wouldn't it be a pity if this gesture came to nothing?"

Faced with this unenviable choice Señor Braulio bowed his head and left Onofre's office without another word, tears streaming down his cheeks.

In the chapel for prisoners awaiting execution, two members of the Brotherhood of the Purest Blood of Our Lord Jesus Christ brought in their association's cross and lit six candles. In accordance with the rules of their brotherhood they wore tunics and hoods, black leather belts with rosaries and the shield of the brotherhood embroidered on their chests as an emblem. This brotherhood, whose task was to comfort the prisoner in his final hours and then take charge of his body if he had no relatives to claim it, had been founded in Barcelona in the year 1547 in the Chapel of the Blessed Sacrament (commonly known as the Chapel of the Blood) in the church of Nuestra Señora del Pino. (It was at Number One of Plaza del Pino that the brotherhood continued to be based until recently.)

Odón Mostaza was praying face down on the cold, damp floor of the cell. He was in a remote part of the prison, cut off from the outside world. The only visits he could receive were from the relevant authorities, the prison doctor, priests and members of the brotherhood. Also, as expressly laid down by law, a public notary *in the event of the prisoner wishing to make a will or final statement.* Every minute is like a century, Odón thought, but the minutes and the centuries seemed to go by at the same speed. Silence reigned in the prison: all exercise periods had been suspended, as well as any other indoor activities *that might disturb proper meditation.*

Those who were to witness the execution had already gathered in the prison yard: *the judicial secretary, representatives of the government and judiciary, the warden and such members of the prison staff as he designates, the priests and members of the charitable association aiding the condemned man, and three local inhabitants chosen by the mayor, if they voluntarily agree to be present.* Public executions had come to an end a few years earlier, by a royal decree of 24 November 1894. This measure had given rise to fierce criticism: *In this manner,* we read, *the death penalty in Spain has ceased to be an exemplary lesson but offers nothing in return, since the newspaper reports not only arouse curiosity but surround the criminal with a pernicious aura.*

The three local citizens were closely watching the executioner, who was testing the garrotte. This instrument consisted of a high-backed chair, out of which protruded a tourniquet that ended in a kind of metal noose. This was attached round the prisoner's throat and tightened until he was strangled to death. On 28 April 1828, His Majesty Ferdinand VII had issued a royal proclamation by which, *to commemorate the pleasing memory of the Queen's happy birthday*, death by hanging had been abolished in the whole of Spain. Instead, it was decreed that from then on executions would be *by common garrotte for prisoners of ordinary estate, vile garrotte for those punished for heinous crimes, and noble garrotte for those of gentle birth.* Those condemned to common garrotting were led to the scaffold on a horse or mule, with the hood up above the tunic worn over the rest of their clothes. Prisoners condemned to a vile garrotte were led to the scaffold on an ass, or dragged there, if that had been the sentence, without the tunic. Finally, those condemned to a noble garrotte were led on a horse with a saddle and a black caparison. Of course, these distinctions no longer made any sense after executions ceased to be public.

When Odón Mostaza's cell door opened, he refused to raise his face from the ground, and four hands had to lift him. He murmured "Lord have mercy on my soul," over and over, so as to avoid having to think. Once he was outside, he opened his eyes. Ahead of him walked the members of the brotherhood, carrying the crucifix that had been in the chapel. He could see the pale white light of dawn on a cloudless morning. What did it matter to him whether or not the sun shone that day or any day thereafter? At the far end of the yard he saw the garrotte, the group of witnesses and the executioner, who was standing a little to one side. One of the witnesses tossed the cigarette he was smoking to the ground and crushed it with his shoe. Next to the wall Odón glimpsed a dark wood coffin, its lid leaning against the wall. His knees gave way, but the guards holding his arms prevented him from collapsing. Let it not be said that . . . he thought. He straightened up and lifted his chin. You can let go of me, he tried to say, but nothing came out apart from a whistling sound from deep in his chest. Given the circumstances, I couldn't have asked for more, he joked to himself. Each step he took without falling was a victory.

He dragged the sackcloth tunic across the cobblestones. When he had been dressed in it a few hours earlier in the chapel, he had felt humiliated. "Until now I've always chosen my own clothes," he had joked with his gaolers. By law these sackcloth garments were always black, except for regicides and parricides, who wore yellow tunics and a biretta of the same colour, stained with red. If Odón had been executed a few months later, he would have had no reason to complain, because this sackcloth for condemned prisoners was abolished by law on 9 April 1900.

Odón sat on the chair of the garrotte and allowed them to strap him in. The member of the brotherhood carrying the crucifix brought it up to his mouth. He closed his eyes and pressed his lips to it. He did not notice how someone made a discreet movement of the hand.

Afterwards, as laid down by law, a brief report of the execution was drawn up and signed by all those present. The members of the brotherhood withdrew the body for burial. In the coffin they folded Odón's hands across his chest and placed a silver-plated rosary between his fingers. They closed his eyes and smoothed his hair, ruffled by the wind. Seeing him lying there, they said to one another: "Truly, there was no better-looking man in all Barcelona."

At that same moment at the far end of the city, the side door of the women's prison opened to let Delfina out. Señor Braulio was waiting for her in a closed carriage drawn up next to the prison's gloomy walls. Seeing her cross the threshold, he clambered out of the carriage. Without a word, they embraced one another, in tears. "Daughter, how thin you are," said Señor Braulio after some time. "And you father, are you trembling? Are you feeling well?" she asked.

"It's nothing, daughter," said the former boarding house keeper, "it's probably just the emotion. Come on, climb in. Let's get out of here and go home as quickly as possible. But you're so thin! Never mind, I'll look after you. You'll be surprised how I've changed."

A month after Odón Mostaza's execution, Onofre Bouvila once more asked Don Humbert Figa i Morero for the hand of his daughter Margarita. This time his offer was immediately accepted, without reservation.

CHAPTER FIVE

1

The nineteenth century, ushered in by Napoleon Bonaparte on 18 Brumaire 1799, was now coming to an end on Queen Victoria's deathbed. Beyond the royal bedchamber, the streets of Europe had resounded to the hooves of the Imperial Guard, to the cannon fire at Austerlitz, Borodino, Waterloo and other famous battlefields. Now all there was to be heard was the clacking of looms, the purring and explosions of the internal combustion engine. It had been a century of relatively few wars, but on the contrary an abundance of novelties: a century of wonders.

Now mankind shuddered as it crossed the threshold into the twentieth century. The most profound changes were yet to come, but already people were tired of so much instability, of not knowing what tomorrow would bring; they looked on all change with suspicion, and occasionally with fear. There was no lack of visionaries who imagined what the future would be like, what it held in store for those who succeeded in reaching it. Electrical energy, radiophony, automobiles, aviation, advances in medicine and pharmaceutics were going to radically alter everything – communications, transport and many other areas of life. Nature would be confined to well-defined regions; day and night, cold and heat, would be tamed; the human brain would control chance at will; there were no frontiers the powers of invention could not cross; people would be able to alter size and sex as often as they liked, fly through the air at unheard-of speeds, become invisible at their own convenience, learn a foreign language in two hours, live three hundred years or more. Super-intelligent beings from the moon, the planets and other more distant celestial bodies would come to visit us, compare their machines with ours, and reveal their extraordinary forms to us for the first time. In these visionaries' dreams, the future world would be an Arcadia overflowing with artists and philosophers, a world in which nobody would have to work.

Others predicted nothing but disasters and tyranny. The Roman Catholic Church never ceased to remind anybody who cared to listen that progress did not always follow the path dictated by God's will, as demonstrated in His manifestations and revealed to the Supreme Pontiff, whose infallibility had been proclaimed on 19 July 1870. The Catholic Church was not alone in its aversion to progress; most of the world's monarchs and princes shared its misgivings. In all this change they saw the crack through which the subversion of every principle could seep; it was the herald announcing the end of their era. Only the German Kaiser disagreed: delighted by the fifty-ton cannons being mass-produced at the Krupp factory, he thought: God bless progress if it means I can bombard Paris.

The years sped past in this and similar speculation. In the port of Barcelona one August evening in 1913, Onofre Bouvila was pondering precisely on how quickly time flew by. He had gone there to supervise the unloading of certain crates whose contents did not conform to the bill of lading. The customs officials had been tipped off, and their acquiescence secured for a small fortune, but Onofre did not want to leave anything to chance. While he absent-mindedly watched the unloading, he recalled the day he had come to this same dock looking for work. Back then almost every craft was a sailing ship, and he was still a boy; now he could see funnels and masts swaying gently against the fading light of that late summer evening, and he was about to turn forty.

Solemn and solitary, he regarded the ships moored in the port. A clerk in strict mourning came to tell him the crates were about to be unloaded. "Is there any damage to the packaging?" Onofre asked offhandedly. He had gathered from various sources that war was imminent. If that happened, whoever was in a position to supply the market with arms would make an immense fortune in no time at all. So now he was smuggling into Spain prototypes of rifles, shells, grenades, mortars and other weapons. His agents were already sounding out foreign ministries throughout Europe.

Onofre was not the only one to think this way: he would have to forge new alliances, make new enemies, counter dirty tricks and destroy his competitors. He would also have to deal with spies from the future warring nations, who were already beginning to infiltrate Barcelona in addition to the other big cities around the world. "Why am I doing all this?" he wondered. His first son had been born an imbecile. Delivered on the cusp of the new century with the best care money could buy, it was soon obvious he would never be normal. Now he was vegetating near Lerida in the Pyrenees, cared for by a religious institution Onofre financed generously, but in whose extensive property he never wished to set foot. A second son was stillborn. Two daughters had followed. His love for his wife, which until then had withstood so many trials and tribulations, and had led him to commit so many misdeeds, had not survived these repeated disappointments. Margarita had grown fat, consoling herself for being abandoned by eating cakes and chocolate at all hours. There was always someone to offer her the most tempting delicacies in the belief this would help them win Onofre's favour.

These gifts and the constant adulation shown him were a sign of his wealth and power, but in every other way he was still a social outcast. The prominent members of Barcelona society admired him: to them, money was an end in itself. As far as they were concerned it was never a means to win power; it never occurred to them to use it to take the reins of the country or to shape government policy to suit their own aims. If at times the Catalans had ventured into the closed world of Madrid political life, they had done so reluctantly, possibly in response to pleas from the monarchy. On those occasions they had acted as trustworthy administrators and acquitted themselves worthily, even when this clashed with the interests of Catalonia they had previously defended or even their own best interests. Perhaps this was because deep down they had always seen themselves as a world apart, cut off from the rest of Spain, which nevertheless they did not wish, or did not know how, or were not permitted, to do without. It may also have been because everything happened too quickly: they did not have enough time to establish themselves as a class or mature as an economic entity. Now the Catalan bourgeoisie were becoming exhausted before they had managed to put down roots in History, without having changed its course.

Onofre Bouvila, on the contrary, spent money extravagantly, in an arbitrary way; this arbitrariness and other contradictions created confusion and uncertainty in others. At that moment he was listening to the twanging of the rigging, the creak of timbers, the water lapping against the ships' hulls. Many of them transported his own cargoes to and from the Philippines and elsewhere; some of them he owned. In the eyes of polite Barcelona society, none of this redeemed him from his obscure origins. They turned to him whenever they needed him, but quickly pretended to have forgotten this. His name never appeared on any invitation list.

A year earlier, a group of prominent gentlemen, presided over by his old acquaintance the Marquis of Ut, had come to visit him. They had themselves announced in the most pompous fashion: most of them had had previous, often illicit dealings with him; they had dined at his expense; and yet now once more they were pretending they did not know him and insisted on this pantomime of introduction.

"To what do I owe the honour?" he asked them. They were busily giving up their seats for one another, paying each other endless compliments. "You speak, no, no, on the contrary, it would be much better coming from you." Onofre studied their faces as he waited patiently for them to come to the point. Some had been members of the World Fair Board; they were already powerful magnates back when he was slipping into the grounds of the former Ciudadela at daybreak to distribute anarchist propaganda and sell hair restorer. The other board members were dead by now: Rius y Taulet shortly after the World Fair closed, in 1889. He was followed in 1905 by Manuel Girona i Agrafel, who had been the royal emissary, had paid for the cathedral's new facade out of his own pocket and founded the Banco de Barcelona, whose bankruptcy had ruined so many families and decimated the Catalan middle class. Those still alive were all elderly; not one of them suspected that the man now observing them with such irony and disdain had seen them go past as a boy, hidden behind sacks of cement, as if witnessing a procession he would never be part of.

"We are here," they told him, "because we know full well of your love for Barcelona, this city you honour with your presence and your activities. And also because we are aware of your proverbial generosity."

"Tell me how much you want," he said sarcastically.

"The thing is," they said without blinking an eyelid, like the thick-skinned crocodiles they were, "we have been informed by the Foreign Ministry that a personage of royal blood, a member of a reigning dynasty, is due to pay a visit to Barcelona in the near future. This will be a private visit, which means that from an official standpoint there is no budget for it, as you can appreciate. On the other hand, we cannot permit – and the Ministry itself has made this clear, echoing the wishes of His Majesty the King, may God preserve him ... we repeat, we cannot permit this illustrious visit to take place without a proper reception. In short, the maintenance and entertainment of our illustrious visitor, so we are given to understand, at least, will have to be paid for out of our own pockets."

Onofre's first question was who they were referring to. After much hesitation they told him in the utmost secrecy that it was Princess Alix de Hesse, granddaughter of Queen Victoria, now better known as Alexandra Fyodorovna, wife of His Imperial Highness Tsar Nicholas II. This information left Onofre Bouvila cold; he didn't have the slightest interest in the Romanoffs, whom he considered lazy oafs. He was much more intrigued by the exploits of conspirators such as Lenin, Trotsky and others. He was kept informed of their movements by his agents in London and Paris. It had even crossed his mind to finance their hare-brained projects himself, with an eye to future business deals.

His meeting with the Marquis of Ut and his friends seemed to him absurd. What interest could I possibly have in doing what these people are asking of me, he asked himself. What do I get out of being in their good books? He knew they were no fools. On the contrary, many of them were among the shrewdest financiers. Yet, unlike him, none of them could see beyond the end of their nose, make out what was going on beyond the purlieu of their offices. They knew nothing about the world of the poor, the mad and the blind who lived and reproduced in the city's dark alleyways. Onofre knew that world well, and in recent times had heard the drumbeat of a nascent revolution.

"Leave it to me," he told them. "I'll take care of everything."

They were still spouting their thanks as they descended the stairs. A long line of carriages was waiting to take them back to their mansions on Paseo de Gracia. A soft drizzle made the carriage roofs and the horses' tack glisten. A yellow halo formed round the gas street lights and the carriage lamps. Onofre waved them goodbye from his doorway. My entire fortune and all my prestige will be inherited by my daughters, he thought bitterly, and the louts who take them to bed. It serves me right for marrying an idiot.

Now the tsarina and her entourage were disembarking incognito at Puerta de la Paz. The rain had ceased only a few hours earlier. The puddles on the ground reflected the tops of the leafy plane trees, their boughs swaying in the damp, unpleasant breeze. "A foul day to receive Her Imperial Highness," growled the Marquis of Ut. He was sitting smoking with Onofre Bouvila in his mahogany brougham, drawn by four English horses. Behind them an army of cabs and wagons was waiting to take the imperial entourage to the rooms reserved for them at the Ritz.

Onofre made no reply to the marquis's comment: two days earlier, he had received a letter from Joan Bouvila. He thought it must be from his father, but on reading it, he discovered it was from his brother, whose existence he had completely forgotten. The letter said that their father was on his deathbed. *Hurry up if you want to see him alive*, his brother wrote.

Onofre had not seen his father since the brief visit he had paid to the family home in the autumn of 1907 for his mother's funeral. During the vigil he had noticed that young Joan was missing. His father told him Joan was doing military service in Africa, where there were always conflicts with the Moors. When they returned from the cemetery, the neighbours had left the two men on their own for the first time. "I don't know what will become of me now," his father complained. Onofre said nothing. His father paced round the room, left untidy by the mourners, peering around as though expecting to see his wife reappear from behind a piece of furniture at any moment. "I didn't even suspect she was ill," his father said after a while. "She was hunched over and hadn't had much appetite recently, but I couldn't see any other symptoms. One evening," he said, "I came home and found her lifeless in that little chair she used to sit in by the fire. The water in the pan wasn't boiling, so she couldn't have been dead very long, but when I took her hand it was as cold as ice."

While his father was talking, Onofre had gone round opening doors, poking his nose in everywhere. Like most women in the countryside, his mother never threw anything away. The house was a storehouse of useless objects: he found the remains of old bedspreads, worn-out pots and pans, a broken distaff eaten by termites. He remembered the hardships he and his mother had suffered when his father left for Cuba and abandoned them. "I've got urgent business to attend to in Barcelona," he said out loud. "I have to leave now."

On his way to the village, after he had got off the train in Bassora he had absent-mindedly asked for Uncle Tonet, the trap driver. Eventually somebody told him he had died years earlier. Onofre had hired an open-top carriage, which now stood waiting for him outside the farmhouse, surrounded by chickens and hens. "It's time for me to go," he repeated. His father carried on as if he hadn't heard: "You know, I've been thinking." As he paused for breath, the clucking of the hens and the buzzing of flies accentuated the silence. "I thought," he went on when he saw his son was not going to encourage him to continue, "that I could come to Barcelona with you. You know I've never exactly liked life in the country. I'm more of a city type, and now that I'm all alone . . ." Onofre consulted his watch, picked up his hat and cane and headed for the door, his father hot on his heels. "You know I've been around, I'm not just a country bumpkin," the older man said. "I'm sure you could find a job for me. I could help you in your businesses in a modest way; if I had work, I wouldn't be a burden on you."

Onofre left the house, his eyes fixed on the carriage. The driver, who seemed to be dozing under a cloud of flies in the shade of a fig tree, got to his feet when he saw him emerge, and ran to the carriage. He had not unhitched the horse, and was ready to leave at once. "At your service," he said. He was a broad-shouldered man with a round, shaven head, who had fought in Cuba under General Weyler. "The fact is," Onofre's father said, "you're very busy; I could devote the whole day to the children." Onofre climbed up onto the carriage seat. "I'm sure Joan will be back from Africa before long," he said. "When he arrives, everything will return to normal. I'll contact people in Madrid to make sure he is demobilised as quickly as possible."

The carriage driver untied the reins, released the brake and raised his whip. Onofre's father gripped his son's leg: "Onofre, whatever you do, don't leave me here on my own. I don't know how to look after myself, I won't survive an entire winter sitting by the fire with no-one to talk to. Please, I'm begging you."

Onofre put his hand in the inside pocket of his jacket and pulled out all the money he had on him. Without counting it, he thrust the bundle of notes at his father. "With this you can live comfortably until Joan returns," he said. His father refused the money. "Come on, father, take it; I'll get more when I reach Bassora." This time his father accepted, letting go of his leg to take the bundle. Onofre snapped his fingers at the driver and they set off at a trot.

A face lit by an oil lamp appeared at the Marquis de Ut's carriage window. "Don Onofre, could you come a moment? We've caught someone prowling round here," the man said. "What's going on?" asked the marquis. The man, obviously one of Onofre's agents, did not deign to reply.

"Stay in the carriage in case Her Highness moves on," Onofre told the marquis. "I'll go and see what this is about and be straight back."

He set off after the man, who held the lantern high to light their way. They had to step round coils of rope on the quayside and jump over puddles. They came to a group of five men jostling a sixth person, who had lost his glasses in the scuffle. "Let him go," Onofre ordered. "Who is he?" "We don't know," came the reply. "We've searched him, but he isn't carrying a weapon, only a penknife." Onofre Bouvila confronted the intruder and asked how he had managed to gain access to the dock.

"It's not difficult," the other man replied, beating vigorously at his jacket to smooth it down. "The guards are getting in each other's way."

They could tell from his accent that he wasn't a foreigner. Nor did he look like a Menshevik, a Nihilist or anybody else who would want to harm the tsarina. Onofre asked who he was and what he was doing there. He replied that he was a journalist and named the newspaper he worked for.

"I was walking down Las Ramblas and saw all the preparations. I guessed somebody important or vulnerable must be arriving, so I slipped past the guards and hid behind some crates. Unfortunately I was discovered and mistreated. What are you going to do with me now?" he challenged him.

"Absolutely nothing," Bouvila said. "Actually, you were simply carrying out your duty as a reporter. In this case, however, I would implore you not to reveal anything of what you have seen. Of course, I'm willing to compensate you for any trouble this unfortunate incident may have caused you." Saying this, he took several banknotes out of his pocket, counted out three of them and made to give them to the journalist, who refused to take them.

"I don't accept bribes," he exclaimed.

"It's not a bribe," said Onofre, "it's merely a friendly gesture. I have a very personal interest in this matter."

"That's what I'll put in my article," the journalist threatened. Onofre Bouvila smiled condescendingly.

"I leave that up to you," he said. "I would have preferred us to understand one another better. I've always got on with journalists: I am Onofre Bouvila."

"Oh, I beg your pardon, Señor Bouvila," the journalist said. "How was I to know? I lost my glasses somehow . . . Forgive me for what I said, and you can count on my absolute discretion."

Onofre Bouvila's business affairs had appeared in the press for the first and only time in September 1903. There was mention of some murky expropriations during one of the countless remodellings of the port of Barcelona that never came to anything. Nevertheless, a few individuals had made inexplicable profits in the process. After reading the article, Onofre sent a note to the journalist who had written it: *I should very much appreciate an exchange of views with you,* he wrote. The journalist replied with another very short note: *You choose the place, as long as it's not early morning in San Severo.* This was a clear reference to the trap Onofre had laid that had cost Joan Sicart his life. He did not take offence. *You're not important enough,* he answered. *Come and see me at my office, I'm sure we can reach an agreement.* The journalist appeared the following day. "Name the price for your silence and let's get this over with," Onofre said when the man was in front of him, "I've no time to waste." "Who says I'm for sale?" asked the journalist, with the hint of a smile. "You know me only too well, and know what to expect from me," Onofre said. "You wouldn't have come otherwise." The journalist scribbled some numbers on a piece of paper and showed it to him: it was an exorbitant sum, a provocation designed to rile the other man. "You have a low estimate of yourself." Bouvila smiled. "I'd calculated a higher price; here you are." He took a bulky package out of a drawer and handed it to the journalist. Glancing at the contents of the envelope, the journalist remained silent for a few seconds, then stood up, put his hat on and left the office. When he reached the first street corner, he was set on by four men. They snatched not only the envelope but also the money he had taken from home to cover his day's expenses. Then they broke both his legs.

After the journalist had gone on his way, still apologising profusely, Onofre attempted to return to the Marquis of Ut's carriage, but just at that moment the tsarina's retinue moved off. The wagons passed by him with a tinkle of glass and the rattle of hardware; he had to take cover among the piles of merchandise on the quayside to avoid being crushed by the heavily loaded carts. Some goats sticking their heads out of a window brushed his face with their beards; he could clearly smell their foul breath. "What the devil are these goats doing here?" he asked, raising his voice above their plaintive bleating. The mujhik looking after them explained in a language Onofre did not understand. At length a man with puffy features in a hussar's uniform shouted in poor French that His Highness the Tsarevitch, who was accompanying his mother on this trip, did not trust the milk added to his tea in foreign lands. Even the goats' forage came in bales from the distant steppes. Other wagons were carrying the tsarina's favourite furniture: her bed, her mirrored wardrobes, her divans, her piano and her writing desk, as well as a hundred and six trunks of clothes and a similar number of shoe and hat boxes.

Onofre had to wait for the convoy to pass by before he could leave his temporary refuge. He finally found himself alone on the quayside: intentionally or not, in the commotion nobody had stayed behind to wait for him. His shoes, gaiters and trouser bottoms were spattered with mud; some of it had even splashed his frock coat. He found his top hat stuck in a pile of dung and left it there. On Las Ramblas he hailed a cab that took him home. He changed as quickly as he could while the fastest tilbury in his stables was being prepared. Even so, by the time he arrived at the Ritz the banquet he himself had organised and paid for was already under way. Onofre rushed towards the top table, where he could see the tsarina, the tsarevitch, Prince Yussupof and other illustrious guests flanked by their Catalan hosts. When he reached the table, he realised there were no free chairs and no place set for him. Seeing his bewilderment, the Marquis of Ut stood up and whispered in his ear: "What are you doing standing there like an idiot? Your place is down there, on table three." Onofre protested in an undertone: "But I want to sit next to the tsarina!" "Don't talk non-sense," the marquis hissed, alarm written all over his face. "You're not part of the nobility. Do you want to offend Her Imperial Highness?"

This episode came back into Onofre's mind as he watched the cranes hoisting the fearsome German howitzers from the ship's deck, then some gigantic cannon not yet seen on any battlefield: these were the anti-aircraft guns he had managed to purloin from the barracks of the French High Command at enormous expense. Gazing at these outsize crates, he felt a quiver of satisfaction. In recent years such a sensation had become rare; most of the time he was bored. At home in the evenings, shut in his library surrounded by hundreds of books he had not the slightest intention of ever reading, he would smoke Havana cigars and recall with nostalgia those distant nights of revelry when he and Odón Mostaza (whose death he now regretted) would watch the sun come up through the steamed-up windows of a house of ill repute. The two of them sprawled exhausted and replete – sur-rounded by empty bottles, food leftovers, packs of cards and dice, naked women sleeping curled up by the walls and clothing strewn all over the room – in the bemused innocence of youth.

2

In Madrid, His Excellency Mohamed Torres was perspiring freely. Accustomed to the Atlantic breeze that refreshed the flowery patio of his Tangiers palace, he was suffocating here in Palacio de Oriente. He had called in there on his return from Paris, where he had met with Clemenceau. The musk perfume he was wearing made Don Antonio Maura want to retch. Until that moment the sultanate of Morocco had maintained a precarious independence thanks to the rivalry between France and England. Now, however, Germany wanted to install naval bases on the Moroccan coast and to open up markets for its manufactures. Mindful of this threat, in April 1904 the two rival powers had signed a pact, and now France was planning to seize Morocco, cock a snook at the sultan and his grand vizir and turn the sultanate into an extension of Algeria. His Majesty Don Alfonso XIII, listening closely to the laments of the sultan's foreign minister, thought there was a very simple solution.

"My boy, don't let them do it," he suggested.

"Your Majesty is very perceptive," said the emissary, "but we cannot renounce the protection of a great power without a grave risk to the throne and even the head of my lord, His Majesty Sultan Abdul Aziz."

"What do you think, Don Antonio?" the king said, addressing the then prime minister. Don Antonio Maura was faced with a dilemma: to insist on a Spanish presence in Africa meant continuing to sit on a hornets' nest. This was a risky business for an impoverished country still recovering from its recent colonial disasters, and yet to renounce it meant losing the last scraps of prestige it had in the concert of nations. He explained this succinctly to His Majesty. "It's all the same to me," was the monarch's reply. While Don Antonio Maura took him to one side, Mohamed Torres began to admire a monumental diptych hanging on the wall: in it, Judith and Salomé were competing to show off their bloody trophies: swollen tongues lolled from the livid mouths of John the Baptist and Holofernes. He recalled that the Prophet had forbidden any graphic representations of the human form.

The king and prime minster returned from their whispered discussion.

"His Majesty was in favour of abandoning Morocco to its fate," the prime minister said, "but I have succeeded in dissuading him. His Majesty's powers of understanding are proverbial." The sultan's foreign minister gave three salaams. "I have also informed him of other aspects of the question. The fact is, since the loss of Cuba the army has had nothing to do, and idle soldiers always present a threat: they grow bored, don't get promoted and stay around forever. I also told him about the mining concessions and the investments Spain has in your territory," the prime minister added, raising his right hand to his heart. His Majesty Don Alfonso XIII, who at that time was eighteen years old, patted him on the shoulder.

"We'll give that Raisuli what for, eh?"

Now, five years later, at Barcelona's railway station, the mothers of the recruits leaving for Africa were demonstrating again, as they had done during the war in Cuba. They sat on the sleepers and wouldn't let the train depart. Ladies from a Catholic association, who had come to the station to hand out crucifixes to the troops, were encouraging the driver and his stoker to steam over them. "I don't know if the boys would take it kindly if we chopped up their mothers," the two men replied. There were shouts of "Up with Maura!" and "Down with Maura!"

It was a clammy morning in July 1909. Anxious at the turn events were taking, the Marquis of Ut turned up at Onofre Bouvila's home.

"We're done for," he exclaimed. His hair was dishevelled and ungroomed; his tie was undone. "The civil governor is refusing to declare a state of siege, the mob is master of the streets, churches are burning, and as usual, Madrid has abandoned us."

Onofre Bouvila proffered an embossed leather case filled with Havana cigars. The marquis graciously declined the offer.

"Don't worry, nothing will happen," Onofre said. "The worst that could occur is for them to burn down your palace. Is your family away in the country?"

"They're spending the summer at Sitges," the marquis replied.

"And is the palace guarded?"

"Of course."

"There you are then. Take my advice," Onofre told him. "Go and spend a few days with your wife and children."

"I'd already thought of that, but I can't: tomorrow I have the administrative council," said the marquis. Now I think I was crazy to stay, he reflected.

Onofre Bouvila poured two glasses of amontillado. "It's excellent for calming the nerves," he said. "Your health!"

The roar of a cannon could be heard from the street. Could this really be the revolution, Onofre wondered. He remembered the far-off days when he had announced its arrival to the men working on the World Fair. Back then he was young and penniless, and hoped that nothing of what he was predicting would take place; now he was rich and felt old, but couldn't prevent a flicker of hope illuminating his soul. At last, he thought. Now we'll see what happens.

"And yours!" said the marquis, raising his glass. He gulped down the amontillado in one, belched and wiped his mouth with the back of his hand. Onofre Bouvila admired his lack of manners. He's got nothing to prove, he thought.

"What do you think?" the marquis asked.

"What does it look like?" replied Onofre, lighting a cigar and drawing on it with obvious delight. "I don't have a council meeting, and yet I haven't left. I have no intention of quitting Barcelona. What do you reckon can happen?" he added, noting the marquis's furrowed brow. "It's only four rabble-rousers with no weapons or leaders. Let them play their games; they have nothing going for them but our fear."

As Onofre said this, he recalled the demonstration he had been part of more than twenty years earlier. He recalled the Civil Guard with their horses and sabres and the loaded cannon. He didn't share these memories with the marquis. "Just suppose they did win," he went on, peering out of the window: a column of black smoke was rising in the deep blue summer sky. He calculated it must be coming from the Raval district: possibly San Pedro de las Puellas church, or San Pablo del Campo (in fact this was the church that was in flames). "Do you know what would happen? They'd have to come and beg us to help them. After a few hours there would be absolute chaos and they would need us even more than ever. Remember Napoleon."

The marquis had to laugh in spite of himself; Onofre moved away from the window for safety's sake. He had seen a company of soldiers running past, rifles over their shoulders. Some were carrying shovels, others picks: they were from the sappers regiment. He wondered where they could be going with this equipment: it was the workers who were raising barricades. "The time isn't yet ripe," he said, sitting back down in his armchair. "But it will arrive one day, Ambrosi, and not so distant that you and I will not see it. The day the universal revolution breaks out, the current order based on property, exploitation, oppression and the bourgeois, doctrinaire principle of authority will disappear. No stone will be left upon stone, first in Europe, then in the rest of the world. To the cry of 'Peace for the workers, freedom for the oppressed and death to the governing classes, the exploiters and overseers of all kinds' they will destroy all the states and all the churches, together with all the religious, judicial, financial, police, university, economic and social institutions, so that those millions of human beings who now live muzzled, enslaved, tormented and exploited, will see themselves liberated from their oppressors and official and unofficial benefactors, and will at last be able to breathe the air of complete freedom, as groups and individuals."

The marquis stared at him wide-eyed. "What are you saying?" he asked. Onofre Bouvila burst out laughing. "Nothing," he said. "I read it in a pamphlet that came my way years ago. I have a strange memory: I can recall everything I've read word for word. My wife and the girls are in La Budallera," he went on in the same tone of voice, "at my in-laws' house. Stay for dinner; you won't be able to go to your club this evening anyway."

They were in the middle of their meal when they were surprised by a noise that grew louder and louder. The floor shook, the crystal teardrops tinkled as the chandeliers swayed and the plates danced in front of the two men. The butler, whom they had sent to find out what was going on, returned and reported that a regiment of cuirassiers was riding down the street, with their white breastplates and black plumes, their swords resting on their shoulder epaulettes.

"They've brought the heavy cavalry out onto the streets," the butler murmured. "Perhaps things are more serious than you thought, sir."

"You'll have to stay the night," Onofre told the marquis. He nodded. "I can let you have one of my nightshirts; I hope it fits."

"Don't go to any trouble," said the marquis, glancing out of the corner of his eye at the maid clearing the table. "I have my own way of keeping warm."

All night long there was the sound of cannon fire in the distance; the rattle of machine-guns, and snipers' isolated gunshots. The next morning, when they met in the dining room for breakfast, the Marquis of Ut had dark lines round his puffy eyes. The morning newspapers had not arrived. The butler informed them that none of the shops had opened; the city was paralysed, and all communication with the outside world was cut off.

"It won't last," Onofre Bouvila said. "Is the larder well stocked?"

"Yes sir," the butler said.

"Would you believe it!" the marquis exclaimed. "Besieged by the mob, and I only have what I'm standing up in . . ." His eyes shifted to the young girl serving him coffee. She blushed and looked away. "Could you lend me some money?" he asked Bouvila.

"Whatever you need," Onofre replied. "What do you want it for?"

"To reward this delicious creature," said the marquis, jerking his thumb in the direction of the maid. "By the way, I suggest you dismiss her today."

"Why's that?"

"A dud in bed," the marquis said.

Onofre Bouvila caught a look of panic on the girl's face. She could not have been more than fifteen; she had just arrived from her village, but her features and manners were refined, and for that reason she had been assigned to serve at table rather than to heavier duties. Onofre knew that if he did what the marquis was suggesting, there were few options for her apart from prostitution or poverty. "What's your name?" he asked her. "Otilia, at your service sir," she replied. "Are you happy here, Otilia?" "Yes sir," she said. "Very happy."

"In that case, this is what we'll do," he said, turning to the marquis. "You can keep your reward, since you weren't satisfied. Otilia stays here, and I'll double her wages. How does that sound?"

Onofre wasn't doing this out of generosity, or out of self-interest, because he did not believe in gratitude. All he wanted was to show his guest who was master in his house. The two men stared hard at one another for a few moments. Then the marquis guffawed.

They spent what later came to be known as the "tragic week" together. They played cards and talked at great length. The marquis was an agreeable conversationalist, and also a great source of information for Onofre: there wasn't a single noble-born family the Marquis of Ut wasn't related to or whose secrets he didn't know. It wasn't difficult to get him to talk: there was nothing he liked better than to discuss trivial events in great detail. Thanks to his gossip, Onofre glimpsed the cracks in that hermetic, dusty and slightly forlorn world whose doors were always closed to him.

After dinner they would send the butler up onto the flat roof, and if he came down saying there was no danger they would go up to smoke cigars and drink brandy while leaning over the balustrade to watch the glow from the fires in the city. In the end, tired of the monotony, they sent a tongue-in-cheek letter to the civil governor: "Put a stop to this situation, we're running out of cigars."

All in all, it had been a very pleasant week, during which Onofre Bouvila thought he had recovered the incomparable bonds of male friendship. But now, seeing the marquis seated at the top table next to the tsarina, he realised it had been no more than a fleeting dream.

A red silk canopy bearing the coat of arms of the Romanovs had been erected over the top table, and the walls were covered in silk hangings. Plaster of Paris sculptures specially made for the occasion stood in the four corners of the banqueting hall. From the ceiling hung six chandeliers, each with three rows of candles; between them and the candelabra on the tables, the room was lit by four thousand beeswax candles. The cutlery was made of silver, or at the top table, of gold. The dishes were Sèvres porcelain. As he surveyed all this luxury, the exact cost of which he knew only too well, Onofre thought back to that "tragic week". Lost in his thoughts and absent from the celebrations, he was startled by the deep voice of his table companion: "You are thinking about the revolution, dear sir," he heard him say.

Onofre turned to look at the speaker properly for the first time. He was a tall, thin man of around forty, with rough peasant features that had a certain attraction. His tangled beard reached halfway down his chest. He was wearing an indigo blue cassock that made him look even taller and thinner, and he gave off a pungent smell of vinegar, incense and sheep. From his aspect in general and his penetrating, mad-looking gaze, Onofre deduced he had been seated next to one of those ignorant, crafty, superstitious, fanatical and abjectly servile monks who often succeeded in attaching themselves to the entourages of the powerful.

He later learned that the man's name was Grigori Yefimovich Rasputin. At that time he was being protected by the tsarina because he had cured the tsarevitch of haemophilia after the doctors had given up on him. Extraordinary things were said about this Rasputin: that he had hypnotic and prophetic powers, that he could read people's minds and perform miracles whenever he wished. From this moment on, his influence grew enormously, until he dominated the Russian court and became a real tyrant. He handed out appointments and honours; it was not long before careers and fortunes were made and unmade in his shadow. This was until a conspiracy headed by the same Prince Yussupof who was now enjoying *escudella* and *carn d'olla* in the Ritz led to his assassination in 1916. Shortly afterwards, as Rasputin himself had predicted, the revolution that was to signal the end of the Romanov dynasty in the fortress at Ekaterinburg broke out. However, at the time when he accompanied the tsarina during her trip to Barcelona, his influence was just beginning to be felt.

Rasputin told Onofre Bouvila how, a few years earlier in 1905, he had witnessed the Bloody Sunday of sad memory. Standing on the second-floor balcony of the Winter Palace in St Petersburg he was holding the Grand Duchess Anastasia, little more than a baby, in his arms, and was holding the tsarevitch's hand. From the adjacent balcony Grand Duke Sergei was supervising the children. "Make sure they're wrapped up warm, Rasputin, it's very cold out here," he repeated. Grand Duke Sergei was then the most influential person at court, because he enjoyed Tsar Nicholas' complete confidence. (In February that same year, an anarchist by the name of Kalyayev threw a bomb at his carriage as it went by. All that was left of the carriage, the horses and the Grand Duke was a heap of smoking remains.)

From the palace's first-floor balcony, Grand Duke Vladimir, in conjunction with the military high command, was considering from minute to minute the best course of action. "Let's be clever about this," he told the others. When the demonstration poured into the square, he let them advance. "What are their demands?" asked the tsar. "A constitution, your highness," came the reply. "Ah," the tsar said. Then Grand Duke Vladimir ordered the troops to open fire on the crowd. The demonstration dispersed in a few minutes. "I think we got it right this time," said the grand duke. More than a thousand people lay dead in the square.

At table with Onofre, the lunatic monk lamented not having been able to direct the course of action that day. "I know how to avoid the Revolution," he said. He ate voraciously, like an ogre. As the two men talked, Bouvila's initial impression was confirmed, but the madman's personality inexplicably attracted him.

"Are you Onofre Bouvila?"

He studied the man speaking to him on the station platform: a dry, rustic face, lined with premature wrinkles; deep-set eyes, straggly hair. "I'm Joan," the man said. The two brothers shook hands coldly. Joan Bouvila was twenty-six when he met Onofre for a second time, at their father's funeral. He had died the previous night. "It's a shame you didn't arrive in time," Joan said. "He was calling for you right up to the last moment." Onofre made no reply. The Cuban war veteran who now drove a caleche (the same man who had taken him home from the station a few years before, when his mother died) came up to Onofre. He said he still remembered him after all these years and wanted to be the first to offer his services. "We can go on foot," Joan said, "it's just round the corner." Onofre gave the coachman a tip: "For your good memory," he told him. Joan looked askance at his gesture.

The funeral chapel had been set up in the oratory of an old people's home run by nuns. It was a big, solid, stone building with a slate roof. There were bars on all the windows, and the garden was surrounded by a high wall. Two extensions had been built on either side of the main building, and the inmates were crowding at the windows to watch Onofre come up the garden path.

"I don't know how they found out you were coming," said the mother superior, who had come out to receive them at the garden gate. "There are no secrets in places like this. Don't be surprised they all want to see you," she added confidentially. "In his rare moments of lucidity, your father did nothing but talk about you. Sister Socorro, who has looked after him since his arrival here, can confirm that, can't you, Sister?" she said, addressing a little nun with an oval face and very white, almost transparent skin, who had joined them in the gloomy hall. Lowering her eyes in the presence of Onofre and his brother, the young nun opened her mouth, but said nothing.

"On those occasions he always repeated the same thing," the mother superior continued. "That is, that you would come for him. He truly believed you would arrive at any moment. Then, he would say, he would go with you to Barcelona, where the two of you would live in the lap of luxury. As a result, some of the more credulous old men began to envy him and feel resentful towards him. They seemed to think he was being arrogant. But as I say, this only happened occasionally. Your father had a very vivid imagination. A feverish one, I might be inclined to say."

As she was talking they had walked down long, deserted corridors, flanked on either side by closed doors. The tiled floor was remarkably clean, reflecting the religious statues like a calm pool of water. Rounding a bend, they came across a powerful-looking nun wearing a grey apron who was on her knees scrubbing the floor. The freshly scrubbed tiles gave off a pungent smell. When they reached the chapel of rest, Onofre gazed with dismay at the gaunt face he saw in the coffin, lit by the flickering flame of two tall candles: that expressionless parchment face cancelled all his previous memories. "You can close the coffin now," he said.

"In spite of what I've just been telling you," the mother superior said, "during his stay with us, your father did make some friends among the patients. They would now like to attend the prayers, if you have no objection."

Two nuns brought in a group of old men, who shuffled into the room. Not all of them had known Onofre's father during his lifetime; some had sneaked their way into this sad flock so as not to miss the unexpected entertainment. They were all dressed in rags. "We depend on charity, which means our monetary situation is dire," the mother superior explained.

When the ceremony was over and they were about to leave for the cemetery, Sister Socorro tugged at Onofre's sleeve. "Come with me," she whispered. "There's something I want to show you." He let her lead him to a narrow blue-painted door. She opened it with an enormous key dangling from her habit. The door opened onto a dark storeroom. The nun went in and reappeared with a tangle of wickerwork in her hand.

"We teach the patients basket-weaving," she said. "This is what your father was making. He wasn't very good with his hands, so it never got beyond this. The truth is he was already too far gone when your brother brought him here almost a year ago. He paid for the wicker, so it belongs to you."

After they returned from the cemetery, Onofre took his brother to eat in the same restaurant where many years earlier he and his father had by chance met Baldrich, Vilagrán and Tapera. The two men polished off their soup in silence. While they were waiting for the main course, Onofre said: "I was intending to come, but it was impossible. I had a dinner with the tsarina, of all people."

"I've no idea what a tsarina is," Joan said. "But I don't hold it against you; you don't have to apologise to me."

"It goes without saying," said Onofre, "that I'll pay for all the expenses you've incurred."

"I've been thinking about selling our land," Joan commented, as if he hadn't heard what his brother had just said. "To do that I need your consent in writing." He stared at Onofre. When he said nothing, Joan inferred he wanted to hear more before expressing his opinion. "Then I'll go to Barcelona. Don't say anything," he quickly added, seeing that his brother was about to speak. Onofre recognised the look as one characteristic of their mother. Between the two of them they had finished off the carafe of wine, although Onofre had only taken a few sips.

"Don't shout," Onofre told his brother. "We're known in here; everyone's listening in."

"I couldn't give a damn!" Joan roared.

"See what I mean?" said Onofre with a smile. "You're not as smart as you think you are. Calm down and listen to the plan I came here to propose to you." He clapped his hands, and when the waiter approached, asked him to refill the carafe. "I'm well aware what you think; even though we hardly know one another, we couldn't be more different. But we need to understand one another. You're sick of working on the land, aren't you? Tired of the countryside. How could I argue with that?" He passed him the wine, and noticed that Joan drank mechanically, the gleam in his deep-set eyes gradually fading as he did so. "I know very well the land isn't worth anything. The money is in trees. That's what we're going to dedicate ourselves to from now on: forests. They don't create work, they grow on their own. All you have to do is keep an eye out to make sure that nobody else comes and takes the timber first. People pay a fortune for timber in the cities, but somebody needs to be here, keeping an eye on the wood, the source of our wealth."

"I don't know who you're trying to fool with your fantasies," Joan said. "The forests belong to everybody, no-one can claim them for themselves." He had lowered his voice; not even he could resist Onofre Bouvila's forceful personality. Now that they were face to face, the anger building up inside him over the years seemed to be relegated to the background, replaced against his will by a mixture of curiosity and greed.

"Until now they have belonged to everybody," Onofre said. "Or, strictly speaking, to nobody. But if the entire valley were to become a public entity, if instead of a parish it was a municipality, all the land that wasn't privately owned, all the land that previously belonged to no-one, would be communal land administered by the town council, that is to say, by the mayor . . . Would you like to be mayor, Joan?"

"No," Joan said.

"Well, it's time you changed your mind," Onofre told him.

As he stood on the quayside, Onofre Bouvila recalled that conversation and his inexplicable desire to win over a brother he hardly knew, a brother in whose eyes he could see nothing but fierce resentment, and how setting him up as mayor had required a great deal of money and countless underhand deals. The sudden appearance of two customs officials on the dock made him jump. When they saw his reaction, the two men touched their peaked caps: "Begging your pardon, Don Onofre, we didn't mean to startle you," they said. "We're looking for a consignment of tobacco."

Onofre Bouvila had not seen Joan since the day of the funeral. He had not attended his inauguration as mayor and knew nothing of his administration. Timber and cork, abundant in the mountains thereabouts, arrived regularly at his warehouses in Pueblo Nuevo. "And yet," he was thinking as he stood watching the ship being unloaded, "that's all the family I have. My only blood relatives are Joan, an idiot son and two spoilt daughters. Only a fool cuts himself off from his roots completely."

3

He and his brother had gone their separate ways as soon as they had finished their meal. Relations were still frosty, but they had reached an agreement. Now Onofre was strolling alone around the streets of Bassora. Joan had started out on his return home at half past two, taking advantage of the remaining hours of daylight. But Onofre's train did not leave until eight o'clock. This city that had dazzled him as a boy now seemed tedious and ugly, its atmosphere pestilential and the passersby he met uncouth. The soot has got into their brains, he thought. Without meaning to or even realising it, his steps took him to a street lined with arcades. He went into a building, climbed to the first floor and called out. A timid, pious-looking woman answered his call. He asked if a taxidermist had once lived there. She invited him into the waiting room and said yes, the taxidermist he mentioned was in fact her father. He was still alive, though he was quite aged and was no longer working. Father and daughter lived off his savings, modestly but comfortably. She took Onofre to see him, and he asked the old man if he remembered having stuffed a monkey a long time ago. The taxidermist immediately replied that he did: in his professional career that was the only monkey he had ever had the opportunity to stuff. He recalled it had been a difficult job, because he didn't know the details of a monkey's anatomy, and also because it was a small specimen, with extremely fragile bones. This was why he had taken so much trouble over it, the old man explained. It had taken him many hours, but in the end it had turned out very well, as he himself acknowledged without false modesty. After that, months had gone by and the owner of the monkey had not reappeared – he had a clear recollection of him too, he said, even though this had happened several decades ago. He was dressed in white, with a straw hat and a cane, and was accompanied by a little boy. "As you can see, I have a clear mind for my age," the old taxidermist concluded. "Don't tire yourself out," his daughter said. She explained to Onofre in a whisper that her father easily got over-excited and was then unable to sleep until the small hours.

Onofre ignored her and asked the old man: "What happened to the monkey?" He made a great effort to remember, then said at last that he had kept it in a cupboard for a long while to keep the dust off. Then, convinced nobody would ever come to claim it, he had put it on a shelf in his workshop, as a kind of calling card. "And after that . . .?" The taxidermist couldn't recall. His daughter came to his aid. "Yes, father, Señor Catasús ended up with it, don't you remember?"

"Ah yes," said the old man. Señor Catasús and his brother-in-law used to bring big game trophies for him to mount; they were his best clients. "Never anything less than a roe deer", he said. "And sometimes a wild boar." They had seen the monkey and been taken by it. By then it had been on the shelf for years, so he didn't think he was breaking any law by giving it to such special clients.

The Catasús family lived on the outskirts of Bassora, in a mansion that the Cuban war veteran whom Onofre found in the cab rank next to the station said he knew well. When they arrived, Onofre handed the maid his visiting card. While he was waiting in the entrance, it suddenly occurred to him how foolish he was being. "Ridiculous decisions always produce dire consequences," he told himself. "Maybe it would be best to forget this sentimental nonsense right now, while there's still time."

Just then Señor Catasús himself came out to greet him. He was a portly man in his sixties, jovial and good-natured. "Bouvila!" he exclaimed. "This is an honour!" He had heard a lot about him; they had acquaintances in common and news had reached Bassora of the banquet held for the tsarina a few days earlier. "Events like that always cause quite a stir here in the provinces," he said, laughing out loud. "But to what do we owe the pleasure of your visit?" "A private matter," Onofre told him, briefly explaining what brought him there.

"It must seem absurd to you that I'm showing such an interest in the monkey after all these years," he concluded. "No, no, not at all," Señor Catasús said good-naturedly. "It's just that I'm sorry not to be able to satisfy your wish as I should have liked." He told Onofre that, when they had seen the monkey at the taxidermist's, it had occurred to his brother-in-law, who went by the name of Esclasans and owned a distillery, to use it to promote a new brand of spirits. He had persuaded the taxidermist to let him have the stuffed monkey, planning to use it on the product label. However, the lawyer representing his interests in Barcelona wrote to tell him that this trademark had already been registered and by pure coincidence was used for an aniseed drink of the same name. For a while after that, the monkey had been a children's toy, but as they grew older it was stowed away in the attic. Finally, moth-eaten and battered, it was thrown away.

"What is remarkable," Catasús concluded, "is that after all this time you've been able to trace the whole history of that monkey." He glanced at the wall clock as if he wanted to get rid of Onofre as soon as possible, but was unsure how to go about it. Onofre was also trying to think of some pretext that would allow him to leave. "But I see there are still more than two hours until your train leaves," Catasús said, "and we're just round the corner from the station, as they say. Why don't you come in? We'd be delighted if you cared to share a snack with us. As you can see, we're having a little family gathering."

Onofre followed Catasús into a large dining room with a coffered ceiling and oak furniture; twelve or thirteen people were at table. His host proceeded to introduce them, but Onofre paid him scant attention. Some were Catasús's children, together with their spouses; others were more distant relatives. Finally he was presented to a quaint individual whom Catasús introduced as Santiago Belltall.

"Santiago is an inventor," was all he said about him. From the ironic tone Onofre thought he detected in Catasús's voice, and the amused glances of the others, he surmised Santiago Belltall must be one of those poor or unfortunate relatives whose eccentricities inadvertently turned them into the butt of the family's jokes. The inventor, whose name was to become inextricably linked to Bouvila in the future, was twenty-eight years old at the time, although he appeared twice that age. He had the undernourished, haunted look of a man who was neglecting to eat and sleep because of an obsession. He had a mop of greasy, straw-coloured hair, bulging watery eyes, a long nose and a broad mouth with thin lips and protruding teeth that accentuated his comic appearance. His old, patched woollen jacket, a lurid but frayed tie, trousers that were too short for him, and rope sandals did not exactly inspire respect either. Even though it was obvious he got by on other people's charity, he barely touched the rolls and cakes on the table in front of him.

The two men stared at one another for a good while. For a moment

Onofre thought he was seeing another obsessed young man he had never really got to know, a man who was about to emigrate to Cuba, his head filled with fantasies, only to return with his spirit broken but his fantasies still intact. This image momentarily superimposed itself on the one of the sad wreck of a man whose burial he had just attended. An illogical thought crossed his mind: I've been searching without knowing why for a non-existent monkey; now chance has brought me this stuffed dummy in its place.

Before they could exchange anything more than the usual courtesies, Catasús began to tell the story of the monkey. Almost immediately he was interrupted by one of the guests, who declared that monkeys were highly intelligent animals. He had read in a travel book that the ancient Egyptians, despite not believing in a God, worshipped monkeys. Another gentleman said he knew for a fact that, unlike in ancient Egypt, in China and Japan people ate monkey meat, which was considered a delicacy. A third guest said that was nothing: in certain parts of South America they ate alligator and snake meat. Another person said that was probably in Chile. One of his father's sisters, he said, had married a wool merchant, and they had emigrated to Chile. His wife corrected him, saying that the relatives he had mentioned emigrated to Venezuela, not Chile. It was a sad state of affairs, she added, that she had to remind him of these things, when in reality they were only her relatives by marriage. The gentleman who had first mentioned snakes then described the method of cooking them: once the snake was dead, he said, it was cut into pieces of about a hand's length with a saw; the ends of each of these pieces were sewn up, and then they were fried in fat or oil, like sausages. In fact, he said, this and cereals were the staple diet of the inhabitants of that region of South America. A lady complained that white spots had appeared on her skin. Another one recommended she went to take the waters at Caldas de Bohí. A young fellow added that he had been told that the streets of Paris were jammed with automobiles, and that you often saw dead dogs, cats and even donkeys that had been run over. The fashion for automobiles, added a middle-aged gentleman who until then had not uttered a word, was bound to bring misfortune to many families. Nearly everyone present agreed. Señor Catasús said that even so, there was no way of resisting progress, especially in the field of science.

So the evening dragged on. Onofre Bouvila didn't say a word, occasionally glancing out of the corner of his eye at Santiago Belltall. He was silent as well, but unlike Onofre, made no effort to pretend he was interested in the conversation. He was in his own world; every so often his eyes suddenly sparkled in what seemed a perilous way, but since nobody was paying him any attention, none of them noticed. At other moments his brow furrowed and a sad look came into his eyes; this too went unnoticed. Sometimes several seconds went by between these alternating emotions, and then it was his weariness that came to the fore. Belltall himself was unaware of the scrutiny the newcomer was furtively subjecting him to.

The meal was interrupted when a young boy suddenly burst into the dining room. This boy, who could not have been more than three or four years old and was wearing an embroidered smock, ran to bury his head on his mother's lap and broke into loud, inconsolable sobs. His mother finally managed to calm him down and to get him to tell her, between hiccups and sobs, why he was crying.

"María hit me," he said.

He pointed a podgy hand towards the door he had left open when he came in. Beyond it was an empty, circular hall, lit by a skylight. From where he was sitting, Onofre Bouvila could make out a thin, ungainly little girl in the hall. She was wearing a short, threadbare frock that showed her skinny legs and a pair of dirty, darned stockings. He realised at once who she must be. Sensing she was being scrutinised, she glared at him. Although she was far away, he could see she had round, caramel-coloured eyes.

Santiago Belltall had already stood up and strode over to his daughter. Ignoring the dictates of etiquette, Onofre Bouvila also left the table and stood in the doorway, attempting to hear what the inventor and his daughter were saying. Catasús came up behind him.

"Don't worry, Bouvila," he said. "This inevitably happens whenever they come. She's not entirely to blame. María is seven years old and is starting to understand too much. It's an awkward age for someone in her situation."

"What about her mother?" Onofre asked.

Catasús shrugged and rolled his eyes, suggesting it was wiser not to dwell on the subject. A sudden noise made the two men turn their heads. Belltall had just slapped his daughter. A violent man, Onofre thought. The girl was trying hard to keep her balance and, above all, not to cry. But she adores him, Onofre decided, perhaps for that very reason. Violence is her weakness.

The inventor returned to the dining room. He was very pale, and launched into an endless, incoherent apology; he mangled his words so badly that his listeners guffawed. Standing beside him, Onofre Bouvila put his hand on his shoulder; through the cloth, he could feel his collar bone. "Leave, and get the girl out of here," he whispered in his ear. The inventor shot him a furious look, to which he responded with a serene smile. Stay calm, was his silent message. You don't make me laugh, but I'm not frightened of you either. I could have you killed, but I prefer to defend you. Without Belltall noticing, Onofre slipped his visiting card into his jacket pocket. The inventor shrugged off his hand, collected his daughter and dragged her roughly with him towards the door at the far end of the hall.

Onofre took advantage to say goodbye as well, thanking the Catasús family profusely for their hospitality. On the way to the station, his cab overtook the inventor and his daughter, who were deep in conversation. Confident that neither of them would notice him, he watched them until the cab turned a corner.

Now millions of men were preparing to butcher one another in the trenches of Verdun and the Marne, and Onofre Bouvila was doing his best to provide them with the means to do so. A year had gone by since that meeting at Señor Catasús's house: he no longer even remembered Santiago Belltall and his daughter. Cranes had lowered the cannons onto the wagons; they were covered by a tarpaulin firmly tied to iron rings on the sides. A team of eight mules was pulling them along the quay to Bogatell. Men carrying torches led the way, others guided the mules by their bridles, and still others were guarding the convoy, pistols in hand.

4

The streets of Paris were no longer jammed with automobiles, as Catasús's nephew had claimed. Now darkness reigned, and an ominous silence. For four years there had been incessant warfare in Europe. All able-bodied men had been called up; factories were short of workers, nobody tilled the land and every last head of livestock had been sacrificed to feed the troops. Had it not been for their colonial empires and for supplies from neutral countries, the adversaries would have had to lay down their arms, defeated by starvation, until the one left standing, the one that had managed to equip itself for longer with munitions and provisions, would be able to proclaim itself master of the world.

Many in Barcelona took great delight in this situation. Anyone who had something to sell could become rich overnight, a millionaire in the blink of an eye. The city was a ceaseless hive of activity: from dawn one day to sunrise the next, in La Lonja and El Borne, in consulates and legations, commercial offices and banks, clubs and restaurants, salons, drawing rooms, dressing rooms and foyers, in casinos, cabarets and brothels, hotels and inns, in sinister alleyways, the deserted cloister of a church, in the bedroom of a perfumed, wheezing whore, offers were made, prices fixed at random. There were bids, bribes were paid, threats made, and the seven deadly sins invoked to seal a deal. Money passed from hand to hand so swiftly and abundantly that gold was replaced by paper, paper by words, and words by pure imagination.

Many believed they had won a fortune and others believed they had lost one, although in reality neither was true. At the poker, baccarat or *chemin de fer* tables, real or fantasy fortunes changed hands several times in a matter of hours. The most exquisite delicacies (things never seen until then in Spain) were consumed without ceremony (there were those who took caviar rolls to the bullfight). Every imaginable adventurer, gambler or *femme fatale* made their way to Barcelona.

Only Onofre Bouvila remained aloof from this bonanza. He was hardly ever seen in public. The most unlikely rumours spread about him: some said he had earned so much money that he had lost his mind; others that he was gravely ill. Other rumours were more imaginative: it was said in all seriousness that he was following the war step by step and had offered to buy the Habsburg throne from the Emperor if Austria lost, as he calculated would happen. It was also rumoured that he had financed the uprising in Russia that had toppled the Tsar, and that for this Germany had deposited a hundred kilos in gold bars in a Swiss bank and granted him the title of archduke.

None of this was true. A private army of agents and informers kept him up to date of what was taking place on the battlefields and in the high commands, in the trenches and behind the lines. Because of this, Onofre knew too much; the war had ceased to interest him. He did see dark clouds on the horizon, though. He constantly said the worst was still to come: by that he meant revolution and anarchy. Out of the smoking ruins that Europe had become, he saw in his imagination a starving, vengeful mass of people rising, anxious to reconstruct society on the basis of order, honesty and distributive justice. He considered himself the inheritor of western civilisation and was in despair when he imagined its destruction.

He came to think he had been appointed to prevent such a catastrophe happening, to believe that this singular destiny was reserved for him. It's impossible that my life should have been a succession of extraordinary events, all for nothing, he told himself. He had started out in the least auspicious circumstances and had succeeded in becoming the richest man in Spain, probably one of the richest in the world. Now he believed he was called upon to fulfil a higher mission, seeing himself as a new messiah. In this sense he could indeed be said to have lost his mind.

He let his booming businesses take care of themselves, and spent days and nights elaborating a plan to save the face of the earth from chaos. To this end he could count on his wealth, his indomitable energy, his lack of scruples and a lifetime's experience. All he needed was a big idea to bring together all these disparate elements. Since this idea did not come readily to him, his bad temper grew and grew: he hit his employees with his stick for no reason and hardly ever saw his wife and daughters. Finally, on 7 November 1918, two days before the Weimar Republic was proclaimed, the idea that had haunted his daydreams for so long suddenly crystallised before his eyes in the most unlikely fashion.

*

Poor Señor Braulio had never recovered from the death of the man he loved. He had given up all his activities and lived hand in glove with his daughter Delfina in a modest two-storey house with garden on a quiet street in the old village of Gracia, which was now part of the city of Barcelona, almost entirely surrounded by the Ensanche. The two of them left the house only rarely. Delfina would go every morning to La Libertad market, doing her shopping in near silence. She pointed to what she wanted and paid the asking price without demur. The women vendors, unaware of the terror she had inspired years earlier in another market, regarded her as a model customer.

At dusk father and daughter would appear arm-in-arm in Plaza del Sol, stroll around it under the acacias and go back home without having said a word to anybody. They feigned not to notice the greetings and kind words the locals proffered, motivated in part by friendliness and in part by a wish to strike up a conversation that would permit them to penetrate the air of mystery surrounding the couple.

After their stroll they would lock their garden gate with padlock and chain. Lights could be seen at the windows of the house for a few more hours, until around ten o'clock. They received no visits or correspondence and didn't subscribe to any newspapers or magazines. Nor had they ever set foot in the local church. This stubborn isolation obviously led to a great deal of conjecture. It was commonly held that Señor Braulio had a substantial income, and that at his death, which was sure to occur within a short space of time, his daughter would inherit his entire fortune. This made Delfina a good catch, a desirable quarry for bounty hunters. However, those who initially tried to make advances came up against such a barrier of indifference and silence that they soon gave up.

The years slid by for Delfina with the frozen, inexorable slowness of a glacier. Gossips said she was waiting for her father to die to enter a religious order, and would take all her wealth with her as a dowry. At that moment, they said, when the doors of the enclosed convent closed behind her, the possibility of finding out who she was and what tragedy had ruined her life would have gone forever.

Towards the end of October 1918, Señor Braulio and his daughter were no longer to be seen in Plaza del Sol. After a few days, the rumours that had lain dormant for several years were revived: the poor man must be very ill, they said. They predicted he hadn't long to live; they had seen him in a very bad way the last few times he had been out; death was already imprinted on his face, or so they said. Somebody suggested the daughter might be the one who was ill, and this possibility only made the neighbours all the more curious. A doctor arrived in a carriage. Delfina herself came out to open the gate. "Ah, so he's the one who's sick," said the gossips, "just as we thought." Two more doctors arrived at the house. "They're conferring," the neighbours concluded. This consultation marked the start of an endless succession of specialists, nurses and assistants. Delfina continued to go to La Libertad market every morning. The women there asked her how her father was, and expressed their wishes for his speedy recovery, but she merely pointed to what she wanted, paid and left without a word.

The rest of October and the first week of November passed in this uncertainty. A new and uneasy routine had replaced the previous tranquil one. Finally the curious neighbours found their long wait rewarded, when amid great excitement a wonderful automobile drew up outside the house. Having constantly seen his photograph in the press, they recognised the man who stepped out of it at once. They asked themselves what relationship there could be between this powerful magnate and the reclusive, timid couple. "She sent for him," somebody said, but nobody was listening: they had all gone to inspect the automobile. It had red leather seats, sable travel blankets;

its horn and headlights were of solid gold. The driver was wearing a grey dustcoat with an astrakhan collar; the footman a green jacket with gold braid.

The house was invisible from the gate. No-one had pruned the trees or pulled up the weeds. A palm tree, a laurel and several cypresses were growing in the front garden, as well as a hundred-year-old almond tree that was almost a fossil. To the right of the almond tree was a muddy pond; in the middle stood a battered, blackened dolphin covered in slime; not a drop of water issued from its mouth. A multi-coloured swarm of dragonflies flew over the pond. In contrast to the garden, the house appeared well cared for; from the street no-one could not see any paintings on the walls or curtains on the half-open windows. Everything was bright and cheerful, but appearances were deceptive. Only those things the faint light filtering in through shutters and blinds picked out were clean and tidy – beyond that was only dust and decrepitude. Spiders had invaded every corner, moths were devouring the filthy, repulsive items of clothing, cockroaches gorged on rotten food, reproducing by the thousand every day in the larder. This ghastly contrast was a reflection of Delfina herself, the embodiment of her decline.

"It wasn't me who called you here, it was my father. He wanted to see you one last time," she said from the shadows. She had come out to open the gate, her face covered by a thick veil. She did not want him to see her features before she revealed the truth to him. Inside the house, she looked like a ghost. Onofre Bouvila regretted not having a weapon on him, and having left the footman who carried them for him in the automobile. These were the first words he heard her speak, but he immediately recognised the voice of the old boarding-house maidservant. "Nobody forced you to come. You alone know why you agreed to this meeting," she added. "Go up and see him, but don't worry – he has a nurse with him. I'll wait for you down here."

Onofre climbed a flight of stairs. On several steps the marble veneer had come away, leaving the urine-soaked joists uncovered. Orienting himself by a dim phosphorescence he could see above him, he made for the only open door on the landing. He went in and could make out Señor Braulio lying in a canopied bed. On the bedside table an arc lamp behind a gauze screen gave off a violet glow; in this light the prostrate man's face looked as white as flower petals. The nurse was snoring in an easy chair. Bouvila had no need to approach the bed to realise Señor Braulio had been dead for hours. He walked round the room: in the opposite corner to the bed was a lacquered dressing table with ivory inlays. On it he could see pots of creams, make-up and rouge, a pair of tweezers, an eyelash curler and a collection of combs and brushes. A black lace shawl was hanging from the oval mirror. In the top drawer he found a tortoiseshell comb: in his final years, Señor Braulio had liked to boast that he had modelled for Isidro Nonell for his famous portraits of gypsy women. Now Nonell was dead, so there was no way of proving the veracity of this preposterous affirmation. Next to the comb lay a razor-sharp knife: Señor Braulio's unhappy life had wound its way between glamorous daydreams and violence.

Onofre felt a hand on his shoulder and almost cried out. "I didn't hear you come in," he gasped. Delfina made no reply. "He was already dead when you sent for me, wasn't he?" he asked, but again she said nothing. "What have you given the nurse?" Delfina shrugged.

"The last time we met," she began, "I told you that one day I would reveal a secret to you. I can tell you now, because we'll never meet again. With my father dead, there's no reason to."

"I don't know what you're talking about," Onofre said curtly.

A long silence followed: this secret had filled Delfina's thoughts during her painful years in prison and afterwards during the grey years of voluntary reclusion. It had been the only thing keeping her alive. Now she discovered Onofre had no recollection of her great secret and had never felt the slightest curiosity to know what it was. Of all the possible reactions she had dreamed of, adjusting and refining them until she created a veritable imaginary narrative based on a single moment, this was the only one she had never contemplated. Now it seemed to her all those years had passed in vain. In the prolonged silence she once more evoked the unique image she had treasured her whole life, conjuring up one last time that so-oft-repeated scene. She could feel how he had torn off the fraying nightdress she had washed and ironed day after day for just such a moment. She could see from her mattress his naked, sweaty body, his eyes glinting malevolently in the tenuous first light of that spring in the year 1888, the dawn reflected in the sooty windowpane of the boarding-house attic.

She had been waiting for that visit for months, and this was her precious secret. She had loved him from the moment she saw him cross the entrance hall. Throughout those months she had heard his stealthy footsteps on the landing of the floor below. She had got up every night and left her bedroom, unable to sleep or bear the interminable wait, and hidden whenever her father had gone out on a spree.

Now she relived Onofre's hands at her waist, the tingling roughness of his mouth on her lips. She swooned when he sank his teeth into her body; later on, in prison, she watched as time erased the marks of his bites from her breasts and the bruises on her thighs and calves. She had thought she would die of melancholy and despair.

Her secret was no more than that: there had been no need for all the machinations he had employed to make her his: she would have given herself to him without a second thought if he had asked her to do so. That was why she had thrown the wicked Beelzebub out of her attic window: that cruel, painful action had removed the only obstacle holding him back.

She had chosen the moment of her father's death to finally reveal her secret, hoping that afterwards for a moment at least he would be hers once more. She had decided to end her life after that, keeping a phial of powerful poison in her pocket. With it I will put an end to my miserable existence, she reflected. As I haven't had even one moment of joy since then, I'll end my days with a bitter symmetry.

Her plan had been foiled by a few casual words from Onofre. The first time she had wanted to give herself to the man she loved, only to be brutally violated, robbed by him of the chance to offer herself. Now, thirty years later, when for the second time she was about to lay bare her feelings, she was crushed yet again by his indifference. Before saying anything, she raised the veil from her face.

"You haven't changed," she told him. That cancelled their debt.

But Onofre Bouvila wasn't even listening; his mind was on far more serious matters. Germany was on the verge of surrender: the country with whom his secret sympathies lay was now in ruins. More than two million Germans had been killed in the war; another four million had been wounded and left incapacitated. The country was in turmoil. A few days earlier, the sailors at the base in Kiel had mutinied; the Socialists had proclaimed an independent republic in Bavaria; Rosa Luxemburg and her Spartacists were sowing revolt and creating soviets. The moderates, meanwhile, were negotiating an armistice behind the back of the Kaiser, who had sought refuge in Holland. The Austro-Hungarian Empire lay as lifeless as Señor Braulio on his deathbed. Only Onofre had life and means enough to resuscitate its soul, the victim of its own history, its leaders' reckless heroism.

Against all this, Delfina's heartache seemed a mere irritation. He dismissed her theatrical silence; the memory of that blissful night that for her was turning to ashes was to him no more than a dimly remembered anecdotal incident. He was about to tell her this when he noticed the wild gleam in her sulphur-coloured eyes, eyes that reflected the cataclysm and despair of her frustrated impulse. He briefly relived the anxiety of those far-off nights when his passion for her had set his heart pounding. At that instant, his idea crystallised.

He hastily tore off her veil; the tulle drifted down to the floor. He eagerly studied her face by the light of the arc lamp next to her father's dead body. She began to unhook her dress with trembling fingers. When she was in her petticoats she raised her eyes to see what he was doing, and found him lost in thought. Her body no longer aroused the slightest hint of desire in him. "What do you want with me?" she asked. All he did was smile mysteriously.

Several years earlier, the Marquis of Ut had turned up without warning at Onofre's house and made him a very unusual proposal: "Would you like to have a dog piss on you?" he asked. It was a cold, unpleasant winter's night. The rain came in squalls, beating against the windowpanes. As was his custom, Onofre had retired to his library. Logs were burning in the fireplace; their flames magnified the shadow of the marquis, who had gone over to warm his chilly bones. He was in evening dress, with coral shirt buttons.

"Good idea," Onofre said. "Give me ten minutes to get ready."

The marquis's carriage was waiting outside. They drove in the rain from one end of the city to the other, before reaching a small triangular square where two streets merged: Plazuela San Cayetano. There was nobody about, and the houses, their windows shut tightly against the rain and cold, looked uninhabited. When the postilion, who always rode in front of the marquis's carriage on a white horse, jumped to the ground, his boots landed in a large puddle. Leading the horse by the bridle, he went over to a wooden gateway and rapped on it with his riding crop. A few moments later a shaft of light shone from an uncovered peephole. The postilion said something, listened to the reply and signalled to the coachman.

The Marquis of Ut and Onofre Bouvila climbed out and ran to the entrance, avoiding the puddles and the rainwater cascading from the gutters. When they reached the entrance, it opened to let them in. As soon as they were inside, it swung shut again, leaving the postilion outside.

The two men wrapped themselves in their cloaks to conceal their identities, then removed their top hats. They found themselves in a courtyard lit by braziers. There were patches of damp on the walls, and strips of material that had once been paper pennants. Above the opening at the far end of the yard leading to a dark corridor hung a colossal bull's head. The animal's skin was glistening in the rain, but one of its glass eyes was missing, and its name tag was reduced to no more than two bits of faded rag tacked on underneath. The person who had let them in was a man of around fifty, who walked with a limp as if one leg were shorter than the other. In fact, his limp was due to an accident at work: a machine had crushed his hip twenty years earlier. Now, since he could no longer work, he earned a living by any means possible. "Your honours have arrived just in time," he said with a solemnity that betrayed not the slightest hint of irony. "We're about to start."

They followed him down the dark corridor and came out into a square room lit by the bluish flames from gas jets placed on the floor. The jets formed the footlights of a semi-circular makeshift stage. There were several other men in the room, all of them cloaked. Some of them furtively made Masonic signs, to which the marquis responded equally surreptitiously. The master of ceremonies jumped over the flames to land at the centre of the stage, almost burning his trousers due to his bad leg. Several members of the audience laughed nervously at this. The man called on them to be silent and pay attention. Once they had complied, he announced: "Esteemed gentlemen, if you have no objection, let us begin. After the performance, my daughters will offer you refreshments," he added, before jumping back over the floodlights and disappearing behind a curtain. A few seconds later, the lights went out and the room was plunged into darkness.

A short while later, a greyish beam of light crossed the room and was projected on the whitewashed wall. The beam of light started to take on ill-defined shapes that looked like copies of the patches of damp out in the courtyard. These patches began to move, producing murmurs in the audience. They gradually became recognisable: in front of them the spectators could make out a fox terrier as big as the wall itself that appeared to be observing them with as much curiosity as they were gazing at it. It was similar to a photograph, but moved the way a real-life dog would have done, poking out its tongue, pricking up its ears and wagging its tail. After a few more seconds, the dog stood sideways on to the room, lifted a hind leg and began to urinate. The audience ran for the door so as not to get soaked. In the total darkness reigning once more in the room, this stampede led to collisions, bumped heads, spectacular falls.

At last the light came back on and calm was restored. The man's three daughters were onstage: three attractive young girls wearing dresses that exposed their chubby arms and slender ankles. Their appearance was greeted without much enthusiasm: those present had at first been intrigued by the spectacle, but soon felt cheated. Neither the three girls' charms nor their daring outfits were sufficient to rescue the evening; the spectators consumed very little, and overall takings were paltry.

As with many other contemporary inventions, several countries claim to have given birth to the kinematograph. Whatever the truth, its first steps were extremely promising, until disappointment set in.

This reaction was due to a misunderstanding: those who first had the opportunity to see a screening did not confuse what they were seeing with reality (as the legend invented *a posteriori* has it), but something even better: they thought they were seeing moving photographs. This led them to believe that thanks to the projector, any image could be set in motion. *Soon in front of our astonished eyes the* Venus de Milo *and the Sistine Chapel, to quote just two examples, will come to life*, we read in a scientific journal from 1899. A wildly inaccurate article appearing in a Chicago newspaper that same year reads as follows: *Then the engineer Simpson did something incredible: with the aid of his kinetoscope (which we have referred to a thousand and one times in these pages) he succeeded in making the photographs in his family album begin to move. How astounded would your friends and relatives be to see your uncle Jasper strolling calmly round the dining-room table in his coat and stovepipe hat, when he was buried many years ago in the church cemetery, or cousin Jeremy, who died a heroic death at the battle of Gettysburg.*

In August 1902, that is, three years after these absurd articles, a Madrid newspaper reported the rumour that a local impresario had reached an agreement with the Prado Museum to present a variety show with Velázquez's *Meninas* and Goya's *Maja Desnuda*. The correction the same newspaper published the following day did not prevent a flood of letters for or against this initiative; this furore was still going on in May 1903. By then, however, what the kinematograph really represented was common knowledge: a derivative of electrical energy, a curiosity with no practical application.

For a few years the kinematograph existed in an embryonic state. Restricted to places such as the one the Marquis of Ut took Onofre Bouvila to in Plazuela San Cayetano, its chief function was to serve as a hook for a clientele whose true interests lay elsewhere. After that it became completely discredited. The few theatres that four hopeful businessmen opened in Barcelona had to close their doors after only a few months: their only customers were tramps who took advantage of the darkness to snatch a nap indoors.

The man with the injured leg was sheltering in the doorway from the rain that had been pouring down for the past few hours. Every so often he raised the oil lamp he was holding above his head and waved it. Plazuela San Cayetano was lit up by a flash of lightning: he could see the trees bent over by the wind and the pavement covered in a sheet of dark water. Suddenly, in the middle of the square, he saw two black horses pawing the ground, spooked by the noise of the storm. Two men descended from the carriage, and he showed them in. Lighting the way across the yard and down the corridor, he led his two visitors to the same room where a few years earlier he had shown the film of the incontinent fox terrier. By now the projector, acquired more in hope than thanks to any real business acumen, was lying forgotten in the basement. He only dusted it off occasionally to show some dreadful films that had originated heaven knows where, films that the marquis and other eccentrics enjoyed and later claimed were "extremely instructive". In reality, this kind of film was merely pornographic and degrading.

The projection room had been restored to its original decor: a maroon plush sofa, a ceiling mirrorball, leather armchairs, marble pedestal tables and an upright piano fitted with a bronze candelabra. The man's eldest daughter, whom the years had converted into a serene, plump beauty, was playing the piano with languid, chubby fingers. The middle daughter had shown a special talent for baking pastries; the youngest did not know how to do anything, but had still retained the freshness of youth.

"It's a dreadful night," the man said. "I wouldn't be surprised if there were floods, we get them every year. I've lit the salamander:

the rooms will warm up in ten minutes. If you wish I can offer you a novelty: my middle daughter has just baked a kilo of *panellets*."

Onofre Bouvila declined the offer. His companion had no such scruples; he indicated through signs and guttural gurgling that terrified the lame man that he would gladly accept. While he was satisfying his gluttony, the owner limped off to answer a furious knocking at the entrance. "Come in, your honour," they heard him say at the far end of the corridor. "The other gentlemen are here already." A third man, whom Onofre Bouvila recognised at once by his bearing and gait, came in, enveloped in a cloak.

"Gentlemen," said Onofre, "since we're not expecting anybody else, I think we can uncover our faces. I can vouch for the discretion of everyone here." To lead by example, he unbuttoned his collar and threw his cloak onto the sofa. The other two did the same: they were the Marquis of Ut and Efrén Castells, the giant from Calella. The three of them spent a long while exchanging greetings, then Onofre Bouvila said: "I took the liberty of bringing you here on this hellish night, because what I am about to propose has something hellish about it. And the opposite as well."

Efrén Castells interrupted to beg Onofre not to confuse him with complicated nonsense. "Either you come to the point," he threatened, "or I'll eat another kilo of *panellets* and go home for supper." Onofre smiled. "What I'm going to suggest is eminently practical," he assured them, "but it needs a prologue. I'll try to be brief. I'm sure you are aware of the pathetic situation Europe finds itself in . . ." He went on to vividly portray the desolate panorama that had been causing him such despair in recent months. The marquis objected that he couldn't give a fig what was happening in the rest of Europe, and that if France and England were wiped off the face of the earth along with all their inhabitants, he would be the first to celebrate. Onofre Bouvila tried to convince him that the era of fervent nationalism was a thing of the past and that times had changed. The marquis reacted angrily: "Are you giving us International Socialist propaganda now?"

Seeing the discussion was becoming heated, Efrén Castells butted in. His mouth was so full of marzipan and pine nuts the other two couldn't understand a word of what he was saying, but his sheer size commanded respect and they immediately simmered down. "As proof of what I'm saying, I'll simply point this out," Bouvila went on: "Now that the war is coming to an end, what is to become of us? We have built up an arms industry for which suddenly, overnight, as they say, there is no demand. What does that mean? It means factories closing and workers being laid off, and then the inevitable consequences: street disturbances and bomb attacks. You'll tell me we've faced similar problems in the past and succeeded in overcoming them. And I tell you that this time things are going to take on unprecedented dimensions. This phenomenon will not be confined to any national boundaries: it will happen on a universal scale. It will be the Revolution we have heard so much about."

The eldest daughter was still sitting at the piano; the Marquis of Ut was nodding off to the rhythm of a barcarolle. The youngest one was lying sprawled on the sofa. She had put her legs up on the pedestal table and her skirt was raised almost to her knees, impudently showing the soles of her ankle boots and her silk stockings. Seeing this, Efrén Castells' jaw dropped.

"Why did you bring us to a place like this to force us to listen to your doom and gloom?" he asked. Bouvila smiled but did not reply: he knew that the Marquis of Ut wouldn't have been seen with them other than in a low dive like this.

"You can leave the room if you wish," Onofre Bouvila said. "We have plenty of time."

Efrén Castells signalled to the girl, and the pair disappeared behind a beaded curtain that hid the door to a darkened bedroom. The swishing of the beads was enough to wake the marquis up. He asked what had happened to Castells. Onofre pointed to the curtain and winked. Waking up properly, the marquis asked: "What will you and I do until he comes back?"

"We can talk," Onofre said. "When he returns, I'll outline the plan I've come up with. It's important Efrén Castells goes along with everything, because he'll be the one who assumes all the risk without realising it. So we two have to appear to be in complete agreement. He needs to believe that the three of us are in this together; he shouldn't suspect he is simply a tool in our hands. If there are any differences, you and I can settle them in private, as we've always done."

"Understood," said the marquis, who felt an atavistic attraction to conspiracies. "But what the devil is this plan of yours?"

"I'll tell you later," Onofre Bouvila said. At that precise moment the Calella giant reappeared, followed by the girl. The marquis immediately got to his feet. "I'll be right back," he muttered. Taking the girl by the arm, he dragged her off towards the curtain. Efrén Castells dropped back into his seat and lit a cigarette.

"Why did you ask that effeminate fop to come?" he wanted to know, pointing his chin at the chair the marquis had just vacated.

"His collaboration is essential if our plan is to succeed," Bouvila replied. "You must show you're with me in everything I propose. If he sees we're united, he won't dare protest. We two can settle any differences later in private, as we've always done."

"Don't worry," the giant said. "But what exactly is this famous plan of yours?"

"Ssshh!" said Bouvila, glancing at the bedroom door partially concealed by the beaded curtain. "He's coming back."

His Holiness Pope Leon XIII had decided to make a stand once more, to confront certain currents of opinion and ethical positions that had flourished under the aegis of modernity, and which his predecessor His Holiness Pius X had tolerated. With this objective *in mente* he shut himself away in his chambers. "Don't let anyone disturb me," he told the captain of the Swiss guards on duty that night. The Pope wrote until dawn and then gave to the world his encyclical *Immortale Dei*.

This had occurred in 1885, but Onofre Bouvila still clearly remembered the Sunday when as a boy he had heard this encyclical being read in San Clemente church. As befitted such an important text, it was read first in Latin. The faithful, all of them locals from the valley, men and women, adults and children, healthy or sick, listened on their feet, heads bowed and hands folded across their chests. Afterwards they crossed themselves and sat back down on the wooden pews. This always produced a great amount of noise, because the pews were not screwed to the floor and the legs were uneven. Once silence was restored, the rector (the same Don Serafí from whom Onofre had received the baptismal waters) read the infallible text once more, this time in Spanish (Catalan had not yet been reintroduced into ecclesiastical rites, with the result that in Catalonia many people believed that Spanish and Latin were variants of the same language of divine origin and tried, unsuccessfully but painstakingly, to grasp the meaning).

Onofre's mother was sitting beside him. She was wearing her best black dress, with its pattern of tiny flowers, to attend Mass. Now, more than thirty years later, Onofre saw these flowers superimposed on the dispatches from the Western Front that kept him informed of the losses caused by German submarines in the Atlantic and the entry of the United States of America into the European war. Back then he had felt for his mother's hand, and once he had her attention, had asked what the priest was reading. "Something the Pope has written to us," his mother told him, "so that we obey him in everything he

337

says." "A letter?" the young Onofre enquired, and when his mother nodded, he asked: "Did Uncle Tonet bring it?" "Of course, who else?" his mother whispered. "And did he send it just to us?" he asked after a while, when the question occurred to him. "Don't be silly," his mother said. "He's sending it to the whole world. He doesn't know anything about us, not even that we exist." Onofre responded: "But he loves us all the same," repeating what the rector had beaten into him. "Who knows?" his mother replied.

Her husband had left for Cuba nine years earlier, but that was not what was on Onofre's mind at the time (and still less now in his memory). He knew the Pope lived in Rome, but beyond that his knowledge of geography had to be supplemented by his imagination. He thought of Rome as a far-off place, a castle or an inaccessible palace on top of a mountain a thousand times higher than the ones surrounding their valley. It could only be reached by crossing a desert on the back of one of three animals: a horse, camel or an elephant. These images came from the illustrations in a book of Sacred History the rector used to reinforce his teachings. What had astounded Onofre as a child was that from such a remote place, the Holy Father could send his letter so quickly to the humble parish of San Clemente, which he did not even know existed.

As Onofre recalled this towards the end of the Great War, he felt the same astonishment. "That is power!" he muttered, knowing he was alone in his office. Only this ubiquitous power could raise defences against the forces of subversion threatening the world. That power had formerly been reserved exclusively for the Church, and the Church seemed to be resting on its laurels, riven by internal disputes, drifting without a helmsman. Yet it was the Church alone that could penetrate the earth's most hidden corners. In the tiniest, most isolated farmhouse or wretched hovel there was always a holy image pinned to the wall, an invocation that demanded acceptance and obedience. And all that, Onofre said to himself admiringly, had been done by Jesus Christ two thousand years earlier with the help of a handful of unhappy Galilean fishermen.

In fact, despite all the information at his disposal, Onofre didn't have the faintest idea where Galilee was. Even if his entire fortune had been at stake, he could not have placed it on a map. Others had tried to do the same as Christ: Julius Caesar, Napoleon Bonaparte, Felipe II . . . They had all suffered defeat and the most humiliating failure. They had put their trust in the force of arms and had spurned the spiritual might that was able to create an invisible bond holding together those thousands of millions of particles otherwise destined to disperse in opposite directions, to spread throughout infinite space or to collide with one another. Now he, Onofre Bouvila, would resurrect that network: from a seed of the spirit he would help a powerful tree to grow, with infinite branches, infinite roots.

The lame man's youngest daughter was sobbing in the kitchen. During the night she had been forced to submit to the marquis's depraved desires four times, and had had to bear Efrén Castells colossal thrusts on no fewer than nine occasions. This had led to slight haemorrhaging and severe pains; her elder sister had been forced to abandon the piano and replace her in the bedroom. Now she was helping the middle daughter cook more *panellets*. The giant had already consumed fourteen kilos, despite complaining that pine nuts roused his sexual appetite. Through the window a new day was dawning; the sky was overcast, heavy with rain.

Despite all the interruptions, Onofre Bouvila had managed to finish outlining his plan. The marquis had dark circles under his eyes. Neither he nor the giant from Calella had understood the idea or what was expected of them when it came to carrying it out. They both entertained serious doubts as to their friend's mental health, but neither dared say a word, fearful that any comment would lead to a fresh outpouring of the flood of solemn nonsense they had been forced to listen to for seemingly endless hours. Onofre Bouvila was smiling: the sleepless night did not appear to have dampened his spirits. Now the bargaining began, and he knew he would end up getting his way.

This marked the beginning of the most ambitious project of his life, and also of his greatest disappointment. It started off on the wrong foot and went downhill from there. In the end, all his friends and allies turned their backs on him, and he found himself alone once more.

5

A long line of automobiles had formed a queue in the narrow street. The winter sun glinted on their radiators, while now and again a lonely cloud was reflected in their polished mudguards. The automobiles advanced a few metres, then stopped. They remained at a standstill for a while, then edged forwards again. When they reached the end of the street, they turned right into an even narrower and darker one, where the sun never shone. There, shortly before the corner, they finally came to a halt in front of an iron door over which hung a tiny gas lantern, unlit in the middle of the day.

A doorman in livery, top hat and gold buttons opened each automobile door, doffed his hat when the passenger emerged, bowed deeply, closed the door, replaced his top hat, raised a whistle to his lips and blew a loud blast. This was the signal for the driver to set off again, and for the next automobile to take its place. And so on, one after another. When the automobile that had just left reached the end of this second narrow street, it turned right again and went down another very short one which led onto a square. There the automobiles that had already set down their passengers were waiting under the acacia trees for a second blast on the whistle. A bar at one corner of the square had put tables, chairs and some parasols with blue, yellow and red struts out on the pavement. It was serving beer and wine with soda water to the drivers, who could also, if they wished, eat stuffed olives, anchovy fillets, potatoes with peppers, pickled sardines and such like. As the number of automobiles in the square increased, so did the number of drivers enjoying an aperitif at the bar. By twelve-thirty there was no room for any more vehicles or drivers.

Fortunately, by then, everyone who was meant to arrive had done so. The passengers, after alighting with the aid of the ceremonious doorman, had been led from the iron door to their seats by some young ladies whose appearance caught everyone's attention. Not because they were young and attractive, but more because they were wearing straight, loose dresses attached to their shoulders by thin straps and descending like cylinders without in any way emphasising busts or waists. These dresses were covered in white sequins and ended an inch or so above the knee, exposing not only the young women's arms, from shoulders to fingernails, but also their long, muscular and veined legs, more suited to cyclists than any lady worthy of the name. Added to these extravagances was garish make-up that appeared to have been smeared on, and very short, straight hair held in place by a silk ribbon.

The gentlemen arriving couldn't get over it: "Have you seen what a fright they are?" they said to one another. "Looking like that, I can't tell if they're coming or going." "Good God! Nowadays there's no way of knowing whether they're men or women." "If this kind of thing carries on, I'll become of the other persuasion." 'What can you expect, my friend, it's the dictates of fashion." "All I can say is that if ever I see my daughter in rags like these, I'll rearrange her face with a good slap." "This is bound to have consequences." "Time will tell." "What a poor start," was the general verdict.

The Marquis of Ut was regretting having lent his name to such a spectacle; he was sorry he had ever let himself be persuaded by Onofre Bouvila's obstinacy. Neither of them was visible to the audience in the auditorium at that moment: it was Efrén Castells who had officially invited all the guests and was the one showing his face. The giant from Calella had a good reputation among Barcelona high society. He was extremely serious in all his business activities, prudent with his investments and punctual and honest when it came to paying. He had never been involved in any kind of scandal, economic or otherwise. He was regarded as a model family man: he was known to have lapses, his keenness for women was legendary and he was rumoured to be prodigious in this respect, but everybody simply attributed this to his exuberant nature. He spent money lavishly, but not too extravagantly, which also won him approval. He gave quietly to charity and had become a shrewd art collector respected by critics, artists and dealers alike. At this moment, however, he was risking that prestige in front of all his admirers. "I wouldn't want to be in his shoes," the marquis murmured. Onofre Bouvila did not contradict him: the pair were spying on what was going on down below from behind a lattice screen in a box.

Many of those invited only now realised they were in the stalls of a theatre that they had entered from the back via the stage door. "What are we doing here?" they wondered. "Is this a private function? At midday? What's going on?" Two spotlights converged on the stage. In front of the closed curtains stood Efrén Castells; up above the audience in a morning coat, he appeared even larger than he was. A joker began to sing the popular Catalan song "*El gegant del Pi ara balla, ara balla*" ("The Giant of the Pi is dancing") to loud laughter from everybody else. "This is going to be a farce from start to finish," the marquis muttered. "In his place, I'd already have died of shame." Onofre Bouvila smiled: "He's thicker-skinned than you imagine," he said. He had a sudden memory of Efrén shouting out to buy the magic hair restorer Onofre was selling in the grounds of the World Fair. Afterwards he always gave him a peseta for his collaboration. It's exactly the same now, he thought. It's always the same. With his booming voice Efrén Castells had no problem silencing the audience as soon as he saw they had grown tired of singing. They didn't know how to continue their joke and were willing to listen.

"Dear friends," he began. "I trust you don't mind me calling you friends . . . you all know I'm a simple man, and there's not one among you who would deny that in my dealings I always placed friendship before profit. Don't worry, I didn't invite you here to ask for money." At this, they all looked at one another uneasily. Onofre winked at the marquis: "I told you he'd take the bull by the horns," he said. "What's important is that he gives it the *coup de grâce*," the marquis retorted. "Nor do I want you to waste your valuable time with empty phrases. I'm not a great talker, and with you I have always preferred the open, down-to-earth language of sincerity. All I ask is your attention for a few moments. I'm going to show you something you have never seen before. Something you've never seen before!" He repeated himself to discourage the laughter provoked by the possible double meaning of this phrase. "But what you are about to see for the first time you will see thousands and hundreds and dozens of times in the future . . ." "What's he talking about?" said the marquis. "Numbers aren't his strong point," Bouvila replied, "let him do it his way." "Today you are going to have the privilege of this exclusive offer. You know what that means in the world of commerce, but there's no need to thank me. I won't say any more: now the lights will go out. Don't be afraid, you can stay in your seats, nothing will happen. I'll be back later to explain what this is all about. Thank you for your attention."

As he left the stage, the curtains were drawn back by an electric motor. When they had completely parted, the audience saw the front of the stage was covered by an enormous screen with no visible seams. It was made of a material that did not appear to be metal or canvas, but a combination of the two, like asbestos. Then, as Efrén Castells had announced, the lights went down. There was the whir of a machine starting up, and the sound of a piano, which someone was playing behind the screen.

"Damn and blast it!" rang out a voice in the audience. "They're going to show us a film!"

This warning created widespread panic. "If it's the one with the dog, I'm off," somebody shouted. The hubbub drowned out the piano as the first images began to flicker on the screen. The scene was that of a humble dwelling, little more than a tumbledown shack, lit by a wavering candle. Pushed against the far wall was a narrow, unmade bed. In the centre stood a table with four chairs; on the table were a work basket, balls of wool, cotton bobbins, scissors and scraps of material. Together, they gave the viewer the impression of a life of hardship and squalor. This brought hoots of laughter from the audience. They could now see a woman dressed in black seated at the table with her back to the audience. She looked middle-aged, and rather plump. Her shoulders were heaving; sobs shook her stocky frame and her dishevelled hair was tossed from side to side. Somebody shouted, "Give her a cup of tea!" and this remark again set the rest of the guests laughing. "God help us!" murmured the marquis. "Stay calm," Onofre Bouvila snapped at him.

On screen, the woman raised her arms to the roof of the shack, tried to get to her feet, then collapsed back on her chair, as if her joints could not support her weight, or she lacked the mental strength, or both. The laughter in the stalls grew louder and louder; every gesture the woman made only served to create more of an uproar. Efrén Castells burst into the box where Onofre Bouvila and the Marquis of Ut were sitting. Even in the darkness his wild, staring eyes were plain for them to see.

"Onofre, for the love of God," he moaned, "tell them to cut the projection right away!"

"If anybody so much as tries, I'll have him shot," Onofre muttered through clenched teeth.

"Can't you hear how the blasted audience is laughing?" the giant said. His shoulders were heaving just like those of the woman in the film. Grabbing him by the lapels, Onofre shook him as hard as the difference in their sizes permitted. "Since when did you lose your nerve?" he thundered. "Keep quiet and wait!" It was then that the three of them realised the laughter was dying down. They pressed up against the lattice screen and peered anxiously at what was going on down below. The desperate woman had finally struggled up from her chair. She turned round, and her face filled the screen. A hush fell over the audience. As Efrén Castells had promised, for the very first time they were seeing something that for years the entire world would admire at all hours and everywhere: the harrowing face of Honesta Labroux.

Her physical attractions were non-existent. At a time when the charms of a real, buxom woman were being eclipsed by the fashion for androgynous youngsters with narrow hips and jerky movements, she offered a well-rounded, heavy and rather mannish body, vulgar features and mannered gestures, prim and coy expressions. Her clothes were equally vulgar. Everything about her was common and cheap. And yet, between 1919 and 1923, when she retired from the cinema, scarcely a day went by without her photograph or a story about her appearing in the newspapers. Every illustrated magazine announced articles (which she never authorised) and interviews (which she never gave to anybody) to boost sales. Each day she received twenty kilos of letters: some were declarations of love and offers of marriage; others were heart-rending pleas, but there were also macabre threats, repulsive obscenities, warnings of suicide if the sender did not receive such and such a favour, curses, insults, blackmail.

To avoid being besieged by admirers and psychopaths, Honesta Labroux regularly changed her address and never appeared in public. In fact, no-one beyond her inner circle could claim to have seen her except on screen. Rumour had it she was locked in and closely guarded twenty-four hours a day, that she was only allowed out to go to the studio for filming early in the morning, hands bound, gagged and with a sack over her head so that not even she knew exactly where she lived or where she was going. "It's the price of fame," people said.

This air of mystery, the secret surrounding her true identity and her past only made the twenty-two full-length films she appeared in during her brief, meteoric career seem all the more true-to-life. Only a few poorly preserved fragments of these films have survived. Apparently they were all identical to the first one. This pleased rather than disappointed her public; any change immediately provoked out-bursts of anger in the cinemas, and even violence. If there was an evolution in her film career, it was a gradual descent into the depths of sentimentality. A terrible actress, she shook her head and gestic-ulated in the most appalling fashion while Mark Antony lost the Battle of Actium because of her and an asp that looked like a sock wriggled its way to poison her opulent bosom; or while her lover was dying of consumption and a gang of evil Chinamen slipped a sleeping draft into her drink in order to sell her into the harem of an effeminate, acrobatic sultan; or while her alcoholic gambler of a husband thrashed her with his belt after telling her he had bet and lost her honour on the green baize table; or while a gaucho on the point of being hanged revealed to her that she was his mother. In these films, all the men were cruel; all the women cold and heartless; all the priests fanatics; all the doctors sadists, and all the judges implacable. And yet she pardoned every last one of them in her sickly sweet, interminable deathbed scenes.

"Who on earth is going to be interested in this nonsense?" the Marquis of Ut had said when Onofre Bouvila read them the script of the first full-length film that his studios went on to rehash *ad nauseam*. Onofre had shut himself in his study and worked there alone day and night. He planned everything: the plot, scenes, sets, costumes, down to the minutest detail. After a few days, his wife wanted to know what he was up to, but when she went to his study, she found it locked. Alarmed, she knocked on the door: "Onofre, it's me. Are you alright? Why don't you answer?" Met only by silence, she had started pounding frantically on the door with her fists. This noise brought the servants running, and when she saw them around her, she shouted: "Open up, Onofre, or I'll have the door broken down!"

In response, his calm voice could be heard: "I've got a revolver in my hand and I'll shoot the first person who disturbs me again," he told them. "But Onofre," said his wife, only too aware he was perfectly capable of carrying out his threat, "you haven't had anything to eat or drink for two days." "I have everything I need," he answered.

One of the maids asked permission to speak to her mistress. When this was granted, she said that, as her master had instructed, she had brought him two weeks' provisions and water. She added that she had also provided him with changes of clothes and all the chamber pots the local hardware store had in stock. The master had told her not to say anything to anybody; he did not want to be disturbed for any reason. Onofre's wife bit her lip and simply said: "You should have told me before." She thought she detected a note of sarcasm in the girl's voice and a glint of defiance in her black eyes. She can't be more than fifteen or sixteen, but she's already behaving as if I were the maid and she was the mistress. Margarita was convinced everybody was making fun of her, behind her back and to her face. I wager he cheats on me with this one, she thought. She must smell of garlic and cheese; he prefers those smells to the French perfumes and bath salts I use every day. No doubt when they're in bed they cover their heads with the sheets to intoxicate themselves with the body odours they give off after they've been shunting up and down like two locomotives. They'll do it over and over, like that night when he climbed through the window into my bedroom at papa's house. I bet he's told her about that, I bet he's profaned the secret of our first night together with all the sluts he's had since then. They probably split their sides laughing about it until dawn. I ought to send her packing without a second thought, she concluded, but she did not dare do so.

She'll be offended; she'll understand the real reason for her dismissal and she'll insult me in front of the other servants. She'll think, I've nothing to lose, and she'll tear me to pieces. She'll say the swine's name, tell the staff everything and I'll be a laughing stock. Then she'll tell him. He won't go against my wishes, but he'll set her up in an apartment and visit her every evening. Soon he'll find any excuse to spend the whole night with her and tell me he's been obliged to spend the night working, as he has so often. Margarita did not realise that this cowardly attitude of hers was what had made her forfeit his love in the first place.

A fortnight after this episode, the same maid went to tell her the master was emerging from his self-imposed retreat. Margarita was taking tea with her eldest daughter and their dressmaker when the maid came in with the news. She had already forgotten her jealousy and disgust, thinking: This girl is very loyal, I must reward her in some way.

Her daughter and the dressmaker were also heavyweights: together they waddled like three hippopotamuses down to Onofre's study. They reached the door just as he was coming out. During the previous fortnight, he had not washed, combed his hair, nor shaved. He had slept only a few hours, and hardly touched his food. He had not changed his clothes either. He looked haggard and swayed about as if he had just woken from a deep, disturbing dream or was emerging from a trance. An unbearable stench wafted out of the office and down the corridors like a soul in torment, terrifying all the maids.

"Agustí, prepare my bath," Onofre told the butler. He did not appear to have noticed that his wife, his daughter and the dressmaker were there. He was carrying a bundle of handwritten sheets of paper, full of crossings-out and corrections. When the maids came scurrying towards him with buckets and mops to clean the study, he held up his hand to stop them. "There's no need to clean," he told them. "We're moving house."

On screen, Honesta Labroux was now lending her face and gestures to that very script, embodying the fantasies about which the Marquis of Ut had been so doubtful. Onofre Bouvila had grown angry when the marquis asked who would be interested in such nonsense.

"Everybody," had been his stinging reply.

It was true: the whole audience was in tears. Those hard-headed businessmen could not stop weeping. Later, it was said that this unprecedented reaction would never have been elicited were it not for Honesta Labroux's magic. We will never know exactly what that magic was. In a letter written many years later, Pablo Picasso affirms that the enchantment came from her gaze, her mesmeric eyes. This seems to confirm the rumour picked up by some of his biographers: namely that Picasso knew her personally. It was said that in a moment of madness he abducted her in a laundry van (with the help of Jaume

Sabartés), then took her with him to the village of Gòssol in Berguedà, returning her safe and sound to the film studios two or three days later. During those days he made various sketches of her and began an oil painting; these it is said were the origin of the highly prized works of his so-called Blue Period.

Even more improbable than this love affair is the one a magazine claimed Honesta Labroux had years earlier with Victoriano Huerta. This treacherous general had usurped the presidency of Mexico after ordering the assassination of the rightful president Francisco Madero and his deputy Pino Suárez. General Huerta had lived for some time in Barcelona after the revolt headed by Venustiano Carranza, Emiliano Zapata and Pancho Villa had forced him to abandon the presidency and flee the country. Drunk and quarrelsome, he roamed the taverns in Barcelona's Barrio Chino. In his calmer moods he plotted his return to Mexico.

German secret agents were planning a diversionary tactic that would take the attention of the United States away from the war in Europe, and wanted to use Huerta as a decoy. They provided him with the opportunity he was looking for. With the money he had accumulated during his brief months as president, now stashed away in the vaults of a Swiss bank, he had bought arms and ammunition from Onofre Bouvila. Onofre had received payment and delivered the goods, but had also informed the North American government of its delivery. A detachment of US marines had intercepted the shipment in the port of Veracruz, causing numerous casualties among the civilian population. When the arms were returned to Bouvila, he sold them on to Carranza, who was now fighting his erstwhile allies Villa and Zapata.

According to the same magazine, before she dedicated herself to the cinema, but while she was already working for Onofre Bouvila, Honesta Labroux had danced one night for Huerta. He had fallen head over heels for her; had offered her fabulous sums of money and even promised to restore the monarchy in Mexico when he returned there and install her as Empress, like the hapless Carlota, but all in vain. This scene had taken place, the magazine asserts, in his suite at Barcelona's Hotel Internacional, built in an incredible sixty-six days to receive visitors to the 1888 World Fair. The ceiling and walls of the suite Huerta was staying in had several bullet holes in them, which led to the hotel management issuing him with a strict warning. He was also rude in word and deed to the hotel staff and did not settle his bill. It was said that on their night of passion he was walking around barefoot with his trousers undone, revealing a yellowing, ragged vest; his appearance made it hard for her to believe his promises.

This story, like the one with Picasso, is probably apocryphal. In reality, Picasso went to spend several months in Gòssol in 1906, and Victoriano Huerta died a drunken death in an El Paso prison in 1916. In those years, Honesta Labroux had not yet been launched to stardom by Onofre Bouvila; her screen name hadn't even been invented. She was still living a life of reclusion with Señor Braulio in a modest house in Gracia, waiting for him to die so she could give herself a second and final time to the love of her life and then end it all.

It was the man to blame for this decision who persuaded her not to do so; the man whose behaviour all those years earlier had led her to such extremes of despair. He did this not with words, but with the same malign, icy stare that during that first night in the boarding-house attic had conquered and terrified her, leading her blindly to commit the most ghastly of crimes. Her mother had died that same night, and she was also to blame for the betrayal of the anarchist group to which she belonged. Most of its members had later died in the common graves of Montjuich, staining her conscience with their blood.

Onofre Bouvila had instantly grasped how all this pain and endless suffering shone from her sulphurous eyes. He was also aware that in the second half of the nineteenth century, in those countries where the Industrial Revolution had taken place, the notion of time had radically altered. Before then, a person's life was not strictly measured; as circumstances required or made advisable, people could work entire days and nights without stopping, and then do nothing for an equal length of time. As a result, celebrations could be what nowadays seems exorbitantly prolonged: the harvest festivals could last a week or even two. Similarly, theatrical, sporting or bullfighting events, religious ceremonies, processions or parades could last five, eight or ten hours, or longer. Those taking part could do so without interruption or could leave, or leave and then come back, as they wished.

Now, however, all this had changed. Work began every day at the same time and ended at the same time. There was no need to be an augur to know how the days and hours of a person's life would be, from childhood to old age: it was enough to know what work they did, what their trade was. This had made life much pleasanter. It had eliminated a good many shocks and removed many unknowns. Now philosophers could pronounce: the timetable is destiny.

In return, this great change demanded important readjustments. Everything had to be regular, with nothing left to chance or the inspiration of the moment. And this regularity was impossible without punctuality. Prior to this, it had been unimportant: now it was everything. A weary horse had to be whipped, or a lively one reined in so that a cart reached its destination at the allotted time – not a moment before or after. So much importance was given to punctuality that some politicians based their electoral propaganda on it: "Vote for me and I'll be punctual," ran their slogan. It was not the landscapes, works of art or friendliness of foreign countries that won praise, but the punctuality they could demonstrate. Countries most people had shunned in the past were now deluged with a flood of visitors anxious to see with their own eyes the renowned time-keeping of their citizens, hostelries and public transport.

This readjustment could not have taken place on such a huge scale were it not for electrical energy: this continuous, unvarying current guaranteed regularity and reliability. A tram powered by electricity no longer depended on the health or mood of mules to complete its route with clockwork precision. Now its passengers could happily say to themselves: I know what time it is, so I know how long I'll have to wait for the tram.

These changes had not taken place in the twinkling of an eye: first came the most necessary things, then the more superfluous ones. Entertainment and leisure were left to last: bullfights continued for many hours. If a bull showed itself to be resolute or wily, if it gored horses as soon as they appeared in the ring, the Sunday afternoon bullfight could last well into Monday. In Cadiz in 1916 there was a famous bullfight that began on Sunday and finished on Wednesday, with none of the spectators leaving. As a result, the shipyard workers who had attended lost their jobs. This led to strikes, riots and the burning of some convents. The workers were taken on again, but it was clear things could not continue as before. Onofre Bouvila was well aware of this.

Before his re-encounter with Delfina, before she took off her dress, threw herself into his arms and fixed him with those sulphurous eyes that were to transform his ideas, it had often crossed his mind that the kinematograph could be the new form of entertainment that mankind had been searching for. The kinematograph combined three elements that made it perfect in this respect: it ran on electricity, it did not rely on audience participation and its content was always exactly the same. Ah, Onofre mused, to be able to offer a spectacle that is always identical, that always begins at the same time and ends exactly when it is supposed to, always the same as well! And to have the public sitting in silence in the dark, as if they were asleep or dreaming: a way of producing collective dreams! That was his ideal. No, that's too good to be true, it's impossible, he thought. He had seen the film with the dog and a couple of others, and was forced to agree with the pessimists. Nobody went to see any of those films if there wasn't something additional immediately afterwards, if the projection wasn't followed by *sardana* dancing or sack races, if a young bull wasn't let loose, or meat barbecued on the spot. That won't get us anywhere, he said to himself.

In fact, others were thinking the same way. In Italy in 1913, the first film conceived of as a grand spectacle had been shot. This film, which was called *Quo Vadis?*, took up fifty-two reels and lasted two and a quarter hours. It was never shown in Spain, for such an odd reason it is well worth a digression.

The year 1906 saw the debut in a Paris variety theatre of a dancer who went on to win international renown. She was Dutch and her real name was Margaretha Geertruida Zelle, but she claimed to be an Indian priestess and had adopted the artistic name of Mata Hari. As with all exotic dancers, she received many propositions, but none so extraordinary as that made to her by a gentleman one summer night in 1907. "What I'm going to ask of you is very special," the man said, twirling his waxed moustache. "Something that probably nobody has ever asked of you." Mata Hari poked her head over the screen behind which she had taken off her organdie tunic and silver breastplate incrusted with amethysts and turquoises. "I don't know if I'll be exotic enough for you, darling," she said in French with a strong Dutch accent.

When she emerged from behind the screen, the gentleman raised his monocle to his left eye. His visit had been preceded by bouquets of roses (six dozen of them) and a diamond choker. Mata Hari was now wearing the choker as a sign of acceptance, together with a kimono that had a black and gold dragon embroidered on the back. She sat down at the circular mirror on the dressing table, a mirror where princes, bankers and field marshals had seen the lust-filled reflection of their own eyes.

She slowly removed the supposedly sacred rings of her priestly attire, some of them showing human skulls, and dropped them into a sandalwood box. "And might I know what it is you expect of me?" she asked coquettishly. "I'll whisper it in your ear." He came so close that the tip of his moustache left a tiny indent on her cheek, but his eyes were burning not with desire, but cold calculation. "I represent the German government," he said. "And I want you to spy for us."

It was not long before this conversation reached the ears of the English, French and North American intelligence services. Mata Hari's fame as a spy soon surpassed even her renown as a dancer. She received engagements from all over the world, and earned more than Sarah Bernhardt, something that would have been unthinkable only a few years earlier. For a time, the rivalry between the two divas was the talk of Paris. When, in 1915, Sarah Bernhardt had to have a leg amputated, it was said she exclaimed: "Now at last I'll be able to dance as gracefully as Mata Hari." The Dutch spy danced only once in Barcelona, at the Teatro Lírico, winning more plaudits from her public than from the critics.

In the end, the Allied secret services decided to dispose of her, and laid a trap. A young staff officer pretended to have fallen under her spell as so many others had done before him. He showered her with gifts. They were seen together everywhere: riding in the Bois de Boulogne, having lunch and dinner at the most expensive restaurants, in a box at the opera, at Longchamp racecourse and so on. She never asked her lover how he could lead such a life on an officer's modest pay, perhaps taking it for granted he had additional income from a large personal fortune. Or perhaps she responded to his feigned devotion with genuine affection: that is the only explanation for how such an experienced spy could swallow such conventional bait.

One night, when they were resting in bed, the officer suddenly announced he would have to leave her for a week, possibly two. "I can't live for so long without you," she said. "Don't go wherever it is you're supposed to go." "My country needs me," he said. "Your country is here in my arms," she replied.

In the end, he reluctantly revealed to her the mission taking him from their love nest: he had to go to Hendaye. There he was to intercept a film the Bulgarians were trying to smuggle to German agents based in San Sebastián. When they arrived at Hendaye, he would be waiting for them: he would snatch the film, and the agents would be rounded up and shot on the station platform.

No sooner had he finished explaining this than she hit him over the head with a small statue of Shiva, the cruel god, the destructive force: the young officer fell to the floor, blood streaming from his face. Thinking she had killed him, Mata Hari threw a *renard argenté* coat over her nightgown, donned a toque and a pair of rubber boots and climbed aboard her black 24hp Rolls Royce (which she owned together with another three automobiles and a twin-cylinder motorbike). All these had been given her by prominent figures in public life from France and other countries – paid for by the taxpayers.

The moment she left, the officer jumped to his feet and ran to the window. From there he signalled to agents posted opposite the house. He was not dead, nor even wounded: foreseeing such an outcome, the French secret service had replaced all the heavy objects in the room with rubber replicas and given the officer several capsules of red ink for him to simulate bleeding.

Now Mata Hari's Rolls Royce was speeding along a road next to the railway line in the snowy fields of Normandy. In the distance she saw a horizontal plume of smoke: it was the train, speeding towards Hendaye. The chase was being observed by an aeroplane in which the handsome officer and three agents were travelling. By accelerating in an almost suicidal manner, the Rolls Royce had caught up with the train and was now level with the guard's van. The fearless spy was standing on the car's running board. She had torn her nightdress into strips and used them to secure the steering wheel to stop the vehicle veering off the road. She had also taken a stone she had picked up from a roadside ditch and propped it on the accelerator pedal. On the windscreen she wrote *Adieu, Armand!* – the name of the officer she thought she had sacrificed to do her duty. Leaping off the running board, with one hand she grasped the iron rail at the back of the train. She watched the Rolls Royce continue its mad career, leave the road and finally come to a halt in the middle of a field. Miraculously, it did not suffer the slightest damage in this incident, and to this day can be seen in the small *Musée de l'Armée* at Rouen.

Clambering inside the guard's van, Mata Hari tried by the light of a muffled lantern to discover where the film was. She was expecting to find one or two strips of celluloid, possibly a dozen frames. Instead, she came across several stacks of cylindrical cans: the fifty-two reels of the Italian *Quo Vadis?* When the Allied agents rushed into the van they found her exhausted, her hands red raw. The wind sweeping in through the open door had blown away her toque and was ruffling her curly hair. She had succeeded in throwing out twenty of the fifty-two reels; they were now buried deep in the snow.

This was why the film never reached its destination and was

never shown on Spanish screens. The war had halted production throughout Europe, and no more such films were made. It was now Onofre Bouvila's responsibility to resurrect the industry, but it was not until fate led him to cross paths with Delfina a second time that he was sure of the way to do so.

6

The downpour had returned, accompanied by the echo of distant thunder. The rain beat against the shutters and bounced off the awning covering the kitchen yard. In the kitchen, the lame man's three daughters were asleep against the warm wall, tenderly entwined. In the main room the three men were still arguing.

"You're crazy," Efrén Castells told Onofre. He was the only person who dared say such things to him, and Onofre did not take offence. He gently stroked the photographs he had taken out of his jacket pocket and placed on the table for the other two to see.

"I warn you, these photographs don't do her justice," he told them. "I realised that myself from the start. I made her put on twenty kilos to see if that gave her greater ... how shall I put it ... greater physical presence."

He had taken her to a country property in Alella he had rented specifically for that purpose. It suited his plans as it was surrounded by a very high, thick hedge of trimmed cypresses. He told Delfina she had suffered a lot. "What you need now is rest," he said. "You've been looking after your father for years, God rest his soul; the moment has come for someone to look after you." There was nothing Delfina could say to this. She had spent many years in prison, and afterwards had lived in total isolation, devoted as Onofre said to looking after her sick, feeble-minded father. She was accustomed to having no control over her life, and the only escape she could imagine from blind obedience was death.

When Onofre took her to the house, a chauffeur, cook and a maid were already installed there. Delfina registered no surprise that despite there being a chauffeur there was no automobile, or that these servants lived in the main floor of the house, whereas she was relegated to the draughty bedroom upstairs. "They're completely trustworthy," Onofre Bouvila had told her. "I've given them instructions and they know what needs to be done. You don't have to worry about anything, just do what they tell you." All she could say was thank you. She told herself: Maybe this is like us being a married couple; this is what being married to a man like him must be like.

Over the following months she thanked anybody who talked to her. In the morning, the maid would serve her a big breakfast in bed: chorizo omelette, potato purée, toast with olive oil and a litre of hot milk. Then the maid would dress her and leave her in the garden, settled in a wicker armchair in the shade of a mimosa tree. She would wrap a bright yellow angora shawl round her shoulders; attracted by the colour, butterflies and bees would fly round her. Then she had lunch and lay down for a siesta. She would wake up with the sun low in the sky, to be served tea or chocolate with cake. Afterwards she took a short walk round the garden, always followed at a discreet distance by the chauffeur.

On one of the first days she had tried to start up a conversation with him. "Didn't Onofre say if he was coming to see me?" she had asked. The chauffeur looked her up and down before replying. "If you're referring to the master," he said haughtily, "he is not in the habit of informing me of his plans, and I don't tell the master what he should do." He's put me in my place, Delfina thought. She thanked him and continued her walk. On another day she wanted to push aside the cypresses to see the street outside, but the chauffeur led her back. This bothered her less than not knowing if Onofre would come to visit her. He didn't go to see her because he was shut up in his study writing the script for the film she was to star in. Meanwhile, his hired staff continued to fatten Delfina up. At night they gave her a sleeping pill so that she would sleep soundly for many hours. She had no idea she was eating too much: in prison she had been so starving she had lost all sense of proportion. If now she had once again been given a chunk of bread, a piece of rancid cheese, a herring or a bit of cod in brine, she would have been more than satisfied. Similarly, the Pantagruelian feasts she was made to eat seemed perfectly fine to her. She had no notion that there were choices in life or that people sometimes had the opportunity to exercise them. Any sense of self had been destroyed in her. In the end she decided to write Onofre a letter, to tell him everything she had not managed to say in the room alongside her dead father's body. When she finished it, she handed the letter to the chambermaid, begging her to post it as soon as possible.

That night in the kitchen the servants sat down to read the letter, but they couldn't understand a thing. They were three crooks, who carried out their duties with bad grace. One or other of them was always drunk, if not all three at once. Despite the fact that they loathed one another, they were always together, as they were unable to spend a single instant alone. The chauffeur fornicated alternately with the chambermaid and the cook; occasionally, when he had drunk too much, with both at the same time. Whenever that happened, the two women fought over him, tearing each other's hair out, ferociously scratching and biting one another. The shouting and racket from these bestial orgies sometimes managed to wake up Delfina, but as she was still drowsy from the sleeping draft, she was not fully conscious and believed she was still in prison, where she used to be woken every night by infernal screams. She had succeeded in overcoming the terror these shrieks produced in her by incorporating them into her own dreams, and tried to do so again now.

That night, she wrote in the letter that never reached Onofre Bouvila, *I also wanted to cry out, but I restrained myself. That cry stayed deep inside me and I have been hearing it every night since then. I'm not saying this as a reproach – it is not only a cry of pain, but also one of boundless joy. And yet it tore me from the peace that sleep might bring me: I know it is only in death I will find rest. But no, I have no wish to lay claim to a courage I lack. I cannot lie to you: I have lived through difficult moments in my life, and have sometimes been tempted to disown the grandeur of my destiny, namely my love for you. That is not meant as a reproach either. I have always thought that if you were not as you are, if you had behaved differently, my life would have been different to what it was, and there is nothing that causes me as much pain and horror as the thought that a single instant of my life might have been different, because that would mean in that instant I would not have loved you as much as I have loved you. I don't envy anyone and would not change places with anyone, because nobody could have loved you as much as I have loved you.*

While the servants were reading this, several drops of wine fell onto the sheet of paper. "Curse it," they said. "What would Señor Onofre say if he saw those stains?" In order not to be found out, they threw the letter on the fire.

The Marquis of Ut said: "I have to go." He struggled to his feet: the lack of sleep and the damp weather had stiffened his joints. "Don't you have anything to add?" Onofre Bouvila said. The marquis glanced at his watch and frowned, then considered that in reality he had no pressing engagement, and relaxed. "If we've got this far, I may as well stay to the end," he sighed. Onofre Bouvila smiled gratefully. "Sit down and tell me what's worrying you." The marquis stroked his stubbly cheeks. "There's something I don't understand," he said at last, his voice slightly slurred. Ideas occasionally escaped him, and if he was tired he found it hard to concentrate, something difficult enough for him at the best of times. Now he was gazing in a puzzled manner at the photograph of Delfina, a dolled-up matronly figure leaning on a parasol against a background of cypress trees, staring vacantly ahead of her. He dropped the photograph, smacking his lips and clicking his fingers.

"What would that be?" Onofre said patiently.

"What's my role in all this?" the Marquis of Ut said.

Perhaps if all businessmen realised that sooner or later they were bound to die, that would be an end to all economic activity in the world. Fortunately this thought never crossed the Marquis of Ut's mind. Freemason, rogue and libertine, deep down the marquis was a dyed-in-the-wool conservative. His total lack of opinions carried great weight in the most reactionary circles. These small cliques, made up of aristocrats, landowners and some sections of the Army and clergy, exercised a decisive but negative influence on Spain's political life: they never intervened except to forestall change. They simply made public opinion aware of their existence and of what could happen (usually something tragic) if their absolute opposition to progress were challenged. They were like lions dozing in a cage. They did not follow any ideology, and any attempt to rationalise their position was poorly received. In their eyes that would have meant questioning whether this attitude was correct, just or necessary, and that represented a breach of the natural order of things. "Let others justify themselves," they would say. "We have no need to, because we are right." Any innovation, even if it coincided with their interests, horrified them; to embrace them would be tantamount to suicide.

Onofre Bouvila knew from experience it was impossible to discuss anything of this sort with them. He had occasionally suggested to the

Marquis of Ut it might be wise to introduce small reforms in some area or other, with the sole aim of avoiding greater problems. The very idea roused the marquis's ire. "Why on earth do you want to change the world?" he would say. "Who do you think you are, God Almighty? Bah, aren't things fine as they are? You're rich, and after all, we all grow old and die: you look after your own affairs and let those who come after do their worst!"

The marquis's arguments were inconsistent, but nothing in the world could make him alter them. The fact that these subversive propositions came from Onofre Bouvila merely reinforced his views. "When all is said and done," he told Onofre, "you came from nothing. You're a peasant who has been permitted to make bucketloads of money. That's gone to your head and you think you have a right to everything, but what has all this got to do with you?" The marquis saw this as proof that in the future he needed to tread more carefully, to be stricter.

The fact that the marquis felt able to be so rude to a friend whose generous hospitality he never refused, and to whom he owed important favours and large sums of money, aroused Onofre Bouvila's admiration and envy. As with Efrén Castells, he could not take umbrage with the marquis either. "Why are you so narrow-minded?" was his gentle rebuke. "Your inflexibility will bring about your own destruction."

At this, the marquis would shout and wave his arms about like a lunatic, threaten him that his patience had reached a limit and that if he carried on talking like that he would be obliged to send his seconds to call on him. Indeed, when he was in such a fury, the Marquis of Ut would not have hesitated to kill Onofre. Since for the marquis and his fellow conservatives the existing order was the natural one, all disorder by necessity must come from outside the system and had to be eliminated by whatever means. On such occasions, they always used the example of a sick organism, humours and amputation, a confused metaphor that neither sociologists nor surgeons could understand.

"Louis XVI said the same when they came to warn him of what was going on in the streets of Paris," Onofre Bouvila had said, more to disconcert his friend than with any conviction. But the Marquis of Ut responded without turning a hair that all Frenchmen were sons of whores and that he couldn't give a damn what happened to them. "Not even the king?" Onofre Bouvila had countered.

"Ah no, not that," the marquis had said, rising to his feet. "Nobody touches the House of Orleans in my presence."

By now, however, the situation in Europe was no longer a laughing matter. What had taken place in Russia, Austro-Hungary and even Germany itself could not be taken lightly. Only a profound, bold change would allow everything to stay the same.

"So what is this bold, profound change of yours?" the marquis said. "Making films with that fat cow?"

Onofre Bouvila was still smiling in a conciliatory fashion: he wasn't yet ready to confide the true extent of his plans to the marquis.

"Trust me," he told him. "All I ask of you is that you don't send troops into the streets, that you convince your friends I'm not crazy or acting in bad faith. Give me a period of grace to prove what I can do. But during that time I need there to be calm in your ranks. If there are a few small disturbances, let the masses enjoy themselves. Pretend you don't notice: it's all part of my plan."

"I can't commit myself to that extent," the marquis said, tiredness making him unusually defensive.

"I don't want you to do anything," Onofre said. "I simply want you to talk to your friends. Will you do so, for old times' sake?"

"Let me think it over," the marquis said. Onofre knew he could not ask anything more of him, so he left it at that.

*

Now the theatre was full of the Marquis of Ut's friends, and he, Onofre and Efrén Castells were spying on their reactions from the screened-off box.

"It seems to be going alright," the giant from Calella said.

Onofre Bouvila nodded. Of course it is, he said to himself. Yet again his intuition had triumphed.

When she was driven to the film studio, Delfina made no objection or showed the slightest interest: they could have been taking her anywhere. The studio had been built on an empty lot between San Cugat and Sabadell, not far from where today the Autonomous University of Barcelona stands. The cost of its construction was extremely high, because all the technical equipment had to be imported. Two pioneers of the Catalan film industry had been involved – Fructuoso Gelabert and Segundo de Chomón – but neither of them had wanted to direct Onofre Bouvila's absurd film.

In the end an elderly out-of-work photographer was hired. This was Faustino Zuckermann, a tight-fisted, ill-tempered central European. The choice proved an excellent one: from the start he intuitively understood Onofre's project. He was tyrannical with Delfina, and not a day of shooting went by without him reducing her to tears for some reason or other. In addition, he was a drunkard prone to sudden fits of uncontrollable anger. When he was thus afflicted everybody had to get as far away as possible to avoid injury. On one occasion, he broke three bones in the wardrobe mistress's hand; on another, he threw a chair that split a runner's head open. Onofre Bouvila rejoiced at the atmosphere of fear that Zuckermann created in the studio: he knew this would produce a more delicately perfumed bloom.

It took a long time to achieve decent results. Barcelona was dreadfully behind when it came to film technology. The first attempt took three months to emerge from the laboratory, and when it did, it was clearly a disaster. Some sequences were too dark; others were so bright they hurt the eyes, the images staying imprinted on the retina for hours afterwards. Or again, brownish blobs would float across the screen, while elsewhere movement had been reversed. The actors walked backwards, filled their glasses with a liquid that came out of their mouths, and so on; or they walked on the ceiling while others strode across the floor.

Onofre Bouvila was not deterred by this disaster. He ordered all the useless reels be burned, and for shooting to start again immediately. He was told Faustino Zuckermann was in no fit state to work: he could hardly stand up. "Then let him direct sitting down," Bouvila said, a move which was later copied by many famous directors. For this second attempt, everything had to be begun from scratch, because the sets and costumes for the previous film had also been burned on Bouvila's express orders. He wanted the whole process kept secret and for nothing of what went on in the studio to get out. The film hands faced terrible threats, but the financial rewards were high.

At last Onofre Bouvila was told the second film was ready, and if he so wished he could view it in a projection room inside the studio. Hearing this, he dropped everything and had himself driven there in a limousine with tinted windows. At the end of this first screening, Bouvila called Faustino Zuckermann to see him. The old photographer gave off an unbearable smell of red wine and raw onion; his breath seemed to come from the centre of the earth.

"Congratulations," Onofre said. "Everything I wanted is there: the hopes and fears of all mankind." Faustino Zuckermann's bloodshot eyes staring at him drunkenly helped convince Onofre he was right: They're identical, he thought, the same yearning, the same despair. It won't be long before this light still glowing deep in their eyes is extinguished. It will be reduced first to embers, and then to nothing more than a heap of cold ashes. But before that happens, this final moment will have been fixed forever on film.

This was the film that was now bringing tears to the eyes of the oligarchs congregated in the theatre thanks to the Marquis of Ut.

CHAPTER SIX

1

The man who came out to meet Onofre Bouvila was past the age when appearance owes more to circumstance than the passage of the years. There was not a hair on his head, which was spherical and the colour of dark clay. He had pinched features; his eyes were a pure blue. He was wearing a pair of corduroy trousers held up by a rope tied around his waist, a faded flannel smock and rope sandals. He leaned on a gnarled stick as he walked, and stuck into his improvised belt was a jack knife so big it made the rest of him seem inconspicuous. Close on his heels was a small, repulsive-looking dog with a stubby tail and weak legs. The dog never took its eyes off its master, who every so often returned its gaze, as if seeking approval for what he was doing or saying.

The man replaced his cap and turned his back on Onofre Bouvila. "Be so kind as to follow me, sir," he said. "It's this way. As I think I warned you, the path isn't in very good condition."

Onofre Bouvila set off after the man and his dog. The chauffeur who had brought him to this clearing in the woods made to follow them, but Onofre stopped him.

"Stay here," he said. "And don't worry if I'm away for some time."

The chauffeur sat on the running board, laid his peaked cap to one side and began rolling a cigarette as the two men and the dog walked down a path soon hidden from view by bushes. Despite his age, the man moved agilely over roots, stones and undergrowth.

Onofre Bouvila on the other hand frequently had to stop whenever his jacket caught on a bramble. If this happened, the man turned back, lopped off the briar with his knife, and apologised profusely. Onofre Bouvila already considered his jacket ruined.

The film industry he had created in 1918 reached its peak two years later, at the end of 1920. That was its moment of splendour, its apogee; after that, things started to go downhill. To everyone's amazement, in 1923 Onofre transferred his share of the company to Efrén Castells, who had been his associate from the start, and announced he was retiring not only from this venture but from all his other businesses. Those who knew him well, or in the absence of anyone who could make that claim, those who had regular dealings with him, were less surprised by his decision. In hindsight they detected the first signs of it in the sudden announcement that he was thinking of moving house. They now recalled that moment, and saw it as no accident that this move coincided with the beginning of his most ambitious project.

"This used to be the service entrance," the old man said. "Your honour will forgive me from bringing you this way, but it will save us having to climb the wall."

Onofre had seen hundreds of houses in his stubborn search, but nothing had prepared him for what now confronted him. This mansion, high on the slopes of La Bonanova, had once belonged to a family whose name was apparently either Rosell or Roselli. Built at the end of the eighteenth century, little of the original structure remained following the house's enlargement in 1815. The extensive park also dated from then. Romantic in conception, and rather haphazard in its implementation, it covered approximately eleven hectares. To the south side, that is, to the left of the main house, there was an artificial lake fed by a Roman-style aqueduct that brought water directly from the River Llobregat. The lake drained into a moat that wound round the garden and in front of the house, on which it was possible to go boating in skiffs or punts under the shade of the willows, cherry and lemon trees that grew on either bank. There were many bridges across the moat: the main stone bridge with three arches that led to the house's front entrance; the slightly smaller one known as the "water-lily" bridge, with its pink marble parapet. Then there were the "Diana" bridge, so-called because it was crowned by a statue of that goddess taken from the ruins of the Greek colony at Ampurias; the covered bridge, made from teak; and the Japanese bridge, which made a perfect circle with its reflection in the water.

The lake and moat had been stocked with many kinds of brightly coloured fish, and rare varieties of butterflies had been imported from Central America and the Amazon. By dint of great effort and skill unusual in Catalonia at the time, these had been acclimatised to the native vegetation and climate. In 1832, a grotto was added, greatly admired in its day. This addition followed a then fashionable family tour of Italy, from where the Rosells originated or had settled during the Catalan rule of Sicily or the Kingdom of Naples (when in all likelihood the family name had undergone changes like the one already referred to). The offspring of the Barcelona branch of the family traditionally travelled to that country when the eldest came of marriageable age (a custom not dictated by whim or inclination, but from an explicit desire or clear strategy of not wishing to inter-marry with other Catalan families, which in their eyes was bound sooner or later to lead to the dispersal of the family fortune). This grotto consisted of two parts or chambers. The first was huge, with a ten-metre-high vault and curious formations of stalactites and sta-lagmites exquisitely fashioned from stucco and porcelain; the second, smaller one was bare but was even more extraordinary, being situated next to the lake below water level. Part of the rock wall had been replaced by a large rock crystal, some fifty centimetres thick, through which the bottom of the lake was visible. When sunlight penetrated the water, weeds and coral, shoals of fish and a pair of giant turtles brought from New Guinea could be seen. These turtles survived the change of habitat and, as is their custom, lived to extreme old age (in fact until well into the twentieth century), although they never bred.

"My father," the man said, "was a beater for the Rosell family. Later, when he went deaf, he became a gamekeeper. So you see, sir, I was born into service to the Rosells."

In addition to these wonders, the garden had countless twists and turns, pavilions, summer houses, mock temples and glasshouses, as well as deliberately maze-like avenues where anybody strolling could unexpectedly come upon the equestrian statue of the Emperor Augustus, or the stern faces of Seneca or Quintillian on their pedestals. Through the hedges, secret conversations could be heard, loving rendezvous surprised, or passionate kisses spied on in the moonlight. On the seven terraces of lawn extending up the mountainside paraded pairs of peacocks and Egyptian cranes.

"But the first job I remember having," the man went on, "was as pageboy to Señorita Clarabella when I was six years old. If my memory serves me right, back then Señorita Clarabella must have been thirteen or fourteen. Even though she spoke several languages, Señorita Clarabella always addressed the servants in Italian, which meant we never understood the orders she was giving us. That apart, my duties were not onerous: all I had to do was to take her seven lapdogs for walks. Seven pedigree dogs, sir, all of them different. You should have seen them."

The house had three storeys, each of them of twelve hundred square metres. The main front, facing south-east towards Barcelona, had eleven balconies on each of the upper floors and ten large windows flanking the entrance on the ground floor. With all these enclosed balconies, windows, transoms, skylights and doors, there were more than two thousand and six panes of glass, which required constant cleaning.

Now many of them were broken, the house interior devastated and the garden a jungle. The bridges had collapsed, the lake had dried up, the grotto had fallen in, all the exotic fauna had been devoured by the vermin and rats that now lorded it over the property. The skiffs and carriages were nothing more than piles of splintered wood in the doorless sheds. The Rosell family crest was little more than a time-worn, mouldy excrescence on the frieze above the main door.

"Tell me what happened," Onofre Bouvila said. They had risked life and limb crossing the bridge and were now standing outside the main entrance. The man sat on a stone lion that had no head or tail, with the dog at his feet; he rested his head on his hands, which were folded on the top of his stick, and gave a deep sigh. Onofre Bouvila knew he was in for yet another long and curious story.

"Even though as is well known, the Rosell family, sir, refused to marry within Catalonia," the old man began, "so as not to become related to their compatriots, something which always created bad blood, as if being born in the same region and under the same sun gave people the right to pronounce on the private or even senti-mental lives of others, or to judge them, or whatever; as I was saying, sir, they were not disdainful or inward-looking, quite the opposite in fact. So it was rare for me not to meet some visitor or other at dusk when I was returning from the two hours exercising the dogs as I was required to do, even during the months of great heat – in the meadow that used to be up there, the first one touched by the shadows from those poplars, which are much taller now than they were, back then, obviously."

He spoke in long, rambling sentences, as though he found it hard to recapture his memories or share them with a stranger. At times he fell silent, caught up in his thoughts, and when that happened he turned as red as a schoolboy, his naturally ruddy skin taking on an almost indigo hue. When the awkward moment passed, he would shake his head, raise a hand from the stick he was clutching and point to the overgrown meadows as if his memory could magically restore them to the carefully tended fields of yesteryear. He imagined he was still seeing people strolling through the park, and carriages bowling along. "Whenever that happened, you can imagine how hard it was for me to restrain the excited dogs; they tugged on their leashes, wanting to play. And often they won out, and despite them being so small, since I was small too and not exactly expert, they would drag me across the soft lawns, barking and jumping, and with me snivelling, much to the amusement of the visitor who glimpsed this merry scene as his carriage crossed the bridge and the big double doors opened wide to let him enter the house."

At this point, Onofre left the old man still talking and stepped into the entrance hallway. Light came flooding in through the bare big windows. The floor was strewn with dry leaves. A few random objects had survived the ravages of time: a brightly coloured ball, a bronze vase, a chair and a few other trifles. The lack of anything more substantial was plain and painful to see. Onofre Bouvila wondered how many objects it took to make a house, some of them crafted from carefully assembled components. In terms of man hours, a mansion like this must have taken several lifetimes to complete; its destruction made those lives a useless investment, a total waste, Onofre's business instinct suggested. He was roused from these reflections by the old man, who had silently rejoined him and now took up his tale once more.

"And the fiestas, sir! The picnics and banquets!" He pushed aside the leaves on the floor with the tip of his stick, to reveal a foot and the lower part of a girl's calf in a mosaic. If he had gone on clearing away the leaves, he would no doubt have uncovered a mythological scene that filled the hall, but that would have taken him several hours. He gave up and instead went on haltingly describing those bygone receptions and fiestas as they walked from salon to salon. As was to be expected, he said, he was not permitted to attend these usually nocturnal celebrations, but he used to steal out of his room, in his nightshirt and barefoot despite the chill, and hide somewhere where he could see without being seen. These escapades were made all the easier due to the commotion such events caused: the servants had their hands full, and none of them had time to worry about a youngster like him.

In the Hall of Mirrors, swifts had made their nests in the ceiling beams and mice were scurrying along the mouldings. This sight appeared to make the old man even sadder. He fell silent, and when he spoke again it was hastily, as if he wanted to bring what was clearly a painful visit to a swift conclusion, possibly because he was there with someone else for the first time in a long while.

"One summer's day," he said, "a fateful summer day, as I was coming back from my evening walk with the dogs, I found the house in an uproar. Everybody was rushing about, which at first made me think another big celebration was being prepared. No, I thought, that's impossible, because we had just hosted two big events, one on top of the other: Saint John's Eve, and the visit of the troupe from the San Carlo theatre in Naples, whom Señor Rosell had invited to come and put on a performance of *Le Nozze di Figaro* by Señor Mozart during their summer layoff, something which had meant a lot of hard work, because we had to accommodate and look after not only the singers, the choir, the orchestra and the stage hands – about four hundred people in total – but also the instruments and costumes; following this it seemed likely we'd want to avoid any more disruption for a good while. But that can't have been the case because there I was, unable to believe my eyes, in the midst of a battalion of carpenters, plasterers and painters: all those needed to prepare for a lavish occasion. Excited at this unexpected spectacle, I ran inside the house, followed by my seven dogs, looking for someone who could tell me what was happening or was going to happen, until finally I came across a pantrymaid to whom I was, I think, somehow related, since marriages between male and female servants of the same household were not uncommon – a fact which, by the way, gave rise to picturesque situations such as my aunt once removed also being my first cousin, and one of my mother's brothers being my nephew as well, and so on. Be that as it may, this pantrymaid to whom I was somehow related, and who might even, now I come to think of it, have been my mother, since my father, on the rare occasions he emerged from the woods, used to sleep with her, which of course does not prove anything, was at that moment plucking a pheasant, whose head she had chopped off neatly with an axe, that she, that my purported mother, still had on her lap, told me that earlier that afternoon a rider enveloped in a cape and wearing an old-fashioned three-cornered felt hat, leaped from his mount before it ended its frenzied gallop, and without bothering to tie it up or hand the reins to the groom, who, alerted by the thunder of hooves on the bridge, was already running to help him, a situation the horse had taken advantage of to take a quick dip in the moat, had whispered a password in the butler's ear that had meant the doors to the house were flung open for him, and allowed him to have a hasty conversation with Señor Rosell, whom he had rudely awakened from a nap, after which the master had given orders to make preparations for a grand ball that same night (that same night!) in honour of an illustrious guest whose name, however, had not been revealed to the staff.

"'The rider galloped off again, closely followed by messengers sent out to personally invite guests,' said the pantrymaid who was possibly my mother. 'But who is it?' I asked with the hungry curiosity of my tender years, to which my mother responded that she couldn't tell me, it was a secret, and that even if she did agree to whisper it, it wouldn't mean a thing to me, since the name, a few syllables of which she had managed to hear when listening behind a door, was completely unknown to me. I insisted so much – appealing to her maternal instincts, always assuming our relationship justified them and that she in fact possessed them – that in the end she gave in and told me the person in whose honour all the preparations were being made was none other than Duke Archibaldo María, whose claims to the Spanish throne had for many years been supported by the Rosell family."

Up on the first floor there were only a few dry leaves, but there was a thicker layer of dust, as if it came from the objects themselves. So much dirt can build up, Onofre Bouvila reflected. I don't know what would happen if everyone or almost everyone neglected to clean the part of the planet they inhabit. Maybe that is the true destiny of mankind: maybe God put man on earth for him to keep it clean and tidy. Maybe everything else is a fantasy.

"Back in those days, to declare in favour of one or other pretender to the throne was no trifling matter, like having a favourite bullfighter is nowadays. No, it was a grave political choice, the consequences of which could be dire, if the civil wars being fought back then went against one," the old man went on. "The thing was," he continued after a pause, "the pretender in question, the one whose visit had been announced, had promised in some incomprehensible document, a mishmash of ideology, harangue and political programme known for some reason as an 'edict' and promulgated in Montpellier, to grant Catalonia 'restricted independence' or something of the sort, a system apparently copied from the one which used to and still does bind India to the British crown. And it was on the strength of this vague promise that the Rosell family were risking their lives and fortune.

Now this pretender to the throne had suddenly announced his arrival, creating a terrible dilemma for the household: on the one hand they had to welcome their guest as befitted his real or possible status, yet on the other, they had at all costs to keep his visit a secret, since the authorities and rival factions were as one in putting a price on his head, this conundrum only adding to the confusion of the preparations, which sorely tested the family's imagination, refinement and *savoir-faire*."

The floor here was covered with shards of porcelain that crunched beneath the two men's feet. Picking up one of these fragments and studying it, Onofre realised it came, like all the rest, from a Sèvres or Limoges dinner service of no less than two hundred items, not counting soup tureens, sauce boats, serving dishes and fruit bowls. "The dining room is on the ground floor, so how did the dinner service come to be up here?" Onofre asked. His companion did not reply, steeped as he was in his memories.

"The moment we saw him, we realised this Archibaldo could only bring misfortune on our house," he said eventually. "At that time, the duke was forty or forty-five years old and had spent his whole life in exile. This furtive, transient existence had turned him into a debauched, amoral creature. As he was crossing the bridge, he was so drunk he fell off his horse. I don't think he even noticed the skiffs gliding along the moat, on which servants were holding aloft candelabra and candlesticks to create a moving circle of light. His equerry, a gypsy-looking man called Flitán, leaped from his saddle like a circus performer, helped the duke to his feet and dragged him to the bridge's parapet. Leaning against it, His Highness vomited copiously, just as Señorita Clarabella, on her father's instructions and with gestures she had been rehearsing all afternoon with her dancing master, curtsied in a most gracious manner and on a black-and-white silk cushion offered him a gold copy of the key to the house, together with a white lily . . . I don't know whether I have already told you, sir, that it was a sweltering hot summer's night, a fateful night indeed. The duke had not shaved in days or washed in months. His clothes gave off a sour smell, thick clumps of snot dripped from his nose, and when he laughed – more like a snarl than an outburst of joy – he revealed a set of sharp, rotten teeth: never has a royal house been so poorly represented. The duke weighed the golden key appreciatively in his hand, then passed it to his equerry. He threw the lily to the ground, pinching the cheek of Señorita Clarabella, who immediately turned bright red, mechanically repeated her welcome curtsy and ran to hide behind her mother."

They climbed to the second floor up a staircase whose banister was reduced to stumps sticking up from the steps. When they reached the floor, the man, who until then had been walking laboriously through the rooms, dragging his feet and dawdling in every room, suddenly swerved and stood in front of Onofre Bouvila as if to intercept him.

"This is where the bedrooms were," he blurted out: until that moment he had not given any explanation as to the layout of any of the rooms. "The family bedrooms," he said hastily, afraid he had been rude. "The servants of course slept upstairs, in the attic. That was the hottest part of the house in summer and the coldest in winter, but in return for those minor inconveniences, it had the best views over the whole estate. I slept up there as well. My room was separate from the others . . . I'm not saying that to boast: in fact, I slept with Señorita Clarabella's seven dogs, but that meant I didn't have to share with any other servants, and so was spared any horseplay, whippings or acts of sodomy – not entirely of course, but yes, most days. I think I can say that while I lived here I was subjected to horseplay, whippings and acts of sodomy only once a week approximately, which is not something others in my position can claim. The rest of the time I was left alone. I used to sit on the windowsill with my feet dangling out, looking up at the stars or peering down in the direction of Barcelona, hoping to see a fire, because otherwise it was so dark it was impossible to tell from my vantage point there was a densely populated city in the distance. Later on electric light came in and things changed, but by that time nobody was living in this house. "Come on, sir," he said, seizing Onofre by the sleeve, "let's go up to the attic and I'll show you where my room was. Let's leave these rooms for now, there's nothing of interest here, believe me."

There were holes in the attic roof, through which the sky was visible. Bats nesting inside came zigzagging in through these holes, while those not swooping around were sleeping head down from the rafters. Rats with fur as spiky as thorns scuttled across the floor: they were big enough not only to take on a cat, but to finish it off. As a precaution, the man picked up his little dog.

"That night I couldn't sleep," he went on as if he had never paused in his tale. "From my room I could hear music from the ball downstairs. I was looking out of my window in the way I described to you. Beneath me, on the flat ground on the far side of the bridge, I could see, dimly lit by the myriad stars studding the sky on that summer night, that fateful night, sir, the carriages carrying the select group of guests, all of them, it goes without saying, diehard supporters of the duke. Beyond them, on the mountain slopes, countless points of slowly moving light, like a procession of lazy glow-worms – except that, woe is me, these were not glow-worms but the lanterns of General Espartero's men. The general, alerted to the duke's presence by an accursed traitor, had given orders to surround the house. Thanks to an irony of fate, no-one had noticed this dastardly move apart from me, poor innocent that I was: at the age of six, what did I know of the rules of betrayal and war? Let me catch my breath, sir, and then I'll resume my story," he said, pausing and wiping his eyes with a striped handkerchief he took from his pocket. Then for no apparent reason, he also wiped the dog's eyes, though it turned its head away. Stuffing the handkerchief back in his pocket, he went on: "I was listening to the music until I grew sleepy and went back to bed. I've no idea what time it was when I woke up with a start. The dogs I slept with had woken up before me and were prowling round the room, scratching at the doors, chewing the mat covering the floor and whining as if they could sniff vague dangers in the air. Outside, everything was dark. Peering out of the window, I saw the tiny lights that had fascinated me earlier had disappeared. Lighting a candle stub, in my nightshirt and barefoot, I crept out into the corridor, shutting the dogs in behind me: I didn't want them to escape and run all over the house, which seemed fast asleep. Down that very staircase you see over there, sir, I crept down to the second floor. I don't know what took me there, but suddenly a hand grasped my arm, and another covered my mouth, preventing me running away or shouting for help. My candle fell to the floor, where someone immediately picked it up. When I got over the shock, I saw the person who had hold of me was none other than Duke Archibaldo María, and that the other man who had picked up the candle stub and now lit his diabolical face with it was the barbarous Flitán. He had a dagger clenched between his teeth, which filled me with indescribable terror. "Don't be afraid," the duke whispered in my ear, blasting my face with fetid breath so impregnated with alcohol I was afraid I would pass out. "Do you know who I am?" he asked, and when I nodded slightly he appeared satisfied and added: "If you know who I am, then you will also know you must obey me in everything." When I nodded again, he asked if I knew where Señorita Clarabella's bedroom was. My affirmative response produced a brief exchange of looks and smiles between the two men, the meaning of which was completely lost on me. Well then, take me there as quickly as possible," said the duke. "Señorita Clarabella is expecting me. I have to give her a little message," he added, accompanying his words with a coarse guffaw echoed by his equerry.

"Naturally I obeyed. Outside her bedroom door, they handed me my candle and warned me to go straight back to my room. "Go to sleep and don't tell anyone about this," the duke warned me, "or I'll tell Flitán to cut out your tongue." I ran back to my room without once looking round. I came to a halt outside the door: this encounter had made me uneasy in a way I couldn't explain. At the end of the attic corridor where I was standing was the room where the pantrymaid who might or might not have been my mother slept. I tiptoed into the room, which she shared, as I have already said, with other maids, went over to her bed and shook her. Half-opening her eyes, she peered at me angrily. "What on earth are you doing here, you little brat?" she muttered, and I was afraid that she wasn't my mother after all , in which case all I could expect was a good hiding. Even so, I replied, "I'm frightened, mama." "Alright," she said, less angrily, "stay here if you want, but not in my bed: can't you see I have company tonight?" She raised a finger to her lips and pointed to the man snoring beside her, a man who by the way was not my father the gamekeeper, which of course doesn't prove a thing, so I stretched out on the mat at the foot of the bed and began to count how many chamber pots I could see from there.

"I was violently awakened a second time: my mother was shaking me. All the maids and the men who for whatever reason were also in the room were rushing about searching for their clothes by the dim light coming in through the skylight. When I asked what was going on, the only explanation my mother gave was a slap across the face. "Don't ask so many questions and hurry up," she said. Throwing a shawl over her nightgown, she left the room like that, dragging me with her. The stairs creaked and groaned as the servants stampeded down and gathered in the basement. There we found Señor Rosell and his wife. He was still in evening dress, or had put it on again. He was holding a drawn sabre in his right hand, while his left arm was wrapped protectively round the shoulders of Senõra Rosell, who was weeping into his starched bib. She was wearing a long blue velvet dressing gown. As I passed by him, I heard the master mutter: *Povera Catalogna!* I looked everywhere to see if I could spot Señorita Clarabella in the midst of this crowd, something my small stature made extremely difficult. I heard people around me saying that General Espartero's men had just crossed the bridge and would soon be breaking down the main door.

"As if to confirm this assertion, we heard a thunderous pounding from the ground floor, right above our heads. I hid mine in the forest of knees all around me. Señor Rosell said calmly, 'Quickly, quickly! Don't dally, our lives depend on it.' We all crowded into a pantry where I had previously seen that beans, lentils and chickpeas were stored in hooped wooden barrels. I couldn't get over it: I had never imagined so many people could fit into such a small space. As I drew closer, I realised what was going on: there was a trapdoor in the floor that was usually hidden under the barrels but was now lifted, allowing us all to climb down a secret passageway known only to the lords of the house, a way of escape when the house was surrounded, as was presently the case. My mother signalled to me: Don't just stand there, come on, run, she seemed to be saying. And I would have followed her, sir, if I hadn't suddenly remembered I had left the seven little dogs shut in my room some hours before, when I first ventured out and ran into the duke. I told myself I had to go and get them, otherwise Señorita Clarabella would scold me. Without a second thought, I turned on my heels and ran up the four flights of stairs between basement and attic."

Onofre Bouvila went over to the window and looked down. Undergrowth and bushes had blurred the estate's outlines: a green mass stretched beneath his feet down to the outskirts of Barcelona. From up there he could clearly see the limits of the villages the city had swallowed up; beyond them lay the Ensanche with its trees, avenues and luxury houses; further on still was the old city, with which after all these years Onofre still identified. On the horizon lay the sea. Chimneys in the industrial zones belched out smoke against the dark evening sky on the fringes of the city. The street lamps came on one by one as the lamplighters pursued their leisurely rounds.

"I'm not interested in the rest of your story," Onofre snapped, glancing imperiously over his shoulder at the old man. "I'll take the house."

2

Either by sheer chance or because it was in the stars, the collapse of Onofre Bouvila's film empire coincided with the completion of the rebuilding of the mansion. With infinite tenacity, oblivious to time, energy and expense, he had the house interior stripped and then reconstructed as it had originally been or should have been. He had no description or plan, or any other guide apart from the dictates of logic and the uncertain memory of the old man with the little dog. Onofre listened patiently to the opinions of architects, historians, interior designers, cabinetmakers, artists, dilettantes and charlatans who came flocking with promises they could resolve the constant crises: they all had contradictory views about everything. After listening to their views and rewarding them splendidly, Onofre took what seemed to him the best option, never allowing his own preferences to dominate.

Over the next few years he gradually saw life return not only to the house and garden, but the stables and sheds, the lake and moat, bridges and pavilions, flower beds and vegetable garden. Inside the house, the ceilings and floors were restored if what remained of the originals so permitted, or recreated in those places where time had taken such a toll on the work of man that they were no longer identifiable. Onofre distributed the porcelain and glass fragments among his agents and sent them off to the four corners of the earth to search for their exact equivalents. These agents, who only a few years before had gone round these same cities offering artillery shells and mortars to the highest bidder, now set the bells jangling on the thresholds of the damp basements of goldsmiths and antique dealers. Onofre brought painters and sculptors from workshops and attics all round the world to Barcelona, as well as restorers from art galleries and museums. A fragment of a vase no larger than a hand travelled twice to Shanghai. He had horses brought from Andalusia and Devonshire and harnessed them to replica carriages specially made for him in Germany. Everybody thought he had lost his mind: nobody could understand what drove him to immerse himself in this insoluble jigsaw puzzle. And no-one could contradict him: neither usefulness, convenience nor expenditure were arguments to which he paid any heed. Every single thing had to be exactly as it had been in the days of the Rosell family – about whose whereabouts he had never bothered to enquire. Whenever anyone expressed surprise and asked how a man like him, who was trying to replace ancestral religion with the kinematograph, was now going to such trouble to recreate something that ran counter to progress, something progress had in fact left behind forever, all Onofre did was smile and answer: "Precisely." There was no shifting him.

One day, while inspecting the works, he began chatting to an interior designer. This man told him he had been searching in vain for a majolica figurine of little value. He had, however, heard he might be able to find one in a certain Parisian establishment, but had preferred to ignore the suggestion rather than spend a disproportionate amount of time and effort on such a cheap object. Onofre Bouvila obtained the address of the Parisian establishment from the designer, sacked him on the spot, then climbed aboard the automobile waiting on the bridge for him and told the driver: "To Paris."

Until that moment, Onofre Bouvila had never left Catalonia, not even to go to Madrid, where he had so many business dealings. He dozed off on the back seat; after crossing into France the weather turned cold and he wanted to buy a travel rug to cover his legs, but found it impossible because he had no French money. He continued on to Perpignan, where a bank not only advanced him the necessary cash, but also provided him with a letter authorising him to make unlimited withdrawals wherever he went. After they left Perpignan, it began to rain incessantly. They spent the night in a village they came to as the sun was setting.

When they reached Paris the next day, they went straight to the address the slapdash designer had given Onofre. He immediately found the majolica figurine and bought it for a risible amount, then had himself driven to the nearest luxury hotel and booked into the *suite royale*.

He was in the bathtub when the hotel manager came in, dressed in a morning coat with a gardenia in the lapel. He had come to ask *Monsieur* Bouvila if he required anything in particular. Onofre asked for his dinner to be served in the suite and for the hotel to provide some female company for the chauffeur, who was staying in another room on another floor. "He has a tough day ahead of him," Onofre said. The manager waved his hand airily. "*Et monsieur?*" he said, didn't he also need company? "Someone discreet and obedient," said Onofre, trying to imagine what his friend the Marquis of Ut would have done in such a situation. The manager raised his arms to the ceiling. "*C'est la spécialité de la maison!*" he exclaimed. "*Elle s'appelle Ninette.*"

When some time later Ninette arrived at the suite, she found Onofre sprawled on the bed, fully dressed and fast asleep. She took off his shoes, undid his waistcoat and shirt collar and covered him with the bedspread. As she went to switch off the light, she saw on the bedside table an envelope on which Onofre had written: *Pour vous.* Inside was a bundle of banknotes. Ninette put the envelope and the money back on the table, switched off the light and left the suite without a sound.

"Travel is boring, and besides, it doesn't broaden the mind like they say," Onofre concluded the next morning. The hotel manager suggested he shorten the return journey by flying to Barcelona in an aeroplane. As yet there was no regular service between the two cities, but if money were no object, the manager told him, everything could be arranged. Onofre was driven to the airfield, where he negotiated the hiring of a biplane with a Belgian pilot. Onofre's chauffeur set off by road for Barcelona, while he and the pilot climbed aboard the aeroplane. Headwinds forced them to fly over Grenoble, and from there they managed to reach Lyon, where they refuelled and drank several brandies in the aerodrome bar to warm up. As they crossed the Pyrenees they very nearly had a serious accident, but eventually landed safe and sound at Sabadell aerodrome. To Onofre's astonishment, Efrén Castells and the Marquis of Ut were waiting for him by the runway.

"Good Heavens! Thank you so much for coming," Onofre said. They shouted something to him, but he couldn't hear a word: so many hours in the air had left him temporarily deaf. He was staggering as he walked from the aeroplane; the Calella giant almost had to carry him. "What I don't understand is how you knew I was arriving today," Onofre said.

They told him they had been searching for him everywhere. Thanks to the banks, they had followed his trail to Paris; there, the hotel manager had sent them a telegram informing them that: *Bibelot acheté monsieur baigné Ninette déçue monsieur volé.*

Now the three of them were heading towards Barcelona in Efrén Castell's automobile. Ensconced in the bucket seat, the giant was urging the chauffeur to go faster. "What has happened?" Onofre Bouvila wanted to know. "Something important," said Efrén. "And thanks to your stupid escapade we've already lost precious time." He said this with a seriousness ill-suited to his breezy nature.

"Let's put our hoods on," the marquis said. He pulled an inlaid wooden box from beneath the seat and from it took three black hoods adorned with the Maltese cross. With the hoods on, they had to crouch down so that the tips were not crumpled against the roof of the car. The headlong dash came to an end on the slopes of Tibidabo, outside a red-brick mansion with imitation towers, battlements and gargoyles. Two guards with rifles slung over their shoulders opened the iron gate and closed it again once their automobile had passed through. The three men got out at the main entrance, ran up the marble steps and entered a circular hall with a high ceiling. Their hasty footsteps echoed as they crossed it. They hurried on, opening and closing doors; servants in breeches, their faces covered with white satin masks, bowed and indicated the way.

Finally they entered a large room in the middle of which stood a long, narrow table. Seated round it were a number of men who were also hooded. Onofre Bouvila, the Marquis of Ut and Efrén Castells sat in three empty friar chairs. The person presiding asked gruffly, "Is everyone here?" to which the response was a ripple of assent. "Let us commence then," said the chairman, crossing himself. All the others followed suit, after which he began: "Representatives of our brothers in Madrid and Bilbao have come to this extraordinary chapter, so it is my honour and my pleasure to welcome them to Barcelona." A murmur of approval followed this statement. The chairman banged a gavel on the table and went on: "I assume all those present are aware of the situation."

By 1923 the social crisis in Spain had become so acute that some thought, there is no going back. Onofre Bouvila was one of the few who did not agree with this pessimistic diagnosis. "There's always been a social crisis," he argued. "That's the way this country is, and there's nothing to be done." He was of the opinion that, appearances notwithstanding, nothing really serious was going on. "Let things take their course," he would say. "Everything will sort itself out, with no more violence than is necessary." To Onofre, the more confusion and complications the better – that was how he had got where he was.

The Marquis of Ut and his ilk thought the opposite: they had inherited the privileged positions they enjoyed and lived in constant fear of losing them. They considered extreme measures as justified if they helped maintain stability. The spectre of Bolshevism robbed them of sleep. Ah, Onofre Bouvila thought whenever an argument led in this direction, if Bolshevism were to triumph here as it did in Russia, I would be Lenin. He had unshakeable confidence in his ability not only to recover from any setback but to take advantage of any obstacle. Of course, he could not say anything of the sort to the Marquis of Ut and his colleagues now gathered around the table.

"You have to be very stupid to let things get this far," was his only comment.

"The present situation is like the fable of the grasshopper and the ant," said the marquis, raising his voice. "The lower classes ask for something, and we give it them. The next day they come and ask for more, and we give them that as well. And so on until the rabble thinks: 'Why not have the lot?' That day they will rise up in arms, slit our throats and stick our heads on spikes. It all smells fishy to me."

This analysis was greeted with a murmur of approval. The hooded man sitting to the right of Efrén Castells added that the workers had gone crazy, and were no longer content simply to ask for the moon. "What they want now is to chop off our heads," he said. "Chop off our heads, rape our daughters, burn down our churches and smoke our cigars." All the hooded men pounded the table with their fists.

Once they had calmed down, Onofre Bouvila began to speak. "I know what working men want," he said gently. "They want to become bourgeois. What's so wrong with that? The middle classes have always been our best customers." At this there was a murmur of dissent. The fate of the working class meant nothing to Onofre, but he couldn't bear being opposed: he decided to argue his case, even though he knew the final decision had already been taken. "Look," he said, "you all think the worker is a bloodthirsty tiger, waiting for the right moment to leap out on you; a wild beast you have to keep at a distance at all costs. But I tell you that's not so: deep down, they're people just like us. If they had any money they'd go out and buy for themselves what they in fact produce. Production would increase exponentially . . ."

At this point, one of the hooded men interrupted him to say that he had already heard an economic theory of that sort. "I didn't understand it," he said, "but it seemed terrible to me. Later I learned it came from England: need I say more?" Another man objected that this was not the moment to get caught up in an academic discussion. "Anybody can support whatever economic theory they like," he said, "but what needs to be done needs to be done." The Marquis of Ut reiterated that the situation was similar to the fable of the grasshopper and the ant; "Or is it," he added after ruminating a while, even though by this stage nobody was listening to him, "like the one about the ass?"

Onofre Bouvila renewed his attack: "The matter is entirely in our own hands," he said. "If we accept the workers' demands within reason, they'll be eating out of our hands; if, however, we show ourselves to be inflexible, how can we guarantee their reaction won't be violent and disproportionate?"

"The army is our guarantee," said another of the hooded men, who had not spoken before. He had a slurred voice Onofre Bouvila thought he recognised. "The army is there precisely to intervene when most necessary. When the fatherland is in danger, for example." Onofre Bouvila dropped a pencil he had been toying with. As he bent down to pick it up, he looked round under the table and saw the man was wearing thigh boots. That's not good, he thought. Now I *know* who he is.

"The moment chaos reigns is when the army has to step in to impose order and discipline, because chaos is a real danger to the fatherland, and the sacrosanct mission of the army is to come to the aid of the fatherland when the fatherland needs it," this hooded man went on. There was a note of conviction in his voice, mixed with a certain inebriated insistence that brooked no contradiction. "Let our slogan be: against chaos, discipline; against disorder, order; against bad government, order and discipline." This proclamation brought his speech to a close; it was followed by a respectful silence.

"I suppose," Onofre Bouvila said finally, "we'll have to dig into our pockets."

From the steps of the railway carriage, the general turned to salute the hooded men who had come to see him off. Seeing the whole station platform awash with a sea of hoods, the general rubbed his eyes and raised his hand to his eyes in disbelief. It can't be delirium tremens, he thought. Not yet. Then he recalled what he was doing there and why all the hooded men had followed him. He straightened up; the train whistle blew.

"Gentlemen, either they'll have my guts for garters, or tomorrow I shall command Spain," he said solemnly. Beneath their hoods, his supporters smiled: they had already telegraphed their banks and were confident the *coup d'état* would succeed. The station had been cordoned off by infantry, and there were no porters or travellers on the platform. Cavalry units were patrolling Barcelona. Machine-guns and light artillery had been set up in the working-class districts and the nerve centres of the city. Silence reigned everywhere.

As they were leaving the railway station, Onofre asked Efrén Castells to take him home, because he had no automobile. The giant from Calella hesitated. "Of course," he said finally. "You only have to ask. Get in." Onofre Bouvila heaved a sigh of relief. He had no wish to be shot down in cold blood on the station steps. Inside the car he felt relatively safe. "For a moment there I thought you were going to leave me high and dry," he confessed. "We're friends," the giant replied. They removed their hoods and stared at one another. Onofre felt a stab of regret: he recalled the bearded bear he had first met at the World Fair years ago, and compared him to the slack features of the bald, prematurely aged financier beside him now. I wonder what I look like, he thought, smoothing down his unkempt mane of hair.

Unaware of what his friend was thinking, Efrén Castells advised Onofre to go into hiding for a few days. "So you too think I'm in danger?" Onofre asked. The giant nodded. He said he might not be very clever, but in his view it was possible.

"Primo de Rivera isn't bloodthirsty," he added. "If he has his way there won't be much violence. Most likely everything will go well and we won't even notice the change. But it could be that . . ." the giant went on, his face darkening not so much from concern as from the effort it cost him to formulate such a lengthy argument: ". . . it could be that when he gets to Madrid he'll meet resistance, not from civilians, but from other military men who also want to seize power. There could even be civil war. You're very powerful, and Primo knows he can't count on your unswerving loyalty. You weren't very prudent tonight," he admonished Onofre: "I don't know why you had to spout such nonsense."

"Because I believe it," said Onofre Bouvila, glancing at his friend tenderly. "And because I'm too old to keep on pretending. Be that as it may, on this occasion you're right: I'll go to France. I've just got to know Paris; it seemed like a horrible place to me, but I'll adapt if I have to."

"They won't let you cross the border," Efrén Castells said.

"The aeroplane I came in isn't leaving until early tomorrow," Onofre said. "If after we pass by my house you take me to Sabadell and don't tell a soul, you'll be doing me a huge favour."

"Alright," the giant said, "but I'll take you straight to Sabadell. It's best not to waste time: by now Primo or somebody else could already be searching for you." "Possibly," Onofre answered, "but first let's pass by my study. You and I need to sort some things out." When Efrén Castells said this wasn't the moment, he insisted: "It's now or never."

When they reached Onofre's house, he jumped out, but prevented the giant from following him. "Go and fetch my father-in-law. Get him out of bed and drag him here if need be. He's become impossible, but we need a lawyer."

Onofre entered the house as quietly as he could: he did not want to wake his wife and daughters; the mere thought of a tearful farewell set his nerves jangling. It would be worse still if they insisted on going into exile with me, he reflected as he felt for the bell pull. He summoned the butler, who appeared in nightshirt and cap. "There's no

need for you to get dressed," he told him. "Light the fire in my study."
The butler scratched his head. "A fire, sir? But we're in September!"

While the butler put some logs in the fireplace and lit the kindling
with a match, Onofre removed his jacket, rolled up his sleeves, took
a revolver out of the drawer and made sure it was loaded. Then he
laid it on the desk and dismissed the butler. "Make me a coffee, but
try not to wake anybody: I don't want to be interrupted. Oh yes,"
he added as the butler was leaving the room, "in a few minutes Don
Efrén Castells and Don Humbert Figa i Morera will arrive. Show
them straight into the study."

Once he was alone, Onofre began systematically opening drawers
and filing cabinets. Taking out sheets of paper, he glanced at them
and threw some on the fire. Every so often he prodded the ashes with
a poker. A grandfather clock struck midnight in a distant room. The
butler returned to announce that Efrén Castells and Don Humbert
Figa i Morera had arrived.

"Show them in," he said.

His father-in-law entered, tears in his eyes. He was wearing a dark
coat over a pair of striped pyjamas. Since his wife's death he had gone
soft in the head: he no longer understood what was going on around
him. He had been unable to take in what Efrén Castells had tried
to explain to him. All he had heard was that his son-in-law had to
flee the country, and was weeping at the thought of what fate might
befall his daughter and granddaughters.

"Onofre, Onofre, is it true what this brute here tells me? That
García Prieto's government is about to fall and that you have to go to
France to avoid being shot?" Don Humbert cried out. "Good Heavens,
what will become of my poor daughter and granddaughters? I told
my dear wife, God rest her soul, that we were doing the wrong thing
marrying off our little girl to someone like you, that the hunchback
would have been a much better match. Do you remember who I

mean, Onofre? That polite and shy young lad who lived in Paris. What was his name?"

Onofre calmed his father-in-law down. There was no need to worry, he said. Primo de Rivera, the Captain General of Catalonia, had left for Madrid a few hours earlier. The garrisons in Catalonia and Aragón were backing him, Onofre told his father-in-law: "We have to wait and see what happens in Madrid. If he meets with opposition, it could be war, but I think everything has already been settled: neither the high command nor the king are going to stand in his way. The upper echelons of the country are with him," Onofre said, without a trace of irony. "I am with them too, and they ought to know that," he added sadly, "but they don't trust me. In fact, they're more afraid of me than of the working class; I'm the one they hate most." Lost in thought, he lit a cigar and went on: "I should have foreseen all this."

On 30 October 1922 the blackshirts had made their famous entry into Rome. Now, a year later, on 13 September 1923, Don Miguel Primo de Rivera y Orbaneja was attempting to follow Mussolini's example. Since he did not have millions of followers, he had to turn to the army. "That's the difference between them," said Onofre. "Primo isn't a bad fellow, but he's a bit stupid, and like all stupid people he's suspicious and timid. He won't last. But while he does, I have to make myself scarce," he concluded. "Sit at my desk, Don Humbert. Get a pen and paper and draw up a deed of transfer: I want to hand all my business affairs over to Efrén Castells here."

"What nonsense is this?" Don Humbert Figa i Morera exclaimed. The butler knocked at the door: he was bringing the coffee Onofre had ordered, but had taken it upon himself to add two more cups in case Don Efrén and Don Humbert would also like some. It looks as if it'll be a long night, he mused. He had already heard rumours. Tension hung in the air like a low mist; carrier pigeons were crisscrossing the skies; the leaders of the subversive groups were running about the city sewers in search of refuge. Anarchists, socialists and Catalan nationalists met at the intersections of stinking drains, recognising each other by the greenish glow of their lanterns. They exchanged hasty greetings and hurried on.

"It's the only way to avoid possible confiscation," Onofre Bouvila said.

"But what you're asking makes no sense. How are we going to put a value on all your assets?" groaned Don Humbert.

"Make up a figure: a symbolic price, what does it matter?" Onofre said. "The important thing is for it all to be left in safe hands."

After doing some calculations and discussing it for a while, they agreed on an amount in pounds sterling, which the giant from Calella promised to transfer the next morning to one of Onofre's Swiss bank accounts. Don Humbert Figa i Morera was sobbing as he drew up the contract. He had to stop several times and said it was as if he were witnessing the break-up of the Ottoman Empire, a recent event that had filled him with huge regret. He added that he had always felt deeply attracted towards that empire, which was incomprehensible since he couldn't even place it on a map and knew absolutely nothing about it. The name alone carried echoes of pomp and magnificence. Onofre urged him to stop rambling and get on with his task. "It'll soon be daybreak," he said. "By then I need to be far away. You're to take the contract to the notary and have it legalised," he told his father-in-law. "I entrust the two of you with the safekeeping of my family," he added in a neutral tone that did not prevent Don Humbert bursting into tears once more.

Eventually the contract was signed by the two parties and witnessed by Don Humbert and the butler. Once this was done, Efrén Castells accompanied Onofre Bouvila to Sabadell aerodrome. They left Don Humbert back at the house, with instructions that when his daughter woke he should explain Onofre's absence and allay any fears she might have.

Now Efrén's automobile was speeding through the empty streets. Day was dawning, but the lamplighters did not dare come out on their rounds, and the streetlights were shining as if it were still night-time. The only person they passed on their way was a young newspaper boy: he had been told to distribute his papers as usual so that the nation would have news of what had happened a few hours earlier in Madrid.

There, the military had acclaimed Primo de Rivera, the government had offered its resignation to the king and he had charged Primo de Rivera with the formation of the new cabinet. The front page of the newspaper gave a list of the generals who made up this cabinet and announced that all constitutional guarantees had been temporarily suspended. Most of the remaining pages in the boy's newspapers had been censored.

When they reached the aerodrome, they had to wait some time for the bewildered pilot to arrive: between the hotel where he had spent the night and the aerodrome he had been detained eight times by eight different patrols; in the end, the Civil Guard had escorted him all the way to the aeroplane. "*Parbleu, on aime pas les Belges ici*," he protested when he saw Onofre Bouvila. When he told the pilot he wanted to return to Paris with him, the man was delighted, because he had been resigned to making the journey alone. Efrén Castells and Onofre embraced, and the latter climbed into the aircraft, which took off without delay.

They had been flying for half an hour when Onofre told the pilot to veer to the west. The pilot told him that was not the direction for Paris.

"I know," Onofre replied, "but we're not going to Paris. Do as I say and I'll pay you double."

This argument had convinced the Belgian, and now the aeroplane was circling round a mist-filled valley in the mountains. As they descended, Onofre Bouvila shouted instructions to the pilot: "Be careful with that hillside, there are very tall holm oaks there; steer more that way and see if we can follow the river," and so on.

Eventually, through the wisps of mist, they caught sight of a recently used threshing floor. As the plane landed, it sent up into the air a flock of black birds that had been picking at the sheaves stacked in the field. There were so many of them that for a moment they blocked out the sun. Onofre Bouvila gave the pilot an IOU he could exchange at any French bank, jumped down from the craft and indicated what direction he should take. Without switching off the engine, the pilot turned the aeroplane round, taxied for some distance across the field, then took to the air, leaving behind a whirlwind of dust and straw.

An hour later, Onofre Bouvila reached the door of the house where he was born. It was now occupied by a farmer, his wife and eight children. They told him the mayor lived in a new house next to the church. Onofre thought he recognised the couple, but they did not seem to know him.

3

When he knocked, a woman came to the door. She was about thirty years old, intelligent if rather coarse-looking, but not unattractive. She was wearing a knotted kerchief round her head and had a feather duster in her left hand. Onofre thought his brother must have got married without telling him. The woman looked more surprised than concerned to see him: That shows he's never mentioned me to her, he decided. Out loud he said: "I'm Onofre Bouvila." The woman blinked. "Joan's brother," he added. Her expression changed: "The master is sleeping," she said, "but I'll tell him you're here at once." It was obvious from her tone she was not Joan's wife. Maybe she's his mistress, a concubine, Onofre thought. She doesn't look like a spinster. Perhaps she's a young widow who desperately needed a man: protection, economic security and all that. She had left him on his own in the doorway, so he went into the house. Above the door was a framed tile with the inscription: Ave Maria. The entrance smelled of dust, no doubt stirred up by the woman's feather duster. A lamp, wrought-iron umbrella stand and four straight-backed chairs were the only furniture in the hall, which led on to a passageway with four doors: two on each side. The woman was knocking on one of these, and called out: "Señor Joan, your brother is here." She said this in little more than a whisper, but not to avoid Onofre hearing her. After a moment a cavernous voice replied from inside the room. The woman put her ear to the door, then turned to Onofre: "He says he'll be right out and that you're to wait for him." She pointed briefly to the dining room visible at the far end of the corridor, then stepped aside to let Onofre past.

In the dining room there was a square table, on which stood a frosted glass lamp. The chairs were pushed back against the wall. There was also a dark wooden dresser, a sideboard with a white marble top, and an iron stove with enamel tiling, which gave the room a well-to-do feel. On the wall over the sideboard was a carved image of the Last Supper. Glass double doors gave on to a rectangular yard, with a magnolia and an azalea growing in it. At the far end of the yard stood a tiny privy. The kitchen was to the right of the dining room. Everything looked clean, tidy and cold. Onofre was observing all this when all of a sudden the church bell rang, so close it made him jump. The woman, who had been watching him from the corridor, gave a little laugh.

"I suppose it's a matter of getting used to it," Onofre said. She merely shrugged. "Do you live here?" he asked, and she pointed to one of the doors. It was not the same one as she had just knocked on, but that didn't prove or rule out anything, Onofre thought.

At that moment his brother appeared in the corridor. He was barefoot, wearing a pair of worn corduroy trousers and a navy blue smock with half the buttons done up. He crossed the dining room without a word, as if he hadn't even seen his brother or the woman, went out into the yard and shut himself in the privy. The woman had gone into the kitchen and was now filling a metal bucket with water from a tap. Even though Onofre had just spent a night in one of Paris' most elegant hotels, the fact that there was now running water in his home village gave him an intoxicating sense of material well-being. When the bucket was full, the woman picked it up and carried it out into the corridor. Then she came back and started to light the fire with kindling and pieces of coal, fanning it with a straw fan.

How slow everything is here, Onofre thought. He was used to carrying out important business deals in half the time he had been in the house. Here, time has no value, he told himself. His brother came out of the privy, still doing up his trousers. He washed his face and hands in the bucket, then flushed the water down the toilet. He dropped the bucket in the yard and came into the dining room, while the woman went out to retrieve it.

"Did you come in an automobile?" Joan asked his brother.

"In an aeroplane." Onofre smiled.

Pursing his lips, Joan stared at him for a few moments.

"If you say so, it must be true." He sighed. "Have you had breakfast?" Onofre shook his head. "Neither have I," Joan said. "As you see, I've just got up; I went to bed late last night." At first it seemed as if he was going to tell Onofre why he had been up so late; he opened his mouth, but said nothing. A smell of toast came from the kitchen. The woman came in and put a board with cold meats on the table, and a hunting knife to slice them. At the sight of the food, Onofre's stomach started to rumble, and he realised he hadn't eaten in many hours. "Help yourself," Joan told him, correctly interpreting his grimace. "Make yourself at home." Onofre wondered if this was genuine: at that moment he fervently wished it were. He told his brother that after all the years of struggle he felt he had come back to his starting point.

The woman brought in a dish filled with pieces of toast, followed by an oil bottle and a salt cellar and several cloves of garlic out of an earthenware bowl to rub on the toast. Finally she got out a bottle of red wine and two glasses. The wine succeeded in reviving Joan, making him talkative in a way Onofre had never seen before.

By the time they finished breakfast it was almost midday. Onofre could barely keep his eyes open. His brother told him he could take one of the bedrooms; although no-one had spoken of it, all three of them knew he had come for an indefinite stay. The bedroom he was given was the one the woman had pointed to earlier when he had asked her if she lived in the house. Onofre fell asleep with this coincidence going round in his brain. He immediately recognised the ancient rustic wardrobe in the room: it was the one in which his mother used to keep their clothes. He thought of opening a drawer, but didn't dare do so at that moment, in case they heard him in the dining room. The sheets smelled of soap.

In the days that followed, Onofre devoted himself to doing as he pleased: he ate and slept whenever he liked, took long walks in the countryside, talked to people or avoided them; nobody bothered him. His presence in the village had not been a secret for long. Everyone had heard about him; they knew he had left for Barcelona many years earlier, and it was said that he had become rich there.

Not even that aroused the villagers' curiosity; more or less all of them had heard or personally witnessed the story of the brothers' father, Joan Bouvila. He had gone to Cuba and returned claiming to have a fortune that turned out to be non-existent, so there was no reason to believe his son was any different. Onofre enjoyed this uncertainty and did all he could to foster it. Besides, he was not sure those who thought he was penniless were wrong; deep down he suspected Efrén Castells and his father-in-law might have taken advantage of his absence to strip him of all his possessions. It was highly likely Don Humbert had falsified the contract, just as he had done at Onofre's suggestion to secure the properties owned by Osorio, the ex-governor of Luzón. Then it was his turn, now it's mine, Onofre said to himself philosophically.

His brother was scornful when he heard him say these things. "All that hard work to end up here," Joan would say. "Bah," Onofre replied. "It would have been just as hard being a street-sweeper or a beggar." It was only now that he was starting to glimpse the true nature of the brutal society he moved around in with so much authority and apparent ease. The open cynicism of his youth had given way to the grim pessimism of his mature years.

"You've always been an imbecile," his brother would tell him at these moments of self-doubt. "Now finally I can tell you so to your face."

Generally, Onofre did not react to these outbursts. His attention seemed focused on the smallest details: the stove dying out in the corner of the room, the play of light as a cloud passed over the rectangle of sky above the yard, the sound of footsteps in the street outside, the smell of charred wood, a dog barking in the distance. Sometimes, though, his philosophical acceptance switched to a sudden rage, and he heaped insults on his brother.

Joan was only dimly aware of these attacks; he was a drunkard and was relatively lucid only for two or three hours a day. During those hours he would dispatch his business as mayor shrewdly and dishonestly. The villagers had become resigned to this state of affairs: they looked on it as progress and tried to stay well away. Joan Bouvila had never attempted to use his position for anything more than to be able to live without working, but even in such a tiny community, political reality had impinged upon that modest aim. He now found himself one of the village's most influential inhabitants. There were more of these than Onofre had first thought: the rector, the doctor, the vet, the pharmacist, the schoolteacher, and the owners of the village store and inn.

The village had grown considerably since Onofre left. These leading lights knew who he was, and each of them tried to win him over. They fawned over him abjectly, allowing him to show his disdain for them quite openly. Not a night went by without a visit from one or other of these petty schemers. These visits were a torment for the young rector, a slow-witted, greedy and hypocritical priest, who from the pulpit had condemned the woman living with Joan. Now, given the fact that Onofre was living in the house, the rector found himself obliged not only to turn up like the others, but to be extremely polite towards her. Onofre and his brother amused themselves at his expense.

"Look here, Father," Onofre would say, "I've studied the Gospels but I haven't found anywhere where it says Jesus had to work to eat. What kind of moral teaching is that?" Hearing such blasphemy, the young priest bit his lip, lowered his gaze and dreamed of vicious revenge. Onofre, who found it easy to read his mind, could barely refrain from laughing.

The other visitors were more astute. The pharmacist and the vet loved to go hunting: between them they had several greyhounds and other pedigree dogs, as well as half a dozen shotguns. They occasionally invited Onofre and Joan to go with them. Since Joan was invariably drunk, his company always proved dangerous.

For his part, the store owner each week received newspapers delivered on the van that now travelled between the village and Bassora. This enabled Onofre Bouvila to follow the course of the political events that had led to his exile. These newspapers took their information from other newspapers, and were always out of date and unreliable. This did not appear to bother their readers; besides, political news always took a back seat in these publications, which gave prominence to local events and other more banal information.

This reversal of values irritated Onofre at first, but after a while he began to think that perhaps this ordering of priorities was not as misplaced as he had at first thought. By now he regarded as futile everything that until recently he had seen as so important. These thoughts occurred to him whenever he managed to escape the obsequious parasites constantly besieging him and sought refuge in his childhood hiding places. Many of them no longer existed; others still did, perhaps, but he was unable to find them; yet more were in places he could not reach given his age. Even the ones he did find were small and wretched: it was his childish imagination that had turned them into such enchanted places, shrouded in dangers and marvels. Now, on the other hand, he saw them as they really were, and rather than moving him, this left him exasperated and depressed.

Only the nearby stream kept for him all the enchantment of his memories. He had gone there almost every day with his father when he returned from Cuba; now, as then, not a day went by without Onofre visiting it. He would sit on a stone and watch the water flow by and the trout leaping. He could hear its clear tinkling sound, which had always seemed to him on the verge of forming words. On many mornings, sheets were hung out to dry in the sun on bushes on the far bank; the white glare against the dark undergrowth hurt his eyes.

He also found the countryside smells intoxicating. In the city, the smells, like the people, seemed to him to compete aggressively, with the most insistent overpowering all the rest – factory emissions, a woman's perfume and so on. In the country on the other hand, the most varied odours mingled to create a single scent that filled the air. Out here, smelling and breathing were one and the same.

It was autumn, and the path to the stream was already strewn with dry leaves; mushrooms of all shapes and colours were growing at the foot of the trees. Onofre drank in these sensations that brought back dim and distant memories, flitting across his mind like the shadows of birds in flight. When he attempted to follow the trail of any of these recollections, he soon became lost in a thick fog. This led to a recurring daydream: he thought he saw his mother and father reaching out to guide him to a brighter, safer place. But their hands never managed to grasp his own.

In one of the drawers in his room at his brother's house he had found a piece of coarse wool that had once belonged to his mother. She had used it as a shawl, precisely in these changeable autumn days. By now the wool had become stiff and rough and reeked of damp and dust. When Onofre was lost in his memories and daydreams, he would take the shawl from the drawer and cover his knees with it. He could sit for hours like that, absent-mindedly stroking the shawl. At times like those it occurred to him that if he had not chosen a life of adventure in his youth, he could perhaps have enjoyed an existence rich in emotions and tenderness. He felt no remorse for the bad things he had done, only for abandoning what would now be precious memories for other goals. As well as being too late, this remorse was nothing if not selfish.

One evening, as he was coming back from the stream, he saw a man propped up against a tree trunk by the side of the path. With his head slumped against his chest, the man looked asleep, but there was something unusual about his posture that made Onofre leave the path and approach him. He could tell from the cassock it was the rector, the young priest he liked to taunt with impious comments. Even before he reached him, Onofre knew he was dead; a closer inspection showed this was not from natural causes: somebody had shot him at point-blank range, probably with a hunter's shotgun. The cassock was matted with coagulated blood where he had been hit. He also had blood on his right hand, his forehead and cheek, although there was no sign of any wounds there. Doubtless, when he was shot, he had raised his hand to his chest and then his face, before finally expiring.

Even though violence was nothing new to Onofre, the discovery of this crime disturbed him tremendously. The fact that he was the one who discovered the body seemed to him like an ill omen, or the result of some evil plot to link him to the murdered priest. The inner peace Onofre thought he had found in the village had been shattered. He ran from the scene of the crime, and did not stop until he reached the front door of his brother's house. Joan was sitting in the dining room drinking wine while the woman prepared supper in the kitchen. Once he had got his breath back, Onofre told his brother what had happened. He noticed the woman had left her preparations and was listening closely from the kitchen doorway. He also saw her and his brother exchange a rapid glance.

From the day he arrived Onofre had often had the opportunity to talk to her, and was not surprised to learn she was the one who in fact ran the household. She had to put Joan to bed almost every night, because his drinking rarely let him get past midnight in a conscious state. For Onofre, on the other hand, drink created a state of anxiety that robbed him of sleep, and the woman herself did not seem to need rest. So she and Onofre would sit in the dining room, or if it was a warm night or less damp than usual, out in the yard.

They would converse at length, sometimes until the early hours, surrounded by the cloying smell of the azalea. Though not very intelligent, the woman had the feminine ability to instinctively know things men are always unaware of, however much they try to fathom them. She was able to spot the stark reality beneath appearances, and would share these insights with Onofre. Thanks to her, he had gradually learned that beneath the village's apparent harmony lurked base passions and long-standing hatreds, jealousies and betrayals. According to her, congenital illnesses made the peasants in the valley degenerate; they were cold, merciless creatures who allowed their old folk to starve to death, carried out infanticide, and tortured their pets simply for pleasure.

Onofre refused on principle to believe any of this; he thought it was inspired by her obvious resentment at the world; nor could he exclude the possibility that these gloomy revelations were part of a more or less deliberate plan on her behalf. Be that as it may, what she told him only served to heighten the state of unease he found himself in. Sometimes, like his brother, he sought in drink the comfort that his thoughts seemed determined to deny his body. One night he awoke in his bed at daybreak and discovered to his horror that the woman was sleeping peacefully by his side. He had no recollection of what had happened the previous night. When he woke the woman up to ask her, she pulled a face but said nothing.

He pushed her roughly out of bed and then out of the room, and began to wonder about the possible consequences of this unexpected event. Whether he had been rash or the victim of a ruse, the fact was that events had taken an unwelcome turn. Despite this, he could only admire the woman's effrontery; he was starting to feel an attraction for her that was more dangerous in the long run than any occasional indiscretions alcohol might lead him to.

Of course, there was not the slightest spontaneity in the woman's behaviour. In no way was she innocent by nature: she knew perfectly well what her position was in that house, and the reaction to it in the village. And yet she was not a calculating or scheming sort of person: she merely tried to benefit from the few advantages she possessed, to play her poor hand with the apparent coolness of a professional gambler who knows his survival depends on a mixture of luck and skill.

In all this time, and despite the trust that had grown up between them, Onofre had been unable to work out the nature of the relationship between the woman and his brother. He knew that, as he had suspected at the outset, she was a widow, and that she had entered Joan's service out of necessity; the rest was shrouded in mystery. Everything seemed to suggest his brother's drunken state made it unlikely they had any carnal relations, but if that were so, why did they keep up the ambiguity with regard to the rest of the village? It was obviously detrimental to her, and yet she seemed to connive in it. She's probably patiently waiting for the moment to ensnare him, Onofre told himself. She knows that sooner or later she'll trap him. And then she'll be the mayoress and will gain revenge for all these years of humiliation and bitterness.

Whenever he thought in this way, Onofre was filled with melancholy pessimism. Poor people like us have only two alternatives, he told himself. Honesty and humiliation or wrongdoing and remorse. Such were the musings of the richest man in Spain.

Later on, he learned that the woman's husband had also died violently; however much he insisted, she refused to provide him with further details. This partial revelation unleashed all sorts of fantasies in Onofre's mind: perhaps she was not entirely unconnected with that violent death, although she did not appear to have benefitted materially from it. Perhaps his own brother was caught up in a crime that now chained him irrevocably to her.

Life in the house became increasingly unbearable for Onofre.

Then he discovered the rector's body, which left him feeling even more insecure. He persuaded himself that the woman, by beginning a relationship with him she knew from the outset was bound to be impossible and short-lived, was merely forcing Joan to resolve the ambiguity of their situation. However, this logical explanation did nothing to dissipate his growing fear that he was the victim of a plot.

Now the meaning of the look Joan and the woman had exchanged on hearing about the rector's murder acquired greater significance. When he told his brother the rector had died from a gunshot wound, which restricted the list of possible killers to the pharmacist and the vet because they had firearm licences, Joan had burst out laughing. He informed Onofre that every house in the valley had a small illegal arsenal. This sudden expansion of possible suspects was another source of worry for Onofre: now rumour and conjecture would abound, and his name would doubtless come up. His arguments with the rector were well known, and although they had never been serious, but merely a pastime as far as he was concerned, it was highly likely that malicious gossip would twist this into a bitter hatred between the two men. The suspicion that fell on him would be augmented by the notorious bad blood that had always existed between the rector and the woman: this eventual ramification established yet another link between Onofre and her.

He found himself in a very serious predicament. In truth, he was not worried about the risk of being accused of a crime he had not committed: he was far too accustomed to avoiding being charged with crimes he had committed to lose any sleep over the death of a little rural priest. What tormented him was the thought that this crime would never have happened without him. He was the one who had given the killer encouragement and the possibility of an alibi. In his search for peace, Onofre had brought discord and violence to the valley; he had poisoned the atmosphere. He could not escape his destiny: once set on the path he had chosen, he was condemned to follow it to the bitter end.

The next day he left the village in the van from Bassora. The rector's lifeless body had been rediscovered that morning, and yet it had not occurred to anyone to keep him in the village or question his right to leave. Onofre could not help seeing this as concrete proof that everyone thought he was guilty. His brother bade him farewell with the same indifference as when he had greeted him on his arrival; to Onofre this lack of emotion showed how incapacitated he was. Nor did the woman reveal any feelings at seeing him leave, but her eyes were red from prolonged weeping and the deepest despair. As he rode away in the van, Onofre wondered if after all what was behind her attitude was simply the awakening of a love with no future, and that everything else was the fruit of his tormented imagination.

4

When he reached home, Onofre found his family in uproar: they had been searching desperately for him for days. Believing him to be in Paris, they had telephoned the Spanish consulate and embassy there, as well as all the luxury hotels. They had also contacted the French authorities. The commotion created by these drastic measures eclipsed any surprise at his return: they hardly even seemed to notice him.

Onofre finally managed to get somebody to explain the reason for this unusual solicitude. A handsome young man from a very good family had out of the blue asked for the hand of his younger daughter, who had just turned eighteen. Onofre sighed. The tussle over my remains is starting. He did not think particularly highly of his daughters and was already resigned to the idea he would have to see them married off to fortune hunters.

He had to take this proposal seriously, however, and so gave instructions for the suitor to come to his study that same evening. After that he retired to get some rest. The butler woke him to announce the arrival of Efrén Castells. The giant burst into his study carrying a briefcase stuffed with papers: he had come to talk business. The very thought of this made Onofre's heart sink.

"You did well to disappear," Efrén began. "They really were after you." He waved his arm. "Fortunately that first moment of great danger died down as quickly as it flared up," he said. For several days even he had not felt safe. Mysterious automobiles had patrolled the streets late at night; at times, when the city was at its busiest, it suddenly felt silent, and people talked in whispers. Soon, though, everything had returned to normal.

The giant opened his briefcase and began taking bundles of files out of it. "I've come to report back to you—" he began. "There's time enough for that," Onofre interrupted him, but Efrén Castells insisted on bringing him up to date about the peculiar economic situation they found themselves in.

"At first they wanted to strip you of everything," the giant said. "Then, when they saw the deeds we had drawn up, they didn't know what to do: I could see the bewilderment and indignation on their faces." Those same people who would not have hesitated to send Onofre to his death were now paralysed at the sight of legal documents. Onofre was not in the least surprised at this apparent contradiction.

"They consulted their lawyers," the giant went on, "and spent several days and nights discussing things. They couldn't find any way to get their hands on you. In desperation they asked for my collaboration, but I held fast, and in the end we came to an agreement.

I pledged to remain in charge of your affairs, and in return they guaranteed to respect my independence. I also had to promise them I would get your consent to our agreement; everything now depends on that." Having said all this, the giant kept a respectful silence.

"So I'm being put out to pasture?" Onofre Bouvila said.

"That's how it seems," said Efrén Castells.

At eight o'clock that evening, Onofre's daughter's suitor appeared in his study, quaking in his elegant boots. He looked weak and not too bright, and found it hard to string two sentences together. At first sight he seemed to be neither a scoundrel nor an honest man. Onofre began by treating him in a friendly way, which disconcerted the young man. His father had told him that whatever happened, he was not to lose his composure: "If he insults you or criticises our family, don't pay him any attention." Now, faced with such a warm reception, the young man didn't know what to do or say.

Onofre too was lost. Shortly after Efrén Castells had left, he had been visited by his father-in-law. Don Humbert Figa i Morera had repeated the same arguments as the giant from Calella. "The main thing is to be patient," he had recommended. "Take this parenthesis as a well-earned vacation. Devote yourself to family life and the pleasures of home and fine food." After him, Onofre's daughter and wife had appeared. "My father has told me what's going on," his wife said. "I'm so glad you've decided to accept things without a fuss." Onofre had detected a note of satisfaction in her voice: If these set-backs bring you closer to my daughters and me, all well and good, her tone seemed to imply.

His daughter had come straight to the point: "Be kind to him, papa," she had begged him. "I love him with all my heart. My happiness depends entirely on you."

As he studied the suitor, Onofre recalled her words. He'll be a puppet in my daughter's hands, he thought. A lapdog. Perhaps that's what she wants, she's old enough to know. Alright, I'll give my blessing and win the gratitude of all my family. Before long the house will be invaded by grandchildren; maybe Don Humbert was right and the time has come to enjoy my home comforts, Onofre told himself. Out loud he said: "Not only am I completely opposed to this absurd marriage, but I forbid you to see my daughter again. If you try to contact her or anyone else in this household, be it a family member or a servant, I will have my men follow you and break every bone in your body in some dark alleyway."

Fate had provided Onofre with a victim on whom he could vent the anger building up in him all day long, and he was never one to waste such an opportunity. The devil take my family, he thought. Then, addressing the suitor, who was finding it hard to believe his ears, he went on: "The prohibition I am now expressing is irrevocable. Don't expect me to change my mind over time: that is something I have never done nor will ever do. If, despite my warnings, you should insist on seeing my daughter or sending her a message, I shall find myself in the painful obligation of having you shot. I think I have made myself clear. The butler will see you to the door."

This interview to some extent restored Onofre's good spirits; he later even attempted to mollify his wife. "Don't worry," he told her, "if they really love each other and he truly is worthy of her, he'll come for her despite my threats. If that happens, I won't do what I said – on the contrary, there'll be a wonderful wedding and I'll make sure they want for nothing. But I don't think we'll hear from this lad again: believe me, my dear, he's a good-for-nothing, and he would never have made the girl happy. There'll be others. Come on, stop crying and go and console her. You'll see, she'll soon get over it."

Apart from such occasional amusements, family life held little attraction for Onofre. He devoted his time to completing the reconstruction of the Rosell family mansion, which had been suspended while he was away. By chance, this mammoth task was finished in mid-December 1924, a few days after Onofre turned fifty. The garden was no longer a jungle, and had regained its former harmony. Newly varnished skiffs rocked gently on the moat, and the graceful outlines of several pairs of swans were reflected in the lake's crystalline waters. Inside the house, doors opened and closed gently, lamps sparkled in the mirrors, freshly painted cherubs and nymphs peered down from the ceilings, carpets muffled the sound of footsteps, and the shining surfaces of the furniture absorbed the light filtering through the lace curtains.

At last the moment had come to move there. Onofre's daughters tried to resist: they refused to leave the city. "Who will come to see us in that godforsaken place?" they moaned. "As long as I'm rich, they'll come to see us in hell if necessary," Onofre retorted. In fact, what his wife and daughters were most afraid of was being left on their own with such a despotic, tyrannical man, who seemed to enjoy making them suffer.

The mansion itself filled them with foreboding. Even though the reconstruction could be considered perfect, there was something disturbing about such a faithful copy, something pompous about the excessive ornamentation, something crazy about the wish to reproduce someone else's anachronical existence, something vulgar about all those imitation paintings, vases, clocks and figurines. None of them were gifts or heirlooms. Nor were they the fruit of chance discoveries or caprices; they were not reminders of the moment when they had been bought, or of when they had become part of the house. Everything in the mansion was the product of an iron will; it was all fake and oppressive.

Once the noise of the building work had ceased, once the bricklayers, labourers, plasterers, painters and restorers had gone and the

413

mansion been set straight and cleaned, it took on a funereal solemnity. Even the swans on the lake had an idiotic air. Dawn only served to make the house look more sinister still.

Onofre Bouvila was delighted with the way everything had turned out. He could live there as he pleased, without seeing or hearing his wife and daughters for weeks on end. He never strolled round the park, and during the day only rarely left the rooms he had reserved for himself.

A few months after their move, his two daughters left home for good. The younger one was the first to go. With the aid of her grandfather Don Humbert Figa i Morera, who adored her to such an extent he was willing, despite his age and frailties, to face the possible wrath of his son-in-law, she went to live in Paris. Some time later she married a Hungarian pianist twice her age with little reputation and an uncertain future. After their marriage they drifted from city to city, pursued by their creditors. The older daughter soon followed her younger sister's example. Despite openly admitting she had no vocation for it, she entered a congregation of lay missionaries who taught and practised medicine in remote corners of the globe. She spent several years in the Amazon region near Iquitos, trying with limited success to combine the practice of obstetrics with an immoderate consumption of whisky. In the end she was repatriated by the Peruvian authorities after certain government officials had been bribed and the victims of her ignorance, her negligence and her vice had all been compensated. From then on she lived placidly in an alcoholic haze in a suite at the Ritz in Madrid, until her death in 1981.

Onofre Bouvila watched his family fall apart with the same indifference he had seen it come together following the death of his second son: a family that to him was nothing more than a cruel disappointment. His wife spent all day and part of the night in the first-floor chapel. She had boxes of frozen truffles and liqueur chocolates sent up to her and ate compulsively at all hours while she ventured through the labyrinth of novenas, triduums, stations of the cross, adorations, forty hours, infraoctavas and vigils to which she devoted her life.

Now the house really did seem deserted. If at first the furniture and objects lacked any emotional life, they soon took on a ghostly existence: at night, noises could be heard in empty rooms, and the next morning wardrobes had been moved and carpets rolled up, as if all those huge, extremely heavy objects had been shifting around under cover of darkness. In reality there was nothing supernatural about this: it was the work of the servants, trying to show their dissatisfaction and disgust. "Let's see if we can drive the mistress really crazy," they said to one another, and began banging saucepans, dragging around furniture and beating chains against the walls.

Onofre Bouvila was oblivious to all this. To escape the mansion's gloomy atmosphere he had acquired the habit of going out every night. Together with his chauffeur and bodyguard he frequented the lowest dives. Fleeing elegance and cleanliness, he sought the company of thieves, crooks and whores. In this way he believed he was recapturing the Barcelona he had succeeded in leaving behind, but in which he now imagined he had once been happy. What he really missed was his lost youth. He tried to convince himself he felt at home in these ignominious, wretched places, even though deep down inside he was repelled by the stinking, poorly ventilated hovels and the sweaty, pestilential beds in which he would wake up with a start. The rotgut wine and adulterated champagne, and the cocaine he took to stay merry all night long, made him ill: he frequently vomited in the street or in the car on the way home at daybreak.

He was also well aware that the charlatans, smugglers and loose women that surrounded him were only after his wealth. When his chauffeur had to haul him out of some brothel or other, the whores who had greeted him with exaggerated displays of delight changed

415

moods in the blink of an eye, and their pimps beat out of him money he would gladly have handed over anyway. Euphoria and lust gave way to greed, violence and rancour. Onofre Bouvila knew this, but allowed himself to be taken in; he did not care about the money he squandered, believing this was the price he had to pay for the right to once more breathe the air of the port, the smell of saltpetre and oil and over-ripe fruit rotting in the ships' holds, to pretend he still belonged in this world.

One night Onofre woke in a tiny room. The walls were covered in filthy wallpaper that had once been orange; a bare light bulb dangled from a wire. His feet and hands were icy, and he felt an unpleasant tingling in his left side. He knew he was dying, and was amazed how precisely he could still register the smallest detail. He heard a whore shouting next to him, but could not remember ever having seen her face before. With a great effort, he grasped her wrist: he was convinced that if she managed to get away she would steal everything he had on him and vanish without telling anyone, leaving him to die. I'll promise her a fortune if she helps me, he thought, but the words stuck in his throat and would not let him breathe. It's not such a bad place to die, he said to himself. What a scandal it will be! What am I saying? I don't want to die here or anywhere else.

The whore had wrenched herself free and picked up the clothes she had left scattered on the floor. She ran out into the corridor, carrying them in her arms. Finding himself all alone, Onofre tried not to let panic overwhelm him. This is the end, he thought. He heard shouts and hurried footsteps outside before he lost consciousness.

In fact, everybody behaved impeccably. As soon as she had put her clothes on, the whore ran to find Onofre's chauffeur. He, in turn, fearful of the consequences if things went badly, went to fetch Efrén Castells. By the time the two men returned to the house of ill repute, the girls and their pimps had dressed Onofre as best they could, although they had not managed to get him to drink a sip of brandy, despite trying with everything that came to hand. Efrén Castells distributed money to everyone; even the watchman and policeman got their share. Satisfied, they all swore not to say a word.

It was four o'clock in the morning by the time Onofre was put to bed at home and his wife informed. Margarita rose to the occasion and behaved in a lady-like fashion. She curtly accepted the improvised, implausible explanations Efrén Castells mumbled, and mobilised the household. As a result, within a few hours the mansion was a hive of activity, crawling not only with specialist doctors and nurses, but also, anticipating a fatal outcome, lawyers and notaries with their clerks, brokers and stockbrokers, real estate agents and tax officials, consuls and commercial attachés, crooks and politicians (who tried to go unnoticed), journalists and correspondents, as well as a horde of priests carrying everything necessary to administer the last rites: confession, the eucharist and extreme unction.

This crowd of people wandered around the garden and house. They entered every room, peered into wardrobes, opened drawers, rummaged among possessions, manhandled works of art, damaging some of them, deliberately or otherwise. The press photographers set up their tripods and cameras in the middle of rooms, blinding everyone with the flashes from their magnesium lights and wasting their plates on portraits no-one could put a name to. The servants were happy to be bribed, revealing true or imaginary secrets to the highest bidder. There were also shysters who passed themselves off as friends of the family or close associates of the sick man. Unwary journalists and businessmen paid them for the most distorted and confused scraps of information, as a result of which shares fell on almost all the stock markets.

Onofre was either completely unaware or only vaguely conscious of any of this. The medication he had been given left him feeling he was floating in mid-air: nothing hurt, and he could not even feel his own body, apart from the persistent cold in his extremities. If it wasn't for this cold, I'd be better than ever, he thought. This sense of well-being took him back to a period in his childhood before his oldest memories. He had lost all notion of time: despite being completely unable to move, he did not mind lying prostrate, and to him the hours did not seem long.

The people who came and went from his room – the doctors constantly examining him; the nurses who gave him medication, injections, food and sedatives, took blood samples and looked after his bodily needs and washed and perfumed him; his wife, spending the few moments she was allowed to be alone with him weeping at his bedside; the men who managed to sneak into his bedroom to ask for some posthumous favour or other, to urge him to make his peace with God, to ask him for some essential detail about a firm or important commercial transaction or just to hear from his lips as a last testament the key to his success – to Onofre they all seemed like fictitious characters, figures that had escaped from some childish engraving, circulating around the rare fixed points of the space he was the centre of.

He was further confused by the murmurs, whispers and hum of voices and footsteps reaching him through the walls, sounds that grew louder whenever a door was opened and diminished when it was shut again. He was unable to distinguish clearly between sounds, smells, shapes and sensations: all of them led to complex interpretations that were not always definite or coherent. The touch of a doctor or nurse's hand, the smell of quinine, the whiteness of a uniform, a curious face brought up close to his own would create an image he found hard to interpret. What does this mean, he would ask himself. What is this jumble of objects doing around me? Why are they here? Somehow liberated by contact with these multifarious stimuli, Onofre was transported vertiginously through boundless space and found himself on the shore of some forgotten moment of his past, which he relived so vividly it became distressingly painful. After some moments, all this slowly faded, like cigarette smoke in the warm air of a room, leaving only his terror at the certainty of death. At moments like these he would have given anything to live just a little while longer. He knew, however, that in his state no bargaining was possible, and this reduced him to despair. How is it possible I can't do anything to avoid such a horrible end, he asked himself. Convinced his life was about to be extinguished as a light goes out with the flick of a switch, and that he might at any moment disappear forever, he would burst out crying like a newborn babe. None of those around him realised this, because his features always remained serene and resolute.

On other occasions, these terrors gave way to unreal, pleasurable visions. In one of these he imagined he was in some ill-defined place lit by a dull, even light like that of a cloudy midday. Unsure why he was there, he saw coming towards him a man he thought he recognised. As the man came closer, Onofre celebrated their re-encounter. "Father," he said, "it's been such a long time." The *Americano* smiled: he had not changed much since the day he had returned from Cuba with his drill suit, Panama hat and the monkey in its cage, except that now he had a long, well-groomed beard. "What is the beard for, father?" Onofre asked. The *Americano* shrugged. I don't know, son, his gesture seemed to say. He opened his mouth, his lips moved slowly as if he were about to speak, but he remained like that, with no sound coming out. Onofre held his breath, expecting his father to reveal something transcendental. But Joan Bouvila stayed mute; in the end he closed his mouth and smiled again: a smile now tinged with melancholy.

Maybe this is what it means to be dead, Onofre thought with a shudder. This immutability. When you're dead everything remains the same. Where there's no change there's no pain, but no joy either. If death means anything, it's the complete absence of joy, that blank look on my father's face. There's no doubt he is dead. That's why being with him, which at first seemed so pleasant, now fills me with sadness. All this shows I'm not dead – or I wouldn't be thinking the way I do. And yet I can't be alive either, or I wouldn't have had this vision. I must be in an in-between state, with one foot in the grave, as they say in the world I'm on the point of leaving. What I wouldn't give to live again. I'm not asking to start over; that's impossible, and besides, I'm sure I would only do again what I did before. No, all I ask is to go on living, that's enough for me. Ah, if I could only live again, I would see everything differently."

5

"I'm not sure it's wise for you to see her," the nun said. "I mean, to let her see you."

"So you know who I am?" he asked.

The nun pursed her lips and went on staring coldly at him. There was no trace of hostility in this coldness, simply a mixture of curiosity and caution.

"The whole world knows who you are, Señor Bouvila," the nun said quietly, almost coquettishly. Each of her features revealed an aspect of her character: detachment, gentleness, patience, strength; her face was an open book. "The poor woman has suffered a lot," she added, her tone changing. "She's quiet now most of the time; she occasionally has a relapse, but then it's only for a few days. Then she again thinks she's a queen or a saint."

Onofre Bouvila nodded. "I'm aware of the situation," he said. In fact, he had only very recently learned of it. During the endless months of his convalescence, when his life, torn *in extremis* from the clutches of death, seemed to be hanging by a thread, the truth had been kept from him: the doctors had said that any upset could be fatal. But they could not prevent him finding out indirectly.

One autumn day when he was fighting off boredom leafing through some magazines at one end of the living-room, his legs covered in an alpaca rug, he had read news of the wedding. At first its meaning escaped him, as almost everything had done for some time now. A maid removed the magazines he had let fall to the floor and drew the curtains to prevent the evening sun shining in his face. When the maid left, Onofre rested his cheek on the anti-macassar, recently ironed and still smelling of fresh basil. He drifted off to sleep: for the first time in his life he now slept many hours. Even the simplest activity tired him; fortunately these periods of sleep were always pleasant.

This time, however, he woke with a start. He had no idea how long he had slept, but judging by the line the sun's rays reached on the marble tiles, it could not have been long. He tried to work out why he was feeling so anxious. Is it something I read in those magazines, he wondered. He rang the little bell that was always by his side: the maid and a nurse came in, looking worried. "There's nothing wrong with me, dammit," he said, irritated by their unnecessary display of concern, "I just want you to bring me the magazines I was reading." While the maid went off to look for them, the nurse, a scrawny, sour woman, took his pulse.

"My wife is punishing me with these harpies," he would tell Efrén Castells when he came to visit him. "What would you prefer?" the giant scolded him. "A pretty young thing who'll give you another attack?" He looked all round him to make sure no-one could hear them and added: "If you had seen yourself as I did when I went to pick you up from that brothel, you wouldn't say such things."

*

"Bah, stop looking to see if I'm dead or alive and clean my spectacles with that gauze sticking out of your pocket," Onofre complained, withdrawing his hand. The nurse and he glared at each other for a moment. This is what it's come to, he thought. Fighting with old maids. He ordered the two women to pull back the curtains and leave him in peace.

He looked frantically for news of the wedding. "I'm very happy," the film star had told the magazine reporter. "James and I will live most of the year in Scotland, where he has a castle." James was a dashing, wealthy English aristocrat. They had met on board a luxury liner, and both confessed it had been love at first sight. For a few months they had preferred to keep their engagement a secret to avoid being besieged by the press. Every day he would send an orchid to her room, so that it would be the first thing she saw when she opened her eyes. The wedding was to take place before winter somewhere they did not wish to reveal; "Then we'll have a long honeymoon in exotic lands," she explained. "I'm very happy," she repeated, and announced her retirement from the silver screen.

"Where is she?" he asked Efrén Castells point-blank later that evening when he came to visit. The giant was nonplussed.

"She is as comfortable as possible, believe me," he said. "It's a very pleasant place, and it doesn't look like a sanatorium at all." Feeling implicitly accused by his friend's sullen silence, the giant from Calella defended himself angrily: "Don't look at me like that, Onofre, I beg you. You would have done the same: what else could we do? There was no other way out. From the start you knew better than anyone this adventure would end like this; it had been a long time coming." He told Onofre things had gone from bad to worse ever since he had handed over the film studios.

They had soon realised Honesta Labroux was unwilling to take orders from anyone but Onofre, but he had left and was not coming back. Now films that had previously been made in four or five days ran into endless problems and took several weeks to complete. Eventually Honesta had tried to shoot Zuckermann. One day when he had treated her even more cruelly than usual, she took a pistol out of her bag and fired it at him. The pistol was an antique; heaven knows where she had got it from. It had exploded in her hand, and it was only by a miracle she did not blow her own head off.

Following this incident, they all agreed there was nothing for it but to lock her up. Onofre nodded sombrely. With the loss of Honesta Labroux, the film industry he had single-handedly created collapsed like a pack of cards. They tried other actresses, but every one of them failed. Whereas before there had been huge profits, now it became difficult to cover their costs. The public preferred films imported from the United States; Efrén Castells himself spoke enthusiastically of Mary Pickford and Charlie Chaplin. They had decided to close down the studios, wind up the company and devote themselves to importing foreign titles. "Let others come a cropper, risking their money on making films," Efrén Castells said. Onofre Bouvila raised the alpaca rug up to his chest and shrugged: it was all the same to him.

"Follow me," the nun said all of a sudden. She had been thinking it over, and her decision was the result of her deliberations: from her tone of voice it was plain she was used to dealing with people without seeking their approval. Onofre walked behind her until they came to a medium-sized room. It was simply furnished and looked clean and comfortable, despite giving off a smell of sickness and decay. The delicate light of a winter's midday filtered in through a window, and the room was quite cold. Three men of indeterminate age were playing cards round a table with a brazier. Two of them were wearing berets; all three had scarves wrapped round their necks. On another table covered in a blue cloth and pushed against the wall was a nativity scene: the mountains were made of cork; the river was silver foil; the vegetation clumps of moss; the clay figures were a jumble of sizes. Next to the table stood an upright piano under a tarpaulin.

"The patients themselves made this crib," said the nun. Hearing this, the three men interrupted their game and smiled at Onofre Bouvila. "On Christmas Eve after Midnight Mass we have a community supper; that is, family members and close friends can come if they so wish. I imagine that doesn't interest you, but thought you might like to know."

Onofre noticed there were bars on all the windows. He and the nun left the room through a different door, which led to another corridor. When they reached the end of it, the nun came to a halt.

"You'll have to wait here a moment," she said. "Men cannot enter the women's wing and vice versa. We never know what state they might be in."

The nun left him there. Onofre searched in all his pockets, although he knew there was no point. The doctors had forbidden him to smoke, and so he never carried any cigarettes on him. He thought of going back to the main room and asking the card players for one. They must have some, and they didn't seem dangerous, he told himself. After all, what can they do to me? As he was thinking this, he turned to study his reflection in the corridor windowpane. What he saw was a pale, hunched old man enveloped in a black overcoat with an astrakhan collar, leaning on the ivory pommel of a cane. In his other hand he was holding a felt hat and gloves. All this gave him an eccentric, almost comical appearance. This disconsolate observation was interrupted by the nun's reappearance. "You can come through now," she said.

Delfina had also aged a lot, and had grown alarmingly thin, returning to her naturally emaciated state. No-one would have recognised her as the famous actress who had dazzled the whole world only a few years earlier, and only Onofre could glimpse in this human wreck the sullen chambermaid of yesteryear. She was wearing a thick woollen housecoat over a flannel nightdress, woollen socks and slippers lined with rabbit fur. "Look who's come to see you, Señora Delfina," the nun said, but Delfina did not react to her words or to Onofre's presence. She was staring at something in the distance beyond the corridor walls, and Onofre found the silence unbearable.

The nun suggested they went for a walk in the garden on their own. "It's a chilly day," she said, "but it will be nice in the sun. Go out into the garden, the exercise will do you both good." To the nun, a film star must have been little more than a prostitute. She only allowed them in the garden without supervision because they were so decrepit they had acquired a renewed innocence, Onofre thought as he led Delfina down the corridor towards the garden. This turned out to be an arduous, lengthy process; she walked stiffly and extremely slowly. Each of her movements seemed the result of an intensely complex calculation, a deliberate decision that was not without risk. I've taken half a step, Delfina seemed to be saying each time. Alright, now I'll take another half. Thanks to this laborious progress, the garden appeared enormous. She's not wrong, thought Onofre. If she's never going to get beyond the garden wall, why hurry? He was the one who grew tired of her exasperating slowness. "Come on Delfina," he said finally. "Let's sit for a while on that bench over there."

"We'll be fine here," he said once they were seated side by side on the stone bench. The trees had lost their leaves; some muskmallow was growing by the sanatorium wall. Onofre felt he had to say something, and so he asked how she felt, was she in pain? Did they treat her well in here, did she need anything he could provide her with? She made no reply, but carried on staring straight ahead with the same blank expression. She didn't even seem to realise where she was or who she was with.

This silence weighed on Onofre more than he could have imagined.

"How much has changed," he said quietly. "And yet nothing has changed. Both of us are still the same, don't you think? Except that now life has stolen what little we had." A black bird flew down to the gravel path, stayed there for a while, then flew off again. As soon as it had gone, Onofre began talking once more. "Do you remember when we met, Delfina? I don't mean the precise moment you and I met, but the year. It was 1887, in another century, can you believe it? Barcelona was a village then, there was no electric light, trams or telephones. It was the time of the World Fair. Did you know there's talk of holding another one? Perhaps that's our chance to set out again, what do you think? Oh, back then I felt all alone, and I was so scared – as you see, in that I haven't changed. Back then, though, I had you; we never got on, but I knew you were there, and that was enough, even if I didn't know it."

Delfina did not move, and Onofre was afraid she had caught cold, though the air was warm and the sun kept off any damp. An ice statue, thought Onofre. That's what she's always been, except for the night I held her in my arms. He took her hand and could feel it was not as icy as he had feared. "You're going to catch cold," he said. "Here, put my gloves on." He took them off and put them on Delfina. She neither helped nor resisted. Onofre was surprised to see they fitted her: he had forgotten she always had very large hands. These are the hands she clutched me with so desperately, he thought. "You can keep the gloves," he said out loud. "They fit you perfectly." Raising his head, he saw the three card players were now crowded at the window gazing intently at the couple. Although they were far away, and were only three sick old men, Onofre let go of Delfina's hand. She joined it to her other one and sat with them folded on her lap. "But there's no point dwelling on the past," Onofre went on. "If I mention it, it's because I've been on the brink of death and I'm frightened. I don't mind telling you that: I've always known you were the only person who understood me. You always grasped why I did what I did. None of the others understand me, not even the ones who hate me. They have their ideology and their prerogatives, and use them to explain and justify every success or failure. I'm an anomaly in the system, the rare chance conjunction of many imponderables. They don't reproach me for what I've done, for my ambition or the means I've used to satisfy it, to climb to the top and become rich. That's what we all want; they would have behaved exactly the same if they'd been driven by necessity or not shied away out of fear. And yet, I'm the loser. I believed that by being bad I would have the world at my feet, but I was wrong: the world is worse than I am."

Spring was well advanced when Onofre received a letter signed by a nun, possibly the same one who had received him during his visit to the sanatorium. In the letter the nun informed him of Delfina's passing: *Death occurred while she was asleep.* She said he was being told of this sad event even though he was neither a relative nor a close friend, *given the special emotional link you had with the deceased.* Despite the fact that since the day he had visited her, Delfina had not regained her voice or been fully conscious, it was not going too far to say that *she died, as it were, with your name on her lips.*

In the deceased's room they had found some handwritten sheets of paper, probably a missive addressed to him, together with *other intimate and obscene jottings we thought it advisable to destroy,* the nun concluded.

Delfina's letter read as follows: *The reality around us is no more than a painted veil, on the other side of this veil there is not another life, but the same one, the beyond is only the other side of the veil, if we only look at the veil we do not see the other side, which is the same, once we understand that reality is no more than an optical illusion we will be able to cross that painted veil, and when we do so we will find ourselves in another world that is identical to this one, in that world there are also those who have died and those not yet born, whom we cannot see now because we are separated by that painted veil we mistake for reality, once we have crossed the veil in one direction it is always easy to cross it in that direction and in the opposite one, one can live at the same time on this side and on the other side not at the same time, the most suitable moment for crossing the painted veil is the twilight hour going that way, and that of dawn for coming this way, this is the best method to see the whole effect, anything else is useless, it is no good pleading or praying, on the other side of the veil the ridiculous division of matter into three dimensions does not exist, on this side each dimension seems slightly ridiculous to our eyes, those who are on the other side of the veil know this and laugh, those not yet born believe the dead are their parents.*

After this, the handwriting became illegible.

CHAPTER SEVEN

1

Although not as large as the Cullinan or Excelsior diamonds, nor as famous as the Koh-i-noor (which is mentioned in the Mahabharata), the Great Moghul (owned by the Shah of Persia) or the Orlov (decorating the Russian imperial sceptre), the Regent was considered the most perfect diamond of all. It came from the legendary Golconda mines, and once belonged to the Duke of Orleans, who had to pawn it in Berlin during the French Revolution. Recovered from the pawnbroker, it was mounted in the hilt of Napoleon Bonaparte's sword.

The night Santiago Belltall came to see him, Onofre Bouvila was holding it in the palm of his hand, admiring its purity and brilliance under a magnifying glass. The Primo de Rivera dictatorship had forced him to retire from active life, and so he had decided to invest his fortune – the funds Efrén Castells had transferred to Switzerland for him – on the international diamond market. His agents now ventured into the Deccan mountains and the jungles of Borneo; prowled around the inns and brothels of Minas Gerais and Kimberley. Without intending to, Onofre Bouvila was again becoming one of the richest men in the world. He could easily have toppled Primo de Rivera to avenge himself for the prohibition he had suffered, but he had no desire to do so. He had always been contemptuous of politics, seeing it as full of messy alliances he refused to be a part of.

Above all, Onofre was bored. As he studied the diamond, he was reflecting that the passage of time brought only increasing thoughts of death. Delfina's passing in 1925 had been followed by that of his father-in-law Don Humbert Figa i Morera early in 1927, and then that of his brother Joan Bouvila in unclear circumstances later that same year. Each of these deaths seemed to him like a bad omen.

Nor did he feel the need to fight against a dictatorship that was sinking fast. Following Mussolini's example, Primo de Rivera had created a single party called the Patriotic Union, thinking it would attract influential figures from all sides and bring together the country's upper echelons. However, the only people he had managed to recruit were hangers-on from the previous regime and a handful of young social climbers. The army had ended up disassociating itself from the dictator it had acclaimed only a few years earlier, and the king himself was desperately trying to find a way to get rid of him. There were conspiracies against Primo at home and abroad; he responded by imprisoning or deporting his opponents, but he was not bloodthirsty and had no wish to kill anyone.

It was only the opposition's weakness, the tight censorship he imposed, administrative corruption, and the justified popular fear of change, that kept him in power. He clung to it like a madman, unable to understand that he owed his position to the momentary coincidence of his peculiar idiosyncrasies with the furthest swing of the pendulum of History. He had governed not so much badly as eccentrically: he had quickly promoted public works, which had relieved massive unemployment and modernised the country. He had been good for the common people. The positive balance of his rule made it even harder for him to understand why he now found himself abandoned. When he saw he had also lost the support of the Crown, he turned to Onofre Bouvila. Through the Marquis of Ut, who was still loyal to him, he tried to win Onofre over, but it was too late.

Santiago Belltall, whose name came to be linked forever with that of Onofre Bouvila, was forty-three years old when he went to see him.

Even though Belltall was dressed extremely poorly, he had bathed and shaved that same day, and someone had cut his hair with more enthusiasm than skill. This sprucing-up made him look even more of a scrounger; only the eyes burning in his gaunt face kept him from appearing ridiculous. When the butler informed him that his master did not receive anybody he had not himself invited, Santiago Belltall produced a crumpled, yellowing card from his pocket and showed it to the manservant. "Señor Bouvila gave it me himself," he said. "I think it's as good as an invitation."

Perplexed, the butler examined the card. "When did he give you this?" he asked. "Fourteen years ago," said Santiago Belltall, unabashed. "To call this an invitation is stretching the point," the butler said. "What did you say your name was?" Santiago Belltall told him: "Though I don't expect your master will remember me," he confessed. The butler scratched his head dubiously, but eventually decided to tell his master this undesirable-looking individual was at the door. He had no wish to disturb Onofre, and yet he was well aware of his keenness for eccentric characters. In this instance his intuition proved correct. "Show him in," Onofre Bouvila told him.

Although it was a warm night, logs were burning in the library fireplace, and the heat made Santiago Belltall feel he was suffocating.

"I don't suppose you will remember me," he said as soon as he entered the library. There was a hint of obsequiousness in his voice; his words and attitude seemed to suggest that someone as important as Onofre could not possibly recall someone as insignificant as him. Onofre Bouvila smiled disdainfully. "If my memory was as bad as you and other dolts reckon, I wouldn't be where I am today," he said, raising his right fist. For a moment Santiago Belltall was afraid he was going to punch him, but there was no menace in the gesture. "We met fourteen years ago," the inventor said.

"Not fourteen years," Bouvila replied. "It was fifteen. In nineteen hundred and twelve in Bassora. Your name is Santiago Belltall and you are an inventor. You have a daughter called María, a rebellious little girl. What have you come to sell me?"

Santiago Belltall was dumbfounded: with these harsh words, Bouvila had anticipated what he was going to say and had rendered the speech he had prepared and practised on his own for hours completely pointless. Despite himself, he turned bright red. "I see I made a mistake coming here," he muttered, more to himself than to be heard. "I'm sorry." But Onofre Bouvila's sarcastic smile at this transformed his inhibition into anger. Leaping out of his armchair, the inventor headed for the door. "You don't know what you're missing," he said out loud.

"What am I missing?" Onofre Bouvila asked sardonically. Turning on his heel, Belltall confronted the powerful financier: now the two of them were talking man to man. "A real wonder," he said. Onofre Bouvila opened the fist he had kept closed until that moment. The inventor was enchanted by the facets of the Regent, their brilliance speckling the other man's damask dressing gown. "What wonder can compare to this?" Onofre murmured.

"The wonder of flight," the inventor replied without hesitation.

By the third decade of the twentieth century, aviation had undeniably *come of age,* as newspapers of the time put it. No-one doubted the supremacy of these machines, heavier than air, over any other form of aerial transport. Scarcely a day went by without some new feat that proved it. And yet there were still many problems to be overcome. However strange it may seem nowadays, safety was the least of these: few accidents occurred, and only a very small number of them were serious or fatal. Most could not really be attributed to mechanical failures, but rather the puerile determination of pilots to show how stable their craft were, and to demonstrate their own skill at flying upside down, in circles or spirals, or at looping the loop, doing acrobatics and nose-diving. The reflexes and athleticism required of pilots at this early stage of aviation meant they had to be very young (fifteen was judged to be the perfect age for test flights), which inevitably led to a certain level of recklessness.

In 1925, one Barcelona newspaper reported: *Since in Paris and in London those whom certain sensationalist publications call flying aces compete with one another by flying their aircraft as low as possible under the bridges of the Seine and the Thames, and since Barcelona has no river and therefore no bridges, our pilots, despite the city council's strict prohibition, have invented a similar but even more dangerous manoeuvre: they turn their craft perpendicular to the ground and pass, like threading a needle, between the towers of the Sagrada Familia cathedral.*

The article goes on to say that whenever this happened, a shabby, hungry-looking old man would appear at the top of the towers, shaking his fist as if ingenuously trying to bring the aircraft down, all the while hurling insults at the pilot. The protagonist of this colourful scene (which some years later inspired what is today considered a classic scene in the film *King Kong*) was none other than Antoní Gaudí i Cornet, who by this time was in the last few months of his life. There was something allegorical about this unequal confrontation: the so-called *modernismo* that this famous architect represented had been replaced by a new, radically different movement in Catalonia, known as *noucentismo*. Gaudí's *modernismo* looked to the past, preferably the Middle Ages; *noucentismo* was turned towards the future. The former was idealist and Romantic; the latter materialist and sceptical. Devotees of *noucentismo* mocked Gaudí and his work, ridiculing it in caricatures and satirical articles. The aged genius suffered, but not in silence. Over the years he had become embittered and eccentric: he now lived alone in the workshop he had created in the crypt of the Sagrada Familia, surrounded by colossal statues, stone rosettes and other ornaments that a lack of funds prevented from being installed in their proper position. Gaudí slept in the crypt in his work clothes, which made him look like a scarecrow, and breathed in the cement and plaster-filled air. In the morning he did Swedish gymnastics, then heard Mass and took communion. His breakfast consisted of a handful of hazelnuts, a bunch of alfalfa or some berries, after which he plunged back into his anachronistic, impossible creation.

Whenever someone came to visit the church, or he saw a group of people looking round it, he would leap from the scaffolding with an agility that belied his years and run to meet them, hat in hand. He would beg for money to be able to continue his work, if only for a few more days. For a peseta he would throw a hazelnut into the air and catch it in his mouth, then turn a backwards somersault. His face was transformed and his enthusiasm was contagious. Sometimes he had to be dragged out of a pool of fresh mortar. "Progress and I are at war with each other," he would tell people, "and I'm afraid I'm the one who's going to lose." In the end he was knocked down by a tram at the intersection of Calle Bailén and Gran Via, and as a result of this absurd accident died in Santa Cruz hospital.

Another problem preoccupying aeronautical engineers was what later became known as the range of flight. "What is the point of flying if you don't get anywhere?" they would say to one another. To resolve that particular challenge, aeroplanes were fitted with fuel tanks so big they weighed the craft down and made it impossible for them to take off. To compensate for this, the fuselage was made lighter, so that in the end pilots literally flew seated on tanks of highly flammable material. They no longer feared bumps on the head or broken bones, but going up in flames.

However, the quality of this fuel was being improved in leaps and bounds; the gasoline was refined and mixed to maximise its performance. These developments soon bore fruit: on 20 May 1927 the US pilot Charles Lindbergh made a non-stop solo flight from New York to Paris. This feat opened up limitless possibilities. Soon afterwards, on 9 March 1928, Lady Bailey took off from Croydon in England at the controls of a Havilland Moth light aeroplane with a hundred horsepower engine. With stopovers at Paris, Naples, Malta, Cairo, Khartoum, Tabora, Livingstone and Bloemfontein, she reached Cape Town on 30 April. She rested there, then in September began her return journey. After stopping at Bandundo, Niamey, Gao, Dakar, Casablanca, Malaga, Barcelona and Paris for a second time, she landed at Croydon, from where she had left ten months earlier, on 16 January 1929.

Nor had the aeronautics industry in Spain lagged behind. The Moroccan war had accelerated its development just as the Great War had done for the warring nations. In 1926, on board the *Plus Ultra*, Franco, Ruiz de Alda, Durán and Rada completed the journey from Palos de Moguer to Buenos Aires between 22 January and 10 February. That same year, between 5 April and 13 May, Lóriga and Gallarza flew from Madrid to Manila in a sesquiplane, while the *Atlántida*, captained by Llorente, flew to Spanish Guinea and back in a fortnight, from the 10th to the 25th of December.

Each of these journeys was a giant leap towards a bright future, but they also brought with them a host of fresh conundrums: compasses whirled round at the abrupt change of hemisphere, traditional maps did not meet the needs of aerial navigation; there was a constant effort to perfect altimeters, cathetometers, barometers, anemometers, radiogoniometers and so on. Not only the instruments, but clothing, food and many other things had to be adapted to the new circumstances.

It was also necessary to be able to forecast atmospheric conditions precisely: a gale or dust storm could be fatal for an aircraft and its crew. Whereas a train or automobile caught out by these meteorological accidents could always come to a halt, or a ship could ride out the storm, what could an aeroplane in flight, hundreds of leagues from the nearest aerodrome and with a limited amount of fuel, do in such an emergency? Similarly, what happened if there was engine failure mid-flight? Scientists wracked their brains trying to come up with answers to these imponderables. They studied with renewed interest the anatomy of certain flying insects, envious of their ability to alight without difficulty on the tiny surface of a pistil, whereas an aeroplane needed a lengthy, horizontal and smooth surface to be able to land without crashing. This was because a landing could not be made at speeds of less than a hundred kilometres per hour: in these early aircraft forward thrust and lift were not independent.

Onofre Bouvila had just finished listening with half an ear to the inventor's explanations. He pushed the bell, and when the butler appeared in the library, told him to put more logs on the fire. He followed the manservant's movements in the same distracted manner.

"I can see you're not entirely convinced by my proposal," Santiago Belltall said once the butler had left once more. This trivial comment seemed to jerk Onofre Bouvila out of his reverie. He looked at the inventor as if seeing him for the first time.

"I'm simply not interested," he said coldly. His inner thoughts had transported him far away; now his only wish was to be free of Belltall. "I'm not saying the idea isn't worthwhile," he added when he saw the puzzled look on the other man's face – his apparent initial willingness to listen had given the inventor false hope – "it's possible that in the future I myself . . ." he added mechanically, without even bothering to finish his sentence.

In the weeks that followed this conversation, Onofre heard news of Santiago Belltall on several occasions. The inventor had offered his idea to other people and had also approached state companies and government offices. Nowhere did he receive anything more than encouraging words and vague promises. "We will study the project with the interest it deserves," everyone told him.

Thanks to his men, Onofre Bouvila learned that the Belltalls, father and daughter, sublet a flat on Calle Sepúlveda. Neighbours said neither of them was in their right mind, that they were good-for-nothings who didn't have a penny. Knowing that sooner or later something was bound to happen, Onofre Bouvila decided to wait.

One leaden evening, with thunder echoing in the distance, the butler announced a visitor: "There is a young lady at the door who says she wishes to speak to you in private," he said in a neutral tone. Onofre could not prevent a shiver running down his spine. "Show her in, and make sure nobody disturbs me," he said, turning away from the door as if to hide his agitation. "Wait," he said, as the butler was leaving to carry out his instructions. "Tell the chauffeur not to go to bed until I tell him to, and ask him to have a car ready in case I need it at any time."

Seeing there were no further orders, the butler left the library, closed the door behind him and made his way to the hall.

"Be so kind as to accompany me," he said when he was there. "The master will see you now."

The woman could not avoid a shudder. I know what's going to happen, she thought as she followed the butler. I hope to God it's nothing more than that.

The moment he saw her step into the library, Onofre recognised her. In truth, he remembered her with alarming precision, as if the years between their first fleeting encounter and this new meeting had been telescoped and only a few minutes had passed. It was as if he had taken a brief nap: Which is what my entire life now seems to me, he thought.

She said: "I'm María Belltall." "I know perfectly well who you are," Onofre said. "It's hot in this room," he added, to say something. "I always have a fire in here. I was ill a few months ago, and the doctors fuss over me. Sit down and tell me what brings you here."

María Belltall hesitated and then chose a straight-backed chair. She was wearing a very short skirt, and the position she would have needed to adopt in an armchair would have seemed forced, ridiculous even.

By the mid nineteen twenties, having started to move up from the instep in 1916, skirts had climbed the calf with the stubbornness of a snail until they reached the knee, where they stayed until the nineteen sixties. This shortening had led to panic in the textile industry, the mainstay of Catalan prosperity. Their fears were unfounded: although dresses required less fabric, women's wardrobes had expanded dramatically thanks to the increasing participation of women in public life, the workplace and in sport. Fashion had been turned upside down: bags, gloves, footwear, hats, stockings and hair styles had all changed. Little jewellery was worn; the use of fans was looked down on for the moment. When María Belltall crossed her legs, Onofre could not help noticing her sheer silk stockings and wondering what her gesture might mean.

"Don't think for a moment," she began, "that my father asked me to come; we're not a tandem, as they call that sort of couple these days. It's simply that I know he came to see you, probably to offer you his latest invention. All I've come to tell you is this: my father is not a swindler, a charlatan or a crackpot, as his appearance might have led you to believe. In fact, he is a real scientist; he may be self-taught, but his knowledge has proper, solid foundations. As well as being a man of genius he is a tireless and honest worker. His inventions are not fantasies or wild schemes. I know it's one thing to say this and another to prove it, and that you probably mistrust what I say because

I'm his daughter. The only reason for my being here is that things are going so badly for us. Life has never been easy, but recently our situation has become desperate. We can't pay the rent or for food. I won't pretend: I've come here to beg of you. My father is growing old, though that's not what most worries me: I can work and have done so; I can earn enough for both of us to live on. But I think the time has come for him to have a chance; I can't let him face old age knowing his life has been pointless. Don't look at me like that: I'm only too aware that this is everybody's destiny, but won't you allow me to rebel against it in my father's name?"

As she was speaking, she got up and paced up and down the carpet. From his armchair Onofre Bouvila could see the logs burning on the fire behind her legs. Eventually María sat down again and continued in a calmer voice: "I have turned to you because I know you're the only person who can rescue my father from the hole he's been in for far too long. I'm not saying this to flatter you; it's just that I know you're not afraid of taking a risk. The fact that years ago you gave him your card is proof you are not put off by the unknown or the new. From that day on," she said, colouring slightly, "I have always remembered your gesture. All I am asking is that you reconsider your decision. Don't reject out of hand whatever my father offered you. Study it, get a specialist to examine the plans, consult technicians in the field and ask them for their expert opinion; let them say if it's worth the trouble or not."

She fell silent, and sat there, stiff and unmoving, breathing heavily. Her discomfort came from trying to guess what Onofre Bouvila's reaction might be: not only was she afraid he would throw her out unceremoniously, but she feared even more that he would humiliate her by demanding she give herself to him. She was well aware of the risk she was running by going there; she had consciously accepted it. What terrified her was what exactly was going to happen next.

439

Despite the fact she had been convinced for years that circumstances had predestined her for this moment, she did not know how to react now she was facing it.

María was struggling to banish an obsessive image from her mind: her mother had abandoned the family home many years earlier, and she had no recollection of her. But ever since, this non-existent mother of hers had been constantly present in her imagination; this person who did not exist had accompanied her throughout her life.

For now, though, Onofre Bouvila did no more than stare at her. She remembered that gaze from her childhood. When she had first seen it, she had been ashamed of everything: her ungainly appearance, her ragged clothes, the wretched conditions they lived in. And yet the way he had looked at her had remained with her ever since. Onofre meanwhile was thinking: I remembered those eyes as being caramel-coloured, but now I see they're grey.

2

A recent legend has it that one fine day in the early years of the twentieth century, the Devil snatched a Barcelona financier from his office and flew with him to Montjuich hill. As it was a fine day, the entire city could be seen, from the port to the Sierra de Collcerola, from the River Prat to the River Besós. Most of the 13,989,942 square metres of the Cerdá Plan had by now been completed. The Ensanche was encroaching on the nearby villages (those villages whose inhabitants had once amused themselves observing the people of Barcelona scurrying like ants along the narrow streets of their tiny city, confined by the walls and watched over by the brooding mass of the Ciudadela). Smoke from factories created a tulle curtain stirred by the breeze, and through this curtain could be seen the emerald-green fields of the Maresme, the golden beaches and the calm blue sea dotted with fishing boats. The Devil began by saying: "All this I give you if you prostrate yourself at my feet . . ." The financier did not let him finish: accustomed to the rapid deals he did every day at La Lonja exchange, this one seemed very advantageous to him. He sealed it on the spot.

That financier must have been obtuse, myopic or deaf, because he did not understand exactly what the Devil was offering him in exchange for his soul, and thought that the offer was for the hill they were standing on. No sooner had the vision faded, or he had woken from his dream, than he started to think how he could make the most of Montjuich, which had and still has steep slopes, but in general was pleasant and leafy. In those days, orange trees, laurel and jasmine grew there. When the notorious castle crowning it was not launching fire, shot and bombs on the city below for some reason or other, the people of Barcelona would climb up it in droves. Artisan families, maids and soldiers would picnic beside its fountains and springs.

After much reflection, the financier hit on what he thought was a brilliant idea: "Let's hold a World Fair at Montjuich. A World Fair as successful and profitable as the one in 1888." By this time, great sacrifices had led to the debt left by that event being paid off, and the city remembered only the splendour and celebrations. The city mayor welcomed the initiative enthusiastically, if a little enviously. Caramba, what a wonderful idea, why didn't it occur to me first, he thought when the financier explained his plan.

The city council immediately approved a subsidy. Montjuich hill was closed to the public. The woods were chopped down, the springs channelled or blocked off using dynamite. Slopes were levelled, and foundations laid for what were destined to be palaces and pavilions. As on the previous occasion, obstacles were not long in appearing: work was paralysed first of all by the Great War, and then by the Madrid government's reticence. On his deathbed, thanks to the intercession of San Antonio María Claret, the financier's soul was saved from the clutches of the Evil One, but the idea of the World Fair languished.

It took twenty years for General Primo de Rivera's public works policy to breathe new life into the scheme. Now not only Montjuich but the entire city became the canvas for his ambitious projects: buildings were torn down, and streets dug up to lay metro lines. Barcelona took on the appearance of the Great War trenches. Thousands of workmen were employed to work on the citywide building site; labourers and bricklayers who came from all over Spain, especially the south. They arrived in crowded trains at Francia station, which had recently been enlarged and renovated.

As ever, Barcelona did not have the capacity to absorb this flood of new arrivals. For lack of housing, they were lodged in hovels known as "*barracas*". Whole districts of them sprang up overnight on the city outskirts: on the slopes of Montjuich, the banks of the River Besós, in dreadful areas known as La Mina, the Campo de la Bota and Pekin. The worst aspect of these new slums was their air of permanence. Even in the most wretched shacks there were rag curtains; whitewashed stones outside marked out gardens, planted with tomatoes, and empty oil drums were used as pots for red and white geraniums, parsley and basil.

To remedy this situation, the authorities encouraged and subsidised the construction of large blocks known as "low-cost housing". In this kind of construction it was not only the rent that was low cost: the materials used to construct them were of the poorest quality. The cement was mixed with sand or rubble; some of the roof beams were sleepers rejected by the railways because they were so rotten; partition walls were made of cardboard or papier mâché. These houses formed satellite suburbs that had no running water, electricity, telephones or gas supply. Nor were there any schools or social or recreational centres, or any kind of vegetation. Since they had no public transport either, their inhabitants went around on bicycles. The steepness of many of Barcelona's streets often exhausted the cyclists, who arrived at work tired, and occasionally expired there. Women and children preferred tricycles, which were safer and more comfortable, although heavier and less practical. The fittings in these low-cost houses were so substandard that fires and floods were everyday occurrences.

The newspapers of the period were full of revealing articles such as the following: *Yesterday Tuesday afternoon, Pantagruel Criado y Chopo, born in Mula in the province of Murcia, a twenty-six-year-old bricklayer currently employed on the German pavilion at the World Fair, exasperated by a quarrel with his wife and mother-in-law, punched the wall of the dining cum living room in his house. It immediately collapsed, and Pantagruel Criado found himself in the bedroom of his neighbours, Juan de la Cruz Marqués y López and Nicéfora García de Marqués, whom he roundly abused. In the course of the ensuing scuffle, the other partition walls of the block fell down, the other neighbours intervened and all Hell broke loose!* More succinctly, the headline of a brief 1926 news item reads: CHILD KILLED WHEN UPSTAIRS NEIGHBOUR FLUSHES WC.

Added to those who lived in *barracas* and low-cost housing were those who sublet, whom the legal tenants allowed to live in a room (always the worst one) and have limited usage of the bathroom and kitchen in return for rent. These subtenants, of whom in 1927 there were more than a hundred thousand in Barcelona, were the ones who, apart from very rare exceptions, suffered the most humiliation and shame. It was against this backdrop of misery, pauperisation and rancour that Barcelona was preparing the World Fair intended to astound the world.

Far from Montjuich, in her chapel blackened by candle smoke, Saint Eulalia contemplated this panorama and thought: My God, what a city! Barcelona had not been very generous towards Saint Eulalia. In the fourth century of our era, when she was only twelve years old, she was first tortured and then burned for refusing to worship pagan gods. Prudentius tells us that as the saint died a white dove flew out of her mouth, and a thick snowfall suddenly covered her body. This was why for many years she was Barcelona's patron saint, until she was ousted by Our Lady of Mercy, the city's patron to this day.

As if this slight were not enough, it was later decided that the virgin and martyr Eulalia, who had protected Barcelona for centuries, had never actually existed. Apparently, she was no more than a copy, a falsification of another Saint Eulalia, born in Mérida in the year 304 AD and burned together with other Christians during the persecutions launched by Maximian. "The saints are thumbing their noses at us," said the people of Barcelona. "This is what it's come to." Eventually even the existence of Saint Eulalia of Mérida – the authentic one, whose day is 10 December – was called into question.

Now the statue to the discredited saint stood in a side chapel in Barcelona cathedral, from where she meditated on everything taking place around her. This can't go on, she said to herself one day. As sure as my name is Eulalia, I have to do something. She asked Saint Lucia and the Christ of Lepanto to miraculously cover her absence, stepped down from her plinth and strode to the city council building, where the mayor received her with mixed feelings. On the one hand he was glad he could count on the saint's solidarity, but on the other he was worried at what she might say about his administration. "Oh, Darius, what calamities you're committing!" Darius Rumeu i Freixa, the Baron de Viver, had been Barcelona's mayor since 1924. "When I took up this position the whole caboodle was already underway," he said, attempting to justify himself. "If it had been up to me, the World Fair would never have happened."

This mayor was not and could not be an impetuous man like his illustrious predecessor, Rius y Taulet. By now Barcelona had become an enormous, complex city. "It was Primo de Rivera and his mania for promoting public works," Baron de Viver went on. "A popular policy that we'll have to pay for, like it or not. It's his fault the city is becoming infested with immigrants from the south." Suddenly remembering the saint herself was from that part of Spain, he hastily corrected himself: "Don't get me wrong, Eulalia, I've got nothing against anybody; to me, we're all equal in the eyes of God. My heart is torn apart when I see the terrible conditions these unfortunates are living in, but what can I do?" Saint Eulalia shook her head slowly and despondently. "I don't know," she said eventually. "I don't know." Sighing deeply, she added: "If only we could count on Onofre Bouvila!" But at that moment, he could not be counted on.

"Perhaps it would be best if I went with you, sir," the chauffeur said.

Calle Sepúlveda came out onto Plaza de España, which was now a terrifying crater marking the starting point of work on the World Fair. The square led into Avenida de la Reina María Cristina, lined with half-built palaces and pavilions. In the centre of the square a monumental fountain was being built, together with the new metro station. Every evening, thousands of workers returned to their hovels, their low-cost housing, the gloomy apartments they sublet. Many others, who were homeless, spent the night exposed to the elements in the streets round the square. The more fortunate among them wrapped themselves in blankets; the less fortunate in sheets of newspaper. Children slept huddled up against their parents or brothers and sisters. The sick propped themselves against house walls to await the uncertain relief a new dawn might bring.

There was the distant glow of a bonfire, and shadowy figures gathered round it. A low pall of smoke filled the air with the smell of fried food that stuck to clothes and hair. The sound of a guitar came from some corner. Onofre Bouvila told his chauffeur to stay with the car. "Nothing will happen to me," he said, knowing these pariahs were not violent. Dressed in a black overcoat with a fur collar, a top hat and kid gloves, he strolled nonchalantly down the middle of the street. The outcasts regarded him with surprise more than hostility, as if he were putting on a show.

Onofre finally came to a halt outside a poor dwelling with bare walls. He rapped several times on the knocker. Showing a coin to the person peering at him through the spyhole, he was let in at once. In the hallway he quickly whispered something to the old woman who had opened the door. She had not a single tooth in her gums, which she showed in a silent laugh. He began to climb the stairs while she bowed and scraped, holding aloft a candle to light his path. As he climbed the stairs, Onofre was in the dark, but this did not slow him down or make him lose his sense of direction; he still had his old nocturnal reflexes.

Eventually he halted on a landing and lit a match; by its spurting flame he could make out a number and knocked on a door. It was soon opened by a frail-looking, unshaven man wearing a threadbare dressing gown over a filthy, crumpled pair of pyjamas. "I've come to see Don Santiago Belltall," Onofre said, before the man could ask him what he was doing there. "This is no time to come visiting," said the man. He began to close the door, but Onofre Bouvila kicked it wide open and struck the man in the ribs with his cane, knocking him against the china umbrella stand, which fell over and smashed. "I didn't ask your opinion and I don't want to hear it," Onofre said without raising his voice. "Go and tell Don Santiago Belltall to come out, then hide yourself where I can't see you." The skinny individual struggled up from the floor, searching behind his back for the ends of the dressing-gown cord. Then he disappeared without a word behind a curtain that separated this hallway from the rest of the house.

Shortly afterwards, Santiago Belltall appeared, apologising profusely: "I wasn't expecting visitors, still less such an important one. The conditions I live in . . ." he added, not finishing his sentence. Onofre Bouvila followed the inventor down a dark corridor to a tiny room. The only ventilation came through a small window that gave onto a covered interior yard, making the room seem airless. In it were two metal beds, a small table with two chairs and a standard lamp. Clothes and belongings were kept in cardboard boxes pushed against the walls, which were covered with plans the inventor had tacked up.

María Belltall was seated at the table, darning a sock on a wooden egg in the dim lamplight. She was wearing a shawl over a plain, old-fashioned woollen dress to protect herself from the cold and damp. A pair of knitted stockings and felt slippers completed her wretched wardrobe. Being dressed like this brought out her pale complexion and the bluish tinge to her skin concealed by make-up during her visit to Onofre Bouvila a few days earlier. Contrasted with this was her red nose, caused by the typical head cold everyone in Barcelona suffers from. When Onofre came in, she raised her head from her darning for a moment, but quickly lowered it again. On this occasion her eyes were once more caramel-coloured, as he thought he remembered from their first encounter years before.

"Forgive me for all this mess," the inventor said, moving nervously between the bits of furniture and only succeeding in increasing the chaos in the room with his violent gestures and agitated state. "If we had known beforehand you were thinking of doing us this honour, we would at least have removed all these scribblings from the walls. Oh, but what am I thinking? I haven't yet introduced my daughter, whom you don't know. My daughter María, señor. María, this gentleman is Don Onofre Bouvila, whom I have told you about. A few days ago

I went to his house to make him a proposal he was kind enough to look upon favourably."

Onofre and María exchanged a furtive glance that would have aroused anyone but the inventor's suspicions. Oblivious to everything, he took their visitor's hat, cane, gloves and overcoat, placing them carefully on one of the beds. He brought a box up to the table, offered Onofre the free chair and sat down, clasping his hands on his lap, ready to listen to whatever their visitor had come to tell them.

As usual Onofre went straight to the point. "I have decided," he began, "to accept the offer you just mentioned." He held up his hand to cut short the expressions of gratitude and enthusiasm the inventor was about to launch into, once he had recovered from his amazement. "By this I mean simply that for now I consider it a reasonable risk to provide you with a certain sum so that you can carry out the experiments you outlined to me. Of course, this agreement has conditions attached. That is what I came to talk to you about."

"I'm all ears," the inventor said.

Baron de Viver, who was a monarchist, received a visit from Saint Eulalia. General Primo de Rivera on the other hand, who out of spite no longer supported the monarchy, was occasionally visited by a crab sporting a Tyrolean hat. Abandoned by everyone, but reluctant to hand over power to anybody else, the dictator was now pinning his hopes on the Barcelona World Fair. "When I took over the government, Spain was a bedlam, a country of terrorists and layabouts. In just a few years I have transformed it into a prosperous, respectable nation. There is work and there is peace, and this will be seen by everybody at the World Fair. Its success will mean those who now criticise me will bow down to me," he said.

The Minister for Development permitted himself an observation: "Your excellency's idea is magnificent, but unfortunately it calls for expenditure beyond our means." What he said was true: in recent years Spain's economy had suffered a dreadful decline; reserves were exhausted, and the peseta's value on foreign markets was laughable. The dictator scratched his nose. "Dash it all," he muttered. "I thought the Catalans were going to pay for the Fair. Race of skinflints," he said between gritted teeth.

With exquisite tact, the Minister for Development suggested that, whatever their virtues or defects, the Catalans refused to spend a peseta for the greater glory of people who were endlessly mistreating them. "God's teeth!" Primo de Rivera exclaimed. "That complicates things! What about deporting those who won't pay?" "There are several million of them, general sir," said the Interior Minister.

The Minister for Development heaved a sigh of relief that his cabinet colleague now bore the brunt of the conversation. Primo de Rivera pounded the table with his fist. "To hell with all your ministries!" he shouted. His anger soon passed, however, because he had just had a brilliant idea. "Alright, this is what we'll do," he said. "We'll pay for another World Fair in another Spanish city: Burgos, Pamplona, or somewhere else." Seeing his ministers gaping open-mouthed at him, he smiled craftily and added: "We won't have to spend much on it. As soon as the Catalans find out, they'll go over-board and spend any amount to make sure the Barcelona World Fair is the better of the two." The ministers had to admit it was a good idea. Only the Minister for Agriculture dared raise an objection: "There's bound to be someone who gives the game away," he said. "He's the one we'll deport," thundered the dictator.

By now work on the Barcelona World Fair was going ahead at full steam; and yet debt was again undermining the city's finances. Montjuich was the wound through which the local economy was bleeding to death. The mayor and all those opposed to the project, those who objected to the waste of money, were summarily dismissed, their responsibilities transferred to people loyal to Primo de Rivera. Among them were speculators who took advantage of the lack of oversight to make fortunes. The newspapers were only permitted to publish encouraging news and praise about the project; otherwise they were censored or impounded at the kiosks, and their editors heavily fined.

As a result, Montjuich was rapidly being transformed into a magic mountain. New palaces sprang up: the Palace of Electricity and Energy, the Palace of Clothing and the Textile Arts, the Palace of Industrial and Applied Art, the Palace of Cinematography, the Palace of the Graphic Arts, the Palace of Industry and Construction (known as the Alfonso XIII Palace), the Palace of Labour, and that of Communications and Transport and so on. Work on these palaces had begun several decades earlier, in the days of so-called *modernismo*; now these buildings shocked the experts, who saw them as sentimental, recherché and in poor taste. The contrast with the nearby foreign pavilions could not have been greater: these had been designed only recently, and reflected the latest trends in architecture and aesthetics. *Whereas other World Fairs have been dedicated to a specific theme such as Industry, Electrical Energy or Transport, this one could well be entirely dedicated to Vulgarity,* wrote one journalist in 1927, shortly before being deported to La Gomera. *In addition to ruining us, we are going to be seen as vulgar troglodytes in the eyes of the world,* his piece concluded. However, harsh criticisms such as this did not deter the event's promoters.

While all this was playing out on Montjuich, on another hill at the opposite end of Barcelona, Onofre Bouvila was struggling with his thoughts in the garden of his mansion. How can it be, he said to himself. Me, in love? And at my age! No, it's not possible … and yet, it is possible, and that fact alone fills me with joy. Who would have thought it! He laughed softly at this: for the first time in his life he thought tenderly of himself, and this allowed him to laugh at his own distress. Soon, though, the smile vanished from his lips, to be replaced by a frown. He could not understand how such a thing had happened; the miracle that seemed to have taken place in his soul left him perplexed. What irresistible hold can that unremarkable young woman have over me, he asked himself. Of course, she's not unattractive, he went on, arguing with an invisible interlocutor, and yet I have to confess she is no great beauty. And even if she was, why should I be so smitten? There's been no lack of beautiful women in my life, real women whose looks stopped the traffic. My wealth has meant it's never been hard for me to buy beauty, to have the best of the best. Yet deep down I never felt anything but contempt for them. This one, though, makes me feel humble in a way that surprises even me. I can't explain it: whenever she talks, smiles or looks at me I'm so happy I feel nothing but gratitude.

When these thoughts crossed his mind he believed this new-found humility redeemed him from all his previous egotism. It's true, he reflected as he looked back on his life, that I have occasionally behaved in an unorthodox manner. The Lord knows that in my record there are pages I'm going to have to account for, and even though no-one can say I've killed a human being with my own hands, several people have died directly or indirectly because of me. Others have been made unhappy, and could perhaps lay their unhappiness at my door. Oh, it's so terrible to realise all this just when it's too late for repentance or reconciliation!

This sudden realisation made him fall to the ground as if struck by lightning. The air was still, the sun was sparkling on the smooth waters of the artificial lake, and its glow made the swans' plumage look dazzlingly white. Onofre's mind was in such turmoil that he could not help seeing the birds as emissaries sent by the Lord with a message of mercy and hope. There will be more rejoicing in heaven over one sinner who repents than over ninety-nine of the just who have no need to do so, they seemed to be reminding him. Deeply moved by this thought, he buried his forehead in the turf and muttered: "Forgive me, forgive me. I've been stupid and cruel, and have no excuse. There is no redemption for my guilt." Like photographs in an album, a series of accusatory faces flashed in front of the eye of his conscience: Odón Mostaza, Don Alexandre Canals i Formiga and his son, the hapless Nicolau Canals i Rataplán, Joan Sicart and Arnau Puncella, General Osorio the ex-governor of Luzón, as well as his wife and daughters, Delfina and Señor Braulio, his father and mother, even his brother Joan. All of them, as well as many others whose faces he had never seen and never would see, had been sacrificed to his ambition and madness. They had been victims of his senseless thirst for vengeance; they had suffered to afford him the ephemeral, bittersweet taste of victory. Can there be enough forgiveness in the heavens to pardon the monster I've been all these years, he wondered, sensing that tears were about to pour from his tightly closed eyelids.

He hardly had time to formulate this question when he felt some light taps on his shoulder. Thinking he was alone, he was startled by this tapping. He did not dare open his eyes, fearing he would come face to face with a majestic angel wielding a fiery sword. When he finally did so, he saw that in fact one of the swans was rapping him with its beak. The swan, surprised at seeing this strange creature lying curled in a ball at the lakeside, had left the water and approached him to see what was going on.

Onofre Bouvila jumped up and the bemused swan beat a hasty retreat. Seen from behind, its waddling walk could not have been more grotesque, nor its honking more unpleasant. Angry with himself for being taken in by such a graceless animal, Onofre caught up with the swan before it could reach the safety of the lake and gave it an almighty kick. The swan flew through the air and crashed headfirst into the water, remaining there with its tail end sticking up as the ripples slowly died on the surface and the feathers it had lost floated down around it.

Brushing off the blades of grass stuck to his clothes, and without bothering to see whether the swan was alive or not, Onofre Bouvila continued his walk. This incident had brought him back to reality. The painful vision of his guilt had vanished, replaced by the implacably self-centred logic he had always applied to everything. Bah, he thought, why am I blaming myself? To listen to me, anyone would think I'm responsible for all the harm in the world. Nonsense, there's nothing further from the truth, he replied to his imaginary adversary. People were unhappy before I came on the scene, and will continue to be long after I'm dead. It's true I've brought misfortune to some, but was I the real cause of it, or a mere agent of fate? If I hadn't crossed Odón Mostaza's path, would that murderous thug have met a less tragic end? Wasn't he gallows fodder from the moment he was born? And Delfina, what destiny would have awaited her if I hadn't appeared one fine day at her parents' boarding house? I'm sure she would have been a scullery maid all her life; at best she would have married a brutal, alcoholic good-for-nothing who would have beaten her all the time and killed her with hard work and pregnancies. Damn and blast it, at least thanks to me all those sewer rats got their chance and were able to enjoy their moment of glory at my expense.

A muffled explosion close by interrupted Onofre's musings. This first one was followed by several more. The birds nesting in the trees flew off, circling high in the sky in a swirling mass, cawing loudly. Onofre Bouvila smiled to himself: Like that poor old man, for example, he added under his breath. But his smile was not as blissful as it had been moments before.

Leaving the lake behind him, he headed for the spot the explosions came from. He deliberately left the well-cared-for lawn and slipped into the wood, where the trees would allow him to proceed without being noticed. He paused to watch unobserved what was going on not far from his hiding place. Men who looked and dressed like mechanics were constantly coming and going from a big circus tent. At the mouth of the canvas tunnel leading inside, still decorated with pennants and bunting, two armed guards supervised their movements. Even though he could not see beyond the tent, Onofre knew that on the far side stood sheds containing extremely complicated machinery. These generators supplied power to the electrical equipment now buzzing and whirring inside the tent. Of course it would have been simpler and much less expensive to obtain power from the electricity supply company, but that would have made it impossible to keep the proceedings secret.

The sheds had been built to protect the machinery from spying eyes, and the generators had been purchased in different countries by means of anonymous companies specifically set up for that purpose. They had been smuggled into Catalonia and the different parts brought furtively to their destination. The coal driving them had also been brought in small quantities and was now stored in bunkers dug beneath the lawns, the woods and the lake.

It had proved more difficult to get hold of the people now working there. Thanks to the flood of immigrants to Barcelona at the time, selecting and hiring labourers covertly had been easy enough, but contracting specialists, technicians and engineers, whose sudden disappearance from their jobs and from public life in general would have been difficult to explain, presented problems that had to be resolved case by case. Some were recruited abroad; others brought out of a retirement forced on them by a variety of circumstances; still others had been sent false offers of employment at American universities. Those who took up the offer soon received a first-class ticket on a transatlantic liner. When the ship they were travelling on left Spanish territorial waters, these prestigious engineers were taken from their cabins at gunpoint and forced onto a rapid launch that brought them back to dry land.

There an automobile took them to Onofre Bouvila's mansion, where they were informed of the reason for the deceit and their abduction, the nature of the work they were being asked to do, the fact that this anomalous situation would only be temporary, and of the generous reward they would receive in return for their collaboration and the discomfort they had suffered. They were all delighted at this happy outcome to their adventures, but the process had been slow, complex and expensive.

No expense had been spared to launch the project, except when it came to the tent, which was the perfect size for the scheme, and had been bought at a bargain price from a circus whose members had been decimated by an outbreak of cholera in the south of Italy. This catastrophe had forced the only survivors – a bearded lady, a female horseback rider and a strongman – to wind up the company and sell off their equipment. Now these three characters, whom it had proved necessary to hire and bring to the mansion to help erect the tent safely, wandered around in their tights, loincloth and sequins, practising their skills as best they could and causing bewilderment, if not panic, among everyone around them.

Onofre was recollecting this picturesque odyssey when he saw her come out of the tent. She was wearing a loose-fitting pink skirt so short it showed her knees as she walked; the folds of material moulded the outline of her thighs. This attracted the stares of the workmen, which annoyed Onofre. The rest of her attire was simple and modest. I must have a word with her about it, Onofre thought, his heart pounding as he looked from her to the workmen. Dazzled by the bright sunlight, she paused for a few moments at the tent entrance, screwing up her eyes. She smoothed down her hair and put on a wide-brimmed hat. Then, for no apparent reason, she set off for the wood where Onofre was hiding. Good heavens, Onofre said to himself in panic, concealing himself behind the trunk of a holm oak. I hope she doesn't see me.

During the months that María Belltall and her father had been installed in the mansion, he had only exchanged a few polite words with her. He hoped this would make it plain he was interested only in the inventor, whose instructions had led to this ever-expanding and extremely odd industrial complex, and with whom, unlike with her, Onofre had interminable discussions.

From the outset Santiago Belltall and his daughter had occupied one of the original hunting lodges situated in the garden, completely separate from the house. They could live there entirely independently, with everything they needed, but no luxuries, as that might have revealed Onofre Bouvila's secret motive, the real reason he had embarked on such a hare-brained scheme at this stage in his life. He had not set foot in their lodging, whose furnishings and decor he himself had carefully chosen: a messenger summoned the inventor to the mansion when the two of them needed to meet.

The secret nature of the project prevented anyone working in the mansion from leaving; in this way Onofre always knew where María was, that even though she did not belong to him, he could be certain she did not belong to anybody else either. The two of them shared common ground, coexisting side by side in a place he owned. For the moment, that was enough for him. He followed all her movements, concealed as he was now.

How strange, he thought, admiring the graceful way she walked, her slender, stylish figure. When I was young and had my whole life ahead of me, everything seemed so urgent. Now, when time is slipping away, I'm in no hurry. I've learned to wait, he said to himself.

That's the only thing that has meaning for me. And yet now things are speeding up.

The previous day he had visited the grounds of the World Fair, and had bumped into the Marquis of Ut, whom he had not seen in a long while. The marquis was on the board of the Fair and was Primo de Rivera's right-hand man in Barcelona. He received instructions from Madrid and carried them out behind the mayor's back. In return for this loyalty he was able to complete murky business deals with total impunity.

When the marquis saw Onofre Bouvila appear in the grounds of the Fair, he grimaced: the friendship that had once existed between the two men had been replaced by resentment in the marquis and a mutual mistrust. Despite this, they both kept up appearances.

"My boy, you're looking well!" the marquis exclaimed, embracing Onofre. "I heard you had a bad turn, but I'm glad you're completely recovered. You look as young as ever!"

"You're looking fine as well," Onofre Bouvila said.

"If only, if only. . ." the marquis said.

The two men walked along arm-in-arm, skirting the trenches and piles of rubble and crossing puddles on planks that bowed under their weight. As they walked, the marquis pointed out the chief attractions of the World Fair: the palaces, pavilions, restaurants and services and so on. What he was most proud of was the Stadium. He explained to Onofre that this construction, only added to the overall plan at a later date, covered 46,225 square metres and was intended for sporting events. Ever since the Fascist ideology had spread throughout Europe, governments had encouraged sporting activities and mass attendance at competitions. It seemed that nations were attempting to imitate the Roman empire, whose customs they adopted as an anachronistic model. The greatness of a country was symbolised by sporting victories. Sport was no longer the preserve of the leisured classes or the rich; it was now seen as ideal recreation for the urban masses; both politicians and intellectuals considered it a way of improving the nation. "The athlete is the idol of our time, the mirror our youth sees itself in," the marquis said. Onofre Bouvila agreed with this theory: "I'm sure of it," he said quietly.

Afterwards they visited the Greek Theatre, the Pueblo Español, and the immensely intricate network of tubes and cables, dynamos and nozzles that were to feed and activate the illuminated fountain. The Magic Fountain, as it was known, was intended to be the most remarkable and commented-on aspect of the World Fair, just as its namesake had been for the previous one. It was situated on a spur of Montjuich hill so that it could be seen from all over the Fair, and consisted of a pool 50 metres in diameter that held 3,200 cubic metres of water, as well as thousands of jets. These jets circulated three thousand litres of water per second, propelled by five 1,175 horsepower pumps and lit by 1,300 kilowatts of electricity. Thanks to this, the cascading plumes continually changed shape and colour. This fountain and the others lining both sides of the Fair's central avenue used as much water in two hours as was consumed in a whole day in all Barcelona, the marquis told Onofre. "When and where has anything so splendid been seen?" he asked. Onofre Bouvila said he could not agree more. His gushing acceptance aroused the marquis's suspicions. What really brings the old fox here, he said to himself. What's behind this sudden enthusiasm? However hard he tried, he couldn't fathom the mystery.

The Marquis of Ut was not to know that a fortnight earlier a strange delegation had turned up at one of the event organisers' offices. This delegation was comprised of a lady and a gentleman dressed with sober elegance, who seemed somewhat intimidated and spoke with foreign accents. They told the employee who received them that they represented a very large manufacturing company, an international consortium he had never heard of, but whose authenticity he could not doubt on seeing the documents spontaneously presented to him. He was, however, surprised to note that beneath the veil the lady covered her face with throughout the interview he could glimpse a thick beard. Naturally, he made no comment about this. For his part, the gentleman, who had hardly opened his mouth, had spent the whole time studying the employee's movements and reactions with a ferocious look on his face. Subsequently, the employee was to recall that this gentleman had a muscular build that bore testimony to his enormous strength. These details did not arouse his suspicions in any way: since he had begun working at the World Fair he had dealt with many foreigners and had grown accustomed to strange faces and eccentric behaviour.

Accordingly, he asked the two strangers how he could be of service. They replied that they had come to obtain the necessary permits to install a pavilion in the grounds of the World Fair. "Our company would like to display its machinery and manufactures there," the lady said. The employee pointed out that foreign companies could only participate as part of their respective countries' pavilions. "If we granted a permit to one company," the employee said, "we would have to give them to whoever asked for one. Organising a World Fair is extremely complex, and there can be no exceptions or privileges," he concluded. To show this was not mere talk, he pointed to a book on his desk: the catalogue of exhibitors, 984 pages long.

The gentleman picked up the catalogue and tore it in two without any apparent effort. "I'm sure we can find a way to iron out any such difficulties," the lady said at the same time, stroking her beard with one hand and opening and closing the black bag she was carrying with the other. The employee saw it was stuffed with banknotes and realised it would be wise not to insist.

Now the pavilion belonging to this unknown company was rising

459

from the ground to one side of the site, taking the place of the Missions' Pavilion, which had been moved. As work on this new pavilion progressed, it began to look very much like a circus tent. It was on Plaza del Universo, right next to Avenida de Rius y Taulet, an excellent location, allowing people to enter and leave the back of the tent on a stretch of level ground (nowadays Calle Lérida) in the utmost secrecy. At all hours of the day and night, evil-looking individuals patrolled round the pavilion, preventing anyone from going near it. Their menacing appearance kept away any curious passersby and dissuaded the Fair's supervisors from carrying out inspections. These details escaped the Marquis of Ut; either he was unaware of them, or if he did know, he did not associate them with Onofre Bouvila or his visit to the Fair.

All this was going through Onofre's mind as he hid behind the holm oak. Yes, everything will turn out just as I planned, he told himself. She is too beautiful and I am too clever and powerful for anything to go wrong. Oh, how gracefully she moves, with what effortless superiority! It's only too obvious she was born to be a queen. Yes, yes, everything will work out fine, it cannot be otherwise. Saying this, he peered superstitiously up at the sky: despite his optimism he thought he saw in that blue, cloudless vault a sarcastic comment on the folly of his expectations.

And indeed, the whole World Fair project seemed destined to end badly. By January 1929 the deficit had reached 140 million pesetas. Baron de Viver saw a bottomless pit opening at his feet: "This situation calls for a desperate solution," he exclaimed. He doused his office with petrol and was about to light a match when the doors were flung open and Saint Eulalia, Saint Inés, Saint Margarita and Saint Catherine burst in. On this occasion the four of them had stepped out of a Romanesque altar piece still on display today in the diocesan museum at Solsona. Saint Inés was accompanied by a lamb, and Saint

Margarita by a portable dragon. All four had died violent deaths, and knew about such things: they snatched the box of matches from the distraught mayor and persuaded him to see reason. They dismissed the absurd ideas feeding his despair: as well as suicide he had been contemplating a popular insurrection, without stopping to think that the two were incompatible. "Primo de Rivera's days are numbered," the saints told him. "That braggart was the Evil One's last throw of the dice," they said. They reminded him of the fable of the frog that puffed himself up so much he exploded. "Anyway, the thing about popular insurrections is that you know how they start, but not how they finish," said Saint Margarita, whose saint's day is 20 July. "Sit at the door of your house and you'll see your enemy's corpse go by," said Saint Inés, who is celebrated on 21 January.

The mayor promised them he would wait and not do anything foolish again. At that moment, this was the most sensible stance: by now, no-one believed in the corporatist state Primo de Rivera had sought to establish, and nobody wanted the dictatorship, which was threatening to create chaos and lead to revolution. The public works programme had ended up producing uncontrollable inflation and the peseta was in freefall. Only the lack of a general with ambition was preventing another coup.

In addition, on 6 February 1929, three months before the World Fair was due to open its doors, Queen María Cristina died of heart failure. As Regent, she had inaugurated the 1888 World Fair, of which everybody now had fond memories; her death was seen as an ill omen. It was also said in Madrid that on her deathbed the queen had advised her son to get rid of Primo de Rivera as quickly as possible; this was bound to have made its mark on the king.

It was in this tense atmosphere that the day of the inauguration finally arrived.

"You ought to go to bed, father. We have a very busy day ahead of us tomorrow, and you'll need all your strength," María Belltall said.

The inventor rose from his armchair, where he'd been smoking an after-dinner pipe. But instead of heading for his bedroom as his daughter suggested, he walked towards the front door. "Where are you going, father?" María asked. Santiago Belltall said nothing, but stepped outside the hunting lodge. Although it was only natural for him to be absent-minded on this of all nights, María decided to accompany him: over the years, she had got used to not letting him out of her sight. Before following him, she went to fetch a shawl to protect her from the chill evening air. Out in the garden, a gusty wind suggested rain was on the way. No, she thought, anything but that! She saw her father walk automatically towards the tent, as he did every night, refusing to go to bed without first visiting it. Invariably, she would have had to scold him and insist he return to the lodge, so that he didn't spend the whole night awake there. On this occasion, however, the visit was purely symbolic, because the machines and fuel had already been transferred to the pavilion at Montjuich and the contraption completely reassembled there. The guard who out of inertia or an excess of precaution was still standing at the tent flap hailed him cheerfully: "Good evening, Professor Santiago." The inventor returned his greeting distractedly. The guard added: "Tomorrow is the big day then, isn't it, professor?" When he heard this, the inventor shook his head: "What's that?" he asked. Resting the butt of his carbine on the grass, the man smiled: "The big day," he repeated enthusiastically. "God willing, everything will work out fine," he added in an undertone. The inventor nodded. How strange, he thought, stepping inside the tent. Everyone is so excited: they all feel part of it, even that thug, who couldn't have played a less scientific role, one more remote from the spirit of our endeavour; and yet now, on the eve of the great event, it seems as if his happiness depends on its success. The guard meanwhile was thinking: He's a rum sort, but there's no doubt he's a true genius; it's only natural that tonight he's so preoccupied. And his daughter's a sight for sore eyes!

All that remained in the tent were tools scattered over the floor, spare lengths of the wooden planks used to crate the machine up, empty boxes and what was left of the ninety-two tons of shavings used to protect the delicate machinery from any blows. The desolate aspect of this disorder in that huge empty space could not have been more depressing. And I, now that I've achieved my lifelong dream, feel only nostalgia and discouragement, Santiago Beltall thought. The empty tent seemed to him the mirror image of his state of mind. On the other hand, he looked back on the endless years of struggle as happy ones: back then he had lived with high hopes, he remembered. Almost at once, he realised this couldn't have been further from the truth. I've sacrificed my entire life for those hopes, he told himself, uncertain whether all that sacrifice had in fact been worthwhile.

The guard's voice interrupted his musings. "Good evening, señorita," he heard him say. That's María, come to look for me, Belltall thought. She's the one who has suffered most from my lunacy: I've always put my dreams of greatness before her well-being. Instead of being given what she had every right to expect, she has had to lavish care and attention on me. Because of me, her life has been a constant renunciation, an unending humiliation. Out of the corner of his eye, he glimpsed his daughter's shadow by the dim glow of the kerosene lamps lighting the tent's interior. Even now, at this very moment, it's my fault she's here, he thought. She's come to look for me because she thinks I should rest. Perhaps this is my chance to get all this off my chest. It won't improve things, make up for the harm I've done her, or help us recover lost time, but it might be some consolation for her to know that her misery has not gone unnoticed by me.

"Father, you should go to bed. It's late, and there's nothing more we can do here," said María Belltall. "Look, everything has been taken to Montjuich. Even the engineers have gone. They'll all be back home by now."

What she said was true: as they completed their tasks, the workmen and technicians had been laid off. Onofre Bouvila sent the aerodynamics experts back where they had come from, promising them a generous bonus if they kept the secret of what they had done and what they had seen others do. The only people left were Santiago Belltall and a Prussian military ballistics expert with whom Onofre Bouvila had been in regular contact during the Great War. His presence was vital in ensuring the project reached a successful conclusion.

"María, there's something I wanted to tell you," said Santiago Belltall.

"It's late now, father. You can tell me in the morning."

"No, tomorrow won't do," the inventor replied.

Their exchange was interrupted by someone entering the tent. It was Onofre Bouvila's butler. Following his master's instructions, he had gone first to the hunting lodge, and finding it empty, had decided to look in at the tent.

"The master is waiting in the library," he said.

Santiago Belltall sighed. "I can't keep our benefactor waiting," he said to his daughter.

"I'll be with you in a moment," he told the butler.

The man shook his head. "I'm sorry, it's not you, but the lady whom the master is expecting," he said frostily. The inventor and his daughter exchanged surprised looks. "Go on, child," Santiago Belltall said eventually. "Don't worry, I'll go straight to bed." Maybe I should pass by the hunting lodge to change my clothes, María Belltall thought.

He didn't even raise his head from his work when the butler announced María Belltall. "Show her in, then close the door and leave us. I shan't be needing you anymore tonight," he told his butler. Left alone with him, and unsure what was expected of her, María approached the desk. When she was close, Onofre Bouvila said: "Look, my love, do you know what this is?"

It didn't escape María's notice that for the first time ever he called her "my love". The wind was beating at the windowpanes. Is it going to rain tomorrow, she wondered. He said: "It's the Regent, the most perfect diamond in the world. It's mine: with it I could buy entire countries. And yet look, it fits into the palm of my hand." Placing it in her palm, he closed her fingers round it. For a brief moment she saw the facets of the diamond gleam as if it had an incandescent filament inside it. "Everything has a price," he said. She opened her hand; he took back the diamond, wrapped it in a white handkerchief and slipped it into the pocket of the dressing gown he was wearing. The slight trembling of his lips suddenly ceased. "I'd like to know the nature of your feelings towards me," he said without pause. "If I only inspire gratitude or fear, don't say a word," he added. María Belltall closed her eyes. "I've been living for the past twenty years just for this moment," she whispered. He sprang up from his seat. "Don't be afraid," he said. "Everything will be alright."

Santiago Belltall woke up covered in sweat. He had dreamed he was losing his daughter forever, that he would never see her again. That's absurd, he told himself as he lit the bedside lamp, there must be some other reason for my unease. Glancing at his watch, he saw it was four in the morning. The wind had dropped and the sky was clear. The night was still dark, but on the horizon a faint grey line was starting to appear, making the stars grow paler. It's going to be a fine day, thank God, he thought, but this wasn't enough to entirely alleviate his anxiety. Something isn't right, he told himself. Getting out of bed, he left the room barefoot, still in his pyjamas. The hunting lodge was silent. Seeing the door to his daughter's room was ajar, he approached it cautiously. Once his eyes had grown accustomed to the darkness, he realised the bed had not been slept in and there was no sign of María. How can that be, he wondered. Isn't she back yet from her meeting with Bouvila? What can they be talking about?

Going over to the window, he looked up towards the house, but could not see any light shining. What's going on up there right now, he wondered. Without wasting any time putting on shoes or clothes, he quit the hunting lodge. In the garden he found his way barred by three men: one of them was the guard who a few hours earlier had greeted him at the entrance to the tent; the second was the circus strongman who had come with the tent in the first place, and the third, whom he didn't remember ever having seen before, was an elderly gentleman with blue eyes and a ruddy complexion, accompanied by a small dog that waddled along awkwardly. This man was the one who appeared to be in charge.

"Be so kind as to follow us, Señor Belltall," he said. "And please don't raise your voice: we have to proceed as discreetly and rapidly as we can."

"Eh?" exclaimed the inventor. "Who the devil are you, and how dare you give me orders? What is the meaning of this outrage?"

"Don't get so worked up, Señor Belltall," replied the man with the little dog. "We're simply following Señor Bouvila's orders. Your daughter hasn't been harmed in any way."

466

"My daughter!" growled the inventor, clenching his teeth and waving his fists menacingly in the old man's face. "What did you say? Why would my daughter come to any harm, you decrepit old swine?" Saying this, he tried to strike the old fellow, but the strongman, anticipating his move, had stepped behind the inventor and grasped him firmly by the arms. Belltall began to shout at the top of his voice: "Help, police! Help, I'm being kidnapped!"

"Nobody can hear you out here," said the older man. "But you'll have to be quiet in the house if you don't want to wake everyone up. Don't oblige us to use chloroform."

This warning brought Belltall back to his senses; he decided to remain silent. Can all this have been an illusion, he was asking himself. Have my daughter and I been nothing more than pawns in a game whose rules we're completely ignorant of? The most terrible answers jangled inside his head, but his mind rejected them with the despair of someone faced by harsh reality after waking from a wonderful dream. No, no, what reason could there be for it all to be a heartless lie, he said to himself. The sky, meanwhile, had turned iridescent: scarlet stripes were appearing above the city, lending it a fiery glow. What's this, he wondered. Is Barcelona going up in flames?

At that very moment, María Belltall was also contemplating the grandiose dawn. It's as if the horizon were on fire, she whispered to herself. Hell has come to visit us. Wrapped in a maroon velvet curtain, she was standing at the bow window in the library. Casting her eyes back inside the room, she saw her clothes strewn all over the carpet. She shuddered as she turned back to look at the ominous sky. What will become of me now, she thought. Suddenly a cry roused her from her musings. "What was that?" she asked. Onofre Bouvila had just finished dressing and was lighting a cigar with studied calm. Before answering, he blew out the match, dropped it in the ashtray and took several puffs at his cigar. "I don't know," he said. "A servant, a carter whipping his mules, what does it matter?" The cry could be heard again, and María Belltall shuddered a second time.

"It's my father," she said, her voice still a murmur.

"Bah, what are you saying?" Onofre retorted. "It's your imagination; you're a little nervous."

She paid him no attention.

"Hand me my clothes, please. I have to go and see what's happening," she begged him.

Onofre Bouvila didn't move. His eyes screwed up, he was watching her through the cigar smoke. He was touched by the sight of her shoulders and neck peeping above the curtain, her obvious fragility, her tousled hair, the way her panting breaths stirred the velvet folds.

"I'll never let you go," he said finally. I won't allow you to abandon me, he thought. "I love you, María, I've been madly in love with you from the very start. I've suffered for your love for twenty years without realising it."

"And my father?" he heard her asking. "What will you do with him?"

"Nothing bad," Onofre said.

"Where is he now? What are your cronies doing to him?" María Belltall insisted.

"Don't worry, they're taking him somewhere safe. Do you think I'm capable of doing anything that might upset you?" he said, his face relaxing in a gentle smile. At that moment, there was the sound of knocking at the door. "Quickly, hide," Onofre told her. "I don't want you to be seen." Raising his voice, he ordered: "Come in." The door opened a crack and the head of the old man with the dog appeared round it. "Everything as it should be?" asked Bouvila. The old man nodded without a word. "Good," said Onofre. "We're on our way."

When the old man had gone and the door was shut once more, Onofre strode over to the desk. "You can come out now," he told

468

María. "Hurry up and get dressed, we've no time to lose." When he saw her hesitate, he added reluctantly: "Oh . . . alright, alright, I won't look." Why was she being so coy at this stage in the proceedings? He turned his back on her as she picked up the various bits of clothing scattered around the floor, but kept glancing at her out of the corner of his eye: he was afraid she might take advantage of a momentary distraction to try to run away or attack him with some object or other. She made no attempt to do either. At the same time, Onofre had taken a handwritten letter out of a desk drawer. He signed it, folded it, then put it in an envelope. He scribbled something on the envelope, licked the gummed edges to seal it and left the letter on the desk where it would be readily seen. He turned to face María just as she was finishing doing up the loops on the garters encircling her thighs. "Are you ready?" he asked. She nodded. "Well then, let's go!" exclaimed Onofre Bouvila.

They went out into the corridor hand in hand. As they began to descend the stairs to the lower floors, he raised a finger to his lips and said quietly: "Shh! We don't want to wake my wife." They reached the front door on tiptoe. The butler was waiting for them, a jacket folded over his arm. Onofre Bouvila removed his dressing gown and put on the jacket. He felt inside the dressing-gown pocket, took out the hand-kerchief wrapped round the diamond and stuffed it into his jacket. He tapped the butler on the shoulder. "You know what to do," he told him. The butler nodded. "Take care, sir," he added, his voice betraying no hint of emotion. Onofre Bouvila didn't reply, but took hold of María Belltall's hand once more. They went out into the garden; the grass was damp with dew. On the far side of the bridge, against the dawn's crimson backdrop, an automobile stood waiting for them. They climbed in. "You know where you have to go," Onofre Bouvila told the chauffeur. Its headlights piercing the mist, the automobile set off.

*

However lavishly the local authorities showered him with praise and the city's dignitaries went overboard with their buffoonery, and even though that day had been declared a public holiday, His Majesty Don Alfonso XIII found it hard not to feel anxious. Installed in Pedralbes Palace, he vividly recalled the terrible events of twenty-three years earlier. Back then he had been very young, and had just celebrated his marriage to Princess Victoria Eugenia of Battenberg. Despite the drizzle, the streets of Madrid were crowded with people wanting to watch his retinue pass by. The august couple had left San Jerónimo church where the wedding ceremony had taken place and were travelling in the royal carriage to Oriente Palace. As they were progressing down Calle Mayor, a bomb was thrown from an upstairs window. It fell in front of the carriage and exploded on the spot. Although it was a tremendous scare, neither he nor his bride was wounded. Realising he was unscathed, he turned to his spouse. "Are you hurt?" he asked. Her wedding gown was stained red from the blood of spectators and soldiers from their escort. Princess Victoria Eugenia shook her head serenely. "No," she said simply in English.

Between twenty and thirty people had been killed in that assassination attempt. As soon as the monarchs reached the palace, they rushed to change clothes. Among the folds of his cape, Alfonso XIII found a finger; he quickly hid it in his trouser pocket so that his bride wouldn't see it. Later, during the wedding reception, he handed it discreetly to the Count of Romanones. "Here," he said, "throw this down the water closet." "Your Majesty," the count exclaimed, "they're the mortal remains of a Christian." "Well then, have them buried in La Almudena cemetery, but I never want to see them again," the king replied.

While the nobility and the diplomatic corps were attending a ball, thousands of policemen were out searching in every corner of Madrid for the regicide. A few days later, his body was found in

Torrejón de Ardoz. The man had been apprehended by a watchman on a country estate: seeing the game was up, the fugitive had first shot the watchman and then committed suicide. There were several inconsistencies in this version, but since everyone wished to forget the event, it was accepted without argument. The would-be assassin was soon identified: his name was Mateo Morral, the son of a manufacturer from Sabadell who had been a teacher or assistant at the Ferrer Guardia Escuela Moderna. From that moment on, Alfonso XIII considered the Catalans a hostile people who behaved violently and unpredictably.

That night in Pedralbes Palace he had placed his shotguns at the head of the royal bed. "Just in case," he told his wife. When it came to shooting he had no rival. On his frequent hunting expeditions he always took three loaded guns with him. With them he could kill two partridges in the air in front of him, two overhead and two more behind his back. Only George V of England could match him. Despite these precautions, Alfonso XIII had slept badly. He was out of bed before anybody came to wake him, and stood staring out of the window at the dawn: the sky looked like a huge bonfire. A magnificent spectacle, the king thought, but God only knows if it's a good omen!

In another part of the same city, General Primo de Rivera was also scouring the sky in search of signs. No doubt about it, he said to himself, it's the aurora borealis: we're on the brink of a catastrophe. And here I am like a useless puppet. He hadn't slept well either, and his mind was befuddled. He called his aide and ordered him to go and fetch coffee. When the man returned, he found the dictator struggling with his knee-length boots. "Allow me, general sir," the aide said, squatting down. Primo de Rivera poured himself a cup of coffee and brought it to his lips. "One afternoon a long while ago, in Tangiers, I go into a tavern . . . for no particular reason, d'you see,

471

simply to have a drink, and as I enter, who do you think I saw? Go on, who d'you think?" The aide shrugged: "I've no idea, sir." "Come on, say somebody, man," the dictator insisted. The aide scratched his head. "However hard I try, I can't think of anyone, your honour," he admitted finally. "Just say a name, the first person who comes into your head," insisted the dictator. "Whoever you say, you'll never guess," he added with a smile. He took a sip of coffee and sighed noisily. "There's nothing like a good strong coffee to start the day!" he exclaimed. In the distance an out-of-tune bugle sounded, followed by a roll of drums, and then a military band struck up a march. "Oh," groaned the dictator, "they always play the same thing, and always badly. Where are my medals?" His aide presented him with a dark wooden box. A crown was carved on the top; it had once belonged to his uncle, the first Marquis of Estella. Primo de Rivera opened the box and ran his eye over the medals with a mixture of pride and nostalgia. "So, aren't you going to tell me who I met in that Tangiers tavern?" he asked his aide. The man stood to attention before replying.

"Buffalo Bill, general sir," he said. Primo de Rivera stared him up and down. "Damnation, how did you guess?" "I'm sorry, general sir," the aide excused himself, "it was pure luck, I swear on my mother's grave." "No need to apologise, my boy," the dictator reassured him. "You haven't done anything wrong."

The Baron de Viver was also preparing to carry out his duties that day, even though he was seething with rage. In his city hall office the previous day, he had received the royal household's chief of protocol. The flunkey had shown him some incomprehensible plans and had blithely given him strict instructions to carry them out. "What a nerve!" the mayor spluttered, alone in his mansion. "Telling me what to do and where, when and how. Who does he think he is? And where do these people think they are? This is my city, you popinjays!" As he said this, he raised his voice, waving his hands high above his top hat and striding in circles round his dressing room. "And who could have come up with this order of procession?" he asked the empty air. "First His Royal Highness, then the royal family, then Primo de Rivera and his ministers, behind them the chief commissioner of the World Fair, his excellency the bishop, the ambassadors and legates . . . What about me, where on earth do I go? In the guard's van?"

The Baron strode towards the door and grasped the knob as if about to leave the room, then froze, let go of it and began to stride round the room again in the opposite direction. No, he told himself, suddenly recovering his composure, something so blatant can't be mere chance or be a question of ignorance or incompetence. This has to be a premeditated insult to myself and the position I hold. And through that position, to all Barcelona.

This thought stoked his anger once more, and his soliloquy verged on the hysterical. "By almighty God, I'll have my revenge," he muttered through gritted teeth. "In the middle of the inaugural ceremony I'll take my trousers down and piss on their boots! Let them shoot me on the spot if they dare!" The Baron's passionate outbursts never lasted; he would soon fall into a gloomy state where everything around him seemed dark and confused. Can things really be as they seem to me, he thought. Or is it all down to my megalomania? What right do I have to say I represent the city? Aren't I the lowest of its servants, the humblest of its employees? I didn't even have to go through a selection process: it was Primo de Rivera himself who appointed me. And doesn't my attitude go against the common good? Oh, I don't know what to think; everything is spinning round; the sun has at last come out from behind the clouds and the glorious dawn is over: now the red glow is melting in the air, giving way to the clear blue of a spring morning. Oh, what is life, he asked himself with a bitter sigh.

His Majesty Don Alfonso XIII was busy donning his gloves as he walked through the salons and corridors of Pedralbes Palace, escorted towards the main entrance by a chamberlain. How ridiculous, he thought. Such a huge palace for us to sleep only a couple of nights in. His lengthy strides obliged his retinue to trot along behind him; only the queen, who was English, could keep up without any apparent effort, and could even maintain a conversation as they rushed along. "Do you realise," he said, without slowing down, "this is the second World Fair I'll be opening in Barcelona. Last time I was a brat barely two years old. I don't remember anything about it, of course, but my mother used to tell me these things." Memories of his childhood were always official ones: his father, Don Alfonso XII, had died even before he was born. "I was born the King of Spain," he was in the habit of saying. At his birth, the midwives and nurses attending his mother had asked for permission before they smacked his bottom to produce the first cry. His father's sudden death had meant he was very close to his mother from the outset. Now she too had died. "At the age of forty-four, everything is happening for the second time at least," he said, stepping into the bullet-proof vehicle that was to take him to Montjuich.

"You can say what you like," said Primo de Rivera, but I'll wager that the person you saw was a joker, and the show a fake." "If you say so, it must have been, general sir," his aide conceded. "But that's what the poster said. I can still see it now: *The One and Only Buffalo Bill.*" "Stuff and nonsense!" retorted the dictator. "Buffalo Bill died in 1917, I can assure you." "Let's see," he added slyly, "were there any Red Indians in the show you saw?" Their automobile was speeding across Barcelona. They were late, and would have to hurry if they were to reach the grounds of the Fair before their majesties. If the king and queen were forced to wait for the dictator, it could upset the delicate balance of Spain's political jigsaw puzzle. The consequences of such a banal incident could be immeasurable. The aide's face lit up.

"Red Indians? I should say there were, general sir. And how they whooped, the sons of bitches!"

"Goodness! And cowboys too?"

"Cowboys as well, sir."

"Are you sure? Cowboys throwing their lassos?"

"And how, general sir!"

The route was lined with a reasonable though not very deep crowd of onlookers. Some passersby had joined them at the last minute, drawn by the sirens of the motorcyclists clearing the way for the dictator's entourage. Yet nobody applauded or waved handkerchiefs at the cortège, and many of them, in the mistaken belief it was the king who was meant to go by, only refrained from showing their disappointment thanks to the heavy police presence.

"And a stagecoach?"

The aide looked bemused.

"A stagecoach? What stagecoach, general sir?"

"Aha, just as I thought . . ." exclaimed the dictator. Just then the automobile braked sharply, threatening to pitch him forward onto the rug. "Hey, what's going on?" Looking out of the window, he saw a gaggle of smiling faces. "Oh, we've arrived. Thank God His Majesty is still on his way. Come on, out you get: what are you waiting for?" he scolded his aide.

Alighting from the vehicle, Primo de Rivera was received with bows and applause. Bugles blew; drums beat loudly. Lost amidst the crush of dignitaries surrounding him, the Baron de Viver stood on tiptoe and craned his neck to see, eyes red from lack of sleep and fury at his mortal enemy. He doesn't look well, he noted. I could swear he's sick. This observation instantly made his ill will towards the dictator evaporate. At that moment, there came the roar of a cannon, followed by another and another, until the twenty-one-gun salute had been completed: the battery up in the castle was greeting the arrival of the king at Montjuich. Baron de Viver found himself swept along to the National Palace with the throng. The opening ceremony was to take place in the ballroom, which was already filled with countless people. Crowds could be seen flooding into the square outside from all directions.

Once the inaugural ceremony was over, their majesties appeared on the balcony and the crowd cheered them for a good while. Some, believing they were anonymous in the multitude, dared to boo Primo de Rivera. Taking this as a sign his protector would soon be toppled, the Marquis of Ut managed to position himself next to the king, so that he could get into his good books once more. Sweeping his arm round theatrically, he pointed out the magnificent panorama spread out before all those on the palace balcony.

"Look, Your Majesty, at what Catalonia can offer you: its citizens, its inventiveness and its hard work," he said unctuously.

"And its bombs," the king retorted, remembering Mateo Morral once more. The marquis wanted to respond, but had no idea what to say. However, at that moment an unexpected sight caught the attention not only of the monarch but of everyone else as well. To the right of the balcony, on the far side of Plaza del Universo near Avenue Ruis y Taulet, stood a circular pavilion strangely reminiscent of a circus tent. Unlike the others, there was no flag or other insignia flying from its roof. Until that moment, this detail and the strange way the pavilion had been erected had passed unnoticed. From inside came a loud throbbing noise, like that of an aeroplane engine starting up. Soon the sound became such a tremendous din it silenced the crowd.

The organisers of the event had no idea what to make of it: there were so many of them no-one knew exactly what they were meant to do, and still less what they were responsible for. They glanced at each other quizzically, most of them already trying to shift the blame onto someone else. Eventually, as the roar continued, and nobody seemed to be doing anything about it, Primo de Rivera himself began barking orders to the military personnel around him. They in their turn passed these on to the officers in their respective units.

Shortly afterwards, the following troops were dispatched in the direction of the pavilion: a detachment of the Guardia Urbana commanded by Lieutenant Don Alvaro Planas Gasulla; a platoon of the Badajoz Infantry Regiment under Captain Don Agustín Merido del Cordoncillo; a Civil Guard company under the command of Captain Don Angel del Olmo Méndez; a royal household cavalry squadron led by Captain Don Antonio Juliá Cubells; a company from the local security forces commanded by Lieutenant Don José María Perales Faura; a platoon from the Montesa cavalry regiment under Don Manuel Jiménez Santamaría; a detachment from the Catalan militia commanded by Sergeant Don Tomás Piñol i Mallofré; together with an unknown number of plain-clothes policemen.

In total, more than two thousand men were now attempting to force their way through the panicking crowd, many of whom recalled the bloody assassination attempts of recent years and the Corpus Christi bombings, and were afraid something similar was happening. They ran to reach safety as best they could. In some parts of the square this led to avalanches of people that were more dangerous than any bomb. For some inexplicable reason a shot rang out, followed by the kind of infernal hullaballoo that usually precedes notorious disasters.

On the crowded palace balconies all the dignitaries' eyes were fixed on the pavilion, whose walls had begun to vibrate as if the whole building was in fact one huge explosive device. The troops advancing towards it found their way blocked by the multitude frantically trying to get as far away as possible. "It's a scandal!" cried the event organisers. "And such a disgrace for the city!" They could readily imagine the headlines the next morning in newspapers all over the world *Barcelona in mourning*, they read in their mind's eye. And lower down: *The tragedy was due to a lapse in security arrangements; that lapse was the responsibility of Don . . .* in block capitals.

But the situation was evolving so rapidly they couldn't spend long on these thoughts: at this point, a hydraulic mechanism caused the pavilion roof to part as if it were made up of two sliding doors, their edges slotting into grooves fashioned in the side walls. A gust of hot air shot from this opening, creating a shimmering column that rose up as far as the eye could see. Eventually the two halves of the roof were completely folded into the walls, leaving the pavilion looking like an open-ended cylinder or bombard.

By this time no-one in the crowd doubted that a never-before-seen machine would rise out of it at any moment. In fact, a few seconds later the contraption did start to appear, and was soon high above the pavilion. It hung suspended in mid-air like a miniature planet. By now it was visible from every corner of the grounds of the World Fair and beyond. The crowd, which after the initial panic had fallen silent, now burst out in exclamations of astonishment and wonder. And with good reason: the machine was oval-shaped, ten metres long and a maximum of four metres wide. These dimensions were calculated on the spot by observers and are still today a matter of fierce debate: they could never be verified because neither the machine nor the blueprints from which it was constructed were ever seen again.

The back half of the flying machine was made of smooth, shiny metal; the front was all glass, held in place by steel or flexible wooden struts. The two halves were apparently joined by a metal hoop half a metre wide, like those used to make barrels. Several hundred light bulbs mounted on this hoop enveloped the machine in a halo of light. It was obvious the rear half contained the engine propelling the machine and keeping it in the air, while the front half held the passengers, whose silhouettes could be dimly glimpsed through the cloud of dust the contraption raised as it climbed. The crowd was dazzled by the sight of this formidable invention. Even His Royal Highness cast off his attitude of disdain and somnolence; he gave an admiring whistle and muttered a "By Jove" to himself.

Everyone present wondered what on earth it could be, and their imaginations ran riot as they tried to come up with an answer. No doubt about it, they said to themselves. They're Martians. They've chosen Barcelona to demonstrate their matchless technical prowess to the world. This choice of destination will make Paris, Berlin, New York and other upstart cities grind their teeth with envy, they thought with malicious glee.

In those days, nobody doubted the existence of beings on other planets. Speculation raged, and the scientists showed little interest in putting a stop to it. These beings or extraterrestrials, as they came to be called, were represented exclusively by comic-strip illustrators, who invariably drew them with a human body and the head of a fish. Most frequently they were naked, but this didn't offend decency as none of them seemed to have any reproductive organs; besides which their skin was scaly. If they wore anything, it was doublets and hose. Noses like ear trumpets did not become part of the iconography until the 1940s, when cinema and the microscope began to show magnified images of mosquitoes and other insects. As far as these visitors from other worlds were concerned – generically known as "Martians" – it went without saying they were far more intelligent than earthlings. They were thought to be peaceful in their intentions, and somewhat naive.

However, all these suppositions lasted barely a minute, because the machine, after rising above the domes of the National Palace, described a semicircle and began slowly to descend over the Magic Fountain. It became clear that those piloting the craft were flesh and blood creatures, and that the apparatus was a variant of what in those days was known as a helicoplane, ornithopter or gyroplane: in other words, aeroplanes that could take off and land vertically. In recent years there had been a number of experiments with this type of aircraft, although so far the results had been unpromising.

On 18 April 1924, the Marquis of Pescara had succeeded in taking off and landing vertically at Issy-les-Moulineaux in France, but had only covered a very short distance: 136 metres. The previous year, that is 1923, the Spanish engineer Juan de la Cierva had invented a less ambitious but more effective apparatus. This was known as an autogiro, a conventional aeroplane in all respects (wings, tail, flaps and main fuselage) to which was attached a freestanding propeller with several blades. This propeller turned on an axle fixed to the top of the craft, rotating thanks to the wind created in flight. Then, when the engine cut out and the aeroplane nose-dived, the column of air displaced by the fall created a turbulence that turned the propeller's blades even faster. This acted as a brake on the speed of the descent. Once a few additional problems were resolved, such as air resistance, stability and other questions, the autogiro proved to be a safe and viable invention: in the 1930s it regularly flew non-stop from Madrid to Lisbon. However, there was a huge gap between a vertical take-off and the ability to hover in mid-air. And that gap had been triumphantly overcome by the strange invention now zooming over the World Fair grounds. It rose and fell as its pilot dictated. It hung suspended at any height like an adjustable ceiling lamp, and flew horizontally without shaking or swerving. This in itself was a wonder, but more astonishing still was that it could carry out these and other manoeuvres with no sign of propellers.

4

In the wasteland around the grounds of the World Fair an entire shanty town had grown up, where thousands of immigrants eked out an existence. Nobody knew who had organised the shacks into streets or aligned the streets so they crossed perpendicularly. Outside the front doors of some of these hovels stood wooden crates where rabbits or hens were kept; the top of these crates had been replaced by a piece of wire netting so that the crowded animals could be seen inside. In other doorways dozed dubious-looking emaciated dogs.

The automobile drew up in front of one of these dwellings, and out of it stepped Onofre Bouvila and María Belltall. As they passed by, one of the dogs growled, but carried on sleeping. Alerted to their arrival by the automobile engine, a dishevelled woman dressed in rags pulled back the sack curtain hanging across the shack's entrance. The hut was no more than four sheets of wood nailed together and rammed into the ground. The early morning light filtered in through gaps in the cane and palm-leaf roof. When the two of them had entered, the woman let the curtain fall again. She stood staring at Onofre Bouvila with a vacant expression: it was plain she had just woken from an untroubled sleep. "What about your husband?" asked Onofre. "Why isn't he here?" Hands on hips, the woman jerked her head backwards, but the gesture was neither aggressive nor defiant. "He left last night and hasn't come back yet," she replied; she seemed about to laugh scornfully. "He spends the money you give him on liquor and whores," she added, glancing at María Belltall out of the corner of her eye. "That's his business," said Onofre Bouvila, taking no notice of her inquisitive look. "It's not up to me to decide how he spends it."

The sack curtain shifted, and the dog padded in. Sniffing at María

481

Belltall's ankles with its damp muzzle, it sneezed loudly several times. "Well, what are we waiting for?" said Bouvila unexpectedly to María Belltall, still clutching her hand. The woman knelt down on the floor, swept aside the dirt with the edge of her hand and uncovered a trapdoor. Shooing away the dog, which was now sniffing at it, she pulled on a metal ring to reveal an opening. Steps cut in the earth led downwards. Onofre Bouvila took a few coins out of his pocket and gave them to the woman. "Hide them where your husband won't find them," he advised her. Her mouth twisted in a grin: "Where would that be?" she said, gazing round the cramped room. Onofre was no longer paying her any attention: he was already pulling María Belltall down the steps with him. At the bottom was a tunnel: they walked a hundred metres along it by the light of a muffled lantern. Then they came to some more steps, ending at another trapdoor. Onofre opened this by tapping on it three times with the lantern handle.

Now they were inside the pavilion. The walls were made of reinforced concrete; it was exactly like the now empty tent where they had been working until a few days earlier in the mansion garden. Unlike the tent, however, there were no doors or windows in this pavilion: the only way in or out was via the trapdoor. The man who had opened the door for them was elderly and rosy-cheeked. He was wearing a white surgeon's gown over a day suit. Seeing Onofre Bouvila, he frowned and pointed to his wristwatch, as if to say: What time do you call this?

Bouvila had met the engineer during the Great War; the defeat of the Central Powers had left him without a job, and for a decade he had got by giving physics and geometry classes at a Marist Brothers school in Tübingen. It was there early in 1928 that he had received a letter from Onofre Bouvila inviting him to come to Barcelona *to take part in a project related to your specialty.* The funds necessary for his transfer were deposited in a Tübingen bank. *I am sorry I cannot be more specific, due to the nature of the project itself, in addition to other important reasons,* his letter concluded. This kind of language reminded the Prussian engineer of the good old days.

Boarding the train at Tübingen, he reached Barcelona after a non-stop journey of four days and five nights, which had done nothing to soothe his habitual bad temper. When Onofre Bouvila finally outlined the project to him, showed him the blueprints and explained what was expected of him, the Prussian tore off his spectacles, threw them to the floor and stamped on them. "The project is stupid," he said, "the person who thought it up is stupid, and you are even more stupid; you are definitely the stupidest man I have ever met."

Onofre Bouvila smiled and let the engineer get it off his chest. He knew his life at the Tübingen school was one long torture: the pupils had nicknamed him "General Boom-Boom" and made him the butt of their cruellest pranks.

Now, thanks to the German engineer's efforts, Santiago Belltall's hare-brained ideas had evolved until they had a solid scientific foundation. He had transformed a brilliant idea into a machine that could fly. For his part, Onofre Bouvila had needed all his patience and authority to settle the fierce arguments that constantly broke out between the Catalan inventor and the Prussian engineer; it was thanks entirely to him that their collaboration had borne fruit.

At last their machine stood ready in the centre of the pavilion, mounted on scaffolding as intricate as a lace mantilla. "It's utterly unique!" Onofre exclaimed. The engineer sighed: it piqued him that so much talent, effort and money should have been devoted to a mere amusement.

Onofre Bouvila, only too aware of the reason for this sadness, paid him no attention: this was no time for academic debates. Outside the pavilion he could hear the salvo greeting their majesties' arrival at the World Fair. "Let's go," he said. The pavilion was filled with men in grimy blue overalls. Each of them was absorbed in his task, oblivious to what any of the others were doing; no-one spoke or paused to have a smoke or to drink. The Prussian engineer had succeeded in instilling his brand of discipline into the team; they were top-notch mechanics, and didn't raise their eyes from their tools even when María Belltall passed by. Suddenly realising why she had been brought here, she made an attempt to escape. Onofre Bouvila restrained her as gently as possible: he could see the terror in her eyes. She doesn't trust her father's invention and she thinks I'm crazy. Maybe she's not wrong, he said to himself.

Now at his feet he could see the whole of the World Fair grounds. "It's strange," he was thinking. "From up here it all seems so unreal; maybe poor Delfina was right and the world is just the same as the cinema. Well, I'll descend a little so I can see people's faces," he decided. Pulling the control levers, he made the craft lose altitude. By now the crowd had calmed down and was closely following his aerobatics. "Look, look, it's Onofre Bouvila," people said to one another when the distance between them and the aircraft narrowed to allow them to make out its crew. "Yes, it's him; it's him! And who can that girl with him be? She looks like a pretty young thing; goodness, that skirt of hers is very short, the hussy!" These and other similar comments were infused with affection bordering on devotion. The stories circulating in Barcelona with regard to Onofre's fabulous wealth and the means he had employed to obtain it had made him a popular hero. When he walked down the street, passersby stopped to look at him discreetly but insistently, trying to judge from his expression whether or not the rumours they had heard were true. When they saw his unremarkable, slightly vulgar face, they asked themselves: Can it be true that as a young man he was an anarchist, a thief and a gunman? That he trafficked arms during the war? That

484

he had several well-known ministers, and even entire government cabinets, in his pocket? And that he achieved all this alone, without any help, starting from the bottom, armed only with his audacity and strength of will?

Deep down, everyone was willing to believe this was how it had been: Onofre Bouvila was the fulfilment of their dreams. It was through him that they could take their collective revenge. "What if in fact he was a crook?" people said. "Is there any other way these days for a man to succeed in a country like ours?"

This was why when they recognised him the crowd began to cheer; the earlier ovation they had given the king was now transferred to Onofre Bouvila. "Look, look how they're cheering me," he said to María Belltall, who scarcely dared open her eyes. "You know, people are very good," he went on, raising his voice above the clatter of the engines. "They're very good – you should see how much they put up with without protesting!"

As he said this, he pressed a button that automatically opened a hatch in the rear of the craft. Dozens of doves flew out. Suddenly finding themselves free, and frightened by the noisy machine, the birds immediately flew off in close formation. When they saw this, nobody, not even the king, could withhold a gasp of admiration.

Content with the effect produced, Onofre Bouvila edged the craft forwards until it was barely a few metres from the National Palace balconies, which were threatening to give way under the weight of all the dignitaries clustered there. He could clearly see their faces, just as they could see his. "Look, look," he said, "it's the King. Long live the King! Long live the Queen! Long live Don Alfonso XIII," he shouted, even though he knew nobody but María Belltall could hear. "Oh, and there's Primo de Rivera!" he added. "Hey, go boil your head, you drunkard!" He began to identify faces he recognised one by one, excitedly pointing them out to his companion. "Can you see that man who's so tall he stands head and shoulders above everyone else?" he said finally. "That's Efrén Castells: the only true friend I ever had. Well, perhaps I had more than one, but all the others have gone now. Bah!" he continued, changing his tone, "let's not be sad, let's get out of here. I've seen enough."

With that, he pushed one of the levers forward as far as it would go, and the craft shot up and backwards. They could view the whole city at their feet: the Sierra de Collcerola, the Rivers Llobregat and Besós, the vast shining sea. "Ah, Barcelona," he said, his voice choking with emotion. "How beautiful it is! And to think when I first came here, almost nothing of what we now see existed! The fields began right here; the houses were tiny, and those crowded neighbourhoods were villages," he said enthusiastically. "You won't believe it, but cows used to graze where the Ensanche is now. I lived there, in a dead-end street that hasn't changed a bit, although the boarding house I stayed in disappeared centuries ago. It was full of the oddest people. I remember there was a fortune teller who one night read my fortune. Of course, I can't remember a word of what she told me . . ." And even if I did, he said to himself, what importance would it have? That future she foretold is already the past.

Those following the machine's progress from Montjuich and those who, alerted by the sound of its engines, had gone out onto balconies or flat roofs, suddenly saw the flying machine change course and head out to sea, as if caught by a wind from the west. Far from the coast it lost altitude, climbed again for a moment and finally plunged into the water.

Fishermen working nearby said they had been terrified to see the machine flying overhead. They had no idea what it might be: some thought it was a meteorite, a ball of fire heading straight for them, but they were unable to say if in fact the craft was ablaze or whether that effect was produced by the sun's reflection on its metal and glass surface. One thing they all agreed on, however, was that when it reached the spot where it went down, the engines had suddenly cut out. The noise had ceased and the lapping of waves had restored a sense of eternity to the sea, they told the press. Everything seemed to be at a standstill, as though time had come to a halt. Then the craft had crashed into the waves like a shell fired from a cannon, they said.

The fishermen who went to the spot where they thought they had seen it fall could find no trace of it: not so much as a slick of oil or petrol floating on the surface. They couldn't agree as to the exact location where the crash had occurred: in their primitive fishing boats they had no way of measuring it.

The coastguard immediately dispatched several vessels. Eager to take part in the rescue operation, several countries offered their aid. What interested them above all was the prospect of recovering the flying machine and getting hold of the secret of how it functioned. None of these rescue efforts was successful. Divers went down and came up empty-handed; when the seabed was dragged, all it produced was sand and seaweed. Eventually a storm led to the work being suspended, and it was not resumed when calm weather returned.

Since the bodies of the crew members were never found, prayers for the dead were said in Barcelona Cathedral. Wreaths were thrown into the dark waters of the port, and the current carried them out to sea. Newspapers carried the usual obituaries: texts filled with overblown rhetoric. Some conveniently expurgated biographical sketches of Onofre Bouvila also appeared, aimed at the edification of their readers. They all concurred that a great man had gone. *The city owes him a debt of eternal gratitude,* wrote one of the newspapers. *Better than anyone, he symbolised the spirit of an age that has died a little along with him,* said another. *His career began with the 1888 World Fair and came to a close with the one in 1929,* commented a third.

How are we to interpret this coincidence? the article concluded, with obvious malicious intent.

In fact, the event that Onofro Bouvila had enlivened with his aerobatics seemed destined to go down as a spectacular failure. In October of that same year, four months after the World Fair opening, came the Wall Street Crash. Overnight, out of the blue, the capitalist system was teetering. Thousands of firms went out of business. Their representatives rushed to the World Fair pavilions and palaces to remove their exhibits before the bailiffs could seize them. Many exhibitors committed suicide: to avoid the shame and pain of financial ruin they jumped from their office windows on the top floors of New York skyscrapers.

So as not to leave the stands empty – which would have given visitors to the Fair a dreadful impression – the Spanish government began to replace the withdrawn articles with whatever came to hand. Soon some of the pavilions were displaying the most absurd items.

These pathetic events pushed into the background the baseless rumours circulating in Barcelona to the effect that Onofre Bouvila had not in fact died, that the accident had been faked and that he was now living comfortably in some remote region together with María Belltall, at whose side he had finally found true love, and whom he worshipped at all hours of the day and night.

A variety of reasons were given for this romantic thesis. Shortly before the accident, Bouvila himself had arranged matters so that not only would it be impossible to locate the wreckage of the craft, but also to uncover its blueprints or the technicians who had helped build it. When army sappers eventually managed to blow a hole in the pavilion's concrete wall, all they discovered were the planks from the scaffolding on which the craft had been mounted. The trapdoor was eventually uncovered, but the tunnel beneath led only to an abandoned shack. No less suspicious was the fact that when the accident occurred, Onofre Bouvila had on his person the fabulous Regent diamond. This, allied to the other dramatic events of that year, led some to speculate that Onofre Bouvila was behind the global economic collapse, even though nobody could say what his motives might have been.

Everybody's attention then turned to his widow, but it proved impossible to obtain any declaration from her. The family mansion was sold to the Barcelona provincial government, which neglected it so badly the house eventually returned to the ruined state it had been in before Onofre Bouvila resurrected it. The widow, meanwhile, had withdrawn to a villa in Llavaneras which many years earlier had belonged to the governor of Luzón, General Osorio y Clemente. She lived there as a recluse until her death on 4 August 1940.

She left behind some papers, but not the letter Onofre Bouvila had placed on the desk in his study eleven years earlier before he had set out for Montjuich.

All the rumours died out as time went by and no evidence surfaced to back them up, while other more urgent problems began to preoccupy the people of Barcelona.

Meanwhile, the World Fair dragged on. Public opinion openly mocked the organisers, and beyond them Primo de Rivera's government, seizing on this pretext to vent their repudiation of him. Despite the censorship, nobody held back from comparing the 1929 World Fair with that of '88: the former came in for savage criticism, whereas the latter was praised to the skies. Nobody cared to recall the problems the first World Fair had created, the disputes and animosity it had given rise to, or the debt it had burdened the city with. Now Baron de Viver regretted not having been firmer. "We've mortgaged our city to the hilt only to end up with a farce so ridiculous we'll all be left looking like idiots," he would say mournfully. It wasn't long before he stood down.

Even Primo de Rivera, who had been the driving force behind the World Fair in whose success he had put so much store, found himself obliged to admit his position was untenable when he realised how unpopular he was. In January 1930 he offered his resignation to the king, who accepted it without bothering to conceal his delight. The toppled dictator immediately went into exile in Paris, where he was to live only a few months longer. He died on 16 March 1930, a few weeks before the first anniversary of the opening of the Barcelona World Fair.

A year later, King Alfonso XIII himself abdicated and left for exile. Other similarly momentous events followed thick and fast. Some were joyous, others grim; in the collective memory, these two extremes gradually merged into one to form a chain or slippery slope inevitably leading to war and disaster. Later on still, when people began to look back at this period with hindsight, it came to be seen that the year Onofre Bouvila disappeared from Barcelona was the start of the city's steep decline.

EDUARDO MENDOZA was born in Barcelona in 1943. He studied Law and worked as a UN interpreter in the United States for nine years. His most acclaimed work is *City of Wonders*, adapted for film in 1999. He has won many awards for his fiction, most recently the Premio Planeta and the European Book Prize for *An Englishman in Madrid*, and the Premio Cervantes in 2016.

NICK CAISTOR is a British translator from Spanish, Portuguese and French. He has won the Valle-Inclán Prize for translation from the Spanish three times, most recently for *An Englishman in Madrid* by Eduardo Mendoza, published by MacLehose Press.

Eduardo Mendoza

AN ENGLISHMAN IN MADRID

Translated from the Spanish by Nick Caistor

Madrid, 1936.

Spain is on the brink of civil war.
The battle for Europe's soul will be
fought on her soil.

Madrid is teeming with foreign spies
and the cobbles are slick with the
blood of idealists.

Enter Anthony Whitelands:
gentleman, libertine, art historian –
the very model of an Englishman abroad.

MACLEHOSE PRESS

www.maclehosepress.com